T0246138

# THE
# HAUNTING
## OF HECATE
# CAVENDISH

# THE
# HAUNTING
## OF HECATE
# CAVENDISH

PAULA
BRACKSTON

ST. MARTIN'S PRESS
NEW YORK

First published in the United States by St. Martin's Press,
an imprint of St. Martin's Publishing Group

THE HAUNTING OF HECATE CAVENDISH. Copyright © 2024
by Paula Brackston. All rights reserved. Printed in the United States
of America. For information, address St. Martin's Publishing Group,
120 Broadway, New York, NY 10271.

www.stmartins.com

The Library of Congress Cataloging-in-Publication
Data is available upon request.

ISBN 978-1-250-28402-0 (hardcover)
ISBN 978-1-250-28403-7 (ebook)

Our books may be purchased in bulk for promotional, educational,
or business use. Please contact your local bookseller or the Macmillan
Corporate and Premium Sales Department at 1-800-221-7945,
extension 5442, or by email at
MacmillanSpecialMarkets@macmillan.com.

First Edition: 2024

10  9  8  7  6  5  4  3  2  1

*For Thaddeus and Skyla.*
*Because being your mum makes writing only*
*the second-best job in the world.*

# THE HAUNTING OF HECATE CAVENDISH

# 1

———— • ————

HEREFORD, 1881

FOR MORE THAN THREE HUNDRED YEARS THE ANCIENT TOMB HAD HOUSED the remains of its occupant without threat of disturbance. Even the hungry rats and slithering worms had been deterred by its impenetrable walls, so that the cadaver within had, over the long, lonely centuries, quietly and gently turned to nothing more than dry bones. On the outer surface of the sarcophagus, generations of spiders had spun their webs, weaving away in the darkness, their layer of gossamer an external shroud for the long-deceased, long-forgotten person within. For so many years, all had been silent as a grave should be. Untroubled as a soul at peaceful slumber. Dark as the deepwater moment before dawn.

But then came that dawn, rising like a vengeful blaze, splitting the horizon, darkness from light, earth from sky, life from death. Sundering the structures that kept each in its place. Dragging souls from the deep. So that soon, with dreadful, unstoppable progress, the dead would rise.

Hecate had been up at daybreak, following the habit her father had instilled in her. She took after him in so many ways; her striking red hair, her restlessness, her hunger for knowledge, her fascination with things arcane and little understood. It was he who had insisted on her outlandish name, silencing his wife's protestations that it was heathen and uncivilized.

"My dear," he had told her quietly but firmly in a voice that would brook no argument, "while I favor the modern pronunciation *Hék*-atee, the origins of the name are both classical and ancient and all speak of a woman of great fortitude and significance. Would you wish to label your daughter *in*significant?" And so it had been decided.

On this particular morning she had good reason to wake early, for this was to be the first day of her new life. The day she would leave the house merely a young woman, but arrive at the cathedral as its new assistant librarian. The thought that she would spend her time with regular access to the magnificent chained library thrilled her. The library was renowned for its collection of antique and obscure books, manuscripts, documents and maps, and it would fall to her to help care for, restore, and catalog them. As if that weren't reason enough to delight in her appointment as helper to Reverend Thomas, Master of the Library, she would also have the opportunity to study the famous *Mappa Mundi*. This was the jewel in the collection; one of the oldest and largest medieval maps in existence, filled with mysterious symbols, legends, wonders, and secrets.

Hecate wasted as little time as possible pinning her hair into an acceptable bun and buttoning up her blue woolen dress. The fine floral print and modest lace details on the cuffs stirred in her a mixture of irritation (at the girlish style) and guilt (at being ungrateful for a gown of good quality). The frills and folderols that were a woman's lot were irksome to her, for she had always considered there were so many more interesting things to be doing than attending to one's own appearance. She barely glanced in the looking glass, doing so only to confirm that her mother would not complain at her efforts, before descending the wide wooden staircase to the dining room.

The handsome redbrick house she shared with her parents and younger brother, Charlie, was first and foremost a family home, ruled firmly by her mother, Beatrice, but sustained by the gentle benevolence of her father, Edward. While the rooms were well furnished, and carefully chosen paintings and vases left no space undecorated, the priority was for practicality and comfort over elegance and show. Or at least, that was the aim of

Mrs. Cavendish. Mr. Cavendish's fondness for collecting curious objects from his travels over a lifetime as an archeologist fought against this somewhat, so that a bronze Egyptian goddess might find herself sharing a shelf with a Staffordshire china poodle, a desiccated scarab beetle, and a plain wooden box containing fire tapers.

Hecate made straight for the sideboard and helped herself to kedgeree.

On seeing his daughter, her father put down his newspaper.

"Ah, how fares my little Hecate this morning? Are you prepared for your first day of employment?"

"Indeed I am, Father," she said, taking her seat at the table and tucking into her breakfast.

"I am pleased to see your appetite has not suffered in the excitement," he said.

Hecate grinned. "I need to keep my strength up. Did you know there are fifty-four steps up the stone spiral staircase to the muniments room?"

"I did not. I shall imagine you springing up them each morning. Of course, you know why it is called such, don't you?" he asked, testing her gently.

"Because, up until this point, it was used to keep all the title deeds and legal documents relating to the cathedral and the diocese, which are collectively known as muniments."

"Up until this point."

"Yes, because now that it houses the collection, it is simply known as the library."

Her father smiled at her indulgently.

Hecate's mother made a small, tutting sound, unable to completely suppress the disapproval she felt toward her daughter's employment. She would never entirely forgive her husband for having secured a position in the cathedral library for her.

"Why you would wish to shut yourself away among dusty books, I cannot imagine," she said.

"Truly, Mother? You only have to look to Father to see where I get my interest from."

"Your father has more than that to answer for. Had he not spoken to the dean on your behalf you would never have been considered for the position."

Mr. Cavendish smiled brightly. "One does what one can."

"Really, Edward!" His wife was losing patience. "It is enough that you have encouraged Hecate in this direction; kindly resist gloating."

Hecate reached over to pat her father's hand. "Gloating is harsh," she said. "But you know Mother would rather me fill my days with visits and social events."

"Am I to be criticized for doing what any sensible mother would do?" Beatrice demanded. "That is to say, assisting my daughter in the search for a suitable husband." Seeing the disparaging look exchanged between the other two across the table, she added, "A happy and prosperous marriage is not to be sneered at."

Mr. Cavendish looked shocked. "We would never sneer at such a thing, would we, Hecate?"

"Absolutely no sneering," she agreed. "Oh, Mother, could you set aside your ambition for me just today and share my happiness? I am so thrilled to have been given this opportunity. I would enjoy it even more if I knew you approved."

Her mother said nothing but sipped her tea. Hecate let the hopeful silence stretch as far as it could without snapping before giving up and changing the subject.

"Where is Charlie?"

"Your brother is indisposed."

"He has a head cold," her father explained.

"Another one?" Hecate feared her twelve-year-old sibling's health might never improve. Indeed, more and more it seemed he was in bed rather than out of it. She saw the concern etched on her mother's face, and noticed the determined way her father went back to his newspaper. Not one of them wanted to face the possibility that Charlie might never be fully well again. It hurt her heart to see her parents so worried. "If he's feeling a little stronger later today, shall we take him out in the trap? Perhaps a ride to the farm to see the cows?"

Edward smiled. "He is certainly fond of the things."

Her mother would not hear of it. "Hecate, you know full well the weather is not yet sufficiently settled for him to venture out. No. He must rest. Dr. Francis will visit tomorrow and I'm sure he will have better news for us after he has seen him."

A pensive silence fell upon the family, disturbed only by the ticking of the grandfather clock in the hallway, and the occasional rumble of Mr. Cavendish's stomach. Hecate tipped back her head to drain her cup of tea, earning a hard stare from her mother, and rose to her feet.

"I shall be late," she said, even though everyone knew she had never been, nor ever would be, one minute late anywhere for anything that she loved. She was known for the frenetic pace at which she traveled, whether on foot or pedalling her beloved bicycle. She considered lateness lost time that could never be recalled, and the very idea of that bothered her enormously. She kissed her mother's cheek, snatched a slice of toast, and paused to hug her father, who patted her hand.

"Off you go, little worker bee," he told her, ignoring his wife's admonishing glare at the pairing of work and their daughter in the same sentence.

In the hallway, Hecate plucked her favorite workaday hat from the stand, and her coat from the cupboard. She shrugged it on as she chomped her toast, her mother's entreaty not to leave the house while eating echoing in her ears as she closed the back door behind her. Outside the day was awash with spring sunshine, though a refreshing breeze served as a reminder that it was but the beginning of the season. As she took the path that skirted the lawns of the walled garden, breathing in the sweet scent of the cherry blossom, she experienced a pang of guilt at leaving Charlie upstairs to face another dreary day indoors alone. She decided she would work with her father to take him out upon her return, regardless of her mother's protestations, certain the air and blossom could only be beneficial to a person's health. The door of the old stable creaked as she opened it. It had been many years since the Cavendishes had kept more than a single pony for their modest trap. Hecate broke her stride to feed the remnants of her toast to Peggy, the plump chestnut mare that was staring forlornly at her empty hay manger. The second stall was now occupied by a set of harness and Hecate's bicycle. She took a moment to reposition her hatpin. Her enthusiastic pedalling and the morning breeze would combine to remove any headwear if it were not securely anchored to her hair. She wheeled the heavy iron bicycle out into the sunshine. It was a source of great pride to her, and not a little consternation to her mother. No other young lady would be seen riding such a thing, either for decorum's sake or for fear of injury.

Hecate had researched bicycles, as she researched anything that was to become important to her, and had discovered an innovative design being made in America. She had used the small bequest from a departed aunt to purchase it and have it shipped over for the express purpose of using it to ride to and from the cathedral each day. That it was called a safety bicycle had gone some way to appeasing her mother. Safe as it might be, it was still of considerable weight, and required some skill, which Hecate had acquired over a matter of several somewhat bruise-strewn days. She stepped through the frame, hitching herself up onto the seat in one practiced movement. Not for the first time she muttered beneath her breath at the silliness of not being permitted to shorten her skirts a little. The matter of her cycling attire was yet another continuing battle she fought with her mother.

Hecate revelled in the speed and freedom she found while riding through the streets of the small city. Avoiding the carriages that vied for space along the main thoroughfares, she wove her way through the crisscrossing narrow streets and avenues that ran like the veins of a leaf, all ultimately heading in one direction: to the cathedral. As she pedalled she raised a hand in greeting or shouted out a hello. The greengrocer was setting up the striped awning above his display of produce and paused to sing out a good morning. The newspaperboy ran alongside her for a moment, both of them laughing as he ultimately failed to keep up. A gaggle of young girls on their way to start a shift at the bottling factory squealed as she steered her bike through the center of the group, Hecate throwing "*sorry*" and "*beg your pardon*" over her shoulder as she went.

After an exhilarating five minutes, she steered down Church Street, juddering over the cobbles, resisting the wonderful aromas drifting out from the pie shop, and at last reaching the edge of the Cathedral Green. As always, Hecate's heart lifted at the sight of the magnificent building. Its pink-tinged stone softened the grand, masculine lines of its high tower and soaring roofs. The gothic arches that formed the entrances, echoed throughout the building, gave it such a powerful connection to the past, and its stately proportions spoke so clearly of the enormous, sustained effort involved in its construction. She could never fail to be moved by it. Out of respect for the fact that the Green had once been a graveyard, she dismounted and walked as sedately as she could bear (which was to say not sedately at all), wheeling her bicycle past the main entrance, along the north wall, around the splendid east facade, circling right to the south door. Here there was a narrow space at the start of the cloisters where she had been given permission to leave her bicycle. On the threshold, she hesitated. This was not a visit to admire the fine carvings and statuary, nor a day for attending a service or concert. This was the start of her working life. Once she stepped through the doorway and entered the building she became a part of the family of clergy and laypeople who loved and tended the ancient place.

A soft meow alerted her to the presence of Solomon, the cathedral cat.

"Good morning, pussycat." She smiled, unable to resist stooping to stroke his bright orange fur. She had met him on her previous visits and heard the story of how he had appeared one day, a tiny shivering kitten, and purred his way into the hearts of everyone. Dean Chalmers had taken some convincing that he should be permitted to stay permanently, but finding an altar cloth nibbled by mice had decided him. Happily, Solomon had proved to be an excellent mouser.

As the tower bell struck the hour, Hecate skipped through the doorway and into the cathedral itself. Immediately as she entered, she experienced the familiar but nonetheless striking changes in the atmosphere. First there was the temperature. The stone walls were several feet thick and did a far better job of keeping the heat out than in. The fragile warmth of the spring day stood little chance of penetrating such defenses. The only warm points in the whole cathedral at this time of year—between winter stoves and summer sun—were the jewel-colored pools of light that fell through the stained-glass windows. She stood in the transept—the square area immediately inside the south door—where she had been instructed to wait for the dean. This being one of the less grand entrances, there was nothing spectacular about the space save for the lofty vaulted ceiling, the intricate tiles, and a tomb set into the right corner on which was carved in stone an effigy of a sixteenth-century dean.

The second atmospheric change was that of sound. Sounds of the world—birdsong, carriage wheels, train whistles, barking dogs were rendered muffled and distant, or in many cases completely silenced. Sounds within the cathedral walls, however, were amplified, acquiring blurring echoes, which rebounded off the interior masonry or ricocheted off the gleaming brass-work. Hecate did her best to move quietly as she paced up and down, too excited to keep still, but the leather of her boots slapping upon the tiles sounded horribly loud to her ears.

"Ah, Hecate, my dear!" The dean approached down the south aisle, his long, dark purple robes of office skimming the floor as he walked, hands outstretched in welcome. Dean Chalmers was the perfect example of someone who had found their ideal place in life. Kind, thoughtful, and dedicated to his faith and to the cathedral he had been in charge of for over a decade. He was known as a man of sound sense and abundant patience who had the knack of being likeable without losing any of his authority. He clasped both of Hecate's hands. "Welcome!"

"Thank you, Dean. I am so happy to be here."

"You will be an asset to Reverend Thomas and make your father very proud, I have not the slightest doubt. Come, I will take you to the library, though of course you already know where it is to be found."

"Yes, Dean. Father took me to see the collection for the first time last year, and then I returned for my interview. I promise I shall do my best to reward the trust in me the master of the library has shown by accepting me for the post."

Together they turned, walking along the transept where colored tiles underfoot gave way to older flagstones.

"Reverend Thomas is a man of . . . quiet passions. He has a preference for silence, which makes him ideally suited for his role," said the dean, shedding a positive light on the librarian's well-known dislike of unnecessary social interaction or indeed conversation in general. "Keep in mind," he went on to assure her, "he is a font of knowledge regarding the collection. It would be a wise person who listened attentively on the occasions he chooses to share that knowledge."

Hecate nodded as they turned left down the north aisle. She glanced across at the spectacular altarpiece and the intricately carved choir stalls, smiling at the thought from that morning, this wondrous place was to be where she would spend so much of her time. They reached a low door set into the wall. Dean Chalmers opened it and then stood back to allow her to enter the stairwell.

The library had, over centuries, both grown and moved, making way for improvements to the cathedral or escaping damage in areas of dilapidation and disrepair. Now the collection resided on the first floor, so that to reach it Hecate was required to trot up the worn treads of the narrow, twisting stone staircase which was housed in a turret. The steps turned in a tight spiral, lining the slender tower that ran up the side of the building. The only light was that from the small arched windows placed at intervals throughout the climb. Hecate counted as she went, breathless not from effort but excitement by the time she reached the second door. The dean tried the latch but it was locked.

"Ah. It appears we are ahead of Reverend Thomas. It is the habit of Mr. Gould, our verger, to unlock the door on the ground floor, but the master of the library is responsible for opening this one. Have you met Mr. Gould?" When Hecate shook her head he went on. "His is an invisible but vital role in the functioning of the cathedral. No church, big or small, can do without its caretaker. I am sure you will meet him later today, not least because he inhabits the vestry, and that is where you will find the stove, kettle, and biscuit tin."

He smiled, and she was grateful for his attempts to put her at ease. He and her father had attended the same school and maintained a lifelong friendship, so that she regarded him almost as family.

The sound of the ground-floor door opening and shutting reverberated up the stairwell. It was followed by irregular footsteps and labored breathing.

"Ah," said the dean, "here comes our key bearer."

The footsteps slowed and the breathing grew louder until at last the master of the library appeared, holding his ring of keys ahead of him. He was portly and short, his black robes accentuating his shape rather than hiding it, and wore the thickest spectacles Hecate had ever seen. He nodded in reply to the dean's greeting, being too puffed to speak. Hecate moved aside so that he could, with a shaking hand, unlock the door and push it open. The three trooped into the room.

To a newcomer, the importance of their surroundings might not have been immediately apparent. It was, of course, a handsomely built, robust space, with thought having been given to light and care taken with its construction. There were three generous, rose-shaped windows with fine stone and iron tracery, two on the east wall, one on the north, allowing the best illumination for close work in natural light. The ceiling was sufficiently high to house tall shelves and allow air to circulate, but not so lofty as to be

overly grand nor to waste heat through the winter months. The two inner
walls were paneled with dark wood, matching the broad, smooth boards of
the floor. Aside from several chests and trunks, and two desks by the windows, all available space was taken up by book-filled shelves. Row upon row
of them stood, straight backed and strong, facing forward, a regiment of
knowledge and wisdom.

On closer inspection, visitors would notice the large metal locks at the
end of each shelf, and see that there were iron chains attached to them. These
chains, with links too heavy to be easily breached yet smooth enough and
slender enough not to harm the books, ran the lengths of the shelves, weaving in and out to pass down the spinal columns of each volume, tethering
them to the cases. For hundreds of years, those same chains and shelves had
ensured the safety of the individual books and the preservation of the collection. Withstanding fire, war, flood, revolution, and even the rending of the
cathedral's faith itself, the library had survived.

Hecate breathed in the faint but distinctive smell of parchment and leather
and linseed oil and glue. It seemed to her that they were the scent of a living
thing. As if the collection were a mythological creature, its beating heart the
words and wisdom and stories it held. She had been in the room only twice before but the feel of it was imprinted on her memory. Her mother might see a
library as a dull place for a young woman to spend her time. She could not disagree more, for she had inherited her father's thirst for knowledge, his curious
mind, his love of puzzles and mysteries, and here were all those things in abundance, waiting for her to discover them.

Reverend Thomas had caught his breath sufficiently to apologize. "Forgive my tardiness, Dean. I was detained by Mrs. White who had much to say
on the subject of the extra work she is required to do because of the current
renovations. Why she thought the matter my concern I cannot fathom," he
said, pushing his wire-framed glasses back into position, as they had a habit
of sliding down his nose.

The dean explained to Hecate, "Mrs. White has been cleaning the cathedral
for many years and does an exemplary job. When there is work undertaken
to the fabric of the building it does, alas, increase her burden."

"Father told me the renovations may continue a while yet," she said.

"Indeed. The major stonework is nearly completed, which should pacify Mrs. White, for I believe it is the dust she rails against. The stained-glass windows, however, will require many months' further restoration. And restoration is something you will learn about here, is that not so, Reverend?"

The librarian looked at his new recruit with ill-concealed skepticism.

"There are many duties required of an assistant here that must be mastered before the delicate and skilled work of restoration can be attempted," he cautioned.

"Of course, and I am certain you will find Miss Cavendish a willing pupil and a great asset. Now, I must away for a meeting with the bishop. Hecate, my dear, I leave you in the capable care of Reverend Thomas. Please give my regards to your father."

So saying he swept out of the room, one hand already hitching up his robe to ensure a safe descent of the steep stairs.

Hecate turned and gave her new employer her brightest smile. "I would like to say once again how very grateful I am for this opportunity—"

He held up a hand. "There is no necessity to repeat yourself, Miss Cavendish. Now, I will show you what you need to see and tell you what you need to know. I do not anticipate that you will retain everything, so please feel at liberty to make notes." Without waiting for a response he began walking briskly, if unevenly, along the rows of bookshelves.

Hecate scurried after him. She reached into her coat pocket and took out her leather-bound notebook and plucked the attached pencil from its slot in the spine of the book. A Christmas present from her brother, she found it invaluable for jotting down thoughts and discoveries and was rarely without it.

"The chained collection is not arranged alphabetically but in order of age," he began, "which provides a more coherent system. At the end of each case you will see indices so that specific volumes may be easily located on the shelves. These are the very oldest tomes in the library," he told her, not stopping but waving a plump hand, "and most are not bound, but are loose leaves collected within a cover, you will discover more on this matter later." They reached the end of the row and doubled back along the next. "Mostly here you will find leather-bound books from the fourteenth century, many ecclesiastical in their subject matter, but the greater number being city records, muniments, and suchlike, with some works of poetry. . . ." He let the word hang, his tone and expression giving an indication that he did not value these items as much as others.

Hecate noted down the gist of what he was saying. More than once she opened her mouth to ask a question, but the librarian moved at a surprising speed, as if keen to have the tour done with, and was already stomping up the third row of shelves.

"These are some of the most valuable books in the collection. Bibles. Gospels. Prayer books. All with the very finest illuminated lettering and frontispieces, many with ornate endpapers." He stopped so suddenly that Hecate nearly bumped into him. "You are familiar with these terms?" he asked, frowning.

"Oh yes, Reverend. My father—"

"Good, that will save some time at least."

As they turned to walk along the next row, Hecate noticed an intricately carved cupboard, set upon a sturdy stone plinth, apparently secured to stone pillars on either side of it. The plinth itself was plain and of little interest, but the cabinet was a thing of striking beauty and workmanship. It was made of a red wood, burnished to a deep sheen, and decorated with inlaid mother-of-pearl and slivers of paler wood, set in concentric spheres, to mesmerizing effect. The front was reinforced with a finger plate that appeared to be made of gold, and it had across its front a bar and lock that seemed out of proportion for the size of the thing.

"Whatever can be kept in there?" she asked.

The librarian not only stopped but turned and stepped so close to Hecate it was all she could do not to move back. When he spoke his expression was particularly stern, his eyes, made enormous by the magnification of his spectacle lenses, quite fierce.

"Those books remain under lock and key at all times. No one is granted access to them."

"No one? Then . . . what is the point of them being here at all?"

"The point is to render them safe!"

"Are they of such great value?"

"They are not the concern of a librarian's assistant," was all he would say further. He continued his progress along the bookcases.

Hecate could no longer resist a lingering look at the mysterious cabinet.

She made herself a silent promise to discover precisely what it housed. If the master of the library would not tell her, perhaps her father could shed some light on the matter.

The short tour continued, and Hecate's attention was refocused on the increasingly beautiful and interesting books that she glimpsed. She hastily scribbled notes, partly so as not to have to ask her employer to repeat himself, but also as an aide-mémoire in regard to the locations of the most fascinating tomes and volumes. With so many housed in the collection, she wanted to design her own system of reading and familiarizing herself with what was now, in part, her responsibility. She felt anew the thrill of being permitted to work with something so ancient and so wonderful, and reached out to touch the warm, worn leather of an enormous book on the architecture of modern Europe, where modern referred to the late eighteenth century. She was forced to trot to catch up with Reverend Thomas. As she rounded the end of another bookcase she had the feeling someone else had entered the room. Looking back, she saw an elderly man, wearing the pale gray robes of a monk rather than the darker ones of a vicar, apparently scanning a high shelf for a particular book. As if sensing he was being watched, he turned and met her gaze. On seeing her, his aged, round face was lit up by a bright smile. She smiled back.

"Miss Cavendish!" The reverend's tone caused her to jump. "If you could attend we will complete our business much more swiftly. We have a deal of information to cover and you have yet to see the list of duties I have drawn up. These do not include gazing into space."

"Sorry, Reverend, forgive me," she said, following as he led her over to a desk beneath the second of the enormous rose windows. When she glanced back, the monk had moved out of sight.

"This will be your place of work. It must be kept clean and tidy. No drinks or food of any kind are to be consumed at your desk. You will, once adequately trained, be engaged in the cleaning and repair of valuable manuscripts, books, documents, and maps. A clean surface on which to work is vital."

"Yes, I see. Of course."

"Aside from natural light, we have gasoliers fitted, but you will no doubt have need of a lamp for intricate work. See that it is kept away from varnishes and suchlike . . ."

Hecate was dimly aware that the librarian was still speaking and knew that she should be paying attention and making more notes. Instead, she found herself irresistibly drawn to what was on the wall behind him. She knew a great deal about the *Mappa Mundi,* but she had never laid eyes on it before. Due to the restoration work taking place in the cathedral it had been removed from the south aisle and crated for some time. Now it sat in its original plain wooden frame, hanging on the wall of the library, its temporary home, only feet from Hecate's own desk.

The layout of the map would be curious to those unfamiliar with it. They might think it drawn from a limited knowledge of the geography of the world and a poor understanding of topography. This was no mere record of a landscape, however. Rather than an aid to navigation of the world, it was an aid to navigation of beliefs and legends, histories and peoples. It was an illustration of the way medieval people understood life and death. Not a map of places but a map of thoughts. A map of the mind. A way to make sense of the philosophies and ideas that people held centuries earlier. While Reverend Thomas rattled through a list of duties, Hecate stepped quietly closer to the map to study its marvelous detail. The images upon it were simply drawn but were so many and so varied that the whole became an intricate and beautiful depiction of lost tribes and mythological creatures standing among Christian saints and angels, beside strange beasts, mighty rivers, citadels, and mountains. She found herself wondering about the mapmaker's choices. How had he decided what to include and what to leave out? She understood why, particularly given the belief system of the medieval age in which he was working, Christ was seated at the top, a supreme benevolent overseer to all that was laid out beneath him. Similarly, the angels sorting saints from sinners was no surprise, and she had listened to lengthy discussions between her father and the dean on the subject. That the great cities of the world were often represented by images of their religious houses fitted this sensibility, too. In this way, Hereford was depicted by a simple drawing of the very building in which the map resided. She was moved by the fact that the image was somewhat smudged, having been touched by pilgrims come to see it over centuries, unable to resist reaching out to it with their faithful fingers. Less expected were the many strange creatures shown entirely out of scale, so that the fire-breathing bull was as big as the Cathedral of Santiago de Compostela, and the manticore was as tall as the elephant. What reasons did the cartographer have for giving space on the map to these beasts of legend? One in particular delighted her. The Latin inscription beside the animal was hard to read, but Hecate was familiar with this mythical being from descriptions she had read in her father's books. It was unmistakably a griffin, with its eagle's beak, wings, and talons, and the ears, haunches, and tail of a lion. She found herself drawn to it, and raised her hand, tempted to touch it, half expecting its feathers to be both soft and warm. The more she gazed at the creature, the more she had the sensation that the reverend's voice was fading, as if he were moving far away. His words were replaced by a breathy sound, like a breeze moving through dry grasses or disturbing the leaves of a poplar tree. The urge to touch the map as those many pilgrims had done became overwhelming.

"Miss Cavendish!" Reverend Thomas barked at her. "Kindly do me the courtesy of listening to what I have to tell you."

"Oh, I do beg your pardon! The map is just so . . . marvelous," she said, forcing herself to turn back to him and muster a bright smile.

The librarian was unable to argue with her point and so instead bestowed upon her a withering frown.

Hecate could see it would take time to win her superior over. The morning passed with her sorting through a box of papers. These were loose pages from three large volumes of parish records from a church in the area. Her job was to discard the illegible ones, dust off the reasonable ones, and collate them in date order. She understood this was a lowly and largely pointless task, but was happy to do it without complaint. She would show that she could be trusted. Time, patience, and hard work would be needed to persuade her superior of her value and abilities. All of which would be a price worth paying to be there, where she was surrounded by such an abundance of wonders.

When the tower bell rung one o'clock, Reverend Thomas closed the ledger in front of him and rose from his chair.

"I take my luncheon with the other vicars choral in the main hall of the cloisters," he explained. "You will have made some provision for your own refreshment." It was more a statement than a question. "You recall neither food nor drink are permitted in the library."

Hecate got to her feet, eager to reassure him that she was safe to be left, but before she could speak a tall man with fair hair and bright blue eyes appeared in the doorway.

"Fear not, Reverend, I am here at the dean's behest to see to it that Miss Cavendish does not starve."

The librarian stared at their visitor. "She cannot join us in the hall!"

"Indeed, which is why I shall escort her to a suitable place in which to dine." As Reverend Thomas seemed uninterested in making introductions, the man stepped forward, hand outstretched, to make himself known. "John Forsyth, another of the singing vicars," he said with a smile.

Hecate took his hand and shook it.

"Hecate Cavendish, assistant librarian, pleased to meet you," she said. It crossed her mind that Reverend Forsyth was altogether too good looking for a clergyman. His long black cassock fitted him perfectly, giving his slender physique a slightly theatrical air, accentuating his height and contrasting with his fair coloring. "It is good of you to give up your time, but I promise you, I am perfectly capable of finding something to eat."

"I don't doubt it for a moment, however, Dean Chalmers would not hear of it. Shall we go?" he asked, stepping aside to hold the door open for her.

They descended to the ground floor and Reverend Forsyth strode along the north aisle, pointing out items of interest as they went. Hecate found that yet again she had to almost trot to keep up. She tried to take in details about the decorated tomb of St. Cantilupe; the stained-glass window in the transept in need of repair; the position of the organ behind the choir stalls, where, he told her, he spent most of his time; the unlit Gurney stoves, which he informed her would be all that stood between herself and a winter chill in the months to come; the tomb of St. Cuthbert set into the north wall, and the beautifully carved paneling that led to the main door. This was the second time in the same day she had trailed in the wake of someone attempting to fill her head with information. John Forsyth was a wholly different guide from the librarian however. Where her superior's haste had been all about returning to his own desk and concerns, this young vicar was full of obvious delight for the cathedral and a wish to share it with her.

They emerged into the spring sunshine and headed off across the Green. Hecate was surprised to find that he did not, in fact, take her to a café or a restaurant. Instead he marched to Askews bakery in Church Street, where he purchased hot meat pies and bottles of lemonade for them both. Their meal obtained, he then took her back across the Cathedral Green, skirting the west wall, and on to the Lady Arbor. This recently refurbished quadrangle was prettily planted with small trees and shrubs, among which were set several benches. He selected one in the far corner and bid her take a seat.

"A lovely place for a picnic," Hecate commented.

"When I cannot endure another bout of feasting and gossip in the hall it is to this haven that I come. This bench is perfectly positioned, you see." He indicated with the wave of a hand as he spoke. "We are able to observe any-one entering the quad, either from the arbor gate or the exit from the clois-ters. However, those two cherry trees afford us the advantage of privacy. Here we may enjoy the finest pies in Hereford without fear of a breach of deco-rum, however many crumbs may fall." To illustrate his point he bit into the unwrapped mutton pie he held, sending a shower of pastry flakes down the front of his cassock.

Hecate grinned and tucked into her own pie, her mouth already water-ing at the savory aroma and anticipation of what she knew to be, as he had said, a snack without equal in the city. For a few moments they ate in com-panionable silence before she could not resist quizzing him about his posi-tion at the cathedral.

"Forgive my curiosity, Reverend Forsyth . . ."

"Never apologize for curiosity. The quest for knowledge is always to be encouraged."

"Ah, but how can you be sure my inquiries are not, in fact, carefully con-sidered questions, but simply impertinent musings? Perhaps I am merely nosey about how you live your life."

He gave her a sideways glance to check how serious she was being.

"Well, in that case you might be an incorrigible gossip and therefore highly entertaining."

"A shocking statement from a member of the clergy!" She feigned aston-ishment, but did not let it stop her eating her pie.

"You are mistaken if you think we clerics are above such things. Faith and gossip are what fuels our work here. Faith is what calls us. Gossip, or as I prefer to think of it, a real and lively interest in our congregation and parishioners, well, that is what gives faith its application. How are we to help the afflicted if we do not know of their affliction? How may we persuade the sinner to mend his ways if we are not informed of those very ways? How can we bring the comfort and guidance of God's word to those most in need of it, if we cannot name them and have no inkling of whose need is, in fact, the greater?" After this little speech he finished his meal and dusted pastry crumbs from his fingers. "So, nosiness or a thirst for knowledge, it matters not, for I am happy to answer your questions in either case."

"I am delighted to hear it. Tell me, then, what drew you to a life at the cathedral? There must be any number of livings available for a man wishing to be a priest, and I imagine the duties would be fewer and the freedoms greater, with your own house, for example, in a village parish. Why did you choose to come here?"

"Aside from the magnificence of the cathedral itself, and the esteem in which it and its clergy are held, d'you mean?" He gave a light laugh then, surprising in its softness. "It was a simple decision for me, once I had accepted I was to become a man of the cloth. I came here for the music. Any parish priest may raise his voice in a hymn on Sundays. Only the vicars choral here at the cathedral perform sung services of great sweetness and beauty twice a day, seven days a week. Only here can I give a great number of my hours to the practice and playing of the wonderful organ. You see, Miss Cavendish, God called me through the gift of his music."

"An irresistible call, then?"

"For me, yes, it was. And I am glad of it. Frankly, I wonder what else I would have been able to offer the world."

"How fortunate then, that your talent has found a home, to the benefit of many, no doubt."

"I shall ask you to repeat that once you have heard me play." He smiled at her. "And you, Miss Cavendish, what is it that brings you here?"

She brushed pastry from her lap. "Can you not guess?"

"Let me see, you have a fierce desire for independence and so wish to enter the world of work?"

"Reverend Forsyth, I believe you have been speaking with my mother!"

He laughed at this. "Or could it be that you, too, are answering a call?"

"To the church? Oh, no. You might blame my father for that. I'm afraid a lifetime of listening to stories of Egyptian tombs, lost tribes and their belief in human sacrifice, and so many other fascinating glimpses into what shapes us . . . all these things have, if anything, steered me away from, well, from the more conventional religion."

"And yet, here you are. So, not to break free of your family, not to find your way to God, and yet, if I am not mistaken, I see a brightness in you . . . something drew you to this place."

He waited then, allowing space for her to give a more serious answer, perhaps.

"My father has a word for it," she told him. "Adventure."

"And you think to find that in a library?"

"Of course! Such a library is not a mere accumulation of books. Up there, in that room, there is a collection to rival any in the world! Ancient manuscripts; records that predate the printed word; fabulous illuminated Gospels; writings of the sages through time; books that speak of forgotten people and their wisdom that might otherwise be lost; books of such rarity and value that they must be chained, or in some instances, kept locked up in a manner that would defy the deftest of thieves. What greater adventure can there be than to travel to mysterious lands, to hear of far-flung peoples and their strange and wonderful lives, to marvel at stories of cities built over centuries only to be abandoned to jungles or fall to ruin under years of siege and onslaughts of the machines of war? How many lives might we ourselves live when transported through the words kept in that library, as if the very ghosts of those who wrote them are whispering in our ears as we read?"

He looked at her differently then, so that Hecate felt herself studied like some unusual bird that had flown into the garden. She stood up, uncomfortable under such scrutiny, irritated with herself for saying so much.

"While my father might encourage my passion for books, my mother tells me that I am prone to talking more than is necessary or sensible in company. I fear I may just have proved her right."

He, too, rose to his feet.

"Well, I for one am delighted that you have come to join us at the cathedral. I look forward to hearing of your adventures, of the mysteries you uncover up there in your aerie."

She glanced at him to see if he was laughing at her but his expression remained open and kind rather than mocking. She heard the tower bell strike the quarter hour.

"Thank you for the pie," she said, already backing away. "It was good of you."

"Let me escort you."

"No need," she said, turning and walking briskly across the quadrangle. And then, concerned she had seemed rude, she spun around so that she continued stepping backward while she called to him. "Surely an adventurer can find her own way back to her desk?"

"Godspeed!" he called after her, and she saw that he was smiling again.

AS HECATE DESCENDED THE STAIRS FROM THE LIBRARY AT THE END OF her first working day, the final, sustained notes of a sung psalm echoed through-out the cathedral. She was familiar with the sublime singing and glorious organ music of the cathedral from attending services, but knew she would never become inured to its power. The beauty of the voices, the sweetness of the high notes and the somber comfort of the low ones never failed to reach her. Despite her father's inclination, she had been raised a practicing Chris-tian so that the liturgy and rituals were part of her normal life. However, she was of the opinion that even a nonbeliever could not fail to be moved by such sounds as were to be found in Evensong. Now, thinking of John Forsyth and his devotion to the music of the cathedral, she had another reason to enjoy it.

She arrived home to find her father in the stables.

"Wonderfully punctual as ever, I see. How was your first day as an em-ployed person?"

She laughed. "Fascinating! I have so much to tell you, and so many ques-tions . . ."

"And I shall be delighted to hear all the details and answer whatever I am able, but first, we must attend to our mission for your brother."

"We are to take him to Kynaston?"

"Indeed we are. Put your bicycle away, quick as you can. Then go and fetch

Charlie," he said, returning to the complicated business of getting the harness on Peggy. Hecate leaned her bicycle against the door of the stall.

"Are we in a particular hurry?"

"Yes and no. No, in as much as the days have lengthened nicely, so we have sunlight on our side. Yes, in that your mother is taking tea with the Benson sisters and may tire of their conversation and return home at any moment."

The two exchanged conspiratorial grins.

She found her brother in the hallway lacing up his boots. Eight years her junior, he had still the gangly frame of a young man in the making. His hair was the same red as her own, but the rest of him was all their mother. When fully grown he would no doubt be quite substantial. Now, however, he was fragile. Hecate would never forget the agony of worry the family had endured when rheumatic fever had almost claimed him. Good nursing and good fortune had seen him win through, but the legacy of vulnerability was there for all to see. The doctor had assured them he would regain his strength and could live well, but he must guard against chills, fevers, and suchlike. Their mother had made it her mission to protect him. Their father saw it as his job to ensure the boy experienced life, even though it be at some risk.

On seeing his sister, Charlie grinned. "I knew you wouldn't be late. Has Father got the cart ready?" He showed little sign of the head cold their mother had mentioned.

"Very nearly. Here, let me." She bobbed down and took the laces from him, pulling tight, her movements quick and practiced.

"Hey, my poor feet!" Charlie laughed.

"Come along, no time for complaining," she said, standing up and reaching past him to grab a boater and muffler.

Ten minutes later, the trio were installed in the small tub-cart, Peggy trotting smartly east along Hampton Park Road. The trap was plain but serviceable and adequate for the family's everyday needs. When covered transport was required, perhaps to take them in their finery to a ball, Mr. Cavendish would summon a cab. It was a matter of disappointment to Mrs. Cavendish that they no longer kept a carriage of their own. The truth was, they could neither afford nor justify it. Their social engagements were mostly of the small variety and within a short cab ride. Their funds would be tested if they were to purchase and maintain such a carriage, and to buy and keep at least a pair of well-bred and trained horses to pull it would be beyond them. Hecate understood that her parents were not poor, as such. She also understood that, however much her mother might declare the humble income she earned from the library superfluous to requirements, it was helpful. The family money her father possessed, along with the small financial success his career as an archeologist had brought him, was sufficient for their modest lifestyle, but no more than that. She was perfectly content with things the way they were, but she knew that at times her mother struggled to keep up with their wealthier friends, and that invitations were sometimes turned down in order to limit expenses.

She tucked a rug over Charlie's knees and slid her arm around his waist, pulling him a little closer. She could hear their mother's admonishments in her ear and was determined to keep him safe, but she and her father were of one mind when it came to what was best for the boy. Already there was more color in his cheeks and his eyes were shining with the simple pleasure of being out of doors. The avenue of fine houses gave way to countryside as they left the city. The road was a good one, well maintained and reasonably free of ruts and holes. The lowland fields to the east of Hereford were lush and fertile, fed by the River Wye and its smaller cousin, the Lugg. The county was known for its produce, particularly its beef and hops, and increasingly its cider apples. On this fine spring afternoon the orchards were beginning to bud and some to blossom, lending a prettiness to the landscape that could not fail to lift the spirits. It took them a little under an hour to reach the village of Kynaston, by which time the pony was beginning to slow, her flanks damp with sweat, her tail swishing against bothersome flies. As the farmhouse came into view, Charlie twisted in his seat, craning for a better view of the fields and a possible glimpse of the Hereford cattle he so delighted in. Hecate experienced a similar delight at the idea of seeing their family friend again.

As if reading her thoughts, her father exclaimed, "And there he is! The man himself."

Perhaps having heard the approaching cart, the owner of Kynaston Farm had come to stand at the end of the drive. And now she could see him, leaning on the gatepost, a hand raised in greeting, his habitual smile topped off by his fine waxed and twirled mustache, his broad shoulders filling out the tweed of his jacket and his ample chest straining the buttons of his yellow-checked waistcoat: the imposing figure of gentleman farmer, Phileas James Weatherby Sterling.

"A trio of Cavendishes!" he exclaimed. "Is there a compelling reason to flee the city, or am I to believe you make the journey purely for the pleasure of my company?" he asked, taking hold of Peggy's bridle and rubbing the pony's ears.

"I am sorry to deflate your pride, Phileas," Hecate told him, opening the little door at the back of the cart and climbing out, "but it is your cattle we've come to see."

Mr. Cavendish laughed. "You cannot compete with their charms, old boy. Pointless to try."

He clutched at his heart dramatically. "I am wounded! Though inclined to agree."

Hecate let him take her hand and kiss it.

"Charlie knows all their names," she said, noting how he held her hand a little longer than was strictly necessary. She made sure not to react. "He's come to check you are looking after them properly."

Phileas turned his attention to the boy. "Ah, I sense a stockman in the making!"

Charlie beamed. "I would like nothing better."

"I'm sure Mother would be delighted," Hecate said, her face clearly stating the opposite.

"And why not?" Phileas wanted to know. "Farming is good honest work, you can't argue against that. Close to God's creations, and putting food in the mouths of the hungry."

"I thought your main income was from beer hops," Hecate teased.

He gave an expansive shrug. "Good, nourishing stuff, beer. But you forget, I do sell my beef cattle. They are the pride and focus of my farm, and as fine company as anyone could wish for."

Mr. Cavendish had also alighted from the cart. "I doubt Beatrice would view it quite like that," he said. Seeing the frown on his son's face he went on. "I suspect she would prefer you to occupy yourself with something less . . . pungent."

At this Phileas let out one of his famous bursts of laughter. It was a sudden roar of a sound, sincere and joyful. It reminded Hecate that it was not, in fact, his cattle herd or his beautiful farm that had lured them from their home. Being in his company was a tonic, though she considered it unwise to let him know just how much she valued his friendship. She was aware that his interest in her had outgrown that of family friend but she did not wish to give him false hope. The fact that he was five years her senior was not an issue for her. Nor did she consider, unlike her mother, that farming, however genteel and lucrative, was not a desirable occupation. The plain truth was, she had no desire to marry anyone. She could not imagine marrying and giving up her post at the library that she had only just obtained, and taking up the duties of a wife.

Phileas led them up the sweeping driveway that circled around the pretty gardens at the front of the house. Kynaston Farm was a medieval black-and-white timbered building of particular charm and character. It was not so big as to be uncomfortable to live in, yet large enough to provoke envy in anyone with a discerning eye for property. Its ancient timbers supported a roof of fine Welsh slate and complemented the handsome mullioned windows.

Hecate had always loved the house. Her affection for the place was also built upon the many happy hours she and her family had spent there. Phileas was renowned for being a superb if unorthodox host. His parties invariably involved games and an abundance of food and a degree of latitude when it came to etiquette that she had always found refreshing.

Today, it was not the house that was their destination but the pasture to the rear of it. They tied Peggy to a post and walked across the cobbled yard, past the towering redbrick oasthouses which stood waiting for the hop harvest, and on to the first of a series of meadows. These lush, flat fields had been carefully fenced with iron railings at no small expense. The four of them stood with the low sun at their backs, their long shadows falling before them upon the verdant turf, taller versions of themselves. With the others, Hecate scanned the field, searching for the cows, wondering how such substantial creatures could hide themselves so well.

"There!" shouted Charlie at last, pointing excitedly. "In the shade of the far oak."

"You've a keen eye, Master Cavendish!" Phileas told him.

Hecate could see them, too, a cluster of dark shapes in the cool shadow of the spreading tree, some standing, swishing their tufted tails, others lying down. "They look so peaceful. It seems a shame to disturb them," she murmured.

He looked at her. "Shall we walk to them?" he asked.

"No!" Charlie was adamant. "Whistle for them, Phileas. Please?"

"Come along, Sterling," her father teased, "let's have your party trick."

"What say you, Hecate?" their host asked. It was a simple question, but the softening in his voice and the way he looked at her as he asked it spoke of other things unsaid.

She smiled brightly. "Go on. This is Charlie's outing."

He nodded. Taking a breath, he put his fingers in his mouth and let out a rich, two-noted whistle that carried easily over the distance before them. The cattle heard it. Some turned their heads. Others fidgeted a little. Phileas waited, showing a knack for dramatic timing. When all the cattle had risen, and most had turned to face him, he whistled once more. It was all the encouragement his stock needed. As one, the herd began to move, walking at first, their broad feet sinking a little into the soft turf with each stride. In a matter of moments, they were all traveling at speed, their combined weight shaking the ground as close to thirty full grown Hereford cows and an almost equal number of the previous year's calves came thundering across the meadow. The herd drew closer and then suddenly, as if they were a troop of well-drilled soldiers, they wheeled right, showing unexpected agility, slowing their pace now, completing the circle to return to stand in front of their beloved owner.

He sprang over the fence and moved among them, scratching an ear here, patting a rump there. "Good afternoon to you, too, my dear ladies," he told them, far too proud of his stock to be coy about showing his affection for them. And they did look splendid with the April sunshine setting their curly red coats ablaze, and their white faces prettily setting off their large, dark eyes. At rest again they returned to their more docile selves. "Come along, young Cavendish, step lively," said Phileas, holding out a hand. Charlie took it and scaled the fence, puffing only a little. Hecate and her father watched as he, too, made a fuss of the cows naming each one as he did so. They took comfort in the boy's obvious enjoyment, for how could anyone so full of life be in danger of losing it?

"Some fine beasts you've got there, Sterling," Edward announced. "Not that I know much about these things. Though I have an opinion on a good piece of roast beef."

"Father!" Charlie was horrified.

"That is the reality of rearing cattle for market, no avoiding it, I'm afraid."

Charlie looked at Phileas. "But these aren't going for meat, are they? Not Iris. Not Flora!"

"No, sir!" he assured him. "These ladies are my foundation stock. And their calves will go out into the world to provide the next generation of Herefords. Have I mentioned that these youngsters are all bound for America?"

Hecate nodded. "Once or twice."

"Herefords are causing a stir over there. Imagine, my fine young cattle roaming the Great Plains . . ." His expression became wistful.

Edward laughed. "I swear, Sterling, you will never find a wife while your heart belongs to these blasted cows!"

Charlie piped up, "You should marry Hecate, then I can visit more often."

"Charlie!" Hecate was infuriated to feel herself blushing. From the corner of her eye she noticed her father watching her closely. "Not everybody wants to get married," she said, leaving them to decide if she was talking about herself or their host.

Phileas did his best to laugh off the insensitive remark. "Oh I don't think many women would consider me a suitable husband."

Charlie thought about it. "They may not be as keen on cows as you are," he conceded.

"No?"

He shook his head. "They like flowers more." A thought occurred to him. "You could show Hecate your orchard. She'd like that."

"You think so?"

He shrugged. "She's a girl."

There was an uncomfortable silence. Hecate did not dare speak for fear of either hurting Phileas's feelings or encouraging her brother's line of thought. She had the horrible sense that her father was letting the awkward pause in the conversation stretch to a breaking point in the hope Phileas would jump in and say something that might make clear his intentions toward her. In the end the moment was saved by one of the younger cows setting up an unprovoked and startling lowing, filling the air with its booming voice, causing everyone to laugh.

Phileas recovered himself enough to suggest that maybe a stroll through the orchard was a good idea anyway. He helped Charlie back over the railings and they made the short walk to the wooden gate to the left of the house. Charlie and his father went in first heading off briskly at a pace Hecate was convinced was designed to leave herself and Phileas alone together. She let him fall into step beside her, though pointedly did not take his arm.

"These apple trees blossom late, to guard against frosts," he told her, gesturing at the rows and rows of little trees that filled the field. "So, not many flowers to see here yet, I'm afraid. But by the end of the month, well, they will put on quite a show."

"I look forward to that," she said.

"And cider is the coming thing, don't you know?"

"Really?"

"Oh yes. Hops will become my secondary crop. Apples will take over. I'll have my own cider this year." He looked as if he might have more to say on the subject but then faltered and changed his mind.

"How wonderful," Hecate said, plucking at a tall piece of grass.

He hesitated for a moment and then went on, "Apple blossom can be most attractive, can it not?"

"Certainly it can."

He began to twirl the ends of his fine mustache. It was a habit she had noticed in him when he was either deep in thought or a little perplexed. Even knowing him as she did, it was hard to tell which was the cause at that moment.

"How is your bicycle?" he asked suddenly.

Hecate stopped and stared at him. "My bicycle?"

"Yes. Fine piece of engineering. American, I believe you mentioned. Very fine."

"Phileas, my bicycle is exceptionally well, thank you so much for inquiring after its health."

"Now you are laughing at me."

"Do you wonder?"

"Dash it all, Hecate. I'm not a man for frivolous small talk. You know that."

"Then why try?"

He waved an arm in the direction of Charlie who was already at the far end of the second row of apple trees. "I might bore you with so many details of the farm. Your brother is right. My . . . interests may not be, well, of interest . . . to ladies."

"First of all, I am not 'ladies'—you've known me since I was eight and we are friends, are we not?"

"Indubitably!"

"Secondly, we came here today because Father and I know how much Charlie enjoys it and he needed fresh air."

"He's a fine lad. Happy to help."

"And thirdly . . ."

"Dear Lord, has there to be a thirdly?"

She put her hand on his arm. "If you start making silly small talk at me I will never speak to you again. Now, tell me about your cider."

A broad smile rearranged his attractive features, his eyes sparkling. "Right. Good! Ha! Cider, yes, of course. So, half these trees are Tremletts and the other half are Foxwhelps. They are pest resistant and known to give a fair yield. More importantly, they will provide a good mix for a dry cider, which is what we're going for here at Kynaston. None of your sugary nonsense. A traditional, golden cider. I think it will be quite the rage. Nothing too heady, of course . . ."

And so he fell to telling her with great enthusiasm about his new enterprise, and they strode on through the old orchard, ducking drowsy bees, happy to have banished the awkwardness that had initially accompanied them.

On her second day of work, Hecate arrived early at the cathedral. She wanted to take the opportunity to explore the building for a short while, to begin to learn its secrets for herself. Having parked her bicycle she slipped quietly through the south door and wandered down the aisle that led to the main transept. This was on the opposite side of the nave and the altar from her ordinary route, so it was an area she knew only slightly. She passed the entrance to the vestry where she had yet to be sent to make tea. She was on the point of turning into the south transept when a large woman with high color came bustling out through the vestry door, pushing a cart laden with feather dusters, rags, and tins of beeswax polish and brass cleaner. Even without the tools of her trade, Hecate would have recognized her as Mrs. White from the dean's description, not so much by her appearance as her manner.

"I shall fall behind with my duties this day and every other, the way things are!" The cleaner dispensed with any greetings in favor of launching into a complaint concerning the restoration work that was in progress. "Stonemasons cannot but produce dust, and that dust must be dealt with. I am one person and one only, with just so many hours in my day," she pointed out, as if her day might be shorter than anyone else's.

Hecate gave her what she hoped was a reassuring smile and held out a hand. "Mrs. White? I am Hecate Cavendish, come to assist the master of the library."

Mrs. White took the proffered hand and gave it a limp squeeze. "It had not escaped my notice that Reverend Thomas has been provided with help, whereas my own entreaties for reinforcements have fallen upon deaf ears. Oh, I do not begrudge your presence, Miss Cavendish, dear me, you will think me a termagant!"

"Not at all . . ."

"'Tis only that I wish to maintain the high standards I have always provided. And now I find I cannot! Corners are being cut, Miss Cavendish. Cut, I tell you!"

"Your distress is entirely understandable, Mrs. White. Perhaps another conversation with Dean Chalmers would be worth your while? I do not believe he would wish to see you so overwhelmed."

The older woman seemed a tad reassured to hear these words and calmed a little.

"The dean is a fair-minded man . . . but I dislike bothering him with my woes," she said suddenly. "I will do as I always have, Miss Cavendish; I will manage. I will endure." So saying she pushed her trolley onward, away along the aisle, its wheels rattling as it trundled over flagstones, then tiles, and back to flagstones once again.

After lingering awhile in the nave to gaze upon the gorgeous goldwork on the altar cloth and the fabulous carved reredos behind it, Hecate took the steps into the north aisle. She passed the open door to the tiny Stanbury Chapel, and as she did so she saw a soldier sitting, head bowed in silent prayer, the light filtered through the stained-glass windows setting the scarlet of his uniform ablaze. She tiptoed past and took the spiral staircase up to the library. The door was unlocked. Reverend Thomas appeared to give the impression he had been there some time, looking up from his desk with raised eyebrows as the tower bell struck nine o'clock, but the fact that he was still puffing from the climb somewhat undermined his subterfuge.

"Good morning, Reverend Thomas," Hecate said brightly, hanging her coat on the hook on the coat stand. "Another lovely day. I was only just saying to Mrs. White—"

"You would do better not to engage that lady in conversation. She is given to exaggeration and chatter, neither of which is a good use of your time."

She opened her mouth to reply but thought better of it, hurrying to take her place behind her desk instead. To her left there was a box containing the documents she had been given the day before. Despite her diligent efforts, it was still more than half full. On her right were two boxes into which she was required to sift and organize the pages once she had identified and logged them. As Hecate settled to her work, so the atmosphere of the room settled around her. It was filled not with silence, but by a busy quiet, punctuated by a loose windowpane being gently rattled by a spring breeze, Reverend Thomas's faintly wheezing in-breaths, the occasional rustling of paper or vellum as the two of them applied themselves to their labors, the distant sound of footfalls upon flagstones, or snatches of singing from the choir practicing in the hall of the cloisters. Underlying these was another sound. It was of such a timbre that Hecate could not be certain it did not exist only in her own head, like the thud of her heartbeat reverberating against her eardrums. It was a soft humming, a vibration of some sort, and it ran continuously, underscoring all the other small noises. In addition, the room had its own smells; old books, leather, turpentine, glue, varnish, beeswax, gas lamps, metal polish. They were familiar to Hecate from a childhood spent in her father's study or in the attic, where he would clean, repair, and preserve treasures and tomes acquired through his years as an archeologist. She breathed in those smells now, steadying her own breath as they calmed her, absorbing the atmosphere of the room while it in turn absorbed her. She became part of it. A tiny cog in a mighty engine. Her own thoughts adding to those recorded in the books and maps, her mind open to the whispers of the ancients whose wisdom and stories sat upon the shelves surrounding her.

She raised her gaze from her paperwork to glance across the room at the locked cabinet. A slant of sunshine threw shadows of the window tracery upon its polished wood and the gold of its finger plate. She could not help wondering what it contained, and the librarian's reluctance to tell her only increased her interest. She had not had the opportunity to ask her father if he knew about it, as upon their return from Kynaston the previous evening he had received a visitor from the city museum. She resolved to ask him the moment she saw him next. Her plan had always been to compose a reading schedule, so that she could work through the most thought-provoking and unusual works in the collection. How could she know where to start without knowing the contents of that cabinet?

She stretched her back for a moment, moving her arms to free them of a stiffness born of close, still work. As she did so she turned her head so that she was looking at the map on the wall to her right. If the library held secrets, the map held mysteries of its own. She fell to picking out the mythical creatures, naming them in her head, committing them to memory.

*Unicorn, phoenix, dragon, sphinx, griffin, manticore . . .*

She stopped, her eyes flicking back to the griffin. She could have sworn she saw it move. Just the tiniest bit. A brief flexing of one of its talons. She stared hard at it, waiting. Nothing. Her imagination was playing tricks. She straightened her shoulders and turned back to the work on her desk.

# 3

OUTSIDE, THE AFTERNOON WAS COOLING AS SHE WHEELED HER BICY-
cle across the Cathedral Green. The fresh air helped soothe her mind, which
still seethed with the stimulation of her second day as library assistant. There
was so much she wanted answers to, and to force herself to be patient was, for
Hecate, the hardest of challenges. She had just reached the narrow entrance
to Church Street when she heard her name being called. Turning, she saw
Clemmie waving to her from the other side of the Green.

The Honorable Clementine Twyford-Harris was, aside from being Hecate's
dearest friend, a rare and wonderful person, in that her presence in a room
could not fail to brighten it, her attendance at a function would ensure its
success, and her smile, when bestowed spontaneously, could thaw the iciest
of hearts. It was not simply that she was beautiful, for many pretty girls of the
town could be said to equal her in their decorative qualities. It was her sincere
warmth coupled with her renowned determination to see the advantages to
everything and play down the disadvantages that made her so well-loved. If
a thunderstorm interrupted a picnic, Clemmie would be the one dancing in
the rain. If the orchestra were prevented from attending a ball because of a
snowstorm, she would have twenty volunteers singing waltzes while she accompanied them on the pianoforte. If a friend was disappointed in love, she
would throw a party to celebrate their narrow escape from a boring match
and line up five more suitors, each more thrilling and unsuitable than the last.

"There you are!" She arrived at Hecate's side, her pale blond hair not in the slightest disturbed by the briskness of her pace. "I swear even when pushing that wretched bicycle you move like the wind. If you'd started pedalling I'd never have caught you up."

The two young women embraced, Hecate enjoying the light but expensive scent her friend wore as it evoked old-fashioned roses and languid summer afternoons.

"You were lucky to find me at all," she said. "I was on the point of leaving when Reverend Thomas asked me to see to it that all the glue brushes were taken to the vestry and washed."

The two fell into step and continued their way down the cobbled street.

"I know you, given half the chance you will spend far too long in that gloomy place. I shall spring surprise visits often to make certain you come out with me and have some fun."

"I enjoy my work."

"That is precisely what causes me the most concern! Hemmed in by dusty books and ancient scribblings, surrounded by tombs, not to mention being prayed at all the time."

Hecate laughed. "It really isn't like that, you know."

"Never fear, Clemmie is here! I have the perfect antidote to all that somber stuff."

"Indeed? And what might that be?"

She slipped her arm through Hecate's and grinned. "I'm about to show you. Come along, this way!" she said, leading her across East Street, apparently impervious to the admiring glances of the men who parted before them like the Red Sea. They emerged into the town square which they crossed quickly, weaving in and out of the late afternoon hawkers and carriages. Crossing Widemarsh Street, Clemmie steered her friend down a short alleyway at the end of which was a café with chairs and tables set up outside it.

"I haven't tried this one before," Hecate said. "Is their cake to be recommended?"

"Put cake from your mind," she replied with an expressive wave of her hand. "This, Hecate Cavendish, is something new. We are not here for mere cake. This is an ice cream parlor!"

"I never heard of such a thing."

"Isn't it thrilling? A whole establishment solely devoted to the selling of ice cream. More flavors than you ever knew existed. And look, we can sit out here and enjoy it, as if we were in Paris!"

"Eating in the street? I don't know who would be the more furious, your mother or mine."

"I know, that's the best bit!"

A waiter came out and escorted them to one of the little wrought-iron tables. The young man took just a tiny bit longer over pulling out a chair for Clementine than he did for Hecate. He handed them menus and advised them regarding the various flavors and quantities on offer. After much deliberation, Hecate chose cherry and Clemmie selected candied orange. When the pink china dishes arrived they were piled high with the exotic desserts, topped with sugared almonds and tiny sticks of jewel green candied angelica. Both girls were delighted with their choices, savoring every spoonful.

"Heaven in a dish!" Clemmie declared, her eyes closed for a moment.

Hecate mumbled her agreement, enjoying the ice cream too much to speak. The last of the day's sunshine fell helpfully into the small square where they and half a dozen other customers were sitting, so that they could indeed imagine themselves in some sunny corner of a continental city. Only when they had both scraped the last morsel from their bowls did they speak again.

"I had a very specific reason for coming to see you," Clemmie said, dabbing at her mouth with the linen napkin provided.

"Aside from the ice cream? What could be more important?"

"It's a close-run thing, I grant you, but, well, Mama is holding a ball."

"Another one?"

"Another one. And you are to attend, I won't let you wriggle out of it."

"I never do!"

"You always try."

"I'm simply not a . . . ball sort of person."

"Nonsense. Everyone likes a ball if it's done properly. You've just been dragged to one too many disappointing ones."

"Often by you, I'd like to point out."

"Oh, Hecate, don't be such a grump. You can bring your whole family if it will make you happier. Charlie loves to get out of the house. You're surely not going to deny him the opportunity for some fun, are you? No. Then it's settled."

Hecate felt her shoulders slump just the slightest. While she loved being in the company of her friend, the thought of a hot, crowded room, full of people she would, for the most part, rather have avoided, and hours of small talk, and being expected to dance with men she had no interest in . . . And yet, she was no more able to refuse Clementine than anyone else was.

Clemmie was talking about lending her a dress.

"Oh, don't worry," Hecate cut in, "Mother will find me something."

"Which is exactly what I am concerned about. Really, Hecate, you are never going to find yourself a husband if you persist in letting your mother dress you. Unless you want to be the one to tell her frou-frou bodices have been *de trop* since the end of the Napoleonic Wars."

"I have no wish to find a husband. How can I convince you?"

"Wishing has nothing to do with it. If you don't find one for yourself, your mother will, eventually, foist one upon you. And if her taste in suitors is anything like her taste in ball gowns, you are in terrible trouble."

"Just because your mother wants to see you well matched . . ."

"All mothers live to see their daughters married off as successfully as is humanly possible. In fact, I have the opposite problem to you."

"You do?"

"Your mother would marry you to some dreary, dry vicar or other in a heartbeat and be satisfied. Mine has such high ambitions for me, nothing less than a duke will do. Why would I care for a high-ranking aristocrat? I can't think why Mama imagines I would be happy in some drafty mausoleum of a house with dusty ancestors staring down at me from all the walls."

"I think it's a little harsh to paint all vicars with the same brush. Some are really quite . . . personable."

Clemmie gasped.

"Gracious, one has caught your eye already! For pity's sake, Hecate, you surely cannot see yourself as a vicar's wife!"

"I do not! I'm only pointing out that, well, you are wrong to cast them all in the same light."

"Same brush, same light . . . nothing changes what would be required of you! Worthy works, visiting the poor, hours spent consoling widows . . . Really, Hecate, you might as well marry the bally cathedral."

Hecate opened her mouth to protest but thought better of it. How could

she explain, even to someone who knew her so well, that the strongest argument in favor of her marrying this particular vicar would be precisely that:
that she would be able to stay at the cathedral. As his wife she would live in
the cloisters and might be permitted to continue to assist in the library. While
she had never wanted to marry, even she had to admit to herself that John
Forsyth was the first person who offered the possibility to satisfy her mother's
plans for her while also allowing her some freedom to follow her own life interests. She did not, however, expect Clemmie to understand. As far as her
friend was concerned, a good marriage, a family, a secure place in society,
these were things that mattered.

"Anyway"—Clemmie was smiling broadly now—"Phileas will be at the
ball. Now, *there's* a husband for you, Hecate. No, do not tell me I am wrong.
I might end up an old spinster thanks to my mother's unreasonable expectations, but I will see you happily installed in Kynaston Farm surrounded by
a gaggle of red-haired children, running rings round a very happy Phileas.
Just see if I don't."

Hecate arrived home to find her mother and Charlie in the drawing room.
Despite the warmth of the day a fire burned in the hearth and she could smell
the menthol infusion her mother insisted on subjecting her brother to.

"Where is Father?" she asked, pausing to lean over Charlie as he sat at a
table working on his ship in a bottle. She hugged him, pleased to see him up
and about and looking quite well.

"Hecate, you're not helping!" he complained good-naturedly, holding up
a stick in tweezers. "I have to keep my hand steady."

"Forgive me," she said, stepping back, smiling at him. "I should hate to
delay the construction of—What is it this time, *The Beagle*?"

"HMS *Victory*," he corrected her. "I'm going to put Admiral Nelson right . . .
there," he said, picking up a magnifying glass to identify the spot.

Her mother looked up from her sewing. "What on earth is that on your
dress?"

Hecate glanced down and saw what her mother had noticed; a pink stain
on her bodice, showing up rather markedly against the blue fabric. She rubbed
at it with a thumb.

"Oh, don't worry. It's only ice cream."

"Ice cream?"

"Clementine took me to the most wonderful place. You'd love it, Charlie. It's called an ice cream parlor and they sell nothing else."

"Just ice cream!" His eyes widened.

Her mother narrowed hers. "And were you, perhaps, required to catch it as it was thrown to you? I cannot imagine how else you come to be covered in the stuff."

"Hardly covered, Mother. I only dropped a little. Everyone did. The sun was making it melt so quickly."

"The su— You were eating it out of doors? In the street?"

"At a darling little table set on a terrace outside a café. All completely respectable, I promise. Now, where is Father?"

Beatrice turned back to her mending. "He is in the attic. He went up there over an hour ago in search of some bone or other. He mentioned the museum."

The attic was Edward Cavendish's place of retreat. His study, while very much his own domain and not somewhere his wife would linger, was nevertheless accessible, positioned as it was on the ground floor, only a few brisk strides from the drawing room. When he wished to put himself beyond the reach of domestic interruptions, it was to the attic that he fled.

Hecate climbed the broad wooden staircase and then took the narrower, creaking one that led to the top floor of the house. Here were rooms that another family might have given over to the housing of servants. The Cavendishes' staff, however, lived out. Stella, the maid, and Mrs. Evans—known always simply as Cook—arrived six mornings a week and left after supper each day. So it was that the rooms that shouldered the roof of the house, their ceilings sloping, were entirely at the disposal of Mr. Cavendish, so that he might store his treasures. And what treasures they were, at least to him and to his daughter.

Hecate followed the sounds of rummaging, passing through the first room and using the interconnecting door that led to the second. The spaces were arranged with boxes and crates and cupboards forming blocks, so that narrow paths ran between them. The stacks were too high to see over, and the fading light of the day falling through the skylight windows set into the roof was largely obscured. Gas had not been piped to the attic, Mrs. Cavendish deeming it an unnecessary expense, so that now Hecate had to fumble through gloom, moving toward the sounds of her father's search in the far room.

"Ah, the worker bee returns to the hive!" He greeted her without looking up, certain the only person who would venture to the attic would be his daughter. He was sorting through a crate of small, wooden boxes, lifting the lid of each to check the contents, his endeavors illuminated by the light of a large brass lamp set down on a trunk to his right.

"Mother said you were hunting for a bone."

He straightened up then, turning to look at her, his unlit pipe clenched between his teeth. "Yes. A thigh bone, in fact. Or, more accurately, several of them."

"Goodness! What creature can have so many?"

"A family of desert gerbils. *Pachyuromys duprasi.* Small fellows. Given to hopping about at great speed, more than anything resembling rotund, miniature kangaroos."

"And they are destined for the museum?"

"They are if I can find the elusive little creatures. I know they came back with all the lesser artifacts from the 1872 dig in Mesopotamia, and I am certain this is the right collection. Alas the ink on the labels has let me down so that I am required to look inside every box. See? Here . . . nothing but smudges."

Hecate took one of the boxes from him and examined the blue marks on it. "How sad, to become nothing more than part of a lesser collection of things in an unmarked receptacle, so far from home."

"Don't let that romantic imagination of yours do the gerbils down. Their cousins would no doubt have been eaten by snakes. How's that for an ending? No, these will have a future, in a curious way. Mr. Squires will feature them in his Egyptian display and knowledge and understanding of the fat-tailed gerbil, to give them their common name, will be increased." He patted his pockets in search of his tobacco pouch, failed to find it, and sucked instead on the empty pipe. "Now tell me, does your work continue well at the library?"

"Oh yes, it really is the most fascinating place, Father. Only . . ."

"Only . . . ?"

"I fear I will be an old woman before Reverend Thomas allows me anywhere near the more valuable books."

"Hecate, this was your second day. Even you must admit a greater degree of patience is required."

"He doesn't trust me, I can see it in his eyes. He's given me heaps of papers to sort."

"Then sort them, and do it well."

"I shall, but I know there will be more to follow. Oh, don't look at me like that. You are right of course. I must prove myself. Earn his trust." She paused and then smiled, mimicking him. "Have a 'greater degree of patience'!"

"Just so. Let me have that," he said, holding out his hand for the box and returning it to the rejected stack. "Tell me what it is you are so eager to have access to. What treasures have caught your eye?"

"There are so many!" she said, jumping up to sit atop a particularly large crate, swinging her feet as she spoke, her eyes bright. "The books themselves, of course. Hundreds! Some centuries old. And most in a good state of repair. The ecclesiastical proportion is high, understandably, but there are other things, too; records of battles, books on natural history and geography—you would love those—even works of poetry, much to Reverend Thomas's displeasure. And the *Mappa Mundi*! Father, it is magnificent. It will take me weeks, months even, simply to learn the names of everything it depicts. It has such . . ." She paused, searching for the word. "Presence," she said at last.

Her father nodded. "It is a marvelous thing. I have seen other medieval maps in my travels. There is a splendid one in the Cairo library, but none can match Hereford's *Mappa*. Such an exquisite example of its kind."

"And there's something else. A cabinet. A locked cabinet. Kept secured to two stone pillars as if the case itself might try to escape. It's a little apart from the other shelves, and the master of the library became quite agitated when I questioned him about it."

Edward raised his eyebrows. "Describe it to me."

"It is no bigger than that trunk over there but significantly heavier, I should imagine. It seems to be made from a hardwood of some sort, very reddish in color."

"Mahogany, perhaps?"

"Possibly. And it has inlay decorating it, beautiful and yet somehow forbidding. The pattern is swirling and geometric. It makes one dizzy to look at it for more than a moment. The lock is, in truth, out of all proportion to the case."

"How so?" he asked, ceasing his rummaging, giving her his full attention.

"It is set upon a broad plate of beaten gold."

"Unusual. Gold is a soft metal. Its use must be purely decorative."

"There may be something stronger beneath it. There is a keyhole, a large one, and a pair of padlocks to either side of that."

"Secure indeed. Intriguing. What exactly did Reverend Thomas tell you about it?"

"He said it was kept locked at all times for safety. His tone was clear; I was not to even think about opening it. I find it hard to understand. I mean to say, I know I will not be trusted with the lowliest illuminated page for a considerable amount of time, but, despite my impatience, I do believe he will, eventually, permit me to read even the most valuable books in the chained collection. But not the ones in that box." She shook her head slowly. "They must have a terrific value for their safety to be so much more important than that of any of all the other wonderful books in the library."

Her father looked at her seriously then. "In my experience, the only things that are kept more securely locked up than treasured things are things that are dangerous."

"Dangerous?"

"Have you considered, Hecate, that the master of the library may not have been speaking of keeping those books safe from you, but keeping *you* safe from *those books*?"

# 4

THE FOLLOWING MORNING, REVEREND THOMAS HAD A SMALL AN-
nouncement to make. He delivered it to his audience of one—Hecate—with
a certain force, as if wishing to underline the point that he was in charge. He
stood in front of his desk, his color still high from climbing the stairs.

"I have taken the decision to dispense with Mrs. White's services as cleaner
here in the library. Now that you have taken up your post I think it more ap-
propriate that you undertake her duties."

"Of course, Reverend. I'd be happy to," said Hecate, and meant it. Rather
than considering such work menial, she saw it as an opportunity to get closer
to everything in the collection.

"No caustic substances or abrasive materials are to be used. In the corner
cupboard you will find everything you need. The books are to be dusted *in
situ* fortnightly, the shelves polished weekly, other pieces of furniture you may
attend to as you have time. The *Mappa Mundi* itself is not, under any circumstances, to be touched, do you understand?"

"I do."

"It requires expert cleaning annually. I see to that myself, and this year
you may observe me in my work. However, the frame will need dusting once
a week, with a dry, soft cloth. No beeswax, nor feather duster. Is that clear,
Miss Cavendish?"

"Perfectly, Reverend."

"Good. You may set aside your paperwork and spend this morning polishing the desks, chairs, and so forth. Once you have finished, with a clean cloth, you can dust the frame of the *Mappa*." He looked at her as if for the first time, taking in her slight build and lack of height, and added, "You will require the small set of steps. Be sure to approach the map from the side, not directly, lest you stumble and cause damage."

"From the side, of course, makes complete sense," she confirmed, nodding. As she fetched the cleaning things from the tall cupboard she recalled her brief conversation with Mrs. White the previous day. Had the dean listened to her pleas regarding her workload and suggested to the master of the library that he could do without the cathedral cleaner? It seemed likely, and how like the librarian to reframe the change so that it bolstered rather than undermined his authority. Hecate cared not who had instigated the new system. What mattered was that now she had the perfect excuse to closely examine everything in the room, including the map and the locked cabinet.

For the next two hours she worked diligently, beginning with her own chair and desk, then two oak coffers, followed by an unimposing cupboard that housed the materials used for map and book repairs. The smell of beeswax polish rose to prominence over other aromas in the room. When Reverend Thomas moved to the tall ladder on the first set of shelves to inspect something, he told her to take that moment to polish his desk and chair. Hecate decided that as soon as he was ensconced in his own work, she would take her duster to the locked cabinet. After her father's reaction to it the night before, she had been itching to have a closer look. Her superior had not specified when the cabinet was to be cleaned, but nor had he expressly told her not to touch it. She reasoned that it could fall into the category of "and so forth" regarding individual pieces. At least, that would be her defense should he remonstrate with her. Polishing his desk took a maddening amount of time, as first she had to clear piles of papers, boxes of pencils, magnifying glasses, and other sundry items he liked to keep close at hand. She glanced up when she had nearly finished and was relieved to see the librarian, still perched atop the ladder, deeply absorbed in reading a parish record from sometime in the last century.

Although she moved toward it swiftly, when Hecate reached the locked cabinet, she hesitated. Her father's words were fresh in her mind—*keeping you safe from those books*. She had pressed him to expand on this startling thought. How could books be dangerous? What words could they contain that required people to be protected from them? He had shrugged then, explaining that he had never seen the cabinet and had no knowledge of its contents. He advised only that she respect the librarian's wishes where it was concerned, for he must have good reason for the warning he had given. Now, face-to-face with the strangely beautiful work of carpentry, she experienced a blend of excitement and wariness. As if she were standing on the top of a tall building, peering over a low wall, the vertiginous drop seeming to pull her forward, the wish to experience the thrill of danger fighting against the innate gift of self-preservation. She decided it was silly to be so timid. Whatever supposed dangers might be hidden inside, the locks were impressive and the box sturdy, and there could be no harm in merely dusting the thing. She ran her cloth over the top of the cabinet, surprised to find she had been holding her breath. She smiled at her own foolishness as she polished the rich red wood. The cabinet itself was not going to reveal anything regarding what it housed. She would have to find the right moment to persuade Reverend Thomas to talk about the mysterious books inside it.

Next she made her way to the *Mappa Mundi*. As instructed, she took out a clean cloth, tucked it into her pocket, and then fetched the set of small wooden steps. Following her remit exactly, she positioned the steps side-on to the map, taking great care never to put the precious artifact in any danger of being damaged. She climbed onto the second step and took out her duster. This was the closest she had yet been to the map, and with the benefit of midday light flooding in from the north- and east-facing windows, so much more detail was revealed to her. Though age had blurred the edges of many of the drawings, and time had faded its colors, the workmanship was still quite breathtaking, and the subject matter endlessly fascinating. Hecate picked out her favorite images; those depicting the mythical creatures. She muttered their names under her breath as she found them.

*Unicorn, phoenix, dragon, sphinx . . .*

She paused when she found the griffin, the sight of him making her smile. Such a curious little beast, part lion, part eagle. Its chest all puffed up with pride, its talons sharp, and yet somehow it failed to look in the least bit threatening. She stared hard at those claws, remembering how one had seemed to move. The creature remained static, one foot raised, poised, as if ready for an action that had not occurred for over a thousand years.

With great care, she took her cloth and leaned forward to slide it along the worn edge of the frame, picking up any dust that sat there, being sure not to simply disturb the motes and send them airborne in case they should resettle on the map itself. She worked slowly, moving the duster into the bevels and grooves of the frame, not letting it touch the vellum on which the map was drawn. She recalled reading about that vellum. There had been a calf specifically bred to provide the skin that would be cured and prepared for the mapmaker. That calf had lived a good life, being well fed to produce the best possible quality calfskin. She liked to think of him enjoying abundant food and green pastures until his time had come. Not everything had gone entirely to plan, however. While the calf frolicked or dozed in those meadows through its bright, single summer, its plumpness did not go unnoticed by an opportunist fly. This fly had settled onto the flank of the young beast and laid its eggs beneath the surface of that supple skin. Those eggs had later hatched, and left behind a tiny, circular scar. Through all the processes, despite all the skill of the deftest tanner, that tiny blemish remained. Hecate knew it was there. She narrowed her eyes, searching for it. At last she found it, a dark knot between the cartographer's lines. Instinctively, her finger still shrouded in the cloth, she reached forward and touched that ancient flaw.

As if it had been waiting for her all those centuries, the map responded to that touch.

The creatures depicted upon it came to life, flapping their wings, rearing up on their hind legs, snorting through great, fiery nostrils, squawking and braying and bellowing and shrieking. They jumped and stamped as if testing the confines of the tiny space in which they existed. At the same time, the dozens of people on the map began shouting or calling, some in anger, some in terror, others in welcome, so that Hecate was assailed by a cacophony of sound, her mind shocked by so much sudden and impossible noise and activity. She instinctively pulled back, almost losing her balance, forced to clutch at the top handle on the steps, only just able to stop herself falling. The second she removed her hand from the vellum the commotion ceased. In the blink of an eye, the beasts fell silent, all movement and chaos stopped. The map returned to its normal, soundless, static condition.

She became aware that there were people behind her talking. She turned quickly, certain the librarian would have heard the noise and come running.

Instead she saw that Mr. Gould had entered the library and the two men were conversing. As her heart rate returned to a steadier rhythm, Reverend Thomas descended his ladder and came to speak to her.

"It appears the dean wishes to see you," he said, peering up at her through his thick glasses. "Miss Cavendish, are you quite well?"

"Oh, yes, Reverend Thomas. I am perfectly fine, thank you," she said, hastily getting off the steps. It was clear no one but she had heard any of the wild sounds that had come from the map. She wished she had time to think about what had happened, but the verger had evidently been sent to fetch her.

"Go with the verger," the librarian told her. "I will put away the steps." He watched her closely as she passed him, clearly unconvinced about her health.

Hecate put on a bright smile and addressed Mr. Gould. "I am pleased to meet you," she told him, holding out her hand. "I understand you do important work here at the cathedral."

He was a nondescript man; the sort one might pass in the street and not notice. He was of middling height and weight, with thinning hair and a sallow complexion. Unlike the master of the library, he enjoyed the company of people whenever he could find it, and loved nothing more than to talk.

"Oh dear me, Miss Cavendish, how kind of you to say so. And how very good it is to meet you, too. Yes, indeed. We are always happy to welcome new people to the cathedral to join our merry band. Every pair of hands is needed, every mind put to good use, isn't that so, Reverend Thomas?" He clutched Hecate's hand in both of his and shook it warmly, reluctant to let it go. She smiled at him. All that came from the librarian by way of reply was a grunt as he folded the steps and carried them away.

"You say the dean wishes to see me?" Hecate asked.

"He sent me to fetch you. Oh, do not be alarmed, for there was nothing in his demeanor to suggest anything amiss. Quite the contrary in fact. Dean Chalmers is a man of great thoughtfulness. No doubt he is eager to make certain you are settling in and happy in your work," he said, glancing in the direction of the librarian. "Please follow me. I am to take you to the crypt."

Before Hecate had time to question him about the venue for the meeting he was hurrying toward the door. She glanced back at the map as she left, still shocked by what had happened, still needing to make sense of it. As she turned to follow Mr. Gould, she noticed that the monk was browsing the second row of shelves. She wondered that she had not noticed him enter the library, but then reasoned she had been too affected by the map to be aware of what was happening on the other side of the room. She made a note to herself to ask Reverend Forsyth about the monk's identity when next she saw him.

As they made their way along the north aisle, Hecate saw a figure coming up from the crypt stairwell. She recognized him as Lord Brocket, the earl of Brockhampton, a local aristocrat and acquaintance of her father's. He saw her and paused to smile, raising his top hat briefly, before continuing on his way. She wondered what business he could have with Dean Chalmers. She supposed it was not unusual for men of good fortune to shore up their souls by making donations to the cathedral.

"Here we are," the verger had begun to chatter again. "Have a care, Miss Cavendish, for the treads here are uneven," he counseled.

Hecate had not been in the crypt before. It was reached via a short flight of stone stairs. Unlike those in the library tower, these were straight and gently sloping and led from the area in front of the Lady Chapel down to the subterranean level. The first thing she noticed was the surprising amount of light. Unusually for a floor that was entirely underground, the space had several windows. They were set high in the wall, showing glimpses of grass through the iron tracery and snatches of blue sky here and there. Another unusual feature was a second flight of steps leading up to another door. This heavy, iron-barred exit gave on to the Cathedral Green. Inside, the space was not, as she might have expected, some gloomy, dust-laden tomb, but a clean, airy room with its own vaulted ceiling, the stone beautifully carved to give a sense of height and space. There were iron gates behind which coffins were kept on shelves, and several impressive tombs positioned at irregular intervals around the four walls. There were a few sarcophaguses in the main space, but the majority of it was given over to pews and there was what appeared to be an altar of sorts against the far wall. The dean heard their footsteps and turned to greet them.

"Ah, Miss Cavendish safely delivered. My thanks to you, Mr. Gould."

"No trouble, Dean. No trouble at all. Happy to be of service."

He bobbed up and down as he spoke, not quite bowing, yet successfully expressing the reverence in which he held the dean. He smiled and kept his eyes cast down. He reminded Hecate of a young hound approaching the leader of the pack, submissive and craving approval.

"I will detain you no longer," Dean Chalmers told him. "I know how busy you are."

Unable to find a reason to linger, the verger nodded, muttered his farewells, and left.

"Come, my dear," the dean beckoned Hecate, leading her toward the plain, sturdy altar. "I trust Reverend Thomas was not too perturbed by my taking you from your work in the library?"

"Not at all, Dean. That is, he did not say so."

"Well then, we will take his silence on the matter as evidence of a lack of complaint. Have you been in the crypt before?" When she shook her head, he continued. "I thought not. And I imagined the place might be of interest to you, given your familiarity with your father's work as an archeologist."

"Indeed it is! I confess it is not as I thought it might be. It is so much brighter, and . . . cleaner."

The dean chuckled. "Mrs. White would be gratified to hear you say that! It is a common misconception that crypts are the domain of spiders and bats. As you can see, this is far from the truth. And the same is the case for many such places. Hereford's crypt is a little more unusual than most, however. You may have noticed this." He raised a hand to indicate the broad table in front of them.

"It appears to be an altar. Which means services must be held down here. Can that be correct?"

"You have your father's sharp mind, my dear. I've always said so. Yes, although no longer in use, it is an altar and services were held here for many years. This humble space served the parish of St. John when there was no other church available. Hence the external door also, and the pews, which are somewhat redundant now."

"How strange it must have been singing hymns down here among the dead," she muttered.

Dean Chalmers pointed up at the impressive vaulting. "As a matter of fact, voices lifted in song often sound better here than they do in the nave. Or so Reverend Forsyth tells me. He sometimes brings the choir to the crypt for practice."

Hecate smiled at the thought of him doing something so controversial. "Do the other vicars choral object?"

"Not in summer. The temperature is quite pleasant when it is uncomfortably hot elsewhere, even in the main body of the cathedral." He paused and then asked simply, "Tell me, are you happy in your position as assistant to the master of the library?"

"Oh yes, Dean. I am so very grateful for my post."

"And Reverend Thomas . . . you find him a fair taskmaster?"

"He has been very patient with me."

"He can be taciturn at times. It is only his manner."

"I'm sure it must be testing to have to explain everything to someone new."

"Quite so. And yet, time invested in his new assistant now will surely afford him greater productivity later. I wanted to be certain you were finding your position . . . pleasant. As your father approached me directly regarding your employment at the cathedral, I consider myself very much *in loco parentis* during your working day. Please do come to me, should anything ever give you cause to feel . . . uncomfortable."

Hecate studied his face, searching for signs of concern, but the dean's warm smile remained in place.

"Everyone here has made me feel very welcome," she assured him.

"Excellent!" He gave a clap of his hands, which echoed through the crypt. "I had best let you return to your work. Come, I will escort you as far as the Stanbury Chapel and then my presence is required in the cloisters where I am told there is an issue with the pipes. A workman has been summoned. You see, my dear, not all my duties are of an esoteric nature." He led the way back up the stairs.

As they emerged onto ground level Hecate noticed a small woman energetically polishing the brass railings in front of the altar of the Lady Chapel. She had not seen her before, but she was clearly employed in the work of cleaning. It seemed Mrs. White's conversation with Dean Chalmers regarding her workload had been doubly successful, for not only was she now excused her duties in the library, but she had a new helper to assist her.

The afternoon passed in something of a daze for Hecate. To begin with, she had returned to her desk and to the mundane task of sorting through the old papers. The undemanding, repetitive nature of her work had a meditative quality about it that allowed her mind to travel elsewhere. And the place it traveled to was, of course, the map. Her head buzzed with thoughts of what had occurred when she touched the scar on the *Mappa Mundi*. Even without looking at it, sitting in such close proximity, remembering what she knew she had heard and seen, caused her skin to tingle. She would not for one moment have thought about telling the dean of her experience. While she was touched by his kindness and concern for her, she could not imagine even starting a conversation about having visions and hearing things on only her third day of work. True, as a spiritual person whose life's purpose was built upon the unfathomable, he might have had an open mind to what she had experienced. That did not, however, mean she would feel at ease discussing it with him. Nor did it rule out the chance that he might consider her in some way ill or hysterical and send her home. The thought of what her mother might say to such a report made her all the more determined to carefully consider whom she told. Her father, she believed, would know what to make of it. He was a man who had in his work found the perfect balance between the unknowable and the practical. He had spent years chasing whispers of stories and snatches of hearsay, but in those quests he had been required to dig in the ground and construct pulleys and shafts and supports that demanded of him the skills of an engineer. He had lived among the gritty, hot, snake-riddled ruins in the desert, facing real hardships and dangers, but he had witnessed men brought to their knees by their terror of some ancient curse or other. Yes, she knew in her heart, her father would believe her. What was more, he might even be capable of offering some manner of explanation for what had taken place.

The sunshine had moved off the windows, throwing the room into shadow, and Reverend Thomas had lit the gasoliers. The light they gave off was superior to oil lamps but came with a soft rasping noise which Hecate did not care for. Rather than the flicker of a candle, the lights appeared to pulsate. For all their advantages, it seemed to her that gaslights were a poor substitute for daylight when it came to any sort of close work.

"I must attend a meeting of Chapter," the librarian informed her. He pulled his pocket watch from beneath his black robe and consulted it. "I will be no more than an hour, so shall return in ample time to lock up the library before the end of the working day. While I am gone you may continue with your paperwork. Should anyone present themselves seeking access to the collection ask them to return tomorrow."

"Yes, Reverend," said Hecate, her pulse already quickening at the thought that she was about to be left alone. Alone to inspect the map!

"On no account are you to leave the library unattended, is that clear?"

"Perfectly, yes," she assured him. She watched him go, listening as he descended the stairs, the whistling wheeze of his breathing diminishing with each step until he was, at last, out of earshot. Hecate remained silent, letting the sounds of the library wash over her, waiting, checking, wanting to be certain her superior had not, perhaps, forgotten something, and was on his way back up the stairwell. Only when she was convinced he had gone and must be halfway to the dean's office in the cloisters did she get up from her chair, turn, and walk over to the map. She stood a few paces off, acknowledging to herself that she was both afraid and enthralled in equal measures. At that moment it appeared perfectly normal, inert, without sound or movement. A beautiful, important, medieval artifact, but a stable, silent one. Could she have imagined it all? Had she fallen victim to a combination of an overactive—what did her father call it?—romantic imagination, and perhaps the odors from some of the cleaning fluids used on older bookbindings? It was a possibility. Except that no such substances had been removed from the cupboard, nor their lids so much as loosened. And for all her wild fancies, she did not believe herself capable of such fantastic daydreaming. No, there was no real doubt in her mind. She had seen the creatures wriggle and writhe and heard them roar and squawk, just as the figures had shouted and called to her. That was the truth of it, and she would never let anyone persuade her otherwise.

"Such a fine example of the cartographer's art. I, too, have stood before it many times, lost in wonder."

The voice behind her startled Hecate, causing her to gasp as she turned. The monk had emerged from between the bookshelves, his pale gray robes sweeping the floor as he came, his arms folded, his hands tucked into his sleeves. As he moved beneath the gasolier the light fell upon his tonsure and his round, crinkly face. Hecate could see now that he was very old, and was surprised he was not stooped and that he walked without the aid of a stick.

"Forgive my joining you unannounced and without introduction. I would not wish to cause you alarm. My name is Brother Michael," he told her. His voice was low and had about it a slight west country accent, with rounded vowels and words that sounded as if they had been rolled around in his mouth before being spoken.

"Hecate," she stuttered slightly. "Hecate Cavendish." Ordinarily, she would have reached out to shake his hand, as she did with every person she met. But this was turning out to be anything other than an ordinary day, and Brother Michael was most definitely extraordinary. She stared at him openly then, finding herself rendered temporarily both speechless and immobile. Now that she looked more carefully, there was something about the way the lamplight fell through rather than upon him, giving the appearance that he was lit from within. His monk's habit rippled as he moved, but not as if his feet were kicking it with each step, more as if it were flowing through the air. More than any of these things, what caused her to have to quell a wave of panic was that she could plainly see Brother Michael cast no shadow. She had the sensation an earwig was wriggling down her spine. She imagined her father's voice telling her to buck up, to stand firm. But then he was not the one who was, at that moment, standing between a magically animated map, and what was, she was completely and utterly certain, a ghost.

She tried to speak. Fought to form some sensible words, but her tongue was clumsy in her dry mouth.

"I understand you are perplexed by my sudden appearance. I promise you, you have no reason to fear me. In fact, the very opposite is true."

"The . . . opposite?" she asked, her voice high and tight.

The monk nodded. "I feel blessed that you have been sent. After so many years of watching over the library unaided, to at last have someone here with whom I might communicate. Someone . . . living."

A fizzing silence opened up in the conversation. Hecate was both astonished and reassured to find that her initial fear was diminishing, while her sense of awe and excitement increased. She summoned her courage.

"You are . . . you are, then, a ghost?" she asked.

Brother Michael tilted his head, his expression a little sad. "A word that has so many interpretations, and none, I fear, helpful. I cannot deny what I am, but for preference I would choose the term 'soul.' In point of fact, that is what we all think of ourselves here at the cathedral; the lost souls."

"*We all?*" She hardly dared press him on the point but felt a thrill of anticipation as she waited for the answer.

"Most of the departed are able to travel to the afterlife without difficulty or delay. For some, that is not the case. Something prevents them from moving on. Something tethers them to this earthly realm, even though they are no longer of it. Their insubstantial forms linger, against their will, and each is kept to a place of significance to them." He paused, withdrawing a hand to indicate the chained books, the movement slow and fluid. "For myself, there could be nowhere more important. My own situation differs in the small fact that it was always my choice to stay with my beloved library."

"Your library? But, I don't believe Hereford Cathedral was ever a monastery? How did you come to be here?"

He smiled, an expression that made his already wrinkled face crinkle so much that his bright eyes almost disappeared. "How much you know, and how marvelous that you do! We shall be the very best of friends, I have not the smallest doubt. You are correct, of course. I was a monk at the abbey in Shaftesbury, sent here to assist in the setting up of the chained library. Fate determined that I was never to leave."

"The very first time the books were chained was . . . the fourteenth century, is that right?" Hecate was astonished at how quickly conversing with a ghost had started to feel normal.

"I arrived in summer, the year of our Lord 1373. There was so much work to be done. The then bishop of Hereford had spent time at our abbey and knew of my love of books. I was so pleased to be here at, as it were, the birth of the library."

Hecate smiled, for a brief moment imagining this ancient phantom experiencing, as she had done, his first day at his new place of work, in the very same library, all those long centuries ago. Something else he had said had struck her as important and she was eager to return to it.

"Brother Michael, you said 'We all.' Are you telling me there are other ghosts here in the cathedral? Other lost souls?"

"Oh yes, we are small in number, a little family of sorts. But of course, you have already seen some of my brothers and sisters," he replied.

Hecate swallowed and a thrilling shiver ran through her. "When and where did I see them?"

"Why, only this very day you walked past Mrs. Nugent in the Lady Chapel."

"The new cleaner?"

"Cleaner, yes, but far from new. The dear lady met her end during the reign of King George III. It is for him she so lovingly tends the cathedral, for she died on the eve of a royal visit."

Hecate gave a small cry of astonishment, an exclamation of delight, though she was uncertain it was seemly to feel that way about someone who had died. "And did she . . . did Mrs. Nugent see me?"

"She noticed you at once and came to tell me, though I had already seen you in here. She was not the only one to wish to speak of your arrival. Young Corporal Gregory spied you as he looked up from his vigil in the Stanbury Chapel and knew that you were special. We all did straightaway."

"Special?" Her mind raced, recalling the soldier in his scarlet uniform apparently at prayer.

"Certainly special, my child, because you have the gift. The gift of communing with the dead."

# 5

HECATE RACED TOWARD HOME THAT AFTERNOON, PEDALLING EVEN faster than was her habit, desperate to share her news with her father. The more she attempted to rehearse how she could start the conversation about having met and spoken with a ghost, the more she realized there was no sensible way to do it. But it mattered not. Her father, of all people, would listen, would take her seriously, would believe her. He was the one person with whom she could share her secret. As she began to climb the hill toward Hafod Road she leaned forward, shifting her weight to aid her pedalling feet. Even so, the bicycle wobbled as she steered around a pothole, and the movement caused her dress to flap against her leg. In an instant, her skirts had caught in the chain, bringing her to an abrupt halt. So sudden was the change in speed, and so deeply fixed to the chain was her dress that both she and the bicycle fell sideways into the mercifully empty road. Hecate cursed under her breath as her shoulder took the brunt of the fall and her elbow connected with the rough, unforgiving stone of the street. For a moment she lay there, held fast, unable to right herself.

"Oh for heavens' sake!" she muttered, forcing herself upward even though it meant using her painful elbow to do so.

"Are you all right, miss?" A young man in a flat cap and brown tweed jacket stepped toward her.

"Yes, perfectly fine, thank you. Ouch!" She flinched as she tried to sit up further, her ankle catching on the pedal as she attempted to drag herself free of the bicycle.

"Let me help you," he said, crouching down to examine the chain. "You came a right cropper, miss. Saw it as I came out my front door. Here, hold still. You're caught good and proper."

"If you could just remove my hem from that wretched chain . . ."

He worked the woolen fabric loose. "There, it's out. Bit oily, I'm afraid. And torn, too." He reached down and took her arm, helping her to her feet.

Hecate brushed herself down and adjusted her hat. She could feel that the wide brim was bent on one side and was aware she presented a somewhat pathetic spectacle.

"I am most grateful for your assistance," she said, mustering her dignity and taking hold of the handlebars. She was sufficiently shaken to walk home rather than ride.

"If you're sure you're not hurt . . ." When she nodded and smiled, the young man touched his cap and went on his way.

Upon arriving home she discovered her father was out with Phileas and that the pair would return together in time to dine.

Beatrice was shocked by her appearance.

"Whatever has happened to you, Hecate? Your hat . . . and your hem is ruined."

"I took a tumble on my way home. It is nothing, Mother, do not concern yourself," she replied, bracing herself to defend her beloved bicycle.

"Nothing indeed! That is your best day dress."

"Which can no doubt be repaired," she said, removing her hat and examining it. "As, no doubt, can my poor hat." She turned for the stairs, trotting up them as evenly as she could, determined not to give any hint of her injuries.

Her mother called up after her. "There is always a cost to pay for carelessness."

"Not on this occasion, for I shall attend to the repairs myself," she called back, reaching her room and closing the door on her mother's further comments on the matter.

Much as she would have rather not had a terse exchange with her mother, she was glad of the excuse to be in her room. She was not in the state of mood required for chatting in the sitting room, even with Charlie. She needed time to think, to try to make sense of her conversation with Brother Michael. As she undressed she replayed the encounter in her head, committing the monk's words to memory, smiling to herself at the enormity of what had taken place. A gleeful giggle rose up inside her. It was true. She had spoken with a ghost. And from what Brother Michael had told her, she had seen, and been seen by, at least two more. She sat at her desk in her undergarments, recalling how real, how solid, Mrs. Nugent had appeared to be as she polished those brass railings. And yet the dean had been oblivious to her. And the sorrowful soldier in the Stanbury Chapel . . . when she had noticed him, he had seemed in every way real, and solid, and ordinary. Except that now she thought about it, his uniform was not of the modern kind.

And then there was Brother Michael. Casting her mind back to when she had first noticed him, she realized he had been watching her since the day she arrived. And he had known, straightaway he said, that she had, as he called it, the gift. What a strange gift it was! And was it that same aspect of herself that was allowing her to connect so strongly with the *Mappa Mundi*? She had collected herself sufficiently, during their conversation, to ask the monk about the map and what she had heard and seen, but they had been interrupted by the arrival of John. He had discovered she was left alone in the library and come to make sure she had everything she needed, so he had told her. She felt a little badly about how she had responded to his solicitous visit. After all, he was only being kind, considering this was but her third day at the cathedral, and being concerned for her. She had not, she knew, been receptive to that kindness. All she had been able to think of was how quickly Brother Michael had faded and disappeared, leaving her, heart pounding, with so many unanswered questions. She felt mounting excitement at the thought that she might see him again the next day. Or perhaps encounter the phantom soldier. Or talk with the industrious Mrs. Nugent. What, she wondered, would Mrs. White make of the fact that she had a lost soul assisting her in her work? Of course, she could never tell her. Beyond her father, she could not imagine sharing her secret with anyone.

And now she was forced to wait. To make use of the time, she turned her attention to her torn dress. Despite assuring her mother that she would see to the repairs, they both knew that her talents at needlework were poor. She lacked the requisite patience, or indeed interest, to have properly mastered the skills that would produce neat and durable results. With a sigh she turned the hem over in her hands. The fabric was mangled and stained with oil. The damaged section would have to be cut out.

"Good," she said to herself. "How much better if the whole thing were several inches shorter?" She opened a drawer in her desk and took out a large pair of scissors. She cleared a space of books and papers and writing paraphernalia and laid out the skirt of the dress. Pausing only for a moment, she took hold of the fabric and started to cut, becoming more and more determined with each snip of the blades. In no time at all she had removed the ragged hem. She lifted the dress and held it up to herself, turning to study her reflection in the large looking glass in the corner of the room. It was shockingly short, revealing not only her ankles but two inches of her calves at least, more if she strode about.

There was a quiet knock at the door and at her response the maid, Stella, entered the room. She was carrying her sewing basket. On seeing Hecate she stopped, mouth open.

"Ah. I see Mother did not trust me with my own repairs. She need not have worried," Hecate insisted, twirling. "As you can see, I have removed the damaged material and in the process rendered the dress far more suitable for bicycle riding."

Stella appeared to be searching for the right thing to say but failed to find it.

Hecate continued. "I'd be grateful if you could turn a new hem for me, though. I confess I would make a poor job of it." She held out the dress and then an idea came to her. "In fact, although shorter, the skirts still present a hazard in combination with the chain, particularly when I execute any . . . irregular maneuvers. What is needed is some way of securing them to my leg on the inside. Some manner of strap, perhaps, about . . . here." She indicated the ideal position. "What do you think, Sella? Could you fashion such a thing?" She gave the girl her brightest smile.

The maid took the dress with a slow shake of her head. "I could, Miss Hecate, but what will the mistress say?"

"You leave Mrs. Cavendish to me. After all, my safety is her main concern, wouldn't you agree? Now, can it be done?"

Stella nodded then, focused on the task. "T'would be a simple matter to stitch in a strap. The tricky part would be making openings in the petticoats that lined up perfectly. . . ."

"I know you have many demands upon your time, but I would be so grateful for your assistance. . . ."

Stella glanced at the scissors on the desk. "Of course I will help you, miss. But please, do not take to cutting any more of your clothes without first consulting me," she added.

"I promise! No need to tell my mother of the finer details of what we are about. Well then, let's set you up under the best light, over here I think," she said, pulling back the desk chair.

While Stella worked away at the dress, Hecate put on a simple blue evening gown, refusing the maid's offers of help. She knew her mother would be scandalized by the length of her skirts and so formed the idea to purchase a new, longer pair of brown leather lace-up boots.

When the grandfather clock in the hall chimed the half hour, Stella hurried away to continue her duties. They agreed she would continue with the alterations the following day. Hecate could barely contain her excitement as the moment to share her news with her father drew nearer. She felt certain he would be as astonished, as full of wonder, as she herself was at what she had to tell him. He, too, would have questions. Thinking of this, she hurried to the pile of books on the floor beside her little sofa. This small selection from her father's study had been her essential reading before beginning work at the cathedral, and all contained some information or other about its history. Quickly, she flicked through the pages of the oldest, weightiest tome, searching for details about the setting up of the library. Alas, it did not dwell on the matter of who might have assisted the bishop and the dean of the day, choosing instead to concentrate on what manuscripts had been included. She continued her search. At last, in a tiny pamphlet regarding the development of the collection, she found a small entry that made her heart race.

"'To assist the Master of the Library in his endeavors, there was sent from Shaftesbury an elderly monk, whose labors at the Abbey had been of great value due to his knowledge of the manuscripts held therein.' Brother Michael," she muttered to herself.

The sound of the front door opening and voices in the hall announced the arrival home of her father. Hecate left the book and hurried downstairs. She found him and Phileas in ebullient moods, handing their hats to Stella.

"Ah, my little Hecate," her father greeted her with an affectionate kiss on the cheek. "Here we are, all workers returned from our tasks."

Phileas took her hand and bowed over it as was his habit, although she had long ago noticed that he did not greet other women in such an old-fashioned and charming way. "I prevailed upon your father to lend me his good judgment."

"Sterling is to be a social philanthropist," Edward announced.

"Oh?" Hecate was finding it hard to attend to what they were saying.

Phileas explained. "Hardly that," he insisted. "The chamber of commerce know I am a man with time to fill and a small amount of influence. They have asked me to oversee a housing project on the west side of the city. I have this day been to examine the site."

"How very laudable," Hecate replied, following them toward the drawing room, hoping to corner her father privately at the soonest opportunity.

Edward expanded on the subject. "The plot of land where once stood Grayfriars Abbey is to be put to good use at last."

"The abbey?" She could not help but be struck by the coincidence that her father, too, had spent the afternoon thinking of long-dead monks. "Well, I'm sure the community would have approved of it providing homes for those who need them."

Her father raised an eyebrow at her. "The present community," he asked, "or the original brethren?"

"Both," she said, smiling, and then whispered urgently to him, "Father, I simply must speak with you!"

He looked at her more closely, taking in the brightness of her eyes and the excitement written clearly on her face.

At that moment her mother swept into the room.

"Oh Edward, you are home at last. Cook is in a bad temper over the salmon drying out should she have to wait longer to serve it. Good evening, Phileas." She went on to insist there was no time for an aperitif, but they must all quickly change for dinner. Their guest could borrow suitable clothing. She shooed them all off toward the stairs, reminding them that should they not be at table within the half hour, they would have to search for a replacement cook in the morning.

Edward saw Hecate's face fall and squeezed her hand as they climbed the stairs.

"We will talk directly after we have dined, I promise you," he said.

"Directly," she repeated firmly.

For Hecate, the meal proceeded at an agonizingly slow pace. As Phileas was joining them, there had been an attempt at lavishness not commonly seen in the Cavendish household on a weekday. Cook sent Stella in with soup, which Hecate recognized as the gravy from the night before worked up. There followed the salmon, which no one dared say was dry. Both her father and Phileas made a point of announcing their appreciation of everything placed before them. Charlie was well enough to display a youthful appetite, and for once Hecate joined him in eating as quickly as possible, wasting little time on talking, earning a disapproving frown from their mother.

"Tell us, Phileas"—Beatrice took it upon herself to make polite conversation—"when do you expect the new houses to be built?"

He dabbed at his waxed mustache ends before replying, "Ah, could be some time, alas," he said. "We have to get many permissions, graves must be moved, and so forth. . . ."

"A worthy endeavor indeed," Edward said. "I am certain your efforts will bear fruit, eventually."

Charlie piped up, "But what will they do with all those bones? If it was a graveyard, there will be skulls and everything."

"Charles!" his mother chided him.

Phileas shrugged. "Young Master Cavendish makes a fair point. The moving of graves is a sensitive business." He glanced at Hecate. "And a gloomy subject for your mother's dinner table perhaps, eh? Here's a thought to brighten us all up. I consider now that spring has properly arrived, it is high time for another of the famous Sterling picnics."

"I think you mean infamous," Hecate commented.

Her mother looked slightly appalled at the idea, but her father was delighted. "Capital! Precisely what we all need."

Charlie beamed. "Oh yes! Will there be circus performers, like last time?"

Phileas's picnics, and indeed any of his social events, were renowned for their wild excesses and outlandishness.

"Indubitably!" he confirmed, then, seeing the look on Beatrice's face, added, "Though perhaps not the fire-eaters. Not this time."

And so the conversation continued around plans for the picnic, and a pudding of meringues and the last of the jarred stewed fruit from the previous autumn were consumed. Hecate feared the men might retire for cigars and she would have to wait out half a bottle of port but her father had recognized the urgency in her voice, perhaps, or the eagerness in her expression. They finished their meal and said their farewells to their guest. As they stood on the front doorstep, waving and watching the cab speeding away, Edward whispered to her.

"Fetch your coat, daughter." When Beatrice sought to protest at their going out at such an hour, he steered Hecate down the drive, striding out, cane in hand, placing his hat on his head and calling over his shoulder. "Just taking the air before sleep, my dear. Aids the digestion, don't you know? It is a fine evening for a walk."

And it was. A milky moon lit the gaps between streetlamps as they walked along Hafod Road, arm in arm. The energetic pace suited them both, and reminded Hecate how alike she and her father were. How much better to hold a conversation fueled by activity.

"Let us have it, then," Edward demanded. "What is so important that I must deny poor Phileas his port?"

"I scarcely know where to begin."

"Some favor the beginning," he replied. "For myself, I prefer to pitch in with the minor acts and build to the crescendo of the top billing." He waved his cane with a flourish to emphasize his point.

"Then I shall state things as you suggest, though in truth I am not certain where the greater importance lies."

They crossed the road and turned left, taking an avenue that climbed a slight incline, the branches of the still bare trees adding scribbled moon shadows to their progress, fine houses obscured by tall hedges on either side.

"The map," she announced. "The *Mappa Mundi* . . . I was up on the small steps, cleaning the frame, which meant I was the closest to it I have ever been."

"I am surprised Reverend Thomas wished you to clean it."

"Oh, only the wooden casing. I was under strict orders not to touch the map itself."

In the pause that followed, Hecate felt her father glance at her.

"And which bit of it, precisely, did you touch?" he asked.

She gave a bashful smile, heartened that he knew her so well, reassured that he did not judge her for it. "The blemish. The mark left in the vellum by the fly eggs. You know of it?" When he nodded she continued. "And the instant I touched it . . . oh, Papa!" she said, falling into her childhood name for him, her grip on his arm tightening. "Everything changed! The map appeared to come to life, the creatures roaring and squawking . . ."

"You heard them?"

"Both heard and saw. The figures called out to me, some of them were so desperate, others quite terrifying, and all the while the beasts leaped about or flapped their wings."

"Astonishing!"

"There was so much noise I was certain Reverend Thomas would hear it."

"He was present?"

"On the other side of the room. But he didn't hear a thing, I'm certain of that. And the second I took my hand off the map, all movement, all sounds, ceased. Just like that," she said, clicking her fingers.

"Fascinating!" Edward said, increasing his pace in his excitement so that Hecate found she must almost break into a trot.

"What do you think it meant?" she asked. "Why did it happen? Do you think it has reacted in such a way to anyone else? What could it signify?"

He thought for a moment and then answered. "You say this was the lesser of the events that took place today. Before giving my assessment I would ask that you apprise me of the second."

Hecate drew a deep breath. To her surprise she found she could not deliver her next statement without first coming to a halt. Her father turned to face her, his expression showing some concern. A couple strolled by, forcing her to wait while her father raised and replaced his hat, and then a moment longer for them to walk out of earshot. She met and held his questioning gaze as she spoke.

"I encountered a ghost," she said baldly.

"Encountered? How so?"

"Saw, conversed with . . ."

"You spoke to the spirit and it responded?"

"*He,* not *it*. His name was . . . is Brother Michael. He is a monk, sent from Shaftesbury Abbey to assist in the setting up of the library. That is, the original library, in the fourteenth century. Because he was known to be good at such things and the dean of the day needed help . . . and then something happened and he never left. Not even after he died . . ." She was aware that she was gabbling, talking too fast, saying too much for anyone to take in. Anyone except her father.

"And this was before or after your interaction with the map?"

"A short while after. Do you consider them connected?"

"I consider the connection to be you, Hecate."

"That's what Brother Michael told me! I mean to say, he believes that the lost souls—"

"Lost?"

"Yes, that's what they call themselves, all the ghosts at the cathedral."

"All the . . . My darling girl, precisely how many ghosts did you converse with?"

"Oh, I only spoke with Brother Michael, but there are others."

"Others you have seen?"

"Yes, Mrs. Nugent, who was a cleaner and so I thought her recently come to work there, to assist Mrs. White. And Corporal Gregory . . . I am told there are others. From what Brother Michael explained, they all know of me, because they have noticed my presence. He says I have a gift."

Her father gave a gasp and then his smile broadened into an enormous grin.

"Ha!" he said, letting go of her arm to punch the air. "I knew it! I saw it in you, some time ago. I was not certain at first but then, I watched you, and yes, I knew it! Oh, this is capital. Capital! And of course, I had been told . . ."

"You're saying that you do not mind that I speak with—?"

He leaped in to finish her question. "Ghosts? Spirits? Phantoms? Specters? Let us name them. You and I need not be coy about such things, not any longer. How glad I am that we have reached this point," he said, regarding her with open pride.

Hecate began to laugh with relief. "Oh, I cannot tell you how badly I needed to share this with you! Although . . ."

"What? You had reservations? Did you not think you would find me sympathetic?"

"I feared you might not let me continue at the cathedral. That Mother might . . ."

"I think it best we do not trouble your mother with this. What say you?"

"Mother has a great many things to manage. Best not to add to them."

"Precisely my thinking."

"But Father, you say we are alike, that you saw this in me. . . . Does that mean that you, too, have communed with spirits? And . . . what did you mean when you said just now that you had been told?"

He took his pipe from his pocket, tamping down the tobacco with his thumb before placing the stem in his mouth. He had no match with which to light the pipe, so it simply remained clenched between his teeth as he spoke. "My dear little worker bee, I have spent my life unearthing tombs, disturbing soil that covered the bones of the lost, and toiling among the mausoleums of the ancients. Do you seriously think I could have done so without, from time to time, encountering their souls?"

"But, you have never spoken of this before. I mean to say, you told me many, many stories of course, but . . ."

"And where do you think those stories came from, eh? Oh, I don't pretend to have your facility for conversing with the deceased, no no. But have I encountered them? Have I felt their presences, whether benign or menacing? Yes, and yes. As to my expectations of your own gift, for gift it is, make no mistake . . ." He paused and Hecate beamed. "In the months before your birth I was engaged in a dig at a site outside the otherwise insignificant town of Idalid. You won't have heard of it, for we found nothing of great importance, and it is a lesser known corner of Mesopotamia. However, something occurred there which was, in contrast, of enormous importance to me. One evening a peddler, or so I thought, came padding through our encampment. The day had been long and unproductive, and I was in low spirits. Missing home and hearth, truth be told. And waiting for news of your imminent arrival, of course. So the peddler found me and revealed herself to be, in fact, a teller of truths."

"You mean, a fortune teller?"

"She resisted such a nomenclator, but in essence, yes. Me being at a loose end, somewhat bored, I agreed to pay to have her tell me what she could. I recall we were seated outside, enjoying the cool of the evening before the chill of the desert night set in. Matravers was with me. Hamsworth, too, I think. We were sharing a tolerable whiskey. She bid me sit on the sand opposite her, where she had arranged herself, cross-legged, swathed in her many colored robes, some with coins and tiny bells decorating the hems. She took my hand and immediately gasped. Matravers laughed, telling me she had seen my countless indiscretions. Which were of his own invention, before you reproach me. But I saw seriousness in the woman's face. She had my full attention. She studied my palm for some time and then she looked at me, and when she did so her face was lit up with joy. It was an astonishing transformation."

"What did she say? What had she seen?"

"In a word, my dearest girl, you. She told me I was to have a daughter with hair the color of a sunrise, and that this child would have a gift. I remember her words exactly because they struck me with such force. She said, 'The child will tread the realm twixt the living and the dead as the goddess Hekate did, and she will speak to those long gone, and they to her.' She refused my money. Said it was a blessing to have met the father of such a child, and that I was blessed myself. So you see, you could only ever have been named for the goddess of ghosts and magic. All these years I have been waiting, watching you for a sign that she spoke the truth."

"All these years," Hecate repeated. She took his hand in hers. "So, you promise you will not stop me, Father? You must see now that I cannot ever leave the cathedral. Not for anyone. Promise you will not let Mother marry me off to someone."

He smiled at her gently then, his voice reassuring.

"No one will force you to leave, Hecate, you have my word. Now," he said, linking his arm through hers once more and continuing their walk, "tell me absolutely everything about this wonderful monk of yours."

# 6

THE FOLLOWING MORNING HECATE DRESSED IN HER WORKADAY BLACK
woolen skirt, as it was the only alternative she had to the dress awaiting Stella's
attention. She was on the point of going down for breakfast when her father
appeared at her door.

"I have something for you," he said, handing her a small leather jewelry box.

"A present?" She took it from him, a little puzzled.

"It was sold to me by the mysterious woman I told you of. She produced
it after our talk and insisted it was meant for you. I had planned on giving
it to you on your next birthday but, well, after what you told me, after what
has happened, I could not wait until the summer. I want you to have it now."

She opened the box. Inside, nestled against a cushion of cream satin, sat a
beautifully wrought cameo brooch set in gold.

"Oh, Papa! How very lovely!"

"Hold it up to the light. Notice the clarity of the shell on which the image
is carved . . . do you see?"

She did as he suggested and the tawny color of the background glowed as
the morning sunlight fell through it, the carving showing up in sharp relief.

Her father could not resist taking it from her to point out the details.

"The image is that of your namesake. Some might mistake it for Diana,
as she, too, was associated with the moon, and there is a crescent set into the
hair . . . here."

"But this is not Diana?"

"Indeed, it is not. Closer inspection will reveal a coil of her hair to be a serpent. Only one, so not enough to point us in the direction of Medusa. And worked into the setting are further clues that confirm her identity. Look."

"Keys . . . a torch, and another tiny snake!"

"Which, as you well know, being familiar with the qualities and particulars of that original Hekate, are indisputably her symbols."

She did know, of course. Had known since she was old enough to ask about her unusual name and to wish to hear the stories behind it. She knew that the goddess was associated with the night and therefore the moon, with ghosts, with magic. Often depicted at a crossroads, she was believed to inhabit the liminal spaces between light and dark, life and death. She was thought to act as a guide through the land of the dead when called upon, and would appear accompanied by her loyal pack of hounds. "The serpents represent her magic," Hecate said, running her finger over the smooth surface of the cameo. "The keys stand for the thresholds she watches over." She beamed at her father, throwing her arms around his neck. "I shall treasure it," she told him.

"Here, you should wear it, now that you are a friend to ghosts." He took it from her and pinned it to the lapel of her tweed waistcoat. "Well then," he said, his voice catching with emotion. He hugged her again and Hecate knew that behind his pride in her newfound ability there was, small and hidden but nonetheless powerful, the fear of a father for his daughter who was venturing into unknown territory.

She stepped back and admired the pin in the mirror before taking his hand. "Come along. If we are late to breakfast we will raise Mother's suspicions."

As planned, she arrived at the cathedral early that day. Her purpose was simple yet fantastic; she intended conducting a ghost hunt. She parked her bicycle before morning prayers had finished and stepped as quietly as she was able over the flagstones and into the Lady Chapel. If she ventured into the nave, she would be seen by the vicars choral in the choir stalls, and the dean as he took the service. Her plan was, should she find nothing in the beautiful, second-grandest chapel in the cathedral, she would next try the tiny Stanbury shrine. As it transpired, she had no need to venture beyond the altar steps before her. There, standing tall and straight, ever watchful, was the lone soldier. She felt her breath catch in her throat. Now that she studied him with the benefit of what Brother Michael had told her, she recognized the uniform as being from the Napoleonic Wars, and saw that the soldier's hair was unfashionably long. She approached him a little shyly, the notes of a sung psalm surrounding her as she walked. The soldier continued looking straight ahead, his unsubstantial body taut, his jawline set, every fiber of his ethereal being giving the impression of someone determined and professional.

"Good morning to you, Corporal Gregory," she said softly. While the vicars were at their prayers and so unlikely to hear her, both Mrs. White and the verger could be anywhere at that moment in the course of their duties.

The soldier's eyes darted in her direction before resuming their forward stare.

"Morning, miss," he said.

"I am so very pleased to meet you," she replied, doing her best to make her voice sound less astonished than she felt. This was, after all, only her second time conversing with a ghost. "Brother Michael spoke of you yesterday. I would very much like to hear your story." When he made no reply she added, "If you feel you can trust me with it."

He turned his head to look at her then, his expression relaxing a fraction as their eyes met. She felt her heart lurch to see how terribly young he was.

"Mine is a sorry tale, miss. A lesson to others, perhaps. You might not think well of me after hearing of it."

"I would not presume to judge you, Corporal."

He considered this for a moment and then began to speak again, and she saw that though it pained him to relive the events of his past, he was, in fact, keen to share it with her. As if the telling of it was in some small way an unburdening.

"I was an eager recruit, not some wild roustabout with brandy in his blood and friends who knew no better. It was the army for me, and glad of it. My father was dean here, and my brother had taken the living in a parish near Bromyard, but it was always the life of a soldier that called to me." He glanced down at his scarlet coat. "Was my proudest day, when I donned the uniform of His Majesty's infantry. We were sent to France within the month. I had scarce learned how to shoot straight, but I cared not, for this was my destiny. I believed myself prepared for what was to come." He looked back at her again and heartbreaking fear was written upon his handsome face. "I was not. The thunderous cannons, the choking stink of gunpowder, the sobs of the dying . . . I was not prepared for the mud that sucked at my feet, holding me fast for the enemy's musket fire. I was not prepared for the relentless onslaught, the pitiless rhythm of attack and retreat, attack and retreat, attack and retreat. Day upon day. And only thin stew or bread to fuel us. I was not ready for any of it, yet I endured. I obeyed every command. I fought as best I could along-side my comrades. Long weeks passed. The more men fell, the more each of us was required to do, so that rest became our greatest wish. Rest and sleep."

At that moment the vicars stopped singing. Hecate heard the dean's mel-lifluous voice bringing the service to a close with a short blessing. She found herself holding her breath, desperate for the soldier to continue his story, not wanting the spell of their conversation to be broken, but knowing that soon they might be interrupted.

"Please continue," she said.

"After many weeks of fighting, we gained ground, moving forward across the war-scarred fields. We took possession of a woodland, one that must have been beautiful before the cannon fire tore at the trees. Still, there were some oaks standing, and clusters of holly and hazel. From here we were sheltered and the slope of the hill gave us a vantage point. Six of us were chosen to guard this post; to keep watch. We followed a rota of our captain's devising. Two of us would keep vigil at any time while the others cooked, cleaned weapons, or slept. There came a lull in the fighting. For a while all was peaceful. We be-gan to recover but still we were weary. One night a fellow soldier . . . his name was Evans . . . was to share the watch with me. I could see he was fighting sleep, so I sent him to rest with the others. I took up my position, my back to a tree stump. All was quiet save for owls hunting, foraging for mice among the brambles. I paid no heed to my own drowsiness. I should have done so. Alas, I did not, and sleep overtook me." He paused, his expression full of sorrow. "When I awoke, there had been a stealthy attack in the darkness. All five of my comrades were dead, bayonetted where they lay. I had been missed by the enemy. Upon discovering my friends I would have ended my own life had I the chance, but an attack had begun. Later . . . much later, a court-martial decreed I pay for my failure with my life. It was a fitting end."

Hecate longed to be able to put a hand on his arm to comfort him. She could hear footsteps coming up the north aisle and the quiet chatting of the vicars.

"What keeps you here, Corporal Gregory? Do you wish to . . . move on?"

"Oh no, miss. This is my vigil now. I will never again abandon my post."

"Hecate!"

The sound of Clementine calling her name made her swing around. She was astonished to see her friend walking toward her, escorted by Reverend Forsyth.

"Clemmie, what a pleasant surprise," she said, leaning forward to exchange a kiss in greeting.

The reverend explained. "I found Miss Twyford-Harris wandering the cathedral in search of you. Knowing your route to the library I brought her this way."

Clemmie nodded. "I thought I'd come and see these precious books of yours. See what it is that demands your attention and keeps you so occupied. Oh, what a darling cameo you are wearing, is it new? Gracious, Hecate, it was not my aim to shock you. You look quite disconcerted to see me."

Hecate was acutely aware of the fact that Corporal Gregory was still standing at her side. It was obvious the other two could not see him. She was uncertain of his ability to see them but it felt extremely awkward. She found herself glancing at him. It was a small action, but one that she noticed did not escape John Forsyth's observation. She felt him watching her more closely.

"I am delighted to see you, Clemmie. And would be even more delighted to show you the library. Do you think Reverend Thomas will permit a visitor so early in the day?" She directed her question at Reverend Forsyth, holding his gaze, smiling brightly. She had the unsettling feeling that he could see how wrong-footed she was and somehow tell that her demeanor was not a result of Clementine's surprise appearance.

"I am certain he would be pleased to show off the collection," he replied. "He takes great pride in it. A new admirer is always welcome."

"Excellent! Thank you so much for rounding up this little lost lamb, Reverend," Hecate said cheerily, taking her friend by the arm and steering her away. "We will go and see the master of the library and brighten his day. Come along." She strode off, allowing no time for dithering, eager to move away from the confusing mixture of the vicar and the ghost. Glancing back, they made a curious tableau; the keen-witted clergyman in his long black cassock standing beside the sorrowful soldier in his scarlet uniform. Both were young men who had been called to their vocations. Both were now part of her new life.

Clemmie was whispering urgently in her ear.

"Goodness, Hecate, I can see why you are taken with Reverend Forsyth! I know what I said about marrying a vicar, but he is rather lovely and quite charming. I might make an exception for him."

She giggled then, her laughter infectious, so that by the time they encountered the librarian Hecate had shaken off something of the sadness of the corporal's story.

Hecate was kept so busy beneath the watchful eye of Reverend Thomas that she was not for one moment on her own in the library. This meant she had no opportunity to study the *Mappa Mundi* closely, let alone touch it. Nor was she able to speak at any length with Brother Michael, though she had twice spied him drifting up and down between the bookshelves. She applied herself to her small tasks and did her utmost to prove her worth to her superior. She had, at least, been able to spend time in other areas of the cathedral and, to her great delight, had encountered more of the ghostly family who resided there. She met again the phantom cleaner, who fussed and fretted about not getting the cathedral ready for a visit by King George III. Hecate quickly realized that some souls had less awareness of their own state or the time in which they found themselves than others. If she mentioned the modern date, Mrs. Nugent became at first confused and then dismissive, as if it was Hecate whose mind was not to be relied upon for facts.

It was during this time that she made the acquaintance of another ghost, whose story touched her deeply. On her way back from an errand for Reverend Thomas she had stopped at the shrine of their local saint, Thomas Cantilupe, to light a candle of remembrance. It was while she was dropping the spent match into the tin receptacle provided, its narrow plume of smoke drifting heavenward, that she had become aware of a presence to her right. Turning, she found a slender woman of late middle years dressed in a gown of so soft a blue it suggested she had stood too long in the sun. It was not the paleness of the woman's skin, nor the whisper of her voice, nor the silence of her footsteps that alerted Hecate to her otherworldliness. Indeed, to begin with the stranger's physical peculiarities seemed to her to speak of aristocratic frailty, perhaps, or the hothouse delicacy common to many women of a certain type. Instead, it was the profound sadness emanating from her that had caused Hecate to realize she was somehow significantly different. So affecting, so pitiful, was the stranger's demeanor that Hecate stepped toward her at once, her hand outstretched, as if she might lend her strength by way of the warmth of her own touch. The ghost, unaccustomed to any manner of connection with the living after so many years of drifting lost and sad, hesitated, not moving beyond Hecate's well-meant reach. So it was that Hecate's vital hand grasped at the insubstantial one of the ghost. She experienced a coldness against her palm and a tremor that ran through her very soul.

She gasped aloud, finding her voice seconds later.

"Tell me . . . what is your name?" she asked, watching as the ethereal lady drifted minutely away from her, the hem of her trailing gown moving ever so slightly above the tiles of the cathedral floor.

"I am Lady Elenor Rathbone," the ghost replied, quite matter of fact. "Of Berrington Hall. Do you know of it?"

"I—yes. Yes. It is a fine house, with notable gardens, I believe."

At this Lady Rathbone's sadness had lifted a fraction, a smile accompanying a happy memory. "Oh how I loved the rose arbor in the walled garden," she said. "It was at its best in late spring."

Hecate glanced this way and that but there was no one else nearby. "My name is Hecate Cavendish," she told her new acquaintance in her brightest voice, "and I am delighted to meet you. Truly I am."

Lady Rathbone looked at her more closely. She reached out as if she might touch her hair. "Such pretty coloring," she murmured. "So . . . charming." She sighed then, her icy breath raising the hairs at the nape of Hecate's neck. "Had I such flaming locks . . . he might have loved me better," she said.

"Who?" Hecate asked.

But the specter put her finger to her lips and shook her head, as if to speak his name was too much to bear.

And then this poignant, mysterious moment had been shattered by the sudden ringing of the cathedral bells summoning the faithful to communion. Hecate jumped, her hand flying to her heart, the jarring volume of the bells' peals shocking after the whispered conversation. Instinctively she looked up toward the bell tower, and when she looked down again, Lady Rathbone had gone. Hecate had asked Brother Michael about this soul that seemed more lost than any of the others she had encountered to that point. He told her the story. She had been engaged and planning her wedding when her fiancé had betrayed her. She had run mad with heartbreak, fleeing her parents' home, taking refuge in the cathedral. Well-meaning people had tried to help but she would not be comforted and fled from them, escaping to the belfry, from where she tragically fell, plummeting to her death. Ever since, in times of crisis for the city, she was believed to toll the bell.

# 7

ON THE TUESDAY, HECATE'S FATHER HAD TAKEN HER FOR SANDWICHES in the Green Dragon Hotel. After their lunch they had returned early to the cathedral and seated themselves upon a central pew in the nave. Reverend Forsyth was giving a short organ recital, so that the space resounded to the sublime music of Bach, expertly played.

Edward leaned close to Hecate as he spoke. The sonata gave them some cover for their conversation, but even so he did not want to risk being overheard by the handful of music lovers who had come to hear the recital.

"It is irksome that the master of the library insists on spending quite so much time in it," he said, knowing how restricted she was by the librarian's presence. "We can only hope he comes to see you as a trustworthy custodian and takes advantage of the increased freedom that will grant him."

"To be perfectly frank with you, Father, I believe it more likely Reverend Thomas is governed by his preference for large luncheons than anything else. Or possibly, his gout, which troubles him increasingly." She quickly added, "Not that I wish him ill health . . . I would do far better in so many ways were I to be furnished with my own set of keys."

"Perhaps you could encourage him to take afternoon naps, in view of his condition. That way you could speak to your spectral monk more often and more freely. I feel he has so much to tell you regarding all the spirits in the cathedral."

"They prefer the term 'souls.' At least, the ones I have met so far."

"Tell me again . . . Brother Michael, Corporal Gregory . . ."

"Mrs. Nugent, the cleaner, though I have spoken to her but briefly. She is so desperate to have the place gleaming for King George, it's hard to persuade her to pause long enough to talk. And then there's Lady Rathbone."

"Ah, yes! The heartbroken beauty! Such a tragic tale. Have you encountered her more than once?" Edward asked.

"Three times, including this one."

His eyes widened. "This one?"

"Yes, Father. She is sitting beside you." She smiled at him as he turned to scrutinize the pew to his left. She knew he could not see what she could; the pale lady in her delicate blue gown listening to the stirring music. She felt a pang of pity for her father. His own experiences of sensing or seeing ghosts had been very real and important to him, yet he had not her gift. He could not see the lost souls around him now. He would have to rely on her to describe them.

Edward reached out a hand as if to touch the invisible person next to him but then withdrew it. He glanced back at Hecate, smiling a little sheepishly.

"I would not wish to do something . . . inappropriate," he said. "Can she . . . can she see me?"

"She can. And hear you. Shall I introduce you? Lady Rathbone, this is my father, Edward Cavendish." She watched as her father turned to face the empty space once again. The phantom regarded him with polite interest.

"What a handsome man," she said, her cool, ghostly breath falling against his cheek as she spoke.

Her father flinched as that phantom exhalation reached it, his hand quickly going to his face.

"Good Lord!" he exclaimed. He turned and beamed at his daughter. "I . . . I sense her presence!"

Hecate put her hand on his arm.

"She is very pleased to meet you, Father. Come," she said, getting to her feet. "It will not help my cause with Reverend Thomas to be late returning from lunch."

Edward stood, unable to help himself staring once again at the spot where he knew Lady Rathbone to be sitting. As Hecate led him away he shook his head. "These are wonderful endeavors you are engaged in here, my daughter. Wonderful endeavors indeed," he said.

Not more than an hour later, Hecate had cause to feel guilty about her careless wish for the recurrence of the librarian's gout. He returned from his own lunch in a mood that had shifted from the region of the taciturn to the territory of the ill-tempered. His progress up the stairwell and even across the floor of the room was significantly more effortful than usual. While Hecate attempted to complete her work, Reverend Thomas puffed and fidgeted in his chair, unable to find a position that afforded him comfort. At last, he gave up the struggle.

"Miss Cavendish, I find I am indisposed," he told her, closing his ledger and picking it up from his desk as he hobbled toward the door. "I shall retire to my rooms. I may yet send for Dr. Francis." He looked at her levelly. "I leave the library in your care for the remainder of the afternoon. Continue with the task in hand. Should anyone require access to the collection ask them to call again tomorrow."

"Of course, Reverend."

"On no account are you to leave the library unattended. Do you understand?"

"Absolutely. I will take the greatest care of—"

"See that you do. I will send the verger to lock up at five. . . ." he told her, his words already fading as he moved out of the door.

Hecate listened to his painful descent of the stairs until she heard the door to the north aisle at the bottom open and close, excitement growing inside her. It was barely three o'clock. She would have the library to herself for two whole hours! She would work quickly to finish the stack of papers so she would be free to examine the map again.

Anticipation lent speed to her fingers as she sifted and sorted and filed away the documents. She would not fail in her small duty. Having charge of the library, however briefly, was a test, and she must pass it well. At last, just when she thought her patience would run out, she put the final sheet of yellowing paper into the box on her right, marked the date on the lid, and set it down on the stack beside her desk.

Now her time was her own. She turned to the *Mappa Mundi*. It appeared calm enough, quiet and motionless. She could hear nothing, nor detect any movement. She examined it closely, repeating to herself the names of the creatures and the places this time, determined to commit it all to memory. At one point she lifted a hand to touch the surface of the map, but a slight apprehension made her hesitate. On the last occasion she had laid a finger upon the vellum she had a duster in her hand, so that her skin had not made direct contact with it. What might happen with that barrier removed, she wondered. How much better might it be to have a friend present? To share the moment. To keep watch over her.

She stepped over to the bookshelves and peered along the rows.

"Brother Michael?" she called gently. "Brother Michael, are you there?"

For a moment there was no reply, and then she sensed rather than heard a disturbance in the far corner of the room. Seconds later, the aged monk glided into view, his round, wrinkly face smiling in welcome.

"How wonderful to hear my name called after so very many years," he said. "And all the more wonderful that I am called by one still treading the earth." He came to stand in front of her, pushing his hood back off his head so that his already-compromised vision was not further inhibited by the generous cowl.

"Good afternoon to you, Brother Michael," she said, her heart beating a little faster as had become its custom at the thrill of having a ghostly companion. "I am happy to have the opportunity to speak with you again. Since last we spoke I have sought out the others."

"Others? Oh, my brethren and sisters. Yes, yes. They have mentioned as much to me. It gladdens my heart to think that we may all welcome you into our home. How fortunate we are that you have come."

"Are you? Fortunate, I mean. What can I do to help any of you? I feel unable to provide any service at all, save for conversation."

"Never underestimate the value of listening to the words of another, my child. Particularly when they are spoken by the lonely. Furthermore, to have a living ally in our midst, well, who knows in what ways you may be of assistance to we flimsy, insubstantial folk?" He smiled at her, attempting and failing to pick up an inkpot to make his point.

"Actually"—Hecate shuffled her feet as she spoke, uncomfortable about asking a favor so soon in their friendship—"I was rather hoping that, on this occasion, you might be able to help me."

The monk silently clapped his hands in delight. "But of course! Ask, and it shall be given. If I am up to the task, that is."

"That is a question I have about myself, Brother Michael. Am I up to the task?" She pointed at the map. "I want to try to connect with the *Mappa Mundi* again, but I confess I am a little afraid." She looked at her hands then. "I don't know what will happen when I properly touch it. I was so excited about what occurred before, but now . . . now I doubt myself. What if it's all simply random? I mean to say, there hasn't been anyone else working here aside from Reverend Thomas for years. What if the map was merely reacting to the novelty of my presence? Or to my youth, perhaps? Or the fact that I am a woman? What if I inadvertently stir something in it which would be better left undisturbed? How am I to know what to do for the best? Perhaps I ought not to interfere. . . . How do I know if I am up to what could be required of me?"

Brother Michael folded his arms, tucking his hands into his sleeves. "There are times we cannot know before we act, my child. The knowing comes afterward."

Hecate thought about this and knew that he was right. Her father had told her she was engaged in wonderful endeavors. He was right, too. And he believed in her ability to withstand whatever rigors were demanded of her in pursuit of those endeavors. Of course such strange actions required courage, but oh, how glorious to have those opportunities! To be given the chance to take those risks and venture upon wild, uncharted waters.

With determination, she stepped closer to the map. She found herself unconsciously pausing to touch her Hecate brooch, as if she might draw strength from her namesake. She was, after all, attempting to cross a most unusual threshold. It could not but help her cause to summon the goddess's assistance, surely? She made a point of emptying her mind of thoughts as best she could, so that she might better receive any communication that came toward her. Slowly, but without trepidation now, she lifted her hand. She had already decided what she would touch this time. Not the map's one flaw. Not its center. Not even the image of Hereford Cathedral, though she had considered all of these. No, instead she chose something else she felt drawn to. A little creature that sat a hand's span above the center, near the left margin. A tiny beast that had already, more than once, signaled to her in its own strange way. She leaned forward a fraction and stretched out her hand, pointing her index finger, moving it until at last it touched the curious shape of the griffin, on the very tip of one of its wings.

She was amused but not alarmed by the high-pitched, somewhat raucous cry of the mythical animal, for it was clearly a sound made in greeting rather than anger. Even the sudden flapping of its wings, stretching of its neck, and swishing of its tail were something she might have anticipated, and she found them delightful. What caused her to gasp, to exclaim with a mixture of shock and joy, was the fact that the griffin bent its legs, lowered its head, and then sprang free of the map.

Hecate ducked as it swooped by, its wings beating erratically, as if the griffin was having to remember how to use them. Now that it was liberated from the confines of the map it became so much more than ink and vellum. Its breast feathers shimmered green and gold. Those on the underside of its wings were scarlet. The rest of it was the tawny gold of a young lion. It swooped straight through Brother Michael, who tolerated the impertinence with a mild "dear me!" Still squawking, the creature, which had grown to the size of a small cat, gained speed, flying the length of the room in seconds, finding its strength with every wing beat. For one awful moment, Hecate feared it might escape the room, or worse, crash into the glass of the windows. It flew directly at the north wall at one point, but veered left at the last minute to avoid a collision. Gaining confidence and speed, it executed two low swoops. During the second one, its talons caught up a piece of parchment from the librarian's desk and knocked over a pot of pencils.

"Have a care!" Hecate called after it, surprised and delighted to see it was able to interact in a tangible, physical way with things around it.

The griffin seemed to be tiring. It flapped on with some effort, and at last landed atop the nearest bookcase, cocking its head to one side, its beady eyes taking in its new surroundings.

Instinctively, Hecate put out her arm, as if the tiny beast were a hawk that might return to its master. "Come along now," she coaxed it. "It's quite safe. Come here, little one."

The griffin lifted a foot but only so that it might step sideways along the top of the bookcase. It had the beak of an eagle, but the body and tail of a lion. Its face was an intriguing mix of the two animals, and the sounds it uttered were sometimes birdlike, sometimes more those of a cat. Just when Hecate thought it would resist her attempt to tame it, it launched itself from the shelf, making a rapid descent, and landed with surprising accuracy on her outstretched arm. She had braced herself for the impact, for the sharp grip of its talons, but it was almost weightless. Almost, but not entirely. As it hopped up her arm and settled on her shoulder she felt its tiny steps, felt its feathers brush against her ear as it made itself comfortable, felt the slightest pressure as it held on to the fabric of her dress.

With great care, she reached up and stroked its downy chest, her fingers detecting the softest resistance, as if it were made of spiders' webs or thistledown. In this way her new friend differed significantly from her ghostly family, for there was corporeal substance to it, however slight.

Hecate found herself beaming at Brother Michael.

"What a glorious, magical thing!" she said, moved almost to tears. "Have you ever seen this happen before?" she asked him. "Has anything ever . . . come out of the map like this?"

"Not in all the many centuries I have been here, no. Not so much as a mouse, let alone such a splendid fellow as this." He chuckled, a gleeful sound that suited him well. He seemed a touch surprised by his own laughter, making Hecate wonder how long it had been since he had heard it.

"Why has this happened, do you think?" she asked him. "What does it mean?"

He gave an elaborate shrug and shook his head. "So many questions . . . alas I have no answers for you. What I think we can both agree upon, with some certainty, is that you, Mistress Cavendish, are precisely where you are needed."

She smiled, nodding. "Yes," she agreed, "I believe I am."

At that moment the sound of the stairwell door opening and closing made her start. She could hear quick footsteps on the stairs and the jangling keys. She felt rooted to where she stood. Brother Michael was at her side. The griffin made no effort to move or hide. She glanced at the map and saw that the image depicting the little beast had vanished! Expecting the verger she was surprised to see John Forsyth enter the room.

He looked at her, taking in at once her bright-eyed expression.

Hecate waited.

"You are alone?" he asked. "I thought I heard voices. Who were you talking to?"

It was all Hecate could do not to laugh out loud. There she stood, in the company of a phantom monk, with a mythical being perched on her shoulder for all the world like a pirate's parrot, and John could see neither man nor beast. She stifled her mirth, noticing that John was not oblivious to the fact that something momentous was taking place.

"I was expecting Mr. Gould," said Hecate, somewhat playing for time.

He held up the keys. "I encountered him and persuaded him to let me help you secure the library." He paused and then asked, "Is there something amiss?"

"Whatever do you mean?" she asked, feeling like a child caught stealing biscuits from the kitchen.

The vicar took a step closer to her. "I mean that your face shines with excitement, there is a light that fills you that is uncommon to say the least, and this is not the first time you have given me cause to think you involved in some . . . unusual activity."

"Truly, I do not know to what you can be referring."

"Do you not? Wouldn't you care to share with me whatever fascinating secret I believe you to be holding on to so tight that you might extinguish it? I grant you have not known me long, Miss Cavendish, but I promise you, I would be a trustworthy confidante. Wait"—he held up a hand—"before you answer, please consider this: I have devoted my life to the study and worship of something unseen, unknowable, unproven, intangible. I spend my days raising my voice in song to the glory of an invisible God, and I believe he hears me. I pray with the faithful, and I trust he listens to those prayers. In addition, one of my duties here at the cathedral is that of diocesan exorcist. As such I have witnessed the extraordinary. Believe me when I tell you, I am a man you may speak to of the . . . unusual."

Hecate hesitated. It seemed that, like her father, Reverend Forsyth was indeed someone who might understand, or at least accept, her gift. How pleasant, how reassuring, it would be to have an ally among the living at the cathedral. But she had known him such a short time. She was a newcomer, her place in the library recently won, and she would not risk it. The fact was that she did not know this man well enough to be able to trust him with her secret. Not yet.

She smiled, keeping her voice light. "I am sorry to disappoint you, Reverend Forsyth, but I am simply engaged in the menial tasks the master of the library sees fit to trust me with. My aim is never to disappoint him. To which end, I should be grateful for your help in turning off the gasoliers and securing the library for the night."

He seemed about to press her further but relented, smiling, his blue eyes remaining watchful.

"As you wish, though please do grant me one thing."

"What would that be?"

"If we are to work together, and become the firm friends I am certain we will be, please, call me John."

She turned away from him to straighten books on her desk, determined to be as casual as possible when she replied, "Of course, that seems sensible. And you must call me Hecate."

"Hecate," he repeated, his smile showing in his voice now. "Here, let me help you with that."

He reached up and turned off the gaslight behind her desk before moving on to extinguish the others along the far wall.

Hecate gently nudged the griffin off her shoulder, gesturing at him to re-take his place on the map. She watched as it flapped its wings, shrinking down to size as it did so, fitting neatly back into position, claw raised, beak open. From the corner of her eye she saw Brother Michael drift away down the furthest row of shelves.

"Well then," she said, clapping her hands together as if at a job well done. "Time for home." Her casual demeanor was not, however, entirely honest, for she felt herself unsettled by John's presence in a way that was new and not, she had to admit to herself, unpleasant.

# 8

---·---

IT WAS A SPACE THAT, IN THE DEEP, STILL-WATER HOURS OF THE NIGHT, should have been devoid of movement, of sound, of life. It should have been filled with nothing more than the slumbering souls of those long passed to another realm. But on this night, someone disturbed that quiet. They broke it turning the key in the ancient lock, pushing open that groaning door on its heavy hinges, moving on hasty feet across the worn flagstones, and unpacking a bag of curious items onto the bare, disused altar. A candle. A mirror. A bone. A flower. A book. Had anyone been observing, they would have seen the figure hunch over this disparate collection, place the lit candle upon the mirror, position the bone just so, lay the book open at a certain page, and hold the petals of the bloom in the flame. But there was no one to witness these potent rituals. No one to hear the hissing of the flower as it burned, or the popping of the seeds inside it as they cracked and jumped in the heat. No one to smell the smoke of the flower's death. No one to hear the mumbled words read from that book. Words that had hardly been spoken for nearly half a century. The figure worked unobserved, as was his wish. But that was not to say he was undetected, for those words had great power when used with skill. And those to whom they are directed cannot resist them, so that when the dead are called, they answer.

\*\*\*

Hecate pushed her bicycle out of the stable, pausing to feed a remnant of toast to Peggy in her stall. The sound of the pony chomping followed her out into the spring sunshine. Stella had done an excellent job of neatening her shortened dress, and Hecate had purchased a fine pair of long brown boots from the outfitters in Widemarsh Street. It had given her no small satisfaction to be able to do so with her own money. A fact that had gone some way to silencing her mother's protests at her new outfit, along with, of course, the matter of her daughter's safety.

"Truly, Mother," she had told her, "it is the coming thing for young independent ladies to travel in such a way. We will set the trend in Hereford, just you wait and see."

"I remain to be convinced. And that hat . . ."

"Stella helped me steam it. I believe it has regained its shape quite well."

"That's as may be, but it has a habit of being blown askew as you ride so that you arrive at your destination with the appearance of someone who has fled danger. Let me reposition that pin." Beatrice had wrestled with the straw boater and the inadequate fixing for a moment before instructing Hecate to wait while she fetched a longer one from her own collection. "Here," she said upon returning, "this will serve our purposes better."

Hecate had taken it from her with a small exclamation of surprise. "Oh, it is very fine, Mother. Are you sure you want me to use it?" The pin was fashioned from high-quality silver, long and strong, its finial formed of curving plant tendrils into which was set a large, lustrous, lapis lazuli stone. "Would you not rather keep it for occasions?"

Beatrice took it from her. "I would rather my daughter did not go about looking like a scarecrow," she muttered, fixing the hat securely this time.

Hecate smiled at her, leaned forward and kissed her quickly on the cheek. "Thank you!" she called over her shoulder as she hurried on her way.

Now, as she jumped up onto the saddle of her bicycle and pedalled off, she delighted in the manner in which she was now able to risk even greater speeds. Her ultimate goal was to own a pair of cycling knickerbockers or culottes, but she recognized her mother was not yet prepared for such a concession.

Her progress through the city was rapid as she was practiced in avoiding the heaviest of traffic, taking a route to High Town that was too twisty for carriages or carts. The wind tugged at her straw boater, testing her expertly positioned pin. The newspaperboy waved as she passed him. The grocer at the bottom of Church Street threw her an apple, which she deftly caught with one hand, throwing a "thank you, Mr. Preece!" over her shoulder as she went. At last she reached the Cathedral Green and dismounted. The sight of the ancient house of worship never failed to move her. If anything, now that it was her place of work and home to her phantom family, she loved the place even more, and could never imagine a time when it would not be at the center of her life.

She parked her bicycle at the entrance to the cloisters and went in through the south door, stooping to make a fuss of the cat as she did so.

"Good morning, Solomon. Your coat is looking particularly fine today," she told him.

Inside, the temperature was still cool, the year not yet sufficiently advanced for the sun's rays to have warmed the thick stone walls. The dean was taking morning prayers, the vicars choral in good voice. Hecate noticed Lady Rathbone sitting alone in the Lady Chapel and paused to whisper hello to her.

"Oh, good morning to you, Hecate," she whispered in reply. "Tell me, is the sun shining outside? And has the apple tree by the west gate yet bloomed?"

"It has, my lady. And indeed it looks splendid in the sunlight today."

Lady Rathbone nodded and smiled, seeming to take comfort in this.

Hecate hurried on. As the choir sang their answers to Dean Chalmers' lines of a psalm, she saw Mrs. Nugent, diligent as ever, her rotund body in no way inhibiting vigorous movement as, cotton duster in hand, she polished the brass on the rail to the chapel.

"Good morning, Mrs. Nugent!" Hecate whispered as she trotted past. "You've brought up a tremendous shine there."

"Must have everything looking its best for the king's visit!" she replied, not for one moment pausing in her energetic polishing. "Must keep going. Must have everything just so!"

"I am certain His Majesty will be impressed," Hecate assured her before turning to push open the low, arched door and step through the narrow entrance to the twisting stone stairs that would take her up to the library. She had learned the little woman's story. She had been employed to clean the cathedral in the late eighteenth century. When a royal visit was announced she worked tirelessly to ensure everything was looking its best. On the day King George was expected she set off from home early to be at the front of the cheering crowds to welcome him. Sadly, she was so distracted by her excitement that she stepped in front of the London stagecoach. After all her hard work she never did get to see the king admire the results of her labors.

Hecate was so taken up with her exchange with Mrs. Nugent that she had failed to notice she was observed. As she turned the corner of the transept into the north aisle she saw that John, from his position in the choir stalls, had been watching her. He must have seen her pause and apparently conduct a conversation with herself. His bright blue eyes met her own gaze and for a moment held her there. She found herself flustered beneath such scrutiny and moved quickly to the staircase doorway.

Hecate found Reverend Thomas on the point of lowering himself onto his chair. The two exchanged their customarily brief greeting and she went to the hatstand in the far corner to hang up her coat. She took her woolen shawl and wrapped it around her shoulders, crossing it over to tie tightly at the back so that there were no loose ends to interfere with her work. She liked the routine that had been established. There was comfort to be had in the rhythm it provided, the solid nature of the expected and the manageable. Of having a place and a set of duties and knowing how to perform them well. The master of the library had begun to entrust her with more valuable items to clean or restore, and to approve her attempts at more delicate and challenging work. She had shown herself to be a diligent worker, quick to learn, eager to please, and he had, somewhat grudgingly she felt, been known to compliment her on the standard of that work. He had yet to entrust her with the keys to the chained books or the library itself, however, a fact that continued to irk her.

While her tasks as assistant librarian mattered to her greatly, what gave her the most joy was the development of her gift. Brother Michael had called it "the gift of communing with the dead" but she did not see it like that. She saw it, instead, as a blessing that permitted her access to those who lived on a different plane. Those who were not troubled by earthly concerns such as food or warmth or money, but had an entirely spiritual existence. She tried to help them when she could, and they were grateful, but in truth she felt she was the one who owed gratitude. Whatever strange ability she had been given, no matter where it had come from, her connection to the map, the friendship of her constant companion, the griffin, and being close to the cathedral's lost souls, these were treasures, privileges, and she was thankful for them daily.

This joy was increased by being able to share her experiences with her father. She had seen him thrive on this new aspect of their relationship, as if he had been rescued from a purposeless retirement by becoming her confidant and support.

Once seated at her desk, Hecate turned her attention to the small map repair she had been charged with, determined to finish the work to Reverend Thomas's satisfaction. The damage was not extensive, but it required careful patching and repainting, and she liked to think her skills, which her father had taught her over many years of helping him with his collection, would satisfy or possibly even impress her employer. The griffin flew from the Mappa Mundi, conducted a circuit of the room, and came to sit on her desk. She smiled at him, glancing to check she was not observed before leaning forward to scratch him affectionately behind one of his tiny lion's ears. She was on the point of unpinning the map to turn it when she heard the sound of one of the cathedral bells ringing. This was not the clock marking the quarter hour, nor the bell ringers practicing their art, but a lone chiming. She and the reverend exchanged looks. Of the several local stories regarding the haunting of the cathedral, the most well-known was that of a phantom who rang the oldest bell in times of danger. For most of the inhabitants of Hereford it was a chilling ghost story. For Hecate, knowing Lady Rathbone as she did, it was fact. Before she or Reverend Thomas had the chance to remark upon the bell, there came, amplified up through the twisting stone stairwell, a series of loud, shrill, and terrified screams.

The griffin took to the air.

Reverend Thomas showed a surprising turn of speed as he leaped from his seat and ran toward the door.

Hecate sprinted after him. As they descended the steep stairs, the screams continued amid sounds of agitated, raised voices and hastening footsteps.

"They are in the crypt!" Hecate said, the thought making her shiver even as she sprinted along the choir aisle and overtook her superior, quickly reaching the entrance to the catacombs. Corporal Gregory stood on guard, imploring her not to enter. She understood her ghostly friend's desire to protect her, but on this occasion she could only run past him. The dean himself had already descended the short flight of stairs from the ground floor to the subterranean level and stood at the center of the main space of the crypt, attempting to calm the hysterical Mrs. White. Ahead of them, John cut a silent but steady figure, a point of stillness in a moment of chaos, as around him the reason for the cleaner's distress was plain to see. Two of the three stone sarcophaguses in the center of the space had been opened, their lids wrenched away and thrown aside as if made of nothing heavier than paper. To the left, one of the iron gates that protected shelves of coffins had been pulled from its hinges and lay on the flagstoned floor. Three of the coffins had been removed from their ledges and dragged several paces across the floor. They, too, were missing their lids. One of the caskets had been reduced to nothing more than a pile of splinters. On the far side of the room, another tomb lay shattered, stones rendered rubble. All six of these burial places—whether worm-nibbled wood or ancient stone or opulent marble—now shared a common factor. Each and every one of them was empty.

Mrs. White had recovered sufficiently to be wailing amid wet sobs. Seeing Hecate, Dean Chalmers steered the cleaner toward her, hugely relieved to find a woman to assist him.

"Miss Cavendish, kindly lead Mrs. White from this upsetting discovery. I fancy a little fresh air . . . ?"

"Of course, Dean," she said, slipping a supportive arm around the older woman's waist. "Come now, let us step outside."

"Oh, such a shock!" Mrs. White declared. "Such a shock. Those poor souls . . . to be so disturbed!"

"Do not distress yourself further." Hecate tried to prevent a fresh outbreak of hysteria. "The dean will know what to do."

"To think such a thing could happen!" the cleaner went on, her voice echoing around the low-ceilinged space, forced down by the carved vaulted stone and funneled up the narrow staircase to inform any who might care to hear what she had to say. "Grave robbers! Saints preserve us, grave robbers!"

The dean lifted his own voice, keen to head off a rumor before it left the cathedral. "Now then, Mrs. White, let us not leap to unwarranted conclusions. We will send for the constable, who will inform the inspector of what has taken place."

Even as the dean sought to reassure everyone present that grave robbers had

not, in fact, breached the security of the cathedral and made off with several
bodies, Hecate could see from the glances he exchanged with John that he
accepted this as the most likely explanation. She herself remained to be convinced. It was not simply that vandalism on such a scale seemed beyond the
scope of most simple grave robbers. It was not only that there was scant evidence of bodies being dragged or otherwise conveyed up the stairs and out of
the building. What led her to the certainty that all was not as it seemed was
the unshakable conviction that, somewhere in the deepest shadows of the
crypt, something lingered. Accustomed as she was by now to the company of
non-corporeal beings, this should neither have surprised nor frightened her.
But it did. For what she sensed, what presence she detected, was not at all of
the kind she regularly spent her time with. This was something altogether different. There came with it such a weighty sense of foreboding, such a cast of
dread, that she found it hard to draw a deep breath. For the first time in her
life, Hecate Cavendish was truly afraid.

Mrs. White had settled to whimpering now and taken out a large handkerchief with which to mop her eyes. "Those poor souls," she repeated.

Hecate helped her up the stairs but as she did so she felt her flesh creep.
The soldier at the top of the stairs had his own mouth open in shock. She
could not speak to him in front of everyone present, but she could tell from
his expression that he, too, felt what she was experiencing. He, too, was able
to detect the danger that still lurked among the catacombs. She could not
leave the dean there unaware of the peril he was in. She could not leave John.
Turning, without attempting to pry Mrs. White's fingers from her arm, she
called back.

"Dean, might it not be wise to leave the area undisturbed? I imagine the
inspector will thank you for protecting the evidence in a place where a . . . a
complicated crime has taken place." She addressed the man who was, after
all, in charge of the cathedral, but it was the vicar whose gaze she met. As she
had hoped, he detected the urgency behind her words. He nodded carefully.

"Miss Cavendish has it right, Dean. I'm certain of it," he agreed. "Let us
go upstairs and secure the entrance against anyone else setting foot down here
before the police officers arrive."

Dean Chalmers nodded and the two crossed the floor of the crypt to the
stairs, where he pulled the hefty ledge and brace door closed, took a key from

the cluster on his belt, and turned the lock with a jarring clunk that echoed through the gloomy space.

An hour later, with Mrs. White sent home, the dean was showing the scene of destruction in the crypt to the policemen. He had sent everyone else away, determined there should be as little disruption to the working day of the cathedral as possible. Before returning to the library, however, Hecate led John into the vestry and shut the door. The room was not available to the public but served as a store for many of the robes and articles required for the services. It smelled of starch and silver polish and mothballs and candle wax.

"Are you quite well?" John asked, his expression one of genuine concern. The black robes of his office and white collar looked severe on some, but on him they seemed somehow somber yet dependable and reassuring.

"Of course," she said, not meeting his eye. She was aware he knew her well enough to sense her unease and had no wish to make herself the topic of discussion. "But, oh, John, what a dreadful thing to have happened."

"So much destruction. Why would grave robbers take time to utterly destroy the caskets? Indeed, what point would there be in stealing dust and bones? Who would pay them for such pitiful remnants? And we have no tradition of valuables being interred with anyone here."

"If it was grave robbers."

"You think otherwise?"

"I sensed a presence. Someone, or something . . . powerful."

"There must be a record of who was interred there. Perhaps it will provide some answers."

"I have seen those records. They are less than helpful," she told him, moving toward the door.

"Do you recall anyone who might have gone to their grave with a grievance? Or someone with a nature for dark deeds or violence?"

She could not help smiling. "Murderers and men of violence are not often laid to rest in cathedrals." She paused and then added, "Unless they were kings."

John gave a rueful shrug. "You make a fair point." He paused, looking at her with undisguised affection. "You know your safety matters a great deal to me, Miss Cavendish," he said.

Her smile broadened a little. "I must go. Reverend Thomas will be checking his pocket watch."

As she slipped out of the vestry and headed back to the library she found herself, as so often was the case, reassured by John's genuine warmth toward her. Nonetheless, she knew that whatever had emerged from those tombs was something more than a restless soul. She also knew that she would do whatever was necessary to seek it out, for if she could not return it to its rightful place, who could?

She found Reverend Thomas in a state of some agitation concerning time in the day lost. She did her best to placate him by settling at her desk and working diligently on repairing the small map without complaint or interruption for the better part of two hours. As the cathedral clock chimed, however, the conservator's hunger overcame his preoccupation with work and he left to go home to the cloisters for his lunch. It was Hecate's habit to walk to Church Street to buy a pie but today she had more pressing concerns than food. As soon as she was alone, she left her desk and threaded her way up and down the rows of shelves and the ancient chained tomes. With the griffin fluttering beside her at shoulder height, she called out softly.

"Brother Michael? Brother Michael, might I speak with you?"

She stopped at the end of a row, waiting, listening, opening her mind and her soul in the way she had learned to do so that she could better communicate with her ethereal friends. She felt rather than heard the old man's footsteps behind her, for while his feet had no weight to them, his presence disturbed the atmosphere of the room. Unlike what Hecate had detected in the crypt, however, Brother Michael's spirit was entirely benevolent. She turned to see him appear alongside his favorite part of the collection: the early illuminated Gospels.

"I should have known I'd find you there," she said.

Brother Michael lifted his eyes to peer for the thousandth time at the worn, leather cover of his beloved book. With a sigh he replied, without looking up, "I confess, I have a fondness for this particular edition of the Gospels that could be seen as a weakness." At last he turned to her, lowering his small, bright eyes, blinking myopically to bring her into focus. With his soft monk's robes, the hood low over his brow, his short stature and small, snub nose, he put Hecate in mind of a mole recently emerged from its subterranean home. For all his slightly comical appearance and mild manner, his mind was razor sharp, and his knowledge of the contents of the library second to none. Hecate knew she was fortunate to have him as a friend. She would never forget their first conversation which came on her third day at the cathedral. It was only after they had known each other a little longer that he told her of how he came to haunt the library. A tragic accident had cut short his stay. The cathedral had been undergoing building work, which was, in truth, its habitual state for centuries. While Brother Michael was carrying out his work in the new library, repairs and extensions to the transept were underway. It had been the monk's sad misfortune to be walking beneath a run of scaffolding at the precise moment it gave way. Two stonemasons were injured in the accident. Brother Michael was killed instantly. His brethren at Shaftesbury at first thought to repatriate his remains to be buried there, but the dean of Hereford protested. It was he who reminded them how much the monk had adored the library he had been so instrumental in setting up. How much better that he be laid to rest in the cathedral grounds. None of the clergy who attended his funeral could know, however, that their brother had chosen not to move on to a better place, because he so loved the books in his care that his soul could not bear to be parted from them. As far as Hecate could tell, he was one of only a very small number among the ghosts at the cathedral in that he chose to remain there and seemed content to do so.

"Has someone moved the copy of *Ecclesiastical Processes for Our Time?* I was searching earlier and cannot locate it."

Hecate stepped forward and put her hand on the shabby blue volume two shelves lower.

"Here it is, see? Safe and sound."

"Ah, good, good! Though why it should have migrated south like a bird detecting the shortening days . . ."

"I believe Reverend Thomas had it on his desk last week. He must have been confused about its home. I shall move it to its proper place when he returns."

The monk shook his head slowly. "Why he insists on taking the key with him when he leaves the library I cannot fathom. You have surely proved yourself trustworthy by now."

"I would hope so," she agreed. "Sadly, I do not think the reverend would ever entrust the keys to someone such as me." To make her point she held out the skirts of her dress and gave a little curtsey.

"Ah, yes."

"I don't believe he has ever quite come to terms with having to work with a woman. Handing over the keys would be a step too far."

"Then we must content ourselves with what access his prejudices allow. I was rather hoping you might release Pitkin's edition of *St. Paul's Letters* when next you are able. Such a thing of beauty both in form and content. It never fails to lift the spirits, eh?" he said, chuckling at his own little joke.

Already, Hecate and Brother Michael had worked a system whereby he requested a particular book and she removed it from the shelves while Reverend Thomas allowed her use of the key. He would not leave her in charge of the priceless collection, but he was happy to have her select volumes for cleaning and regular inspection against mites or damp. In this way, she was able to place whichever book the monk desired open on one of the reading tables, where he could look at it to his heart's content, using his ghostly breath to turn the pages. While she could extract any book and place it on the reading shelves within the limits their chains allowed, the light was so poor, and space between the rows so limited, as to interfere with a proper examination of their contents. Each of her ghostly friends had their own unique qualities and abilities, and differed in how substantial their haunting forms were. The elderly monk had very little impact on the solid world through which he now drifted and was dependent on her help.

"Gladly," Hecate told him, "but today I must ask a favor of you."

"Why of course! How can I be of assistance?" he asked, his chest puffing up a little with importance.

"Something dreadful occurred this morning, in the crypt. Were you aware of it?"

"Ah yes, such a terrible disturbance! I rarely venture beyond the library these days, but something so violent, well, its vibrations are felt throughout the building. There is little of importance to be found down there, surely?"

"Someone thought otherwise. Several of the tombs have been broken open and their contents . . . removed."

"How dreadful! And how curious . . ."

"Indeed. I cannot recall anyone of any note being interred there. I remember seeing a record in the archive of souls inside the cathedral, but none stood out as being important that were laid to rest in the crypt itself. I thought per-haps you might know different."

He shook his head, perplexed. "On the contrary, Hereford's crypt has never housed anyone of particular standing. In fact, over the years, whenever the graveyard has been excavated and bodies removed or reorganized, quite a number of them have been stored in the crypt. These were far from complete bodies or skeletons, you understand. Indeed, such has been the proliferation of boxes of bones that it was merely a charnel house and for a while the place was renamed Golgotha." He chuckled again, but not so heartily this time. "A joke in poor taste, in truth. But, the fact is, such was the confusion of remains housed there it would be impossible to say for certain to whom they belonged."

"So, those coffins, they could have housed anyone?"

"Save for one or two notable exceptions. Of course, there will be a record in the archive of who was buried outside the cathedral, but . . ."

Hecate followed his line of thought. "But it would be impossible to know which bodies had ended up where after the excavations."

"Alas, it was not the most orderly of processes. There was no one of any great experience in charge, it seems." He leaned closer to her, the chill of his other-worldly form settling about her as he did so. "They ought to have employed a monk," he whispered with a smile. "We know how to do these things properly."

"Instead we have a muddle upon a conundrum," she observed.

The ancient spirit turned back to browse along the bookshelves saying, "In which case the dean is fortunate in having you to solve it for him."

Their conversation was halted by the arrival of Reverend Thomas, his face flushed from a hearty lunch and the exertion required to climb the stairs. On finding Hecate apparently doing nothing he was quick to admonish her.

"Miss Cavendish, have you time to stare into empty space?" Reverend Thomas's tone was sharp. "I cannot imagine the dean would approve of any tardiness in the restoration of such a fine gift for the cathedral."

"No, Reverend. That is, I am determined to give this beautiful map my very best efforts and undivided attention."

"See that you do," he said, sitting heavily on the captain's chair behind his own desk. The leather cushion upon it gave a small squeak of protest. The li-brarian muttered a few more words regarding the need for the swift completion of new work, but he had, in fact, lost Hecate's attention. At that moment she had noticed that the *Mappa Mundi* was behaving strangely. At once her pulse quickened again. Could it be responding to the shocking events in the crypt? As she watched, an image near the bottom left of the map seemed to glow, to pulsate with light. Reverend Thomas had his head down over a ledger now and was unaware of the minor miracle that was taking place only yards from where he sat. Hecate got up and stepped quickly and quietly over to the map, anxious to examine more closely its curious activity. On closer inspection she was able to see that it was the drawing of the cathedral itself that was shimmering with a pale light of its own. The depiction marked not only the building, but the city. Now the image had acquired a vivid quality, its colors brighter, its lines clearer. Whatever had taken place in the crypt, it seemed that the map was most definitely responding to it.

She had the opportunity to examine it more closely a little later that afternoon when the master of the library was called away to an urgent meeting of Chapter. It was no surprise to either of them that the committee which was responsible for overseeing the running of the cathedral should need to meet to talk of what had happened in the crypt. Hecate took advantage of being alone to leave her desk and go to the map. Brother Michael had offered nothing illuminating regarding the other possible inhabitants of the crypt. She decided it would help her organize the facts better if she could be certain that it had not indeed been grave robbers who had broken the tombs. And for that, she must either persuade the policeman in charge, Inspector Winter, to share his thoughts with her, or visit the crypt again and see the lie of the land for herself. Given that senior members of the constabulary were not in the habit of discussing cases with young women on the periphery of the matter, the second course of action seemed the most likely to yield results.

When the master of the library returned from the meeting he was even more taciturn than usual, so that the remaining time passed largely in silence. Hecate was relieved when the working day drew to a close. At five o'clock precisely, Reverend Thomas checked his pocket watch against the ringing of the tower bells, closed his ledger, and rose from his chair.

"'*Sufficient unto the day is the evil therein.*' Would you not agree, Miss Cavendish?" he asked, holding the door for her as she hurried through it, hat and coat in hand.

"I would, Reverend," she said.

"Let us hope tomorrow will begin more ordinarily," he said, closing and locking the door behind them, testing the handle an extra time to be certain his beloved library was secure. Hecate thought it best not to point out that the crypt was similarly unfailingly locked.

They descended to the north choir aisle and the librarian repeated his actions with the lock of the second door, after which he muttered a goodbye and took himself off in the direction of the vestry, no doubt hoping for a cup of tea before Evensong. Hecate strode toward the east end of the nave. As she had anticipated, the entrance to the crypt was closed, likely under the instructions of the dean; the heavy red rope used for occasional ceremonial cordons had been tied across the top of the stairwell. Hecate glanced over her shoulder. She was alone. She carefully lifted the twisted rope and ducked beneath it so that she could continue down the worn and ancient stone staircase. The door at the bottom remained locked. There was a small barred window set into the door. She took hold of the cool iron posts and peered between them. There were no candles burning in the dusty space. Unusually, set into the high walls of the crypt were windows, allowing a watery late afternoon light to fall within. When her eyes adjusted to the low illumination it was just possible to discern the dim shapes within. Gradually objects revealed themselves to her in a little more detail, though everything remained softened by gathering shadow, blurred by darkness. The caskets and tombs were as she had seen them earlier; rent apart, smashed, their remnants scattered. There appeared no method or system to the way in which they had been opened, and still she could not see where or how the contents had been removed. The second flight of stairs which led to the door in the external north wall was sprinkled with a fine layer of the dust of the disturbance and yet bore no footprints save for one set, those belonging to John who had sprinted up to check the door when the desecration had been discovered. As that, too, had been securely locked, nothing was explained. Hecate felt her heart thud heavily beneath her ribs. She knew she must open herself to whatever souls might be adrift in that gloomy place but she was reticent. She was reluctant to make herself vulnerable to the menacing presence she had detected earlier. She slowed her breathing and closed her eyes. She listened. She waited. A minute passed, and then another.

It was Corporal Gregory who came to stand beside her.

"A sorry state, Miss Cavendish!" he said, shaking his head sadly. "And one I could neither foresee nor prevent."

Hecate sought to reassure him. "Do not blame yourself, Corporal," she said. She knew his history, and that having such a destructive event take place on his watch would distress him greatly. Although executed by firing squad in France, the soldier had received dignity in death. His grief-stricken father had used his position as then dean of Hereford Cathedral and seen to it that his beloved son was laid to rest secretly within the walls of the Green.

"Did you . . . see anything?" Hecate asked him gently.

He shook his head again and might have had more to say on the matter but a shout from the top of the stairwell caused him to disappear.

"Miss Cavendish! For pity's sake come away, child!" The dean's voice jolted her back to the living.

She whipped around to see him silhouetted against the light from the candelabra and sconces behind him.

"Oh, forgive me, Dean. I wanted to see—"

"These ropes are here for a purpose, my dear. Come now, there is nothing more to be seen." He beckoned to her in the manner of a fussing grandparent. She quickly climbed the stairs and stepped under the rope.

"My apologies, Dean. I had no wish to cause you alarm."

"Do not misunderstand me, I do not believe you to be in any danger. I simply wish to keep the incident as quiet as is possible. To avoid further upset, d'you see? To protect the reputation of the cathedral."

"Of course. I understand. Did the inspector have anything helpful to say?"

He shook his head. "I believe he was as mystified as we all are. But I can tell you this, my dear, and I hope you will reassure your family of the truth: Whatever wickedness occurred in the crypt, there is nothing there to fear any longer."

Hecate turned back to gaze down the dark stairwell once more, thinking about what she had and what she had *not* heard or felt as she had stood at that entrance. "As a matter of fact, Dean, I believe you are right about that."

That night, small clouds, harmless in themselves, were unwitting participants in a brutal act. The streetlamps of the city were not as many nor as effective as could have been wished, so that there were places even at its center that fell between their blurred pools of light. In these intervals moonlight must serve as illumination, but on the moment of this spring midnight, the soft clouds had drifted together. The moon was obscured, and the lampless streets and pathways thrown into deep gloom. The well-to-do gentleman knew the city and did not think to question the prudence of using shortcuts and snickets if they provided him with the swiftest route. So it was that, with the bells behind him chiming the hour, he walked from the Cathedral Green and took the narrow alley that ran in the direction of East Street. The walls on either side were high, and his path turned a tight corner at the midway point. There were no public houses here, no places of business, so that beyond the chimes of the cathedral clock, all was quiet. Even so, the gentleman did not hear the approach of his killer. There were no heavy footsteps to alarm him, nor coarse shouts or curses to alert him to the imminent danger of attack. Instead the first he knew of the violence that was to be brought upon him was when he found himself propelled forward with great force, thrown down upon the cobbles with such a blow that he had not time to save himself. He crashed to the ground, shocked, stunned, too affected to defend himself, his walking cane flung from his hand, his top hat fallen from his head. He struggled to right himself, to at least turn to face his assailant, but as he did so he felt a tightness at his throat. Though he could see no one in the darkness, he was aware of a crushing weight upon him, and of his breath being taken from him, so that he was not able to so much as cry out nor call for help.

And no help came.

# 9

HECATE SLEPT POORLY. SHE HAD WAITED UP FOR HER FATHER TO RE-turn home from an evening at the Rotarians' Society so that it had been past midnight when the two had sat in his study together. She had told him of the disturbing events in the crypt and the pair had debated for hours the possible causes and ramifications of what had happened. Despite their best efforts, they concluded their talk with more questions than answers. Hecate's dreams had been vivid and fractured. She was glad of the sound of garden birds heralding the start of a new day.

The sharp early light promised more bright sunshine, confirming a further step into spring. Hecate sat for a while at the small table in her room making notes. She compiled a list of facts gathered from Brother Michael and her father and her own studies, but still could not draw a satisfactory conclusion regarding the ruined tombs. Brother Michael had not known of any significant burials there. She remained unconvinced that grave robbers were to blame. It was somehow too simple and too flawed an explanation. On top of which, she knew in her heart that the dark presence she had detected was of the utmost relevance. Why should people who had been reasonable, benign souls when alive, become evil or dangerous when dead? No, she knew that whoever had been disturbed in those tombs it was not merely their agitated, restless spirits that she had detected. However otherworldly her own theories, to rule out completely anything more mundane, she decided she should speak to Inspector Winter. While he might not want to divulge information to her, he could not, if she approached the subject carefully, avoid confirming her own suspicions. She had resolved to find an excuse to leave the library and visit the crypt while the inspector was there, as Reverend Thomas had let slip that he would be returning for further investigation that morning. The dark presence she had detected in the crypt was less easy to explain, even to herself. She could not pretend that she had not felt it, nor that it had not frightened her. And yet, might not her shock at what she had found on entering the crypt, coupled with Mrs. White's distress and the dean's own sadness, have amplified what she had felt? She had asked herself if, perhaps, the drama of the situation and the particularly pitiful state of the coffins might not have caused an overreaction. She knew, of course, that it was highly likely a soul or several had been disturbed by what happened. Could she have mistaken sadness and grief for something wicked? After all, Brother Michael had detected nothing untoward at all, and no spirits had appeared to her later in the day.

She sped beneath the old stone arch that spanned St. Owen's Street. The hefty remnant of the ancient city wall looked unfashionable alongside the elegant Georgian houses that lined the length of the road. As she reached the town square she could hear the newspaper boy yelling out the headlines. Even before she could fully discern his words she detected an unusual excitement to his tone. By the time she drew level with his pitch outside the butter market, his announcement was all too clear.

"Read all about it! Gruesome murder in the city! Read it here! Knight of the realm murdered in cold blood! Read all about it! Gruesome murder!" As he shouted passersby stopped to press coins into his hands and take a copy of the paper. Soon a small crowd had gathered. Some stood reading the details of the terrible crime. Others whispered to one another in shocked voices. One elderly lady had to be helped to a bench. A mother led her open-mouthed children away.

Hecate stopped pedalling and hopped from her bicycle. She wheeled it to the stand and picked up a paper. She read quickly, the story indeed bearing out the boy's words.

*Sir Richard Thurston, well known man of business and Herefordshire philanthropist was last night discovered murdered. A constable patrolling the city beat came across a scene of terrible violence, the peer stricken and prostrate upon the street, his assailant fleeing. The officer of the law was unable to give chase, rightly judging that his duty lay with the unfortunate victim. Alas, so grievous and dreadful were the injuries inflicted on the late Baronet that he could not be saved. Speaking on the matter later, Inspector Winter of the Herefordshire Detective Branch confirmed the case was being treated as one of murder and the perpetrator was being sought. Anyone who might have witnessed all or part of the events that took place . . .*

Hecate could not bring herself to read on. Hereford had its share of crime, that could not be denied, but murder was mercifully rare. When such serious attacks occurred they were invariably spurred by a quarrel and inflamed by drink. Robberies happened, and violence was sometimes a factor, but the actual killing of a seemingly random victim was an uncommon event. She could hear those around her discussing their own theories. Sir Richard was well liked in the community and not known for mixing with people of intemperate behavior. He had not been a gambler or a womanizer. Could robbery have been a motive? Was the poor man cut down for his pocket watch or signet ring? Would such a fiendish assailant, left to run free, strike again? As she listened to them conjuring all manner of possible explanations for the attack, she felt a coldness enter her bones. She had no reasoning to offer, no sensible, rational hypothesis. All she had was an unshakable, soul-deep, powerful certainty within herself that this awful killing was in some inextricable way connected with whatever menacing presence it was that she had sensed in the crypt.

On reaching the library, Hecate found Reverend Thomas already at his desk. She knew she was not late, which meant he had arrived early, a sure sign that he was unsettled. He saw the newspaper in her hand and launched forth with what was for him an uncommon amount of words.

"A terrible business. Truly terrible. Brutally attacked. Struck down. Shocking. And so near the cathedral."

"Is that the case?" Hecate had not read far enough for such a detail.

"Only a matter of strides from the Green. The pity of it is, had he been a little further along the street when his assailant came upon him, he might have been within hearing of our own constable. Might have been saved. A terrible business indeed."

Hecate could only nod in agreement as she moved to her own desk, glancing at the *Mappa Mundi* as she did so. She was relieved to see it calm, undisturbed, unchanged. She had removed her hat and coat reluctantly, as the room felt even colder than the previous day. Tempted as she was to keep her outdoor garments on, she knew she would be hindered and made clumsy by them, so trusted to her woolen shawl instead. The library's thick walls and enormous windows did little to provide an even climate for the interior. She anticipated she might spend most of the winter months in coat, shawl, and fingerless mittens, while Reverend Thomas would become ever bulkier with layers of woolen garments beneath his clerical robes.

As she sat gathering her wits, attempting to still her mind as it raced to make sense of what had happened, the griffin appeared. He did not hop onto her shoulder, but sat perched upon her inkstand, feathers ruffled, as if he, too, was out of sorts. Hecate became aware of a movement beyond him. Brother Michael stood at the end of the second row of chained books, beckoning with some urgency. Glancing at her employer, who had his head bowed over a ledger at last, she hurried to her friend. Standing close enough to whisper, she asked, "Brother Michael, whatever is it?"

"Good morning, my dear, oh, firstly, pray forgive the muddle . . ." Here he gestured toward an open box in the corner of the room. Now Hecate could see there were documents scattered upon the floor around it. "I wished to verify a notion, something that came to me as I considered more and more the events in the crypt. My apologies for the disturbance, alas, my capabilities . . ." He let the sentence trail off. The matter of the ancient monk's limited ability to move physical objects was a source of embarrassment and frustration to him. He could only ever use his ghostly breath to turn a page or lift a loose paper and so had often to ask for Hecate's assistance. "But you see," he continued quickly, "there was something about the date that chimed in my memory."

"Yesterday's date? The fifth of April? I'm sorry, I cannot bring to mind anything significant about it."

"Nor was I able to, initially, but, well, when one has so many hours to contemplate . . . At first I thought it must be an obscure point on the ecclesiastical calendar, one that might have fallen out of regular use. But no, I could find nothing. Still, the fifth, I knew it was of note . . . but where to search? It was then I remembered a set of entries in the archive, I believed they were in the parish records. . . ."

"Parish records for which year?"

"Better ask which century. I cast my mind back and yet further back until I convinced myself there had been something that predated even my arrival at the cathedral. Something that would not necessarily be in a bound volume, rather loose papers." He smiled then, his small eyes crinkling at the corners. "Imagine my relief! I was able to disturb the contents of the lidless crates containing those long-forgotten writings. . . . Hence the disarray . . ."

"There is no need to apologize, Brother Michael, I can straighten things in a moment."

"You are too kind, for I know it will take longer . . . and yet, our endeavors will be worthwhile, for I found what I was looking for."

"The significance of the date?"

"Not the meaning itself, but that I was correct in my thought. The date *is* of importance. Or at least, the date *was* of importance. I found an entry in the records that clearly noted it, underlined, set slightly apart from other mentioned festivals and prayer days, in a manner which was curious . . . but, alas, the writing was so smudged I was not able to learn more." He looked crestfallen, aware on sharing his discovery that it was not, in fact, of much use.

Hecate gave him a reassuring smile. "It's a start," she whispered. "It means your recollection is correct. We have only to search the date in other, better-preserved records, to reveal more."

"My thoughts precisely! Which is why I wish to examine a volume of the cathedral records from the beginning of the eighteenth century. Would you be so good as to retrieve it from the shelves and set it where I might peruse it at length?"

Out of habit, they both glanced in the direction of Reverend Thomas. To unchain a book from the shelves they would need that key.

"Do not concern yourself with the good reverend," she told Brother Michael.

"I will think of a reason to request the book and see that it is placed where you can study it. The eighteenth century, you say? Something from the first decade, perhaps?" When he nodded she gave him a smile by way of confirmation of their plan before hurrying back to her desk. She felt encouraged to think that she would have her friend's help. She wished she had been at liberty to talk more with him. Would he have understood her belief that the murder of the night before was connected to what had come out of the crypt? For a spiritual man, the monk was of a pragmatic mind. Would he think her fanciful? She had no proof, no logic to her thought, after all. And yet . . . She turned her attention to her work as best she could, waiting for her moment to descend beneath the cathedral and revisit the crypt.

The long west wall of the library was an internal one with windows high up that opened into the north transept. These were for borrowed light rather than viewing. There was no glass in these windows, but wooden shutters which could be opened to allow air to circulate in the warmer months, and in winter heat from the mighty Gurney coal stoves on the floor below could travel up and lend at least a modicum of warmth. Beyond this, there was a feature of her workplace which Hecate knew few people were aware of. As had been intended, the acoustics of the cathedral carried song and organ music high and wide, flooding not only the main body of the building but also its vaulted ceilings and far corners with sound. A secondary effect of the construction was that voices were also carried aloft. Such was the success of the design that it was not only voices raised in song or to intone prayers or deliver a sermon that traveled in this way, but softer, more conversational words. Words sometimes spoken in the mistaken belief that they would not be overheard.

So it was that Hecate was able to eavesdrop on a short but helpful exchange between Dean Chalmers and the inspector. She had just finished explaining to Reverend Thomas that she wished to remove a certain book from its bonds so that she could treat some foxing she had noticed on its cover, and so was positioned at the far end of a row of shelving. The point where the shelves stopped allowed room for a desk beneath one of the gasoliers and it was here she placed the liberated book. As she was opening it so that Brother Michael would be able to browse it as he pleased, voices from the floor below traveled up and through the open shutters. She listened, recognizing first

Dean Chalmers's distinctive tone, and then the rolling Herefordshire vowels of Inspector Winter's diction.

"My earnest wish is that we can return the crypt to an orderly and respectable condition as soon as possible," the dean was saying.

"I understand that, Dean," the inspector replied, his unhurried pattern of talking removing all urgency from the conversation. "You have my assurance that my constables will work as swiftly as they are able, but you must consider the nature of what it is we are here to do. Every broken piece of wood, every shattered chunk of stone . . . each has its part to play in telling us the story of what happened. I cannot permit the clearing away, removal, or otherwise interfering with what is now evidence."

"Yes, yes. Of course. But surely, if what we are dealing with is a simple case of grave robbing . . . ?"

"We do not, as yet, know that, sir. What we do know is that this is far from a simple case of anything. I would not be doing my job if I did not proceed thoroughly and with diligence. Furthermore, there are . . . new demands upon my time which you will no doubt have heard about."

"Ah yes, poor Sir Richard."

"You will appreciate a murder inquiry must take precedence over everything else."

"Of course."

"So you may be doubly certain I will not tarry in the crypt longer than is absolutely necessary. It is likely I shall be unable to return to the scene after today."

There was a pause in which Hecate imagined the dean biting back words of frustration. When he spoke again his voice was controlled but tense.

"Then I shall detain you no longer. I shall call upon you before Evensong in the sincere hope that you will be able to tell me you have completed your work."

The silence that followed was broken only by the habitual and somewhat inappropriate tuneless whistling of the detective as he left the transept and walked away up the north choir aisle.

Hecate had no choice but to wait until lunchtime. As soon as Reverend Thomas left for the cloisters she made her way down to ground level, trotted quickly and quietly across the choir stalls and through the broad wooden door into the vestry. It had ever been a strange muddle of a room. It acted as an antechamber to the more exalted sacristy, which housed valuable and sacred objects. Here, in this lesser place, were kept prayer books, hymnals, prayer cushions, candles, cleaning equipment, spare mittens and mufflers, and all manner of things mundane and useful. It served as an office, too, with the verger having his record book and key cupboard in one corner of the room, on his desk an untidy stack of papers, and a knee rug hung over the back of his chair, for he always felt the cold. It was here, too, that choir and clergy often gathered to organize themselves before processing through the cathedral or emerging for a service. Perhaps, though, the most important facility the vestry provided was that of the stove upon which a kettle was kept on the point of boiling, for however much God sustained the spirit, as the dean was given to saying, tea and biscuits sustained the body. It was his little joke, and one that those around him tolerated happily, partly because they were fond of him, but mostly because the sentiment ensured there was always tea and not infrequently biscuits to go with it.

She was not sorry to find the room empty, for while she got on with Mr. Gould well enough, he was something of a chatterbox, and she had no time to waste. With practiced speed, she assembled tray, china cups and saucers, a small jug of milk, and one of the smaller biscuit tins, the weight of which suggested a delivery of flapjacks had been made by a caring parishioner that very morning. She was just setting the freshly filled teapot onto the tray when Mr. Gould appeared.

"Oh, Miss Cavendish! What a pleasant surprise," he began, "and a warming cup of tea. Such a good idea. A bright day but summer in the sun, winter in the shadows, and dear me we live our lives in the shade within these walls, do we not? And so busy at our work. I was only saying to Dean Chalmers this morning, I have not seen our young librarian all week, and he agreed with me that Reverend Thomas kept you at your duties really quite long hours—"

She felt mean cutting him off, but needs must. "Forgive me, Verger, I'd love to stay and talk but I've to take these to the crypt," she explained, lifting up the heavy tray.

"Of course, yes, indeed, must keep the constables fueled . . ." He held the door open for her. "Are you sure you can manage that? I could carry it for you. . . ."

"No need. I am equal to the task," she called back over her shoulder as she went. She walked quickly along the south choir aisle, at the end of which she turned left. On entering the crypt she was glad of her shawl, for there was a noticeable drop in the temperature. She told herself firmly that this was merely a consequence of the position of the place, below ground level with no heating, no furnishings, and scant sunlight from its few high windows. The air was musty, the tang of damp and the grit of disturbed ancient dust finding her tongue. Brother Michael's words came into her mind and she wondered why it might be that grave robbers would feel the need to steal bodies on some date of ancient significance. She quelled a shudder and put on what she hoped was a bright, pleasant, but practical expression. There were two constables in dark uniforms brightened by two rows of brass buttons, both engaged in their work, taking measurements and making notes. The inspector wore a long tweed jacket and a dark brown bowler, both of which added to his appearance of someone taller than he was strong. He paced the floor with steady strides, looking this way and that, as if assessing the possibility of something. He saw her and looked as if he might protest at her being there. Fortunately the sight of the teapot changed his mind.

"I thought you would be in need of refreshment yet not wish to break long from your work," she explained, setting the tray down on the nearby tomb of St. Oswald. The elaborately inscribed stone box housed the remains of both him and his wife and was covered in drawings and graffiti born of centuries and worn smooth. It was one of the tombs to have escaped the destruction that had befallen others in the crypt. If the inspector thought it in any way unseemly to use the resting place as a tea table, he gave no sign of it. Hecate poured three cups and handed them around before opening the tin. "Honey flapjack?"

The constables helped themselves with nods of thanks. Inspector Winter hesitated only a moment before following suit.

"Thank you, Miss . . . ?"

"Cavendish. Hecate Cavendish. I assist Reverend Thomas in the library."

He looked at her anew. "Daughter of Edward Cavendish, perhaps?"

"The same. You know my father?"

"Indeed. We sit on the committee of the chamber of commerce. I recall him saying he had a daughter who shared his interest in all things . . . shall we say ancient and obscure?"

She smiled. "I am told we are alike."

This statement seemed to meet with his approval. He took a bite of his biscuit before saying, "I believe you are on my list."

"I am?"

"It is important I speak to everyone who was present at or around the time of the discovery of the break-in. This will ensure I have a comprehensive view of events."

"And is that what you believe it to be? Thieves, breaking in?"

"Now, I did not say *thieves*," he corrected her. He turned and gesticulated with his biscuit, taking in the general scene of destruction. "It is clear there has been considerable damage done to several of the tombs, but we cannot categorically say as yet that anything was stolen." He bit into the biscuit.

Hecate helped herself to one, knowing that she would not get the opportunity for lunch. The oats were still warm and soft, the sweetness of the honey uplifting. It was an unlikely venue for a tea party, and yet there was a shared focus among those present, and a collective willingness to do right by the deceased, that somehow stopped it from being disrespectful. She had many questions she longed to voice, but she held back. He was that rare thing: a person who would not speak before thinking. As such, what he had to say was likely to be worth hearing. He paced the area again, his long legs and lanky frame moving slowly, his biscuit still raised. At the far end of the space he stopped and turned, frowning at the scattered debris. He took another bite of the flapjack. Hecate forced herself to wait. At last he spoke again.

"It seems to me that, were there to have been men moving upon the floor among the wreckage of these tombs, just as I have done, such pieces as are strewn about would have felt the impact of those footfalls. See, here, like so?" He bobbed down to a squat so that he could examine more closely his own footsteps. Something caught his eye and she saw him pick a tiny object from the rubble and hold it to the light for a moment before putting it into his pocket. Hecate moved quickly to join him, taking care to pick her way between the pieces, eager not to muddle his investigations. She could see that the fragile stone pieces, shards of marble, and splinters of wood had indeed crumbled beneath his deliberately placed feet. Those pieces either side of where his strides had taken him, however, were not similarly crushed.

She frowned. "So you are suggesting that whoever was in here somehow traversed the room . . . what, above the floor?" She instinctively looked up. The stone vaulted ceiling offered nothing by way of an explanation. "Might they have used ladders or boards on top of the tombs . . . or swung on ropes? It seems . . . unlikely. Unnecessary even. Is that what you are suggesting?"

He looked at her levelly. "Miss Cavendish, it is not my business to *suggest* anything. I am about the matter of inspecting the evidence and finding facts in that study. The *fact* is, no person set foot on these broken remnants before those who made the discovery of the vandalism." He pointed toward both the stairway that led back into the cathedral and the second one to his right that led to an external door which gave on to the Cathedral Green. "My constables took records, notes and drawings, mapping the path of footsteps we found and they all came from the stairs to the Lady Chapel, across to the point where Mrs. White made her discovery, and back again. They also recorded the route Reverend Forsyth took to check that the external door had not been breached, which, indeed, it had not. There were no further steps." He stood up, his knee joints cracking like rifle fire, the sound echoing in the chamber. "Another point that is raising more questions than answers: What implements were used to open the caskets? It is my understanding that marble, however old, does not splinter when impacted with a hammer, and yet we see here, shards. Similarly, stone such as was used here would require a chisel for any inroads to be made into it, and yet here we see pieces of stone bearing no chisel marks and thrown some considerable distance. Likewise, the wood of the more humble tombs has not been pried with a wrench, for there is no splintering to indicate such a thing, but neither have they been chopped with an axe, for had they been so dealt with, they would have been more greatly reduced."

He let this information settle around him. Both the constables had finished their tea and biscuits and stood listening to their superior. Hecate digested the information, as no doubt did they. The more she thought about it, the more her mind returned to one simple fact. A fact that she hardly dared voice, for her own fear of it, and for fear of sounding like a madwoman to this resoundingly practical and sensible man. She needed to hear it from him, but could he, too, have reached such a disturbing conclusion? She worried that the moment might pass. She must encourage him to speak.

"Inspector, there appears to be only one explanation for what took place here. One . . . conclusion, that is, about how these tombs were destroyed."

He stood as motionless as one of the stone effigies that inhabited the alcoves of the crypt. After this moment of contemplative stillness, he finished his biscuit and brushed the crumbs from his fingers. "I have found, Miss Cavendish, in my many years with the force, that it is unwise to move from fact to speculation. Detective work must stay with the facts, and let those facts tell the truth. There is no room for suggestion, nor supposition."

"Quite so," she agreed, doing her best to keep her voice calm. "But the inescapable fact, the truth of what happened here seems to be, that these tombs were not broken into, they were *broken out of!*"

A crackling silence filled the room. The younger constable grew noticeably pale. The older one was unable to stop himself looking this way and that, as if viewing the scene anew. Hecate did not for one moment take her eyes off their superior, hoping to see a confident rebuttal of this idea in his expression, but she found none. When he spoke again his voice was level as ever, but there was a more somber tone to it.

"I must ask you, Miss Cavendish, to keep such thoughts to yourself. Indeed, nothing that you have learned here this day should be repeated. To anyone. Let us be clear on this point." He held her gaze and she saw something of the steel that was the true character of this seemingly mild man. She wondered if he regretted discussing the case with her so freely, given what it had led them to consider. Hecate could, ultimately, accept the truth of their conclusion. The constables would fear it. The inspector would be the one who must make sense of it.

The cathedral clock struck the quarter hour.

"I must go," she said, gathering the tea things and picking up the tray. As she mounted the steps he called after her.

"Not a word, Miss Cavendish. I shall hold you to it."

She nodded and climbed the stairs. As she left she could hear the low, slow murmur of Inspector Winter's voice as he set the constables about their work.

She found Mrs. Nugent polishing the iron rail. The phantom cleaner paused in her work.

"Lord's sake, but you do look pale, my dear," she said, putting her hands on her hips. "Has Reverend Thomas been setting you to hard work? He's a man to get his shilling's worth out of everyone, that much is clear."

"Oh, no, thank you for your concern, Mrs. Nugent," she said, keeping her voice soft so that it would not be detected by those in the crypt. "I am much taken up with recent events, that is all," she explained, shifting the weight of the tea tray a little as her arms began to grow tired of holding it.

"A terrible business." The old woman shook her head sadly. "Wickedness is what it was. Wickedness."

"Mrs. Nugent . . . do you know something, anything, about what might have—"

"Hecate? Talking to yourself again?"

John's voice from the top of the stairs startled her. She swung around to face him so quickly that one of the cups flew from the tray.

Instinctively, Mrs. Nugent caught it. She held it for a brief instant before setting it down on the tray again.

The ghost stood very still. Although she knew the vicar could not see her, she knew that he would have seen the china cup apparently suspended in the air, unsupported, before returning itself to its rightful place.

Hecate knew it, too. She forced herself not to look in the direction of her spectral friend. Instead she met John's questioning gaze.

His eyes widened.

She strode up the steps, aiming to brush past him.

"Hecate . . ."

"I am sorry, John, but I am in rather a hurry. You know how Reverend Thomas will torture me if I am late back to the library." She would not look at him then but kept a too-bright smile fixed upon her face, trying her best to pretend nothing out of the ordinary had taken place.

He placed his hand gently on her arm.

"I think it's time you shared the truth with me," he said. "Don't you?"

"I . . ." She looked at him and knew that, this time, she could not explain, could not escape his inquiries, could deny the facts no longer. She nodded. "Yes," she said simply.

"I'll meet you at the south door at five," he said, taking the tea tray from her. "I was on my way to the vestry anyway," he assured her. "Now you can return to your post without being delayed further. Until five?"

To her surprise, Hecate found herself letting out a breath she had not known she was holding. The thought of telling him of her gift, of sharing her secret, did not frighten her. On the contrary, she was relieved at the prospect. She welcomed it.

"Until five," she agreed.

# 10

TRUE TO HIS WORD, JOHN WAS WAITING JUST OUTSIDE THE DOOR TO the cloisters. Hecate felt a mixture of nervousness and excitement at the thought of the conversation that lay ahead. He smiled at her as she approached.

"Would you care to walk as we talk?" he asked.

"No. That is, I would prefer to speak with you somewhere private, where we might not be overheard."

"Of course. Well, there are my rooms, but no, that would not do," he added quickly, seeing her expression. "Wait, I have it! The perfect place."

He offered her his arm and she took it. To her surprise they about-turned and reentered the cathedral. Their route took them first to the vestry. She waited while he fetched a large key and then they proceeded to the door in the corner of the north transept which led up to the tower.

"Have you ever experienced the view from the top?" he asked her. "It is quite something, and on a day like today would be seen to best advantage, I believe."

She smiled then, feeling that such a view would be a welcome distraction from the intimate nature of their talk. For she had realized that there could scarcely be anything more intimate than sharing with another one's own, peculiar, supernatural self.

The stairs of the tower were similar to those in the turret that served the library; ancient worn stone steps, twisting tightly, lit only by occasional narrow windows. They differed in as much as they were in two parts. The first flight led to the gallery above the nave. They traversed this and went through a second door, passing the entrance to the belfry, and continuing up. Their greatest difference was in their number. Hecate lost count after she had trodden the two hundredth stair. Her breathing became ragged with the climb and she could taste a trace of damp walls in the air. As they ascended she experienced a sensation of light-headedness that was not brought on by the exertion but by the vertiginous nature of the stairwell coupled with its close confines. The effect was both dizzying, as a great height might be, and stultifying, in the way that a small space often was. The echoes of their footsteps, having nowhere to go, bounced back from the walls, lending a syncopated rhythm to their progress. John made the climb ahead of her, his long black robes sweeping the sandstone. Every ten steps or so he paused, under the guise of allowing himself a rest, while in truth providing a moment for her to catch her breath. When at last they reached the summit he used the key to unlock the low door that led out to the roof.

Hecate raised her hand to shade her eyes, the sunshine sharp after the gloom of the staircase. John took her arm and guided her to the crenellated wall, which was high enough to make her feel safe, yet sufficiently low to permit an uninterrupted view. And what a view it was! She gasped as she turned, slowly, taking in the sweep of the city below, and the verdant pastures beyond resembling the rolling waves of a limitless green sea. John was pointing out landmarks and things she might find of interest, but it took her a while to register that he was speaking.

"There," he said, placing a hand on her shoulder and gently turning her to face west a little. "You can see the gold cockerel atop the spire of St. Peter's Church. Those orchards directly beyond will be in full bloom soon. They are cider apples, for every Hereford man likes his cider, so we cannot have too many. And there, you can see the bend in the river near Breinton, where it is shallow enough to ford in the summer."

Sunlight flashed off the water and a trio of swans took flight, giving her an uncommon view of their slow beating wings.

"What is that?" she asked, pointing. "A new building?"

"That is the city crematorium, currently under construction. Quite an undertaking."

She looked at him. "Reverend Forsyth, is that your notion of a joke?"

He gave a rueful shrug. "I seek only to put you at your ease."

Turning away from him, she moved to the other side of the tower to take in the view to the north and east. He came to stand beside her.

"Won't you tell me now, Hecate?" he asked, his voice little more than a whisper. "Do not be apprehensive. I am, after all, practiced in the art of listening."

She waved her hand slowly, gesturing at the expanse set out before them. "Such a great distance," she muttered. "My mind spreads away so. It is hard to keep one's thoughts tethered, is it not?" When he gave no reply she continued, her eyes still fixed on some distant point. It was easier to speak to him without the distraction of watching his reaction to her words. She shied away from seeing herself—her gifted, strange self—reflected in those pale blue eyes. "You have, I think, noticed some unusual . . . occurrences while in my presence," she said. "Heard some perplexing things, perhaps. Witnessed some curious events."

"Curious, and some might say inexplicable."

"Except that they can be easily explained." Annoyed by her own timidity, she drew a breath and turned to face him. "What you have observed are my interactions with ghosts. No more, no less."

Even in that wide-open space, the air about them fizzed with the significance of what she had said.

John spoke slowly, choosing his words with care.

"You . . . converse with spirits?"

"I do. Though they prefer to be called souls."

"And . . . they are many?"

"Several. Four, so far, though I sense others."

"Have you always been able to speak to the departed?" he asked.

She was reassured by his responses, and by the tone of his voice. He appeared neither shocked nor dismissive.

"Not as such. When I was a child I could glimpse movement on the very limit of my vision. With these glimpses came an accompanying sense of not being alone. And on occasion I would emerge from a vivid dream and whispering voices would follow me into my waking day. I never thought these things significant. They were not frightening. On the contrary, if I had to name the feeling they evoked in me I would say it was one of kinship. As if I had secret friends, even if they were too shy to reveal themselves completely. I did not think to mention these things to my father, but I understand now that he was aware of them. He was watching me."

"And have you shared your recent experiences with him?"

She nodded. "He was not surprised. More . . . pleased." She smiled. "He believes I am fulfilling my potential."

John gave a light laugh at this. "Mr. Cavendish is a rare man, and no mistake. Not many fathers would have ambitions for their daughters in the sphere of spiritualism."

She frowned then, concerned that she had misunderstood his view of what she was telling him.

"Is that how you see me? As some manner of medium, calling to departed loved ones in a parlor draped in red velvet, low lit, with an assistant to rattle doors and blow out candles to thrill those paying for the experience?"

"No, no, not at all!"

"Have you put me in the same category of persons as those with a traveling show, perhaps, touting for customers among the heartbroken?"

"I assure you, I have not."

"These lost souls, *they* came to *me*. They sought out my company, not I theirs. They came unbidden because they were drawn to me. They feel safe in my presence. They know I will help them if they are in need of assistance. Just as I know I may rely upon them."

"Which is why you were not afraid in the crypt?"

She hesitated. She could see from his earnest expression that he believed her, and that he was not mocking her at all. She had told him she was not afraid, but what she had felt among those broken tombs was something quite different.

"I sensed something else in the crypt that day of the first desecrations. I cannot tell you I was unafraid."

"But you felt the presence of ghosts there? Malign ones, perhaps?"

"I do not know. In truth, I believed it was not safe for anyone to remain in that place. I was frightened for the dean, and for you. But, whatever it was is there no longer."

"You are certain of that?"

"Quite. When you found me there earlier today I had been listening to Inspector Winter's theories on the matter of the desecrations."

"Is he still of the mind that grave robbers were to blame?"

"I am not sure he ever was. He came to the unavoidable conclusion that the tombs had not been broken into, but broken out of."

"Good Lord! What can that mean?"

"That is what I intend finding out. It was a shocking conclusion for a man so wedded to solid facts. I fear the inspector may search for the truth in places where it does not lie, for he will resist the possibility of something spiritual being at play."

"Understandably. Though one might think the location of the crime, exceptional in itself, might steer him in a less earthbound direction than his usual inquiries."

"I was sworn to secrecy on the matter," Hecate said, suddenly remembering her promise. "I should not have mentioned it."

John reached forward and took her hand in his.

"You may trust me with your confidence at any time, Hecate. I am happy to listen and willing to assist you in any way I can."

"You do not think me fit for the asylum, then?"

"My whole life has been dedicated to the service of an unseen being. I am the diocesan exorcist, and believe me when I say my role as such has led me to dark and astonishing places. I daily give thanks to the Holy Ghost. I kneel before an image of a man I believe rose from his grave," he reminded her. "Who better than a vicar to appreciate your gift?"

A sharp breeze had got up and Hecate felt it chase around her neck.

"I should go," she said, walking briskly across the lead of the roof toward the doorway. "I am expected home."

"Then let me walk you," he suggested, following on.

"I would rather not discuss this further, not among other people."

"I promise we will not touch upon the matter. Not until you raise it again. It is simply that I find myself reluctant to watch you go."

She was about to refuse him but hesitated, realizing that she enjoyed the thought of spending a little longer in his company. Now that she had shared her secret with him she felt there was a new, almost conspiratorial bond between them.

"Come for tea, then," she said, starting down the stairs. "Mother would be delighted to see you," she told him, her voice floating back up the stairwell to him as she descended.

When they reached the cloister entrance, she stepped past him to fetch her bicycle. As she began to wheel it along he took hold of the handlebars.

"Let me do that," he suggested. When she hesitated, about to say she could manage perfectly well, he added, "Please?"

She gave in, allowing him to be gallant, falling into step next to him as he pushed the bicycle across the Cathedral Green.

A gaggle of schoolchildren dashed past, giggling, chasing one another across the short grass, their pretty clothes and bright ribbons a blur of colors against the backdrop of the lawn. Hecate breathed deeply, forcing herself not to be irritated by the slow pace at which they were walking. Ordinarily she would have sped home in a matter of minutes. It was obvious John wished to make their journey last a little longer. He would have known he would not have her to himself once they reached the Cavendish family house. They walked on in companionable silence and she was grateful for the way they could be at ease with one another without the need for chatter. Even so, she suspected he must have a hundred questions for her regarding her revelations.

Number 24 Hafod Road was the sort of house where people seemed forever to be coming and going. As Hecate and John left the bicycle in the stable and walked through the walled garden, Edward Cavendish came out of the back door. He had on his golfing clothes and strode with great purpose.

"Ah, the little worker bee returned to the hive! And hail to you, Reverend Forsyth," he said cheerily, waving his unlit pipe by way of salute.

"Mr. Cavendish." John nodded.

Hecate was reminded, not for the first time, of the minute but important differences in the way that he interacted with her father compared to the way Phileas spoke with him. John was articulate and nimble minded, but he did not have Phileas's ease, nor his status. He had not the background, the private means, the expensive school of a certain type, the social connections that Phileas shared with her father. The way he addressed him as "Mr. Cavendish" rather than simply "Cavendish" said more about the gulf between them than anything else could.

"John is joining us for tea, Father," said Hecate.

"Capital! Sorry to miss your visit. Alas, I am promised to Lord Brocket for a game."

"So late in the day?" she asked.

Her father strode on toward the stables. "We shall play a swift nine holes and be home before Stella has the table laid for dinner," he called over his shoulder. "Your mother awaits within. I bid you adieu!"

John and Hecate exchanged smiles.

"Your father could have had a fine career on the stage, one feels."

"He'd be delighted to hear you say that. Retirement bores him. Perhaps he'll take up acting."

"I'm sure Mrs. Cavendish would be delighted," he said, holding open the door for her.

They found the rest of the family in the drawing room. A small fire burned in the hearth, no doubt lit for Charlie's benefit. Her brother looked up from his book. Hecate felt a jolt of fear on seeing the dark circles beneath his eyes. She sought to hide it by making rather overenthusiastic greetings, even kissing her mother on the cheek as they all exchanged hellos and gentle inquiries about each other's days. She did not see eye to eye with her mother on many things, but in the matter of their love for Charlie they were united. She knew that whatever fears she herself harbored, her mother would be similarly hiding her own cold, gnawing worry about the boy's fragile health.

Soon they were all seated and Stella arrived with a tray of tea. Mrs. Cavendish waved her away, happy to serve their guest herself. Hecate was certain having John's company would distract her mother from gloomy thoughts.

"Now then, Reverend"—Beatrice poured Indian tea into red-and-gold Spode china cups as she spoke—"how do you take your tea? Let me see if I can guess, a little milk but no sugar . . . ?"

"You have seen right through me already, Mrs. Cavendish." He smiled.

". . . and will you be tempted by some of Cook's fruitcake?"

"It's very good," Charlie put in, hurrying over to the table and helping himself to a slice. His mother frowned, but indulged the lack of restraint, happy to see him eat. Seeing her expression, he added, "It's very good for building people up and keeping them strong."

"How could I refuse after such an excellent endorsement?" John said.

Hecate could not resist teasing him. "Can't have you too weak to lift a hymnal, can we?"

"I'll have you know being a vicar can be physically demanding work. Only yesterday I was required to help Mr. Gould move a bookcase from the vestry to the sacristy."

"Hecate"—her mother's tone had a sharpness to it—"it is unbecoming to make such comments on a man's profession. Here, Charles, pass this to Reverend Forsyth," she said, handing him the tea and cake. If Hecate had hoped that would be the end of her mother's thoughts on the matter of John's vocation, she was to be disappointed. "Such rewarding work; not only to carry out the duties of a parish priest, but to sing in the cathedral. Such . . . uplifting music."

"Indeed it is, Mrs. Cavendish."

"And such an ancient and . . . prestigious position. To be one of the vicars choral carries a certain cachet. Do you not agree, Hecate?" She gave her daughter a look that dared her to declare otherwise.

Suppressing giggles, she replied, "That's exactly the word I would use, Mother. Cachet." She was sitting close enough to John to be aware that he, too, was having to mask his amusement.

Ignoring any possible ridicule, her mother went on. "I have heard," she said while selecting cubes of sugar with silver tongs, "that the new rules now allow the wives of vicars at the cathedral to live with them in the recently refurbished houses in the cloisters. Is that the case?"

"It is," John confirmed. "And they are a welcome addition to our community."

Hecate bit into her fruitcake, determinedly refusing to be drawn into the conversation further.

Her mother was unstoppable. "Why yes, I imagine so. After all, so many figures dressed in black . . . how pleasant to have some colorfully attired ladies among you now. Pretty dresses, a charming smile, an elegant hat or two . . . these things can greatly enhance any company. Do you not agree, Hecate?"

"Oh, absolutely," said Hecate through a mouthful of cake, brushing crumbs from her lap. "I never underestimate the importance of an elegant hat."

John spluttered slightly into his tea.

Charlie had tired of the subject and, in the way that young people do, introduced a new one without preamble, lending it even greater impact than it could ordinarily carry, although the topic was sufficiently shocking without such a tactic.

"Sir Richard's murderer still has not been caught," he said. "Imagine the fiend roaming the city streets at night, searching for his next victim!"

"Charles!" Mrs. Cavendish attempted to silence him.

"He could be someone we know," Charlie went on. "They say the police have found no clues and have no idea where to look next. It could be anyone. Could even be you, Reverend Forsyth!" He laughed at his own joke.

"Charlie," Hecate had to speak up, "it really doesn't do to make fun of something so awful."

John set his cup down in its saucer. "I'm sure the police officers will get to the truth of the matter soon enough," he said.

Charlie was not convinced. "But *will* it be soon enough? Or will the murderer strike again?"

Mrs. Cavendish's tone was serious. "On this I am in agreement with Charles. What use is a constabulary full of policemen in their shiny-buttoned coats if they are unable to apprehend such a villain? Our streets cannot be thought to be safe until such time as they have him locked safely away."

"It was terribly sad for poor Sir Richard, of course, Mother, but it is one isolated event. The law will prevail," said Hecate.

"Well, until it does I would prefer you not to venture abroad unaccompanied."

"But—"

She held up a hand. "I was greatly relieved to see that Reverend Forsyth had escorted you home."

"I would happily do so every day until the matter is resolved," John was quick to say.

"There really is no necessity . . ." Hecate was incensed. To have her hard-won independence limited in such a way was unthinkable.

"I shall be the judge of that," her mother insisted. "Indeed, I have already discussed this with your father and he agrees with my view."

Hecate got to her feet. "Father said I should be accompanied at all times? I cannot believe he would insist on such a thing!"

Her mother's expression hardened. "Are you saying I would invent his consent?"

John attempted to defuse the rising tension. "I am sure Hecate did not mean to suggest—"

"No, I am not suggesting you are lying, Mother. I am suggesting that you delivered this . . . this *idea* to Father while he was distracted. Had he given the matter his full attention he would never have agreed to it! You allowed him to unwittingly consent, taking his lack of interest for him being in favor. I doubt he even heard what you were saying."

Mrs. Cavendish's complexion had taken on a flush of pink that gave away her mounting anger at her daughter's outburst. Torn between chastising Hecate for her rude assumption and not wishing to allow a guest to witness this unseemly family discord, she was momentarily silenced. It was Charlie who came to the rescue with his own observation.

"I shouldn't worry, Mama. For a start, the murder happened at night, and you never let Hecate out on her own after dark, with or without a murderous villain on the loose. And besides"—he paused to take another bite of fruitcake—"who could possibly catch her when she's on her bicycle?"

Mrs. Cavendish opened her mouth to protest but closed it again, lips tight, without uttering anything further on the subject. She saw her daughter's determined stare and folded arms, Charlie's somewhat smug expression after the points he had just made, and their visitor's discomfort, and thought better of fighting a battle she had no chance of winning.

Hecate, seeing the rule would not be enforced, felt bad for speaking so baldly to her mother, particularly in front of a guest. She sat down again and picked up her teacup, glancing at John, who discreetly put his hand over hers and gave it a reassuring squeeze.

# 11

———— · ————

THE NEXT DAY WAS SATURDAY; A DAY HECATE DID NOT WORK AT THE cathedral. Ordinarily she might accompany Charlie on a ride out to Kynaston, or assist her father in the Sisyphean task of cataloguing his treasures in the attic. On this occasion, however, she had been required to visit an ailing neighbor with her mother in the morning. Beatrice frequently reminded her that she must still find time for charitable works and make herself useful, as she put it, and she had long since learned it was quicker to agree than to resist. Besides, on this particular Saturday, she had the joy of a visit from Clementine to look forward to. Her friend arrived after luncheon, and the pair retreated to the relaxed privacy of Hecate's bedroom.

"I swear this place becomes more like the study of an aged gentleman and less like the *boudoir* of a young lady every time I visit. Truly, Hecate, would it hurt to replace some of the soft furnishings? We have an abundant surplus I know Mama would not miss. Or at least consider removing some of the boxes and books? Where is a person to sit among all this?" she asked, waving a lacy cuff at the general muddle.

Hecate looked at the room as if seeing it for the first time. She took in the stacks of books borrowed from her father, the piles of notepaper containing her own scribbling regarding those she had read, the boxes of unknown interesting things that had found their way down from the attic for closer inspection. She raised her arms and let them drop by her sides. "There is a bed to sleep on," she pointed out, "a desk to work at, and somewhere over there I recall a chaise . . ."

Clemmie laughed at her friend and set to moving things to make a space upon the small velvet sofa that had been all but subsumed by clutter.

"It is a wonder you emerge from such mayhem looking at all presentable. Which you do. Just about," she teased, at last able to sit down.

Hecate noticed how pretty she looked. Her dress had just enough gathers and lace to look feminine without being ridiculous and was of course *a la mode.* Her golden hair was piled high in apparently effortless loops that must have required the talents of a considerably skilled lady's maid. Even the way she sat was faultless. She did not envy her friend's beauty, or her wealth, but there were times she felt scruffy beside her. She brushed down her own workaday navy skirts and shook away such frivolous concerns. To look a certain way would require far too much of her time. Time that could be better spent in any number of ways Clementine would no doubt have thought dull.

"I like it the way it is," Hecate said. "I know where to find things," she insisted, taking a black embroidered shawl from where it was draped over the back of her chair. "Here, for example, is the lovely wrap you brought me back from your trip to Spain. Barcelona, was it?"

"Madrid," said Clemmie, clearly unconvinced there was a system at all. She picked up the nearest book on the sofa. It was a slim, leather-bound volume. "*Perpendicular Architecture through the Ages.* Dear me. Have you considered a work of fiction? If only so that you might understand how most women of your age conduct themselves."

"I have no time for novels. May I have that?" She held out her hand and then added, "John lent it to me."

"Ah-ha!" She held the book to her chest. "How intriguing. Oh, has he written an inscription?" She opened it quickly.

Hecate leaned forward and took it from her.

"He has not. As I said, he's lent it to me. Why would he write anything?"

"Why would he miss the opportunity to pen a few words expressing how he feels? Words you would think about every time you pick up that book."

"Clemmie, you do talk nonsense."

"Do I? Or is that a blush I see coloring Miss Cavendish's pale cheeks?"

"*You* clearly spend far too much time reading novels," she said, dropping the book on her desk with deliberate nonchalance. When it slipped from the top of the pile, landing awkwardly on the chair, however, she could not stop herself retrieving it, dusting it off gently, and setting it down with more care.

"Oh, Hecate, you know very well how much Reverend Forsyth adores you. Almost as much as Phileas does. It is such fun to watch!" she declared, clapping her hands.

"Fun for you it may be. I do not find it so."

"But, dearest, to have two eligible men vying for your affections."

Hecate put her hands on her hips and faced her friend squarely. "Phileas is a family friend. I regard him almost as an older brother, a fact of which he is well aware. And I thought you forbid me from marrying a vicar. Anyway, I have far too many things to think about to be bothered with romance."

Clemmie had no interest in what such things might be. Instead she got to her feet and drifted around the room, listing the qualities of both men as she went.

"Of course, Phileas has Kynaston, and I think you would be happy living there. And we would be almost neighbors! But then he does have an unfortunate way of playing the fool which can be charming but also bothersome. Now, John is terribly handsome. . . ."

"Clemmie . . ."

"It's no use pretending he isn't. Those blue eyes! And you could take him anywhere without fear of embarrassment. Except of course that he is a vicar, and, well, only just acceptable. Your mama likes him, which is in his favor, but then your papa likes Phileas. And if you married John you would be rather poor."

"I thought you said you didn't care about the station of a suitor. You said it was his character and whether or not he loved you that mattered."

"Don't be silly, Hecate, I said I'd settle for a baronet instead of a duke if I cared for him. I didn't say I was prepared to live in a monk's cell."

At the mention of the word "*monk*" Hecate immediately thought of Brother Michael. What her friend could never know was that she could not leave her ghostly family. Marrying John would at least mean she could live with him at his cathedral home.

"The cloister houses are not cells. Reverend Higgins married last autumn and his wife is extremely pleased with their accommodation," she said.

"Ah, so you have considered marrying John, I knew it!" Clemmie laughed as if catching her friend out in a game.

Hecate opened her mouth to protest, but thought better of it. It was true, she had wondered what it would be like. The fact that he knew of and accepted her gift was no small thing. She thought about how she felt when she was with him. She felt that she could be herself. She felt that he understood her. She felt pleased to be in his company and enjoyed his wit. But was that love? And Phileas? Her fondness for him was in no way romantic. She could not imagine herself wed to him.

"As I seem singularly unable to choose, much better that I remain single," she said, rather hoping for a change of subject. She found the matter somewhat weighty and complicated without knowing why.

Clemmie, sensing her friend's drop in cheer, stepped up behind her and slipped her arms about her.

"My poor dearest Hecate. Matters of the heart can be quite perplexing."

Hecate rested her head back. "That's just it, I'm not certain my heart is playing any part in it."

"Then you must wait until it does. When you feel your heart lift, that is when you know you have found a man worth your time. Though be careful it is your heart that speaks to you," she added, spinning Hecate around to face her. "A woman must take care not to give in to what is merely desire!" she warned, grinning with glee.

"How will I know the difference? Do you?"

"Of course, silly! When Viscount Bales begged me to elope with him I was all but packed when I came to my senses. Intemperate feelings are delicious, but they are no basis for marriage. We must be on our guard against charming men who would take advantage of that aspect of our natures."

Now it was Hecate's turn to laugh. "I don't suppose either Phileas or John would dream of taking advantage of me!"

Clemmie shook her head. "Don't be so certain," she said, suddenly serious. "A man in love will act in ways you might not have imagined them capable of."

Hecate stepped away to straighten another stack of papers. "And you wonder why I prefer my treasures," she said lightly.

"Better still, let us think about what you are going to wear to Mama's out-of-season ball. I will not let you fall victim to your mother's selection a single time more," she said, moving toward the large wardrobe in the corner of the room.

"Oh Lord, is it that time of year again? The Twyford-Harris balls seem to come round with increasing speed."

"Nonsense. Now, what have you in here. Oh dear . . ." she said, pulling out a gown at random and shaking her head. "Come along, try something on. We must address the extent of the problem before we can correct it."

Hecate gave herself over to Clemmie's insistence, knowing how much her friend enjoyed dressing for occasions, and happy to let her prattle on about French fashions if it pleased her.

Two days later the inspector finished his investigations in the crypt. The dean had instructed a team which included two rather reluctant canons and the verger to carefully collect any broken remnants of tombs and place them in two ancient oak chests in the far corner of the crypt. He then assembled a small gathering of the vicars choral to offer prayers and a blessing. Hecate, standing at the top of the steps, listened to the sung words and gently intoned lines. It was the dean's hope that this would put the spirits and the matter in general to rest, at least until Inspector Winter could furnish them with answers to the seemingly unanswerable questions. She knew, however, that whatever had come out of those tombs was no longer in the crypt, and was far from at rest.

Mrs. White had declared herself unable to ever set foot in the place again, despite the dean's assurances. Hecate stepped forward, happy to offer to take over the small but important task of cleaning the crypt once a week. To others, this was seen as a helpful, possibly womanly gesture on her part. To Hecate, it was the opportunity to spend time in the intensely atmospheric space, perhaps allowing her to find clues the policemen had missed, or even to somehow connect with the spirits that remained there in order to gain an insight into what had taken place. Reverend Thomas had raised a squeak of protest at his assistant being taken from her work, but he was silenced by a questioning look from Dean Chalmers. When the short service was over and everyone else had left the crypt, she took a mop and bucket, broom and duster, and set about the task of cleaning. As she worked she stilled her mind, opening her heart to any souls who might wish to make themselves known to her. Nothing came. In fact, the silence was so deep she considered it more a void. As if nothing spiritual remained in the crypt. The more she worked on, the longer she spent there, the more certain she became that all spectral activity had ceased, the dark presence had left, and there was in its place a tense emptiness. Her hope had been that she would be contacted by a benign spirit. One such as those who had become her friends in the cathedral. One that might shed some light on the disturbing mystery with their unique perspective. By the time she had finished washing the floor, dusting the candlesticks, and polishing the marble of the remaining tombs, however, she had still heard nothing. She paused to survey her work and was pleased with the results. The least she could do for the troubled place was help restore it to order and peace. The dean's blessing had subtly changed the vibration of the space. Her own simple endeavors had added to this in a small but important way. She stood, hands on hips, a little disappointed and yet satisfied that she had, for now, done what she could.

As she had anticipated, she found Reverend Thomas all pursed lips and tutting at the time her new obligation was demanding of her when there was work of her own to be done. Hecate could see her chances of accessing more books in the collection for her own research were dwindling. In an effort to win over her superior, she promised to work through her lunch break to catch up. This appeared to mollify him when he took himself off for his own meal an hour later.

Hecate fully intended to push on with the repair on her desk.

The *Mappa Mundi,* however, had other ideas.

She sensed rather than saw the new activity. Putting down her glue brush, she turned in her chair. As before, the image of the city of Hereford pulsated restlessly, but this time there were other parts of the ancient map which were moving, too. She stood up slowly and moved closer. As she did so, the griffin swooped from one of the library shelves and came to perch on her shoulder. "Keep still now," she whispered to him. There was something about the way the map was behaving that caused her to approach as quietly as she could, so as not to interrupt the activity. She wanted to see what it had to show her. Wanted to understand.

On this occasion, she noticed the water in one of the great northern rivers seemed to be actually flowing, the blue of it brighter than it had been, light catching ripples and waves as the water moved. A little above the river, which was called the Jaxartes, there was a drawing of the golden fleece of Greek legend. A few inches to the left was the space where the griffin himself was depicted. It was what was shown between these two mythological creatures that held Hecate's attention now. There were two people, kneeling down, each holding a long knife or sword. The inscription declared them to be the Essedenes. She knew they were depicted cutting the limbs of a figure, which had always struck her as disturbing. Now that the little figures had sprung to life, raising and slashing with their blades, slicing into the flesh of the arms and legs in front of them, the scene took on a fresh horror. As she watched, wondering what such a thing could possibly signify, the figure on the left ceased his cutting. He turned his head, and with his narrow, kohl-lined eyes, looked straight at Hecate.

For an instant, their gazes met.

She gasped, taking a step back, unable to look away.

The griffin squawked and took to the air.

Hecate felt as if she were locked in an inescapable connection with the terrifying figure. Its vision held her and its glare appeared to be challenging her. For what seemed like a torturously long time but could have been no more than half a minute, she was trapped as surely as if the frightening being had held his sword to her throat.

And then it looked away and she was released.

Hecate staggered back further, bumping up against her own desk, knocking over her glue pot, still staring at the map, watching the figures, not quite daring to look away even though she now could. As suddenly as it had begun, the activity stopped. Even the picture of the city ceased its movement. The drawings were motionless once more. She waited a little longer before summoning the courage to peer more closely at the Essedenes. The depiction of their attack on their victim was as unsettling as ever, but now it did not move.

Without a moment's hesitation, Hecate strode over to the library shelves and called out.

"Brother Michael? Brother Michael, are you here? I need to speak with you. Please, show yourself," she said, looking this way and that, hoping for a glimpse of the monk's hooded habit as he flitted between the rows of an-

tique books. At last he appeared, stepping out of a collection of parish records and coming to stand in front of her as if it were the most normal thing
in the world.

"My dear, whatever is it? You appear extremely vexed."

"I am indeed vexed. And more than a little terrified, truth be told."

"Is it the crypt? Has some other event taken place?"

"Not the crypt." She shook her head. "It's the *Mappa Mundi,* Brother Michael."

"There has been further activity?"

"There certainly has. Tell me, what do you know about the Essedenes?"

"Very little, I confess," he told her, waving a hand in a vague gesture. He
went on, "They were an ancient tribe believed to exist somewhere north of
the Sahara."

"That much I was able to understand from the map. Do you know if they
were thought to be particularly fierce or violent? I mean, of course they are
shown cutting up a body, but depictions of war were often graphic. It doesn't
tell us much about the people themselves, necessarily." The memory of the
way the figure's eyes had seared into her was still fresh. She had often seen
signs and movement on the map, and the griffin had chosen to befriend her,
but she had never experienced such a direct and challenging connection with
one of the people in it.

"I can add nothing helpful, alas. However, there was a book, now let me
think on it . . . yes, a translation from the Greek, I believe . . ." He drifted off
along the shelves, searching. Hecate followed him. "Aristophanes, was it? No,
Euripides, perhaps? I cannot recall, but I am certain there is a book here that
chronicles the existences of forgotten tribes, specifically those in what you
might now call the Middle East." He scoured the rows of books.

"Please, try to remember its name."

"Yes, yes . . . it will come to me . . . lost tribes, forgotten people, customs
and arcane burial rites, something of that sort . . ." The ancient monk drifted
this way and that, peering myopically at the books in front of him. His task
was made all the more difficult by the fact that they were positioned not with
their spines facing out, rather the other way around. Presented with row upon
row of page edges of varying shades of cream or yellow made identification
challenging. When he could not find what he sought on the lower shelves,

nor the middle ones, he flitted upward, taking advantage of his weightless, ghostly form, floating at eye level with the uppermost volumes.

Hecate fought to contain her impatience as she waited.

"Ah!"

"You have it?" she asked.

"I believe so, though I cannot read the title completely. . . . I see the words *Forgotten Peoples of* . . . etcetera, etcetera. I don't recall the name of the book exactly, but I can see the faded sable hue of the leather, and yes, yes, I am certain this is it."

That he had located the book was good news. What was less helpful was the fact that it was on the top shelf. Hecate could reach it by using the library steps, but it was a large, heavy tome. It could not be read unless placed in a stand for fear of damaging it. She would have nowhere to place it at that level. It would have to be removed from the chains that secured it, which meant asking Reverend Thomas to unlock the row. She could not possibly request any further access to books for her own interest until she had completed the repair she had been given. Thanking Brother Michael, she made a note of the exact position of the book. She would think up what she hoped would be a plausible reason for wanting to examine it, but first she must finish mending the tear on the small map. Had she not had so many interruptions that week it would have been done some time ago. At least she knew a few further hours should see it properly restored. It was with some horror then, that she saw, on returning to her desk, the disastrous results of the upended glue pot. She had only half registered knocking into it when she had jumped back, startled, from the *Mappa Mundi*. Now she could see the entire contents of the pot, which had been nearly full, had spread in a ruinous flood across her workstation, coating everything in its path. Including the map. She was in the process of lifting the old parchment up from the desk to inspect the damage when Reverend Thomas entered the room.

For a moment he stared open-mouthed at the sight before him. At last he found his voice. "Miss Cavendish! Would you care to explain what has taken place?"

"Oh, Reverend, I must apologize, I inadvertently tipped my glue pot and . . ." There was no need for her to finish the explanation. The slow dripping of the adhesive from the corner of the map was sufficiently eloquent.

"Such carelessness!" The librarian's complexion had taken on an alarming flush of color. "This is the error of a beginner, and a clumsy one at that."

"I am so very sorry. . . . I . . ."

"I have stressed, have I not, on numerous occasions, the importance of care when using viscous substances in close proximity to artifacts?"

"Yes, Reverend." Hecate gave up all attempts to defend herself and accepted her chastisement, knowing that she deserved it.

Sensing this, Reverend Thomas did not berate her further. Instead he stepped forward to more closely examine the damaged map. Hecate experienced the cold twist of guilt in her gut at what her inattention had wrought. No matter that she had been startled or that her action was accidental. The map was precious and rare and had been entrusted to her care and she had failed in her duty.

The librarian let out a weary sigh.

"Fetch white spirit and clean cloths. The glue must be removed slowly and with a gentle touch. Once you are certain every trace of it has been lifted, a wash of warm water with a few flakes of soap, and then a rinse. Pay attention, for too much water will result in marks and stains. The map must be completely dry before you can complete your repair. Do you understand those instructions, Miss Cavendish?"

"I do," she said.

He finished the discussion with a curt nod, returning to his own desk where he resumed his work and spoke not another word the entire afternoon.

On arriving home, Hecate went straight to her father's study. She found him at his desk.

"Father, what can you tell me about the Essedenes?" she asked, tugging off her gloves and removing her hat as she walked across the room toward him.

"And a good afternoon to you, too, my little librarian," he replied, looking up from his paperwork.

"Yes, of course, hello and all that, but please, Papa . . . can you recall anything about them from your travels?"

Edward put down his pen and leaned back in his chair, casting his gaze upward as if notes from his expeditions might be written on the ceiling. "Let me see . . . a little-known tribe. North African. Given to violence. A race that died out centuries ago."

"That's it? Nothing more?"

He looked at her then, eyebrows raised. "Why the sudden interest?"

"You know they feature on the *Mappa Mundi*?"

"I confess I did not. Though now that you mention it, I am not surprised. The creator of the map displayed a fondness for such . . . untamed peoples."

"Untamed indeed. And violent, you say? Yes, well, they are shown dismembering a body of course. Which all fits with what they made me feel when they looked at me," she said by way of explanation, finally sitting down in one of the small armchairs by the unlit fire.

"Looked at you?"

"I was looking at the map when both the Essedene figures became animated."

"Surely by now you are accustomed to the map's curious behavior toward you, are you not? In which case this 'look' that they gave you must have been something quite different to have you so het up." He left his desk and came to sit in the chair opposite her, leaning forward, elbows on knees, eager to hear what she had to say.

Hecate squirmed a little, disliking the idea that she might react in a frivolous or female way to anything the map might do. "Yes, it was different. It was disturbing. Threatening."

"You felt directly threatened yourself?"

"I do not consider myself in any danger from the figures, it's not that. But . . . there is something about the timing. I mean to say, they have never behaved in this way before. Why now? Why at the same time as the unexplained events in the crypt?"

"You feel there is a connection?"

"Not one I can logically explain," she said. "At least, not yet. I intend studying a book of Brother Michael's recommendation on the subject tomorrow. I was hoping you might be able to furnish me with some information in the meantime."

Edward got to his feet, rubbing his hands together. "Come, let us see what my own collection will yield," he said, and together they began to scour the bookshelves for anything that might prove useful.

# 12

---·---

THE MODEST REDBRICK TERRACED HOUSE THAT WAS HOME TO INSPECtor Winter had as its chief advantage a south-facing garden. Whenever the weather was sufficiently clement, he would step out of the back door of the property and tread the short walk to the potting shed at the far end of the little lawn. He grew vegetables in raised beds and cucumbers in the small greenhouse, but his principal interest lay in flowers, and his favorite of all of these was the auricula. On the north-facing wall of the shed he had constructed an auricula theater. This resembled a set of bookshelves, four in total, each wide enough to accommodate five small terra-cotta pots, which were protected from the worst of the rain by a narrow pitched wooden roof. Here he displayed his very finest auriculas: Black Jack with its dark, velvety petals; flashy Traudl with its orange and yellow bands; the sophisticated pale green of Meadow Treasure; Golden Dawn with its dusting of farina, so hard to achieve and maintain. All his favorites were there, grown from stock some of which his father had handed down to him.

To all the mendacity and violence he was compelled to make sense of in his working life, these delightful flowers offered the perfect antidote. Their simplicity. Their quiet resilience. Their natural beauty. Every Easter he would catch the train to Chester to visit his mother and take with him one of his newest, finest plants. His sister, with her propensity to overwater flowers, was not allowed to tend them. On this morning, as so many, the inspector revisited in his mind the case currently under his auspices, finding the soothing surroundings and benign company of his garden an aid to clarity of thought. As he gently pinched off the spent flowers so that new blooms might take their place, he allowed the facts of the Joe Colwall case to filter through his thoughts. There were, he knew, missing pieces of the puzzle. Why had a previously reliable constable deserted his post and disappeared? Why had Joe shown no signs of any imbalance of the mind before? It irked him that he had not yet succeeded in finding the way forward with the case. And then there was Miss Cavendish and her theories. Should he really give the wild imaginings of a young woman any credence? And yet, there were things which needed explanations and to this point, those explanations appeared only to come from Miss Cavendish. Added to which, she was the daughter of Edward Cavendish, a man whose intelligence and insight he had admired for some time.

He took a small brush and swept away the crumbs of soil he had disturbed during the deadheading process. His plants were thriving under his care, order was maintained. Knowledge, method, application, and attention to detail were what brought about success in his gardening, and these things would, he remained confident, bring about success in his work. He would attend Mrs. Colwall's funeral and see if any new players presented themselves. Whistling, he returned to the house for his breakfast, putting his hand in his jacket pocket as he did so. His fingers found a small object. He stopped, took it out, and held it up to the light. It was then he recalled finding the tiny seed head of a dark, dried plant. He had come across it in his examination of the crypt floor when it was strewn with debris. A flower in any condition was a curious thing to find in such a place. He went inside, but instead of going to the kitchen, he headed for his study. He quickly located the book he most relied upon for the identification of plants. He turned the pages until he found an illustration that matched. Taking up a magnifying glass, he was able to confirm that this apparently charred remnant had come from the flower of *Atropa belladonna*, otherwise known as deadly nightshade.


The following day Hecate armed herself with a tin of Cook's finest Eccles cakes. Reverend Thomas's fondness for sweet things was a weakness she was, on this occasion, willing to exploit. She arrived early and was waiting for him, coat off, shawl tied in place, fingerless mittens added against the cold as despite the advancing spring, the temperature inside the cathedral showed no sign of rising. As she had expected, the small gift put him in a cooperative frame of mind, so that when she presented him with both the fruit-filled pastries and the finished repair work, he was amenable to allowing her choice of book from the library. If he was curious about her selection he did not show it. She and her father had conducted an extensive search of his own library but had found nothing more than two passing mentions of the Essedenes. The importance of the book Brother Michael had directed her to was now all the greater, for where else could she turn for answers?

Hecate watched Reverend Thomas take a key from the ring he wore at his belt and turn it in the padlock at the end of the shelf. It would be possible to take a book from its position and set it down on the reading desk directly in front of the shelf. However, to free the book of its chains and remove it completely required disengaging it from the system. To do this the lock was undone in the plate at the unit's end, which released an iron rod. This slender metal pole passed through rings attached to the ends of the chain links which secured the books. The iron links rattled as Hecate helped him slide free the specific ring from the rod. Reverend Thomas climbed the stepladder and slid the book from its place with no small effort, as it was larger and heavier than a weighty family Bible. With great care, he descended the ladder and handed it to Hecate, who felt the familiar scintilla of excitement at holding one of the ancient tomes from the collection. It had a brown, cracked leather binding, devoid of embellishments or gold inlay, and simple, rough-edged pages. She carried it over to the reading shelf beneath the best light and positioned it reverently on the wooden support. She doubted it had been opened for decades, possibly centuries, and the thought moved her. What arcane writing and forgotten wisdom awaited her inside those worn and forgotten covers? She moved a stool so that she could sit at the right height to best examine the book, and when the librarian informed her he would be taking his lunch break, she hardly heard him, for she was already breathing in the familiar smell of old paper, feeling the fragile coarseness of the pages beneath her fingers, enthralled by the words that were now in front of her.

*Forgotten Peoples of Mesopotamia and Babylonia* was a handwritten work, page after page of meticulous and painstaking manuscripts, mostly text, but with one or two illuminated letters, and some line drawings here and there. It was written, much to Hecate's relief, in English, albeit of an old and in parts impenetrable version. The date on the frontispiece declared it to have been written in "The Year of Our Lorde 1689." She turned the pages gently, keeping them flat, knowing that to flex them was to risk damaging the parched material on which the ancient wisdom was inscribed. As she searched through the titles and headings she thought of the hundreds of hours that must have gone into producing such a volume, most likely by a team of monks. It was easy to imagine them hunched over their work, day after day, their backs aching, trying to keep warm in a building that might not have been dissimilar to the one in which she now sat, writing by the light of candle or lamp and what daylight there was. Her eye caught snatches of sentences: ". . . and the warriors did celebrate theyre victory . . ." or ". . . the King banished them that day . . ." There were lists of those fallen in a battle remembered by no one, and passages praising God for the eventual ending of a pestilence. There were descriptions of tribes who lived in houses on stilts and others who inhabited marshes on boats, harvesting the reeds. At last, Hecate turned a page and a simple ink drawing, the lines faded to brown, sent a shiver of recognition through her. It was not an exact match for the one on the *Mappa Mundi,* but the subject was unmistakably the same. The Essedenes people were shown kneeling, long knives in hand, slicing up the body of a victim, one of them clearly eating the flesh. Quelling a shudder, Hecate read what was written on the facing page. The language was dense and challenging, but she was familiar with deciphering both Old English and unhelpfully stylized lettering. In her mind she translated the writing into something more modern so that she could more easily understand and memorize it. She muttered this version of it to herself as she read.

"'*The Essedenes were a successful tribe of tall, athletic build who inhabited the area north of the Nile and east of Egypt. At the height of their . . . powers, their territory encompassed parts of Mesopotamia, Babylon, and . . . Assyria. They were . . . seen?* no, not that, what is it . . . known! *known for their fierce warriors and hot tempers.*'" She paused, not doubting that this was an accurate description, given the sensations she had experienced when the one on the *Mappa Mundi* had locked gazes with her. She read on, running her finger along each line, the feel of the page against her skin strengthening her connection to every word.

"'*It is said that, among some . . .* fractions? *factions . . . of the people, a be-lief existed that a . . . person's strength could be improved by . . . cannibalism.* Clearly, if what is shown on the *Mappa Mundi* is accurate. *Further . . . they held that to gain the wisdom of their elders a . . . similar tactic could be . . . em-ployed. This led to the practice of . . .* Oh dear Lord *. . . consuming the flesh of their dead parents!*'" Hecate felt bile rising and swallowed hard. Cannibalism was a revolting thought; eating one's deceased mother and father was a thing too horrid to imagine. It moved the notion of eating your own species from the theoretical to the deeply personal. "'*They claimed in their defense against sacrilege that being devoured by their progeny was to be preferred over being left to rot with worms. . . . Another aspect of their faith had to do . . . with . . . re-animating the dead.*'" Hearing her gasp again, the griffin fluttered down to sit on the shelf opposite her. She looked up at him, taking a small comfort in the little creature's company. "Let's all be glad we don't live anywhere near the Essedenes, Griffin. It makes one think some of these tribes were lost for good reason." She bent over the book again. "'*They held services and followed rituals to summon lost warriors . . . and these they called . . .*'" She carefully turned the page. The writing became blotchy, smudged, and harder to read. There was an illustration taking up most of the page, but it was too worn and damaged to make out. "What did they call them?" she asked, picking up a magnifying glass to study the lettering more closely. "It looks like. . . . *resplendent* possi-bly. Can that be right? No . . . '*resurgent*'!" She stopped, turning to look back at the *Mappa Mundi,* boldly focusing her gaze on the images of the Essedenes again. "Resurgent Spirits, raised from the dead, summoned back to life," she muttered. The thought was dreadful, but it made sense to her. At last she had found a connection between the fearsome figure on the map who had moved and stared into her very soul, and the wild destruction that had taken place in the crypt. Both concerned the dead being used in an unusual and shock-ing manner. In the Essedenes' case for cannibalistic rituals, with the spirits breaking out of the crypt, the summoning of the dead. Which led her to an-other inescapable fact. If what she had just read was connected to the events in the crypt, the dead had not risen of their own volition. *They had been called.* Someone had been responsible for raising those spirits.

"But who?" she muttered beneath her breath. "And to what end?"

Desperate to learn more from the precious book, she turned back to what was written. The passage continued with many blotches, foxing, and mildew stains on the paper, so that it was impossible to properly make out the next sentence. The remainder of the page was taken up with the ruined illustration. She moved on to the facing page where to her relief the condition of the paper was much better and the words clearer.

"*'By the beginning of that . . . century . . . the tribe had . . . begun?'* no, become, *'the tribe had become reduced in numbers . . . so that they were no longer a significant power in the region. In fact, their territory had been lost to the neighboring. . . . Voyesenes. These people were, by contrast . . .'* wait. What of the Resurgent Spirits? Surely there is more to say on the matter." She checked back to where she had left off in case she had missed something. It was then she noticed a tiny tuft of thread in the crease of the book. She examined more closely the pages facing each other. The difference between them in terms of condition and damage now struck her as more noticeable.

"There are pages missing!"

She leaned closer to the book, gently turning to the back to see if any loose leaves had been put there. There were none. Exasperated, she shook her head. The very pages she needed, the ones that could have possibly explained more about the spirits summoned, were gone. Had the Essedenes a reputation for success with this ritual? Could they have found a way to succeed where necromancers for centuries before and after had failed? Hecate knew that she would not, only a few short days before, have asked herself such a question. Now, however, with mounting evidence pointing toward a supernatural occurrence to explain what had taken place beneath the cathedral, it was a question that needed answering.

When Reverend Thomas returned she showed him the gap where the pages should be in the book. Together they tutted and lamented the sad damage. Hecate wondered if the pages could have become loose and slipped from between the covers. He agreed it was worth checking in the boxes in which the books had been moved during recent repairs to the shelving, though he did not hold out much hope. In truth, they both were of the opinion that the leaves could have been missing for centuries.

It was while she was in the process of searching for the lost pages in the remainder of the most probable boxes that John came into the library. She could tell at once that he brought bad news. She got to her feet.

"John, whatever is it?"

"I have just this moment received word from Inspector Winter. There has been an incident . . . in my parish."

Reverend Thomas turned to him. "An incident?"

John's voice was somber. "A retired farm laborer, residing in the village of Mordiford . . . he has killed his wife."

"Killed her?" Hecate walked toward her friend, alarmed to see him so shaken.

"In an accident, perhaps?" Reverend Thomas's suggestion carried with it little conviction.

"I am told not," John explained. "There is no doubt it was murder."

Hecate put a hand on John's arm. "Were they quarrelsome?"

He shook his head. "They were the mildest mannered couple you could hope to meet. Had spent all their married lives in the village, liked by all who knew them. Regular churchgoers. Mrs. Colwall . . . on occasion she would help with the flowers at St. Mary's. . . ." His voice trailed off. Hecate thought she had never seen him so shocked. "In recent years her health had faltered. I knew her husband to be a man of great tenderness and compassion, caring for her without complaint."

"How . . . how did she die?" Hecate asked.

"The poor woman was in receipt of terrible violence. Inspector Winter says . . . Mr. Colwall wielded a hammer, with great force . . ."

"How dreadful!"

"I wonder," he said, gathering himself, "Reverend Thomas, could you spare Hecate? I must go and visit the deceased's sister. I know her only a little as she resides the other side of Worcester. It was her misfortune to arrive for a visit. . . . It was she who found her sister's body."

"Of course." The librarian did not hesitate.

"You'll come?" John asked her. "The presence of a woman might offer more comfort. . . ."

"I shall fetch my coat," she said, already undoing her shawl.

The two-seater gig which the dean had, after some petitioning from the vicars choral, supplied for the use of any with a parish church to care for, was old, small, and lacked much by way of suspension. John clicked his tongue to urge on the somewhat nervous bay gelding. The dean had taken a shine to the animal and given him the rather grand name of Bucephalus, arguing that such a legendary association might lend him courage. In truth, the horse's fear of everything, including his own shadow, was all that he shared with his noble namesake.

They traveled in tense silence. Hecate knew John would be bringing his experience as a priest to bear on how he could best help the shocked sister of the deceased and offer her the comfort of God's word. While she herself was there to, in turn, support him and offer what help she could, she had her own questions about the murder. There was something so brutal, so out of character for those involved, so disturbing, that it brought her back to the darkness that had come out of the crypt, and the random nature of the murder of Sir Richard. Could all three things be in some way connected? The link felt tenuous, but nonetheless she could not shake it from her mind.

They drove over the old stone bridge and past St. Mary's Church and into the village. The Colwalls' cottage was down a short track to the right, its garden bordered by a meandering stream that fed into the River Lugg at the point where it joined the Wye. John reined in the horse, left his seat, and tied the animal to the gate post. He moved to offer Hecate his hand but she had already jumped down. A little awkwardly he withdrew his hand and straightened his wide-brimmed black hat.

"Let us go in," he said, leading the way.

At his knock, the door was opened by a tiny woman who appeared to be held together by the two shawls and an apron tightly tied around her frail body. John made the necessary introductions. Red-eyed, Mrs. Tribbet greeted her visitors and bid them enter and sit by the fire. Most of the ground floor of the cottage was taken up by a single room. The floor was flagstoned and the hearth home to a smart cooking range, both things indicating this had not been a place of poverty but of reasonable comfort and security. The heavy air of the cold day was sitting atop the chimney so that the fire did not draw well, sending more smoke than was pleasant back down the chimney and into the room. The smell of coal and wet wood being burned should have filled the house, but above this was the stronger scent of carbolic and bicarbonate of soda. Hecate knew this to be evidence of fierce cleaning efforts in order to remove the stains of death. Even as she took her seat on a ladder-backed chair she noticed signs of what had occurred in that once loving home. The cracked glass of the stitched sampler above the fireplace. On the small dresser beside the window a willow-pattern china set showed not only fresh chips but many spaces in the collection. A delicate figurine sat forlornly on the windowsill missing an arm. The change in color of a rectangle of flags suggested a rug had once been there, and a vision of such a one soaked in blood flashed through her mind. It was clear the old woman had done her best to restore order but she could not hope to expunge the truth of what had happened. For Hecate it was not these small, poignant alterations that concerned her, however. What took a cold grip of her heart was the unmissable, powerful air of menace which lingered in the very stones of the little house.

On the opposite side of the hearth, close to where their host sat, John leaned forward and spoke gently. "Tell me, Mrs. Tribbet, please, if you are able, how we may be of service to you. I knew both Mr. and Mrs. Colwall. They attended St. Mary's for many years, indeed had done so before ever I took charge of the parish. They gave the appearance of being a devout, devoted, and contented couple."

"Oh, reverend sir, they were surely all those things!" Mrs. Tribbet tugged an embroidered handkerchief from her sleeve and proceeded to dab at her eyes as she spoke. "The happiest of couples their whole married lives."

"Your sister had lately been unwell, I recall."

The old woman nodded. "She was troubled by the rheumatism and it had got the better of her. She was not as able to tend the garden or keep house as well as she would have liked."

"And Mr. Colwall looked after her willingly?"

"Oh, he did, reverend sir! A wife could not have wished for a better husband, nor I for a brother-in-law more pleasant and steadfast. Until . . ." Here she stopped and fat tears coursed down her cheeks, evading her attempts to stop them with shaking hand and kerchief.

John took her other hand in his. "Mrs Tribbet, I have no wish to cause you further distress. You have suffered a grave experience such as no one should. I am here to pray for you, pray with you, if you so choose. Or, if there is help of a more practical nature . . . perhaps the packing up of your sister's belongings? The funeral arrangements?"

"Oh, the funeral!" The old woman both nodded and shook her head at the same time, unable to speak through her grief.

Hecate got up and went to her, putting an arm around her trembling shoulders.

"Hush now, dear Mrs. Tribbet. Reverend Forsyth will know what must be done. There will be time enough for you to let him know of any hymns that your sister had a fondness for. In the meantime, let's you and I take a turn about the garden that Mrs. Colwall evidently loved so much. You can tell me your brightest memories of her while the reverend makes notes of how many men and carts will be needed to empty the cottage."

John got to his feet, continuing to reassure the grief-stricken woman that everything would be seen to. Once outside, she became calmer. Hecate had no doubt that the memory of what she had seen in the house made the room an impossibly painful place for her to be. She herself was glad to be away from the dark vibrations that dwelled there now. If she had questioned her own theory that there was a connection between this shocking violence and what had occurred in the crypt, she questioned it no longer. Such a presence could not be mistaken for something else. When Mrs. Tribbet had shown her the apple trees and the beehives, she risked returning to the subject of her sister's death.

"I understand that for you this must be a double blow," she began, "for you have not only suffered the loss of a beloved sister, but of a brother-in-law also. From what Reverend Forsyth tells me, he was, before this . . . aberration, a good man."

Mrs. Tribbet stopped walking and stared into the middle distance as if seeking answers there. "It makes no sense at all. They had been together more than fifty years and in all that time never so much as a raised voice, much less a raised hand. That he should have come to such . . . rage! 'Tis as if some other person had taken charge of him and wielded that h-h-hammer . . ." Her voice faltered over the word.

"Had he been in any way altered, or his behavior unusual, before that night?"

"Not in the least. Why, only two days previous we had met at Ledbury market and passed a pleasant time of laughter and ease despite Mary's worsening condition."

"There was no indication anything was amiss? Are you certain?"

"Nothin' at all, save of course for them both being saddened by the news of Sir Richard's passing."

"Sir Richard Thurston?" Hecate's pulse skipped. "He was widely respected."

"Oh he was, but 'twas more than that. Joe worked on his estate for many years, you see. Up at Hampton Court Castle, before he and Mary moved to Mordiford." She let out a deep, pitiful sigh. "Sir Richard's death was a blow to them both, but especially Joe. And now this . . ." She waved her handkerchief in the direction again and fell once more to silent weeping.

Hecate was aware of a small chink of light fracturing the darkness that surrounded the strange events of the past few days. The link to Sir Richard appeared, on the face of it, a minor one, and possibly insignificant. But it was a link, nonetheless. The two shocking and violent events that had recently taken place involved two men who were known to each other, with a meaningful connection. She strengthened her resolve to investigate further those connections she believed existed, with the curious behavior of the map and, ultimately, the destruction in the crypt.

# 13

THE FOLLOWING MONDAY, HECATE ASKED IF SHE MIGHT BE PERMITTED to finish work half an hour early. She explained to Reverend Thomas that she had an errand to run for her father. When he pressed her for details she had trotted out her planned response regarding collecting something from the museum relevant to an upcoming exhibition there. He had accepted this and granted her permission to leave at half past four, provided she did not make a habit of it.

"The library must be your first concern now, Miss Cavendish," he had reminded her.

"Of course, Reverend. I shall point that out to my father." As she went to fetch her bicycle she had carried the heavy stone of guilt in her stomach. She could not recall ever having told such a blatant lie. She was more than a little shocked at how convincingly she had reinforced it with a further untruth. As she hitched up her shortened skirt and rode away she chided herself for reacting to what she had earlier convinced herself was a little white lie. Something necessary for the greater good that would hurt no one. There was no use, she told herself, being squeamish, given where she was about to go and what she was about to set in motion. In case the librarian happened to be looking out of one of the enormous rose windows behind his desk, she did not proceed down Church Street, which would have been the most direct route to her destination. Instead she continued across the Green in the direction of Broad Street and the museum. Only when she knew she was comfortably out of sight did she turn right and pedal along East Street for a further two minutes.

*MT Sadiki Repairs* boasted a modest facade. The tiny shop was set into a listing, timber-framed house, squashed between two taller, younger buildings that seemed intent on pressing upon it until it took up less and less space, perhaps ultimately disappearing altogether. For now it stood its ground, inhabiting its humble area, beams and lintels swayed and buckled beneath the strain of holding its place. The walls were in need of a coat of wash. Its black beams, exterior and interior it transpired, were similarly overdue the attention of a paintbrush. The small panes of glass in the door were opaque, on both sides, with the grime of ages. Hecate leaned her bicycle against the equally sparkling window, confident she was not contributing greatly to the lack of visibility afforded the display of cobbler's last, boots, laces, and keys. A bell clanked rather than rang as she opened the door. The interior of the little shop was as unimpressive as the face it presented to the world, so that no one could claim they were not delivered what they had been promised. There was a single lamp burning behind the high counter, which was beyond the reach of any sunlight that succeeded in penetrating the rheumy windowpanes. She trod the three available paces of gloom cautiously, breathing in the aroma of boot polish and metal filings. Upon reaching the counter, summoned by the bell, a diminutive man of advanced years emerged from the shadows of the deeper interior in the way of a shy jungle animal compelled to break cover.

"Ah, Mr. Sadiki?" Hecate asked brightly. Without waiting for confirmation she continued. "I am in need of a set of keys and have been reliably informed that you are the person to whom I should come. I had thought of the cobblers in the square, who advertise their services so widely, but no, I was told the master key cutter in town is Mr. Sadiki, and that I should trust none other."

The old man regarded her wordlessly, the unlikeliness of what she was saying apparently having surprised him into silence.

She pressed on, uncomfortably aware of how jarringly chipper she sounded in that small, mute space, and knowing her own nervousness was making her so.

"The facts are these. My father has amassed quite a collection of keys which are vital to his work. He requires access to many secured places, and, within those, several equally secure cabinets. And so forth. And, as I assist him in his work, he wishes to provide me with my own set, which is why I have come to you." She paused to nod at a rusting sign on the wall behind the proprietor, dully illuminated by the lamp, declaring one of his services to be, simply, KEYS CUT.

He turned to look at the sign as if it had, until this moment, escaped his notice.

Hecate plowed on.

"There is, however, one slight . . . complication. My father cannot, not even for one afternoon, give up his keys. No. That would not be possible. And I see that this presents us with a problem, for if you do not have the keys to copy, how will you copy them?"

The question hung in the air.

The man pulled a pair of spectacles from his waistcoat pocket and set them upon his nose, the better to scrutinize the young woman before him.

Hecate squirmed beneath his gaze.

"I realize," she said, "that my request may be somewhat unusual."

"It is out of the ordinary," he agreed, his voice hoarse through lack of use, she suspected, rather than the opposite. "Though not as uncommon as you might suppose," he added.

"Indeed? In that case I am even more confident you will be able to help me."

"I am able," he said, "but ability should not be the master of judgment, now, should it?"

"I'm sorry?"

"There are rules by which I am to abide, else I might find myself hauled before the magistrate."

"Oh?" She strove for a tone between ignorance and reassurance.

"With there being no available keys to copy, the only way to proceed would be to have impressions made."

"Impressions?"

"The key is pressed into a substance that would hold its shape," he explained. "T'would be possible to produce a duplicate in such a fashion."

"I see. And what substance would one use? In such a case?"

"Wax is favored. Soap gives less reliable results."

A silence followed. Hecate hesitated. She did not wish to push too hard for fear the old man would decide against helping her. She knew she was asking something of him that could get him into trouble. She did not have spare money with which to bribe him, and in any case, she sensed he might not be a person to be bought. She must win his confidence.

"My father is an archeologist," she said. "Retired now, but with a splendid collection. Many valuable items. It is these I assist him with. Cataloging, repairing, and so forth. His name is Edward Cavendish, perhaps you have heard of him?"

"I have not."

"No? His work in Mesopotamia is well regarded and widely known. . . ." She faltered, certain she was losing him. "I was so hoping you might be able to accommodate us."

"As I say, 'tis without the bounds of what is lawful. I cannot help you."

Hecate opened her mouth to plead her case further but knew she had nothing more to offer in support.

"Then I shall take up no more of your time," she said, turning to leave.

"Wait." The old man narrowed his eyes at her.

She followed the line of his gaze and saw that he had noticed the cameo she was wearing.

He leaned forward over the counter, his own lack of height making this a somewhat difficult maneuver.

"Where did you come by that?" he asked, pointing, his finger stained with boot polish and leather dye.

Hecate stepped into the pool of lamplight. "It was a present from my father."

Mr. Sadiki blinked as he examined it more closely. "The goddess of magic," he muttered. "Queen of witches. Companion to the dead." He looked up at her then. "A strange choice of gift for a parent to give his child," he observed.

"Not that parent. Not this child." She smiled. "My name is Hecate," she told him.

He stared at her.

She waited.

He drew back a little.

"How many?" he asked.

"I beg your pardon?"

"How many keys?"

"Oh, let me see, um, two large ones—door keys—one slightly smaller, for . . . a different sort of lock, one for a large cabinet, and another for a small padlock. So five in all." She had struggled long and hard with the matter of which keys she should obtain. In the end her conscience had stopped her short of getting a key to the cathedral itself. Her reasoning was that, should her set for any reason fall into the wrong hands, no one outside the employ of the cathedral would be able to use them anyway, as they would not be able to gain entry to the building.

Without another word Mr. Sadiki disappeared back through the doorway into the darkness of the second room. Hecate could hear drawers being opened and shut, boxes being rummaged through. A few moments later he returned. Upon the counter he set down five slender tins of varying sizes. He opened the hinged lid of the first one to show the contents: a block of creamy wax.

"Use one for each key," he said. "You must make two impressions, so that you record both sides of the key."

"Both sides, yes, I see."

"Take care not to damage the surface or the copy will not be accurate." He snapped shut the tin, stacked it with the others, and deftly wrapped them in a sheet of brown paper, tying the parcel with string displaying a dexterity that belied his old eyes and arthritic fingers. He pushed the bundle toward her.

"How much will that be?" she asked, reaching for the purse in her pocket.

"Pay me when they're done."

"Oh, if you prefer." She took the tins. "Thank you. You have been most helpful." She smiled at him again, wishing she could say more to express how grateful she was. "Truly, I am . . ."

"Tell no one. Not a soul."

"No, of course not. I shall return with the impressions in a few days."

He gave a grunt and a nod and then, their business clearly concluded, the curious little man turned and melted back into the gloom of the interior.

When she returned to her bicycle, Hecate found her heart was pounding. Mr. Sadiki was not the reason for her agitated state, this she knew. Far from it, for he had been prepared to help her and had not asked difficult questions. She understood, however, that, even more than lying to Reverend Thomas, this was the first step toward transgression. She had engaged the services of a stranger to do something for her which she knew to be unlawful. Having copies made of one's own keys was of no consequence. Having copies made of those she did not, in fact, have permission to use was another matter entirely. She reminded herself that her motives were good ones. If she was to understand what had happened in the crypt, to fathom the purposes of the Essedenes, to prevent any more killings, she must have unfettered access to the books in the library. All of them. She was certain she was doing the right thing. Even so, she was on edge, so that when she heard her name called she gasped and dropped the package onto the pavement.

"Oh! Lord Brocket . . ."

"I startled you? Forgive me, Miss Cavendish," said the earl, raising his top hat to her.

"That's quite all right. My mind was elsewhere," she said, stooping to retrieve the fallen parcel.

He was too quick for her and snatched it up.

"Allow me. Oh, it is quite heavy. . . ." He rattled it lightly, smiling, as if trying to guess what was inside. Still holding it, he asked, "Have you met my cousin? He has recently come to stay with us at Brockhampton. Viscount Eckley, this striking young lady is the daughter of Edward Cavendish."

"Your golfing partner? Yes, I see the family resemblance," said the viscount. He was smaller than his cousin, slighter, paler, lesser, somehow, in every way. "I am delighted to make your acquaintance, Miss Cavendish," he said, doffing his own hat.

"Viscount," Hecate acknowledged him, doing her best to observe the necessary social pleasantries but keenly aware that the earl still had the tins. Her father had known the local aristocrat many years through his work with the museum and the cathedral, where the peer was a benefactor. She herself had never felt entirely comfortable in the man's presence, though she could not have said why. She held out her hand.

"Forgive me," she said, "I am running to a tight schedule. Must not keep my father waiting."

Lord Brocket passed her the packet but when she had hold of it he did not release it. For an uncomfortable instant she felt trapped. He did not for one second take his eyes off her face, as if he were measuring her reaction, watching, perhaps, for some sign of discomfort. Of fear. She determined to let none show.

Smiling brightly she said, "I understand he has the better of you on the golf course still, sir. It does not do to let him win. He makes far too much of such minor triumphs in the retelling of them."

The earl was sufficiently wrong-footed by her words to lessen his grip so that she was able to take the parcel from him. Dropping it into the basket on her bicycle as she hopped onto the saddle and called back a cheery farewell, she pedalled away down East Street. She felt an unease follow her until she was out of sight of the disquieting man.

Unnoticed by the bustling crowds of the city, something crouched in the shadows, apparently no more than a deeper darkness in the gloom. Had any one of those busy pedestrians paused to, perhaps, tie a loose lace on a shoe, or stoop to pick up a dropped glove, or had an errant child thought to dart from its watchful mother to stray nearer that corner of shade, then that cold presence might have been noticed. As it was, on this bright spring day, the good people of Hereford went about their business, occupying themselves with work or leisure, their minds taken up with their tasks, pastimes, and endeavors. And so they did not detect that unfamiliar company. They did not realize they were observed. They had no notion there was a hunter in their midst, and that they themselves were the prey. That they were spared was the result of two crucial factors. The predator would not strike beneath the revealing rays of the sun, rather it would bide its time until dusk at the very earliest. The second point of protection for the majority of those passersby was the modest rank in society which they occupied. The lowly factory worker, the daydreaming shop girl, the arthritic market trader, the children's nursemaid, the peddler of pans, the portly pieman, and the bent-backed blacksmith—none of these had anything to fear. For the spirit who now searched for its victim sought only a person of wealth, of status, of importance, of influence. Of power.

# 14

---

station a little after ten. As Hecate felt it gather pace and speed southeast toward the capital she took a moment to wonder at how quickly things could change. Ordinarily, this would have been a working day for her; another day spent in her beloved library. Her father had decided, however, that the Essedenes' behavior toward his daughter constituted a possible threat, and called for urgent action. When she had shared with him what she had learned in the ancient book, along with her theories regarding a connection between the necromantic practices of the Essedenes and the destruction of the tombs in the crypt, he had agreed she was onto something both fascinating and dangerous. Her further belief that the death of Sir Richard Thurston and the violent behavior of Joe Colwall were all in some way linked to these things had alarmed him. She had been quite concerned to see the shock in his expression as he warned her that perhaps matters were revealing themselves to be too perilous for her to continue her research alone. She had gone on to tell him of the missing pages in the book and this had, strangely, reassured him. He had already inquired as to whether or not the British Museum held a copy of *Forgotten Peoples of Mesopotamia and Babylonia* so that if it proved useful she might have more unrestricted access to it. Learning of the missing pages he insisted they travel together to London to read the complete chapter in the copy held there. Hecate could see that the more he was able to assist her, the happier he would be, not only for his own curiosity, but out of increasing concern for her safety. She admitted to herself she was glad of his support and his company. The train sped through the landscape of rolling green fields, blossoming orchards, and small villages. They sat side by side in the otherwise empty carriage. She reached over and took his hand and he turned to smile at her. The engine blew its whistle as the train entered a short tunnel and for a few moments they were in darkness, unable to read the other's expression, before emerging into the sunshine again, the smell of smoke and steam blown in through an opening in the window. Swayed by the movement of the train as it rattled along the tracks and over the points, they both fell to watching the passing scenery once more, each lost in their own complicated and frenetic thoughts.

Upon their arrival at Paddington station, Edward hailed a cab and they made the short journey to the British Museum. The library had its home there, with its world-famous Round Reading Room at the very heart of the building. Despite wearing her smartest ensemble of navy wool with a tightly fitted jacket and matching gloves and hat, Hecate felt keenly that she was the country mouse visiting town. The women she saw all looked as if they had stepped from a fashion plate, and the men wore suits of fine tailoring and obvious high quality. She was glad of the silver chatelaine she had borrowed from her mother. The pretty, filigree clip at her waist caught the sun, and the four chains with their useful items at the ends swung rather fetchingly against her skirt as she walked.

Her concerns regarding their suitability for city travel were dispelled, however, by the manner in which her father was received. Every second person they passed, it seemed, knew him by sight, greeting him with a tip of the hat, a hearty hailing, a warm smile, or even a cheery wave. She should not, she realized, be surprised. During his long and successful career as an archeologist, the British Museum had been his second home. Within it, the British Library had provided a place of productive study and essential research.

As they made their way to the heart of the building, Hecate experienced a curious light-headedness. She was compelled to stop and place a hand against the wall to steady herself.

"Are you quite well?" her father asked.

"A little dizziness."

"Insufficient breakfast," he declared. "Come, we shall make a start but break for luncheon in an hour."

"No, let's not interrupt our work on my account. It is nothing," she assured him.

He gave her his arm nonetheless.

Hecate did not tell him that she had been briefly assailed by an onslaught of sound. A noise clearly audible only to herself. It had begun as a susurration, much like the hiss of waves receding from a pebbled shore. At first she had thought it a symptom of the dizziness. The music, perhaps, of her own blood rushing through her veins. But then she had discerned voices. Words. Whispered and breathy, seeming to come from all around her. She had glanced this way and that, but could not make out their source. One word was clearer than all the others, unmistakable and full of urgency.

*Beware! Beware! Beware!*

She went with her father, no longer alarmed, but attentive. Listening. As they proceeded beyond the doors to the exhibitions the voices faded and then fell silent.

The Reading Room itself stood at the center of the quadrangle, with its iconic curved walls and domed roof. As they entered, Hecate was aware of heads turning, eyebrows raising, here and there a newspaper being shaken or a low gruff mumble suggesting restrained but very real disapproval. Women, her father had long ago explained, were not expressly forbidden from entering this hallowed inner sanctum. Nor were they officially permitted. Instead, their inclusion was, on occasion and with the right credentials, tolerated. What irked her most was that this was seen as a hugely generous relaxing of the rules, and any woman fortunate enough to benefit from it should be extremely and effusively grateful. Many female students or professionals were turned away. It was Hecate's good luck that her father was all the *bona fides* she required.

He presented himself at the desk, exchanging whispered greetings with the young male librarian, who was evidently something of a follower of the Cavendish expeditions. As Hecate watched, Edward worked his charm, meekly handing over the ink pen in his pocket, well aware of the rule that prohibited writing devices at such close proximity to valuable books. His confident and personable manner, together with his renown, quickly secured permission for both of them to access the book he had sent a note about the previous day. The librarian acknowledged her with nothing more than a glance through his *pince-nez* before he disappeared to fetch the book. Hecate followed her father to a vacant stretch of desk where they awaited the young man's return. As she removed her gloves she gazed about her, astonished at the towering shelves that lined the arching walls, wondering at all the thoughts and words and recorded deeds that were stored there, waiting to be discovered.

When the librarian returned he was carrying the twin of the book Hecate had read in the Hereford cathedral. As she set it down with some reverence upon the stand on the desk, she recognized the nut-brown leather and the crinkled edges of the pages. This copy, however, was in better condition than the one she had studied. She felt mounting excitement at the thought that she would now get to see what was contained in the missing pages. She had expected her father to open the book, so that as the librarian's leather soles gave muted squeaks describing his progress back to the reception desk, she waited. Edward smiled at her, making a sweeping gesture with his hand that clearly said, *This is your adventure.* She stepped up and opened the book, leafing through it with as much patience as she could muster to find the relevant place.

The pages were there, the book intact, nothing missing at all.

She and her father exchanged beaming smiles as they both leaned in to read. She picked up at the point where the Hereford copy had left off. She had to force herself not to mutter out loud as she stumbled over the challenging archaic English of the text. In her head she made the best sense of it she could, knowing that Edward would be doing the same.

*Here it is . . .* "*These Resurgent Spirits were . . .*" *What is that? Oh, possessed, yes . . .* "*were possessed of great and fearful strength . . .*" *which would explain their ability to break free of their tombs, I suppose.* "*But they were not powerful in themselves, for their . . . lack of corporeal substance made them . . . vulnerable. They had but one goal . . . to find a host.*"

"A host!" On reaching this information, Hecate could not contain her voice, earning *shh*'s and *tut*'s from others in the Reading Room. She stared at her father and he at her before they both bowed their heads over the text once again.

"*Having thrown off the shackles of death . . . the Resurgent Spirits . . . prowled . . .*"

*Oh dear, that bit is too smudged to read. They prowled, then what . . . ? ". . . once chosen, a victim had little chance to defend himself, for the spirit would strike without warning. The intended would be held fast, the breath squeezed from him . . . so that he did . . . fall into a faint. In this deathly . . . attitude, helpless, he would fall prey to the demon spirit as it then took up its place within and became the terrible thing that was an Embodied Spirit."*

The next page was taken up with somewhat lurid drawings of several people depicted in a state of being inhabited by the spirits. They were drawn with wild, staring eyes, gaping mouths, their arms akimbo and feet raised as if in some manner of involuntary dance. Hecate turned the next page, but other than a map, there was nothing. Beyond that, the text picked up where she recalled from the other copy, where it talked of the Essedenes' decline.

Her father leaned close to whisper in her ear.

"A shocking detail, but nothing further?"

She shook her head, her shoulders sagging under the weight of her mood. All she had learned was of the terrible next step the Resurgent Spirits would take, but there was nothing regarding stopping them doing it. Nothing about how those risen might be returned to their graves. Nothing about how to keep people safe from those that now roamed abroad.

Her father, sensing her despondency, put a reassuring hand on her shoulder.

"Never mind," he whispered. "We have not learned a great deal, but what new information we have is valuable. Come."

She was on the point of closing the book when she noticed something. There was writing at the bottom of one of the maps. A long number which included some letters. There was nothing particularly notable about it, but, having seen two versions of this book and so being quite familiar with the hand that had scribed and annotated it, Hecate noticed something odd. The number had not been written in the same ink and with the same sort of quill that had been employed for the manuscript. The lines were thinner, fainter. The loops of the letters were rounder. She glanced over her shoulder to check they were not observed. The librarian had his back to them. Their nearest neighbor along the desk was engrossed in his reading. Quickly, she unscrewed the silver pencil that hung from one of the chains on her chatelaine and opened the tiny silver notebook that was fixed to another. She copied down the number exactly as it was written before snapping shut the notebook, the sharp sound making a minute echo around the circular room. The librarian turned, frowning, but Hecate was already pulling on her gloves.

As soon as they were out of the Reading Room and standing among the bustle of visitors in the museum quad, she opened up the book to examine what she had written, her father scrutinizing it over her shoulder.

"A curious combination of letters and numbers," she said.

"Not to one who has accessed the museum archives," he told her. "That, if I am not mistaken, is an entry into the catalog used to identify minor documents and texts deemed too insignificant to take a place on a public shelf."

"But that is excellent news! Can you tell what it is we are looking for?"

"Let me see . . . the filing system is alphanumeric so row G . . . box or drawer twenty-two. Then the date it was filed, so 1856 in this instance. The lowercase letters refer to either the subject of the piece or the person who filed it . . . 'th.' Hmmm, means nothing to me, but that may not matter. The italic capital will reference the category, perhaps, or subject matter. *N*. Not immediately clear what that . . ."

"Necromancy," said Hecate straightaway.

Edward beamed at her. "Of course it is."

"Can you get us into the vault?"

He stood a little straighter. "If I can gain access to the lost tombs of Mehut the Great I do not believe the archive of the British Museum will defeat me."

"Father, you are so useful!"

"Indeed. Almost as useful as the girl who smuggled pencil and paper past the strictest of guardians. Had you planned all along to take notes? I did wonder at you asking your mother to borrow the chatelaine."

"Did you think I had discovered a sudden fondness for jewelry and girlish adornments?"

"It seemed unlikely. Where are you going now?" he asked as she mounted the stairs back toward the library entrance.

"To watch you persuade whomever needs persuading to allow us access to the vaults. We must see what it is that someone took the trouble to alert us to."

If the librarian was surprised to see them return so soon he did not allow it to disturb his haughty expression. He listened to Edward's request for access to the archives and shook his head, explaining, *sotto voce*, that, even for members of many years' standing, appointments had to be booked some time in advance, permissions had to be gained in writing, protocols had to be observed, and so on and so forth. As he spoke he cast a glance at Hecate and she had the clear impression that her presence was not strengthening their case. For all his reputation it seemed her father was meeting resistance to this perceived bending of the rules. She stepped forward.

"Please forgive my father's persistence, Mister . . . ?"

The young man regarded her with ill-concealed impatience.

"Thorpe," he informed her.

"Mr. Thorpe, we have already taken up far too much of your time," she said with what she hoped was a sweet smile. Charm was not her forte, and it did not help that the conversation had to be conducted in such hushed tones so as not to disturb the library goers. "Come along, Father." She put a hand on his arm. "We will return to Hereford and simply tell the master of the library our request was too improper and inconvenient. I am certain he will understand, after all, he knows better than most the responsibility such a collection demands."

A flicker of interest lit up Mr. Thorpe's eyes. "You are acquainted with the master of the library at Hereford Cathedral?"

"I have the privilege of being his assistant."

"*You* have access to the chained library there?" he asked, now completely failing to mask how impressed he was.

"That, too, is a privilege I cherish. We will keep you from your duties no longer, Mr. Thorpe. Shall I give your regards to Reverend Thomas, one librarian to another, as it were? He will be sorry we were unable to complete our mission, but I have not the slightest doubt he will understand the circumstances which caused you to refuse us entry to the archive."

A battle was being fought inside the young man, and its blows and parries were played out in his expression. Hecate watched him move from a reluctance to give in to their request, through a nervousness about incurring the displeasure of a fellow notable librarian, coming to a restless stop at a need to save face. After a further moment's hesitation, he stepped out from behind the high reception desk, beckoning them impatiently, lifting a ring of keys from his belt as he strode briskly toward the door.

Hecate and Edward were led along a convoluted path that took them back across the quadrangle, through another door into the main body of the museum, down a narrow flight of stairs, through a locked door, and into a nondescript basement area. Here they paused while Mr. Thorpe read the details of the catalog entry. Hecate experienced a momentary panic that he might suspect she had just written it down, but this did not, thankfully, occur to him. He took them into a second chamber and through a further door which opened into a gloomy room, lined with chests of drawers. As her father had rightly surmised, the capital letter led them to the row, and the date and other numbers to a specific drawer. The librarian opened it and removed a small box from inside. This he placed on a table in the center of the room, and lifted the lid. The three peered at the contents.

"Letters," Mr. Thorpe said, as if a little disappointed. He took out his pocket watch. "I shall return on the hour. Kindly do not leave this room until I come to fetch you." He snapped shut his watch and strode for the door, where he paused. "I hope you will be able to tell Reverend Thomas that you found what you required."

"I am certain we shall," Hecate assured him.

As soon as he had gone she and her father took out the bundle of letters and unfolded them. A quick glance told them that they were all addressed to the same person. Edward held one up so that the gaslight fell upon it more evenly.

"Here's our 'th'—Tiberius Harper," he read. "A fine name, but not one with which I am familiar."

"Who are they from? Let's see . . . oh. A monk," Hecate said, experiencing a jolt of connection as she thought of Brother Michael. "Father Ignatius. He signs himself 'your friend' and addresses the other man with quite familiar salutations, look 'My dear Mr. Harper,' 'My good friend,' and later . . . here, just 'Dearest Tiberius.' They started close and grew closer."

"A friendship born of frequent correspondence, it would appear," said Edward, spreading out the many letters across the table.

"Or adversity."

"Now you are jumping to conclusions."

"Father, when did you know two men, one of them a monk, who would so quickly become endeared to one another without an extreme set of circumstances?"

"You make a fair point. Where is the first letter, can you find it? This one is dated May second, 1771. . . ."

She sifted through them quickly. "Here, March 1771. This is the earliest there is." She pulled out a chair and sat at the table. Her father took out his pipe and paced up and down the length of the room as she read to him.

"'*Piedmont Abbey, France. My Dear Mr. Harper, As you were so kind as to contribute to the costs of my travel to my new station here at the abbey, I felt compelled to write as soon as I arrived. It is indeed a splendid place, in reasonable repair for a building so aged. The name of its founder, Robert de Furches, is inscribed above the main door, which is curious as he was not a religious man himself. The brothers have made me most welcome. Alas my arrival was marred by a strange and disturbing event which occurred during my first night here. It was discovered the following morning that several tombs in the crypt had been destroyed and their contents removed.*'" Hecate paused and looked up at her father. No exchange of words was necessary. She read on. "'*I am certain you can imagine the consternation and alarm this incident caused. The local magistrate was summoned, and the Abbot spent some time in conference with him, but neither cause nor motive for the desecration has yet been established.*' He goes on to talk about the routine of the abbey, the food. . . . There is nothing more of significance."

"Try another letter," said her father.

Hecate set the first aside and located the next. "It's dated a week later. '*Events have continued apace. Only a matter of hours after the discovery of the empty tombs, one of our brethren began to behave in a manner which I have been assured was utterly at odds with the man he had always been. He became quarrelsome, outspoken, difficult. Within a very short time he was foulmouthed and aggressive. When this aggression spilled over to violence we were forced to contain him in his cell. While we were doing this, Father Ambrose—the mildest mannered man you could wish to meet—stole two silver chalices, took the horse and cart we use to take our produce to the weekly market, and fled the monastery. The community is in turmoil. As a newcomer, and therefore a little removed from the situation, I am doing my best to be the voice of reason and calm. . . .*'" She scanned the remainder of the letter, found nothing further of importance, and so went on to the next one. "Another week has passed. His handwriting is notably untidy, as if he were in haste to get his thoughts down. '*Before we had time to make sense of any of it, the crypt was once again desecrated. Several tombs had been breached, some containing bodies of monks who had died centuries before, others . . . more disturbingly . . . the resting places of brethren passed in living memory, causing great distress throughout the abbey. One of the oldest members of the community was found dead in his cell, we fear the shock stopped his poor tender heart. A second, one of the youngest here, has run mad. It took three monks and a visiting preacher, James Habington, to restrain him.'"*

"Habington? That name is familiar to me, though I cannot think why." Her father thought for a moment and then shook his head, signaling for her to continue.

"*'He is another now confined, for his safety and our own.'*" Hecate sorted through the letters and found the next. "There has been a longer gap . . . this one is dated April the fourteenth. And look! He mentions the Essedenes!" Her father stopped his pacing to stand close to her as she read on. "*'My Dear Tiberius, at last I have some words of explanation for the terrible events here at Abbey Piedmont, though they bring with them no comfort. The Abbot's investigations, including calling upon an exorcist from Paris, have led to the discovery of heinous practices that would appear to be afoot. A long forgotten tribe, the Essedenes, were believed to have used dark magic in their attempts to raise the dead. It seems that someone has gained sight of an ancient manuscript that records details of their methods, and these have been used with wicked effect, summoning the departed from their places of rest. As if this were not sufficiently distressing, these Resurgent Spirits—for such their Necromancers named them—will stop at nothing to become Embodied in their new hosts. Once there, they vanquish the original soul and replace it with their own, which is inevitably blackened and vile given their unnatural progress. I was with the Abbot himself when one of the brethren was attacked by a Resurgent Spirit. We saw only a dark mass, though we both strongly felt its evil presence and saw the mortal struggle Brother Paul was engaged in. Alas, we could not stop it. For a night and a day we watched as the gentle soul, who had once been a baker in Toulouse, faded to nothing. We have learned there is a chance to save the victim if swift action is taken, but as yet, we know not what that action should be. Only one of our attempts have succeeded, when an exorcism was performed. We must stand helpless as the abbey is consumed by this darkness, or flee to save those of us who remain.'*" Hecate picked up the final letter. "He has only written the date, and a few lines beneath the greeting. '*They have taken the best of us. We have found them to be intolerant of alcohol, and uncomfortable in the presence of animals, which react strongly to them. Another exorcist arrives on the morrow, the first himself having fallen victim to the curse of the Essedenes. I will write again if I am able, though I fear all is lost.'* He has not even signed it," she said, "but he has made some sort of drawing, here, see?" She held the page up to the light and they both scrutinized the simple shape the monk had sketched.

Edward gave his opinion. "A symbol, rather than a depiction of something more real . . ."

"It resembles slightly a handprint," she said, turning it this way and that. "A smudged palm . . . What can it signify?"

Edward sorted through the letters, checking points for himself. "What a terrible business," he muttered. "And see here, Hecate, this struck me. The date, do you see? March 1771. Almost one hundred years before the tombs in the Hereford Cathedral crypt were opened."

"Almost, but not precisely. Brother Michael thought the date significant, though he has not yet recalled in what way. There is a shape to the number. . . . Do you see?"

"A shape? Why, yes. It is a palindrome. You think that significant?"

"I think we cannot rule out anything that might be. Wait." She sifted back through the letters. "The date of the first emergence from the tombs."

"The third of March."

She nodded. "The third of the third. Or thirty-three, if you were to reduce it so."

"Palindromic. Interesting, but . . ."

"How does it help us? If there is a pattern to the dates . . ."

"When did the first desecration in the crypt at Hereford take place?" her father asked.

Hecate thought for a moment, working it out in her mind. She smiled at him. "I recall it well. A Wednesday in April." Her face fell then. "But no, that doesn't work, the fifth of the fourth." She shook her head. "We are chasing down a path that leads nowhere."

"Or possibly in circles."

"In either case, a waste of our time. . . . There is another point that causes me more concern," she said, looking at him. "There is no escaping the fact; if there are Resurgent Spirits roaming the city of Hereford looking for hosts, they have not risen by themselves. They have been called. And called by someone who possessed the incantations, spells, curses . . . whatever words the Essedenes used, someone is using them now. Someone who knows where to find those lethal words."

"The like of which would surely be considered among the most dangerous ever written," Edward murmured.

She nodded, following his inevitable line of thought. "And the only books kept more closely guarded than priceless ones are dangerous ones. Such as those kept in the locked cabinet in the muniments room." She sat back in her chair. "To think that such things have been there, a few strides from where I work every day."

Edward sat on the seat next to her and placed a hand over hers.

"There is something else you must consider, my daughter, however hard. There are only a handful of people with access to that cabinet, and every one of them is known to you."

When Mr. Thorpe returned Hecate and her father left the archives meekly. Both were occupied with their thoughts. Having thanked the librarian for his assistance, they made their way toward the exit, Edward voicing his inclination toward finding somewhere for their overdue luncheon.

"Yes," Hecate agreed, "that would be sensible. Pleasant, indeed. But first, Father, would you mind if we spent a little time here?" She indicated the interior of the museum. "I should very much like to see the ancient Greek exhibits. We have so much to discuss but my thoughts are confused. I think I might find it . . . helpful," she told him. What she did not tell him was that once again she was experiencing the light-headedness that had afflicted her earlier. Once again she could hear the whispered voices.

*Beware! Beware!*

While her mother might have insisted dining was the required course of action, her father was more accepting of the idea that wisdom and knowledge could themselves be sustaining.

"Of course," he said. "Another hour will not see us starve. I believe I know precisely which exhibits you would like to see."

He offered her his arm and they strode, in step, toward the room given over to Greek statuary. As they moved through the museum the voices chattering in Hecate's ear became increasingly excitable and insistent, to the point where she could not make out words clearly. She was thankful when they reached their destination. She let go her father's arm and stepped forward gazing up at the exquisite marble figure in front of her. Even after centuries, it had not diminished in its purity, its simplicity, its power to hold the attention of the viewer.

"Hekate," she murmured, experiencing the strangeness of using her own name to identify another.

The goddess before her was beautiful, her limbs impossibly long but pleasingly so, her curves womanly but modestly draped. There were crescent moons woven into her hair. She held aloft a flaming torch, indicating her ability to shine light upon the dead and show the way through the darkest night. A serpent coiled its way down her arm. In her other hand she held a ring of keys, symbolizing her ability to open doors from one world to another, or to assist those wishing to travel through unearthly realms.

"Your namesake is a fair bit taller than yourself, daughter," Edward noted. "At least, this splendid version of her is. Over there is a much later figure. Not Greek at all, in point of fact, but some curators prefer to group figures together by their identity, rather than their chronological position. A practice I have some issue with, but there it is. And there, in the center of the room—which does show some understanding of this particular goddess's iconography—we have her represented as a trinity. One woman but three figures, three faces, each looking in a different direction, the statue traditionally positioned at a crossroads. Of course, this was a much, much later iteration of Hekate, but, as I say, curators all have their little ways, their need to make their own opinions heard. . . . And here she has hounds at her feet. Another addition to her mythology. Some say they are the hounds of Hades. . . ."

Hecate knew the legends well and had no need to hear her father's words to remember them. Which was as well, since her mind was filled with another voice. It was not, she thought, that she could hear these words spoken, more that they were laid upon her mind so that she simply and immediately understood them. Just as she understood that it was Hekate herself who spoke to her.

*You tread the boundary between two worlds, Daughter of the Moon. Where you venture there is great danger. You must not shrink from your task, but you must protect yourself. Go bravely, child, but go wisely.*

A calmness flooded through Hecate's very bones. She felt it strengthen her. The voice was as familiar as if it had been her own mother's, and as clear as if the goddess lived and breathed.

"I will," she murmured, gazing up at the serene face of the statue. "I give my word, I will do what is asked of me."

"Hecate?" Edward placed a hand on her arm. "What is it?"

She wanted to answer him but could not tear her gaze from the statue. She was aware of him watching her, aware of his calm presence, but beyond that, nothing but the goddess until he spoke again.

"Are you ready to leave now? I would not wish us to miss the late afternoon train," he told her.

"Surely there is plenty of time?"

He took his pocket watch from his waistcoat and flicked it open. "We have been here longer than you might think," he said, showing her that it was almost four o'clock.

She was astonished. She felt she had stood before the goddess for mere moments, but almost an hour had passed. She nodded then. "Yes," she said. "Let us go. I am ready." She saw that he had noticed an alteration in her demeanor but she did not wish to talk to him about it. Not yet. She required time to make sense of what had happened. "Come," she said, smiling at him, a newfound confidence bubbling up inside her. "Let us go home."

# 15

HECATE AND HER FATHER HAD CHOSEN AN EMPTY CARRIAGE COMPART-
ment so that the train journey home from London had been entirely taken
up with discussion regarding the new information they had gleaned. There
had been no time before their departure to take tea, so that all they had to
sustain them was a bag of apples purchased from a barrow at the station. Sitting opposite each other, they both ate hungrily as they summarized the situation, and agreed on the main points. Someone had gone to the trouble of
writing the number reference on the page in *Forgotten Peoples of Mesopotamia
and Babylonia*. That person may or may not have been Tiberius Harper, but
either way they had wanted to direct anyone reading about the Essedenes to
Father Ignatius's letters. It was, Hecate and her father were certain, a warning.
What it was not, however, was a solution. The letters fell short of explaining
how the Resurgent Spirits could be stopped from becoming Embodied, and
how they in turn could be vanquished, or their hapless hosts saved. The evidence pointed to there being a text in existence, both in 1771 and 1881, that
would enable someone to summon the dead. Given the fact that the latest
necromantic activity had been in Hereford Cathedral, it was not unreasonable to suppose both the Essedene curse and the person using it were located
in there. It would have to be someone with access to the crypt and the text
in question. Hecate was convinced it must be in the locked cabinet in the library. Her father had warned against making this assumption, not so much

because the theory was unproven, rather that it meant only one of four people were under suspicion. Only these four had access to the complete sets of keys that would be required to gain entry to the crypt, the library, and the locked cabinet. This short list now replaced in her mind that of the mythical creatures in the map. Instead of *manticore, phoenix, griffin, unicorn,* she had four names of real people to consider.

*The dean, the verger, the master of the library, and the leader of the vicars choral.*

"Not John," Hecate said as the train lurched over an old set of points. "I will not believe him capable of such a thing." When Edward gave no reply she asked, "You cannot believe it, Father, surely?"

"I do not wish to believe any of these men capable of such a terrible course of action. However, until we know who is responsible, we must proceed with the utmost caution. Whoever it is has gone to great lengths to unleash a dangerous power. He will not easily be stopped, and will not, I fear, be beyond violent acts against anyone who should get in his way. You must promise me, Hecate, that you will not put yourself at risk. That you will not confront anyone while alone with them. We need more information and a plan."

"I work with Reverend Thomas and it would seem strange to alter that habit. I am rarely alone with either the dean or Mr. Gould. But John . . ."

"Just until we have the proof we need. I will have your word on this," he said, concern etched upon his expression.

"But I must discuss all of this with John!"

"You are not listening to me."

"Father, it is ridiculous to suspect him. If it will reassure you, let us speak with him together, tell him everything we know."

"And if it is John behind the raising of these spirits we will be warning him that we are close to discovering the truth. We should not share what we have learned with anyone. Not yet."

Hecate leaned back in her carriage seat and took a bite of apple, her stomach rumbling. She understood her father's desire to protect her, but she could not, she would not, believe John to be the sort of man who would cause such destruction, such wickedness, such awful consequences.

"Very well," she said at last, "I will not say anything to him. Not yet. That way you can be at ease regarding my spending time with him." She watched her father relax a little at the fact that he had her agreement on this and she realized anew how concerned he must be for her safety. "There is something else, Papa," she said, seeking both to reassure him and keep no secrets. "When we were at the museum . . . when I stood in front of Hekate . . . she spoke to me."

Instantly, he was alert again, leaning forward in his seat.

"You heard her? You are certain?"

"There was no mistaking her voice, or that she addressed me directly. It was . . . exhilarating!"

"I knew it!"

"You . . . ?"

"I saw the trancelike state you entered. It was clear to me that it was caused by your proximity to the statue. This is capital. Capital! What did she say to you?"

"She warned me. . . ." she told him, watching his expression closely. "She said there is danger, but she also said, I must be brave. I must not turn away from what has to be done." She waited, hoping that her father's natural concern for his daughter's well-being would not override that sense they shared that she must act. That she was in a unique position to stop the Essedenes and whomever was summoning them. "It has to be me," she said.

He nodded. "I see that. We must draw strength from the fact that she has communicated with you."

"She called me *Daughter of the Moon*. What did she mean?"

"You know that she herself is the Goddess of the Moon. She was identifying you as her own child."

She saw then that her father's eyes were filled with tears.

"Oh, Papa! Do not fear for me . . ." She reached forward and took his hand.

"It is not fear that moves me, my little friend to phantoms, but pride," he told her. "I knew before you were born that you were destined to be different. I watched you grow into a fine young woman, waiting for a sign that my belief was not misplaced. Oh, you were always a wonderful child. Curious, brave, full of energy, and ever questing for adventures . . . And there were times when I thought I saw a sensitivity to ethereal things, the way you might turn your head suddenly in a graveyard, or how I might catch you babbling in conversation when you were apparently alone. But nothing . . . certain. Until now," he said, smiling then. "How does such a connection strike you? How does it make you feel, Hecate?"

She returned his smile, joy lighting her face. "It feels as if I shall never face anything alone again." She moved to sit beside him, resting her head on his shoulder. The swaying of the train and the excitement of the long day took hold of her, so that soon she was asleep.


The next morning Hecate returned to her duties at the cathedral. She found the master of the library in an uncharacteristically talkative frame of mind, as he could not resist hearing about her trip to the British Museum. She was concerned, at first, that he might press her for information. Information which she was determined not to share, as she and her father had agreed, with anyone on their list. She need not have worried, however, for Reverend Thomas's greatest wish was, it seemed, to tell her of his own time spent seconded to the British Library and how appreciative the head librarian had been of what he had been able to offer with his own expertise.

As she listened to him speak she was aware that her view of him was forever altered. Every word, every deed, would fall under new scrutiny, seen in a new light. The light of suspicion. The day passed with them both engaged in their work. She was aware of the *Mappa Mundi*'s heightened state of restlessness, occasionally glimpsing figures moving or glowing, but she did not have the place to herself for a moment. More than ever, she knew that obtaining her own set of keys to the library and its treasures was the right thing to do.

She was pleased when it came time to finish work for the day, for there was something she wished to do, and the thought of it pressed on her mind with so many other thoughts that her teeming brain ached. She and Reverend Thomas left the library, shutting off the sunlight from the rose windows as he closed and locked the door. On Hecate's way down the north aisle a movement caught her eye, and she noticed Corporal Gregory beckoning her in the doorway to the Stanbury Chapel. She said her goodbyes to the librarian who first thought to question what she planned to do, and then, seeing she wished to step into the chapel that was traditionally used for private prayer, did not press her. Hecate waited for him to walk out of sight before closing the heavy door and taking a seat on one of the short pews beside the young soldier.

"What is it, Corporal?" she asked. "You seem agitated."

"Miss Cavendish, I have heard you are investigating the terrible occurrences in the crypt."

"Why yes, I feel I must. Things are far from right."

"Indeed they are not! It is my duty to warn you of danger. My duty to protect you and all who inhabit the cathedral. I must beg you to desist from venturing down a path that could bring you to harm."

She saw then the pain in his expression and knew that for him, the proximity to peril not for himself, but for those he saw as under his protection, stirred dreadful memories. She would have taken his hand in hers if it had been possible. Instead she smiled at him.

"I am touched by your concern, Corporal Gregory. And impressed by your sense of duty and your vigilance. Please, rest assured, I will proceed with caution. I have my father's support in what I do. I have Brother Michael's help. And I have you to watch over me. All will be well."

Hecate steered through the city streets with some speed. She was not making haste in order to get home. After what she and her father had discovered, she felt compelled to seek out Inspector Winter. Even as she crossed the square in High Town and turned right past the black-and-white beams and wattle of the famous building in its center, she knew she faced an impossible task. How could she convince the sensible, fact-loving detective of her far-fetched theories? How could she make him understand that the city was under threat from something so otherworldly and unseen? She knew that, as yet, she did not have sufficient evidence with which to convince him. Instead, she decided, she would ask to speak with Joe Colwall, who was being kept in the cells. It seemed to her too much of a coincidence that a mild-mannered man should behave as if possessed by a demon at a time when demons were prowling the city streets. She did not believe in coincidences, and she was certain the logically minded inspector would have no time for them either. If she could make him see that Mrs. Colwall's murder was something out of the ordinary, and that the man in his jail was far from ordinary . . . it would be a start.

Within minutes she reached the drab stone building that served as both constabulary office and jail. She leaned her bicycle against the wall by the front entrance and went inside.

She was greeted by the smell of carbolic soap and bicarbonate of soda, neither of which was entirely successful at masking the stench of urine and sweat that seemed ingrained into the tiled walls and wooden benches. There was a broad, high desk in the lobby, behind which stood an aged policeman with an impressive set of whiskers. He regarded Hecate over his half-moon spectacles.

"Can I be of assistance, miss?" he asked.

"I am here to see Inspector Winter," Hecate told him, removing her gloves.

"He is expecting you?"

"I do not have an appointment, no, but I have information of great value. I believe he will wish to hear it."

"Is that so?" The sergeant picked up a pencil and licked the end of it, opening a broad ledger and selecting a fresh page. "If you would be so good as to tell me what this information is in relation to, I will make a note of it, and see that it reaches the inspector."

"Oh . . . I'm afraid that will not do at all."

"Will it not?" he questioned, pencil remaining poised, gray bushy eyebrows raised.

Hecate tried to imagine putting her theory into words that could be entered into a ledger without sounding like the wild imaginings of a silly young woman. She knew she had to speak to the man himself.

"I am here in my capacity as assistant librarian at the cathedral," she said.

The police officer received this information blankly.

"I understand that Joe Colwall is here in the cells. I should be grateful for the opportunity to speak with him."

The sergeant frowned. "Members of the public are not permitted in the cells. Unless, of course, they have been arrested." He allowed himself a small smile at his own joke.

Hecate would not give up.

"The matter in question is in regard to the . . ." She hesitated, choosing her words carefully. ". . . desecration of the crypt," she said, hoping to imbue the subject with sufficient drama to raise its importance.

Still the sergeant remained unmoved.

Hecate glanced over her shoulder. Even though there was no one else in the reception area, she leaned forward, lowering her voice to a whisper, as if to suggest what she had to say was highly sensitive information.

"It has also to do with the death of Sir Richard Thurston, God rest his soul, who was a close friend of my father, Edward Cavendish."

She could not tell, and might never know, which of these names was the key that unlocked his resolve, but he straightened up, regarded her closely for a long moment, and then set down his pencil. He walked around the end of his desk and held open the door leading to the inner sanctum of the building.

"If you would step this way, Miss Cavendish," he said.

Hecate needed no second bidding. She quickly crossed the threshold and allowed herself to be guided down a narrow corridor to a small room at the rear, where she was left to wait. There was an empty desk, a table lamp, two hard chairs, and a map of Herefordshire on the wall. The single window was too high to facilitate a view out, and the thick bars across it only allowed a modicum of light to find its way in. She decided this might once have been a cell, and the thought made her shiver. A few minutes later, the door opened and Inspector Winter appeared, wearing his familiar brown bowler and heavy tweed jacket.

"Miss Cavendish, this is an unexpected pleasure."

"I appreciate your finding the time to see me."

"Sergeant Highcliffe informs me you wish to speak of Sir Richard's murder, and also that you wish to speak to one of the prisoners we are currently holding here. Can this be correct?"

"Quite correct. I have a theory regarding the terrible murders that have taken place in the city and to confirm it, I should like to interview Mr. Colwall. Briefly. If I may."

The inspector took in this information, his face as inscrutable as that of his officer, so that Hecate began to wonder if they were trained to remain impassive, whatever the provocation. At last he gestured toward the chairs.

"Won't you sit, please?" he asked. When she did so, he took the seat opposite and leaned forward on the desk, his hands clasped lightly in front of him. "Well now, what is it that you have to tell me that could not be relayed through my highly capable and trustworthy sergeant?"

"I believe that Joe Colwall is connected to the death of Sir Richard Thurston."

"You think him a double murderer?"

"I did not say that he killed him, only that Sir Richard's murder and Joe Colwall's violence are linked. And both are connected to the desecration of the tombs in the crypt."

The inspector let out a low whistle. "I see now why you feared confusing my sergeant."

"I am not here to convince you of outlandish theories."

"I am pleased to hear it."

"I would prefer that you come to an understanding of the way things are through your own logical and, I'm certain, highly efficient means."

"So efficient that you felt compelled to assist me?"

"I wish only to present you with evidence that might otherwise escape your notice. I do not believe, as I understand you do, that Joe Colwall is insane. I believe him to be working under the control of another, let's put it that way. Would you be so good as to take me to him?"

"Members of the public are not permitted in the cells . . ."

". . . unless they have been arrested. Yes, Sergeant Highcliffe has already shared that witticism with me."

"The point is, Miss Cavendish, the cells are no place for the innocent. Those incarcerated have a tendency to show the very worst side of themselves. I cannot fathom what you hope to achieve by viewing a criminal confined."

"Not any criminal. Only this one." She got to her feet, causing him to do the same. "I would not ask if I thought it a waste of your time or mine, I promise you."

She waited.

The inspector hesitated.

Hecate felt sure he was about to send her on her way, but instead, after a moment's apparent deliberation, he said, "Come with me."

She followed him as he led her from the dismal room, along another narrow corridor and down a flight of stone steps. She realized then that she had descended to the level of the proper cells. The basement was divided into four spaces of equal size, each with a miserably small barred window in the far wall. More iron bars separated the cell spaces from the basement area in which she now found herself. Inspector Winter beckoned her. She walked to the end of the row and turned to look into the cell. At first she thought it empty, but slowly a figure began to take shape in the shadows. A man, not tall, in dirty clothes, sat crouched in the corner. He was elderly, frail, and muttered continually to himself, his mouth moving as he formed words she could not discern. Sensing he was being watched, the man turned. On seeing the superior police officer he stopped his murmuring, one-sided conversation and got unsteadily to his feet. He walked the three strides to the front of the cell and carefully took hold of the bars. To Hecate it seemed he needed to do so if he were to stand for any length of time, so frail and gaunt was his appearance. As she watched him, however, his expression hardened and became so fierce she was shocked to see the transformation. His eyes widened and he set his teeth together, barely opening them to spit out his words as he spoke.

"Why, Inspector, a visit at last. I was beginning to think you no longer cared for my company."

"You must get used to time spent alone, Joe Colwall. A deal of it lies ahead of you, before the hangman grants you final release from such loneliness."

It was shocking to stand before a murderer, and Hecate had expected it to be so. But she had not been prepared for Joe Colwall's appearance. He certainly fitted the description of someone raging, someone filled with violence. It was hard to see any trace of the mild-mannered good husband John and Mrs. Tribbet had described to her.

"You will be sorry to see me go," Colwall declared. "I believe it delights you to come down here and poke the chained bear with a stick. Is that what sets the blood racing through your veins? Do you crave the proximity to that which you yourself cannot be, yet secretly, you admire?"

"That you consider yourself in the smallest way admirable is a clear indication of your own mania."

"You may comfort yourself in believing me mad, but you and I are not so different. I know the base desires of all men. I've seen the blackness in their hearts."

He turned suddenly then, springing to one side with the speed of a much younger, stronger man, snatching at the pair of bars directly in front of Hecate. He stared at her with a wildness in his eyes and an intensity to his gaze that she recognized, for she had experienced it before. She had felt the same shock once before, on that day when the figure on the map had turned and caught her in his glare. Despite her thundering heart, she would not let him see how shaken she was. She might never again have the opportunity to speak with an Embodied Spirit, for such she now was certain he must be. She must learn what she could.

"I will not call you Joe Colwall, for I fear he is long gone," she said.

The man reacted to this, no longer furious, but intrigued. A grim smile did nothing to add warmth to his expression.

"Who have we here?" he asked, licking spittle from his lips. "I thought you some spectator, brought to see the caged animal."

Hecate did not look away. "I know what you are," she told him. "I know where you came from. What I do not understand is why? And why now? Who was it who summoned you?"

He gave a short bark of a laugh at this. "She is clever, your woman, Inspector," he said. "Or at least, she thinks she is. Thinks she knows things. You would do better not to meddle, girl. I serve one with power such as you could never imagine. My master would crush you beneath his heel and not break his stride. He will not stop for you, nor anyone who gets in his way."

Hecate looked at Inspector Winter to gauge his reaction. Surely Joe Colwall's words would give him pause. Surely he could not dismiss such particular words as the random ravings of a crazed person.

"Who commands you?" she asked the murderer. "Who is it who brought you to this vile end?"

He shook his head then, slowly to begin with, then faster and faster, a frenzied gesture, crazed and mindless. "Your cleverness will not stop us! Nothing will stop us. Not this time!" He fell backward then, thrashing on the floor, the energetic movements too much for the frail, elderly body to withstand.

"Come." The inspector put his hand on Hecate's arm. "He cannot be helped," he told her, leading her from the terrible sight, and up the stairs.

When she had refused a glass of water and satisfied Inspector Winter she was sufficiently steady to safely ride her bicycle, he escorted her to the front door. As she turned to go he spoke, not unkindly but firmly.

"A clear case of madness. Insanity can visit a person at any time, but increasingly we see it in the elderly. I wish that it were more uncommon. Alas, the opposite is true."

"Here we differ in our opinions, Inspector. You see a madman. I see a man possessed." So saying she hitched her skirt up and set to pedalling, steering her bicycle toward St. Owen's Street, hoping she looked steadier and more capable than she felt.

She had gone no more than twenty yards when she saw John walking toward her. He smiled, waving his hand in greeting and stepping in front of her. She had no option but to stop and felt at once cross that he had presumed she would do so.

"Goodness, Hecate, you are in a hurry. But then, when are you not? Have you come from the police station?"

"I spoke with Inspector Winter."

"About the events in the crypt?"

Hecate knew John was attempting to be supportive but she could not possibly launch into the details of her theory while standing on the pavement. Not only was she tired and rattled by her encounter with Joe Colwall, she was also mindful of her promise to her father that she would not share details of their new knowledge with John. Not yet.

"We spoke mostly of Joe Colwall. And now I shall be late home and Mother will fret about it. You know she does not like me being out unaccompanied at present."

"Ah, yes. Of course. I will not detain you longer. I only wished to . . ."

"Forgive me, John, but can we talk another time?"

He looked at her a little sadly then. She understood his concern was for her as he could see she was unsettled by something. His kind heart only served to make her feel cross with herself for being ungracious.

"As long as you remember I am always here to listen to you, Hecate." He let go the bicycle then and stepped from her path. "I myself am on my way to talk to the inspector," he said.

"Oh?"

"I am finalizing the arrangements for Mrs. Colwall's funeral. As her death is the subject of a murder inquiry, I need him to sign a paper so that her body might be released to the family."

Now Hecate felt doubly bad.

"You will let me know when the date is fixed?" she asked. "I would like to attend."

"Of course. I'm sure Mrs. Tribbet would find solace in your presence." He appeared to be on the point of leaving but lingered, not yet content to let her go on her way without expressing his concern for her further. "There is more to this than you have shared with me. I know you too well, Hecate. Please know I wish more than anything to be a good friend to you."

"And you are. Far better than I am to you."

"Then tell me what it is that is troubling you so."

"I want to, truly I do. There is just so much to explain. . . ."

He nodded. "In which case we need quiet time to talk. I have the use of the gig and horse on Saturday. I was to officiate at a wedding but it has been postponed. It would be a pity not to make the most of the turnout. Let me take you for a drive. A picnic, perhaps?"

Hecate thought about what her father had said but she could not, would not suspect John of being dangerous. And she would, she realized, welcome the chance to share with him what she had learned so far. He knew of her gift. Hekate had told her to protect herself. What better way to do that than to enlist the help of those who understood her, and those she could trust?

"A picnic would be very nice," she told him.

He smiled. "If the excitement of such a thing would not be too much . . ."

Realizing she must have sounded insincere she sought to reassure him. "Truly. I will look forward to it."

"More than Clementine's ball on Friday evening?"

Hecate let out a heartfelt groan.

"You had actually forgotten about it!" He laughed lightly.

"I would avoid it if I could, but Clemmie has insisted on my being there. And I know it will do Charlie good."

"I wish you good luck."

"I wish you were going to be there," she said suddenly and meant it. John was not of the correct social standing to have been invited, which seemed a stupid injustice to Hecate.

"Lady Twyford-Harris sets the bar very high," he said.

"She makes an exception for my family," Hecate pointed out. "More's the pity."

"Enjoy yourself. Dance. Laugh with your dear friend. It will do you good. You can tell me all about it on Saturday."

"There will be nothing to tell on that score, I promise."

It was she who lingered then. She wished she could find the words to tell him that she would rather have spent the time in his quiet, intelligent company than endured the frivolity of a ball. She wished she could reassure him that she preferred his conversation to that of any of the dukes or earls or young viscounts that would no doubt bore her.

"Go home, Miss Cavendish," he told her then, turning to walk toward the constabulary building. "I would not detain you and bring your mother's wrath upon my head."

She smiled at this, although that smile faded as she glanced back at the prison building and recalled the wretched and wicked creature that was kept locked beneath it.

# 16

THAT THURSDAY EVENING THE NIGHT SKY WAS HELPFULLY STREWN WITH clouds, affording Hecate some cover as she made her way through town, for once on foot, it being vital that no one saw and recognized her. Sneaking out of the house unseen had not presented any great difficulties. Her mother often retired to bed early, and as Charlie's health was again fragile she had insisted he do the same. Edward was out of the house, attending a meeting of the chamber of commerce with Phileas. In addition, slipping unseen from her bedroom to roam the city was something Hecate had been doing since she was a young girl, so that she had perfected the art of leaving the house undetected when the occasion merited it. She had thought long and hard about telling her father of the keys. She had taken him into her confidence in so many important ways, but she was uncertain of how he might react. It was testament to the singularity of her parent that she knew he would be accepting of all things supernatural or arcane, but less so of her doing something that was, after all, against the law. And would she not, if she informed him of her intentions, make him an accomplice? She would not risk bringing his reputation into disrepute. Let this jeopardy be hers and hers alone.

She reached the cathedral a little after eight o'clock. As she approached the south door, her leather satchel held tight against her hip to stop its contents rattling, she could hear the first notes of song drifting out from the choir stalls. The door was shut, but she knew it would be unlocked. There was a rehearsal in progress which required the attendance of all the vicars choral. It was the south door that they would use to and from their rooms in the cloisters. Hecate glanced about her. There was no one to be seen. She took hold of the heavy iron ring and twisted it. The latch lifted and the door swung open. The ancient hinges gave only a small squeak of protest, so regularly used was this particular entrance, and, at the dean's insistence, well maintained. She went inside.

The interior of the cathedral was a little cooler than the night air outside. With no boilers lit, this was not uncommon in the early weeks of spring. Lately, however, people had begun to notice that however warm and sunny the days, the space within the cathedral walls did not rise. Hecate believed the chill came from the darkness that had been disturbed in the crypt. She promised herself that one day sunbeams would once again spread their warmth through the stained glass of the windows. One day the wicked curse that afflicted this holy place would be lifted.

As she walked quickly down the south aisle she passed within a few feet of where the vicars sat, their voices lifted in song. They could not see her, as she was obscured by the construction of the rear of the choir stalls, and by the great organ itself. The music filled the air, great surging chords as John played the organ, sweet contralto notes, vibrant tenor melodies, and rich bass lines rose and fell, swooped and soared. The beauty of the music gave her courage. She might be doing something secret. She might be betraying the trust of people whom she cared about. It mattered not, in the greater scheme of things. She had told the goddess she would do what was needed, she would do what was asked of her. This was a part of what she had been called to do. She turned left and hurried toward the vestry door. Through the patterned glass set into its top half, she could see that a lamp had been left lit inside. She did not let this worry her. Mr. Gould was not a part of the choir, but she knew his habits. She was confident he would have returned to his quarters in the cloisters hours ago and was most likely sleeping off a late supper and a tankard of beer. After such rehearsals it was John's habit, she had learned, to lock up, sparing the verger the bother of waiting for the session to finish. It was Hecate's good fortune that the choir gave a performance of popular choral music every Easter to raise funds for the upkeep of the organ.

Expecting the room to be empty, she gave a yelp on seeing a figure standing by the key rack. For one awful moment she thought Mr. Gould had broken his routine and was still at his post. It took her a few seconds to realize that what had surprised her so was in fact nothing more than a cassock set up on a hanger to air. She paused for a moment to allow her galloping heart to calm itself.

"Well then," she muttered, taking a deep breath and striding forward. She went around the cluttered desk and stood before the ranks of hooks and keys. Reaching into her satchel she took out one of the tins Mr. Sadiki had supplied her with. When she lifted the first key from where it hung—beneath a label reading NORTH AISLE STAIRCASE—her hand was trembling. She flipped open the lid of the tin, exposing the pale wax inside.

"Miss Cavendish!"

Hecate jumped at the sound of her name being called, wheeling around, dropping the key which clattered onto the tiled floor.

"Oh! Corporal Gregory . . ." She closed her eyes, offering a quick prayer of thanks to God or anyone else who was listening that it was only one of her phantom friends that had discovered her.

"What are you about, miss? Do you have need of assistance?" the young soldier asked.

"Thank you, Corporal. Now that you are here, I should be grateful if you could keep watch. Position yourself in the south aisle and return here to alert me if anyone threatens to enter the vestry."

"Right away!" he said, clicking his heels together and then leaving the room as he had come into it, through the door without troubling to open it.

Hecate picked up the fallen key and brought her mind to bear on her mission once again. As Mr. Sadiki had instructed, she laid the key flat onto the wax and pressed it firmly. When she lifted it there was a pleasingly deep and clear impression left behind. She turned over the key and repeated the process with the other side. Her hand still more than a little unsteady, she returned the key to its proper place. Next, she selected the one labeled MUNIMENTS ROOM. This impression she made with more confidence, the process a little quicker. Even so, the whole procedure felt tortuously slow. She heard the choir finish a piece of music and waited, not wanting to risk making a sound during such quietness. There was a short exchange between Dean Chalmers and John and then the choir launched into another piece. She moved on to the LIBRARY key, followed by the LIBRARY CHAIN one, which was lighter and shorter. She could not immediately see the other one she required. She ran her finger along the rows of hooks, surprised that the cabinet keys were not with the others for the library.

"Where are you?" she whispered. She came to the last key on the last row. Nothing. "Not here!" She put her hands on her hips and cast about the room, trying to imagine what separate, hidden place might reveal them. "Where would Reverend Thomas choose . . . ?" she asked, and was surprised when Mrs. Nugent appeared before her to answer her question.

"'Tis not hard to imagine, my dear," she said. "Better ask, what is more precious to the master of the library even than his beloved books?"

Hecate thought for a moment. "His stomach?"

The ghostly cleaner gave a girlish giggle. "Indeed!"

Hecate strode confidently to the biscuit tins. The third one, smaller than the others and set on a higher shelf, yielded a leather pouch. She shook the contents onto the desk. One medium-sized iron key and another tiny brass one. "Treasure!" she exclaimed, and then beamed at the cleaner. "And you are a treasure yourself, Mrs. Nugent!" she told her, before quickly taking the remaining tins of wax from her bag. To save time, she set them down on a small clear space upon the desk, side by side, lids open. The first key was heavy enough to press easily. She dropped it back into the pouch, which she set in the tin, and took hold of the little padlock key. It felt smooth and almost delicate between her fingers. She would have to take care not to damage it. Just as she lowered it toward the wax the singing came to an abrupt halt. There were some shouts, a minor commotion, and sounds of coughing. Then, footsteps, running.

Corporal Gregory bounded through the door, materializing in front of her. "Mistress, make haste! The dean!"

Panic rising within her, Hecate turned this way and that, searching for a place to hide. None of the cupboards was large enough, and there was no time to try the window. She could hear the dean's footfalls now. He would be at the door in seconds. She grabbed the biscuit tin and dived beneath the desk, crouching behind the stacks of parish magazines and service orders that half filled the space. There was so much dust she felt a sneeze threatening. The door opened. Too late she remembered the last tin. It sat upon the desk, in full view, lid open, the creamy wax gleaming under the lamplight. She could see the dean's boots and the hem of his maroon cassock and white surplice as he all but ran to the stove. As she listened, her heart pounding loud enough surely to alert him, she heard him lift the water jug and pour some into a beaker. Hecate held her breath, fighting back a burgeoning fit of sneezing. Dean Chalmers sprinted back through the door, not even bothering to close it behind him, bearing his remedy to the stricken clergyman in the choir stalls, whose coughs could still be made out.

As soon as she was certain the dean was out of sight, she emerged from her hiding place. She pressed the key into its waxy bed, forcing herself not to hasten so much as to blur the impression and so render it useless. At last it was done. She snapped shut the tin and dropped it into her bag. The chatter from the choir stalls seemed calmer now, the vicar evidently having recovered. There was some laughter and more talk, but, to Hecate's horror, they did not begin to sing again. On the contrary, she could hear sounds of shuffling and more footsteps. It seemed the dean had called for a break in the rehearsal and the vicars were stretching their legs or seeking refreshments. She knew they could discover her at any moment. If they reached the south aisle, her route out of the cathedral would be effectively cut off. She thrust the biscuit tin back onto its shelf and dashed through the door. At the junction with the aisle she paused. It was still clear. There was no option but to run as quickly as she could. She sprinted down the gloomy space. She could hear someone coming down the steps from the nave. Glancing back she saw John step into the aisle.

And he saw her.

She froze.

He stared at her, frowning, his mouth open as if he might call out her name.

She shook her head, putting a finger to her lips to silence him.

The dean, in conversation with another vicar, started to descend the steps. In seconds she would be in view. There was no escape. She stared back at John. She had to trust him.

*Please!* she mouthed.

John hesitated. Hecate thought to flee but knew she could not reach the corner of the aisle without being seen, and running would make any explanation she could think of even less plausible.

"Oh, Dean, I wanted to show you the sun damage to one of the tapestries, behind you, hanging from the lectern." John's quick thinking turned the dean on his heel, sending him back the other way.

Hecate seized the moment and ran.

By the time she reached *MT Sadiki Repairs*, she had slowed to a ragged trot. She took a moment to perch upon the shabby windowsill, catching her breath, giving herself time to recover. The narrow street was deeply dark, the shop being between the reach of two lampposts. From a nearby tavern came raucous laughter, the smell of beer borne on the breeze. She closed her eyes, reliving in her mind the moment when John had seen her. She had seen surprise in his expression, of course. Puzzlement. Followed by concern, for what could she be doing that required stealth? And then, unmistakably, hurt. For she had not chosen to confide in him. Even though they had spoken earlier that very day. Even though she had trusted him with her secret and he had not betrayed that trust. She was glad they would spend time together on Saturday. She had much to tell him. He had shown himself to be a caring, trustworthy friend. He deserved better from her.

She opened her eyes and dusted paint peelings off her skirt. Putting her hand to the window she attempted to peer inside but all was in darkness. As her eyes adjusted to the shadows, however, she detected a chink of light showing through the door to the room at the back of the building. She began to hammer upon the door.

"Mr. Sadiki!" she called through the letter box. She hammered some more, banging on the wooden frame, rattling the glass panes as she did so. "Hello, are you there?" she called. She paused, listening, but heard no movement within. She was about to start knocking again when she saw light moving inside and detected slow, shuffling footsteps. She moved back a little from the door and waited while bolts were drawn and a key turned.

Mr. Sadiki stood in the entrance, a small lamp raised. He had the disheveled appearance of one roused from slumber.

"Forgive me for disturbing you so late," Hecate said as she reached in her bag for the tins. "I wanted to get these to you as soon as they were done. I wasn't sure if the wax might soften over time . . . the impressions blur . . ."

"Come in off the street!" he snapped, standing aside so that she could step into the shop. As soon as she was over the threshold he shut and bolted the door.

Hecate attempted to put his mind at ease. "I am confident I was not seen," she said.

"Indeed." He indicated the counter. "Put them there."

She did as she was told, opening the lids so that he could inspect her work.

He set the lamp on the wooden surface and adjusted the position of his spectacles. For what seemed a worryingly long time, he examined the impressions. At last he clicked shut the lids, one after another. Wordlessly, he walked across the room, drew back the bolt, and held the door open.

Dismissed, Hecate moved to leave, pausing when she reached the doorway.

"When shall I collect the keys?" she asked. "There is some urgency . . ."

He stared at her before replying. In the low light he appeared less frail and elderly, his eyes having a hard focus to them. She sensed an inner strength perhaps born of a harsh life, and wondered at how this strange little man came to know and care about the goddess Hecate.

"Monday," he told her. "Come early."

"Thank you," she said, stepping onto the street. "I really am so very grateful. . . ." she continued, but she was talking to a closed door, her words going unheard beneath the sounds of bolt and lock. She adjusted the strap of her now empty satchel, looked up and down the narrow road to confirm to herself that she was not observed, and set off for home.

The following day, the crypt was empty when Hecate reached it at lunchtime, but she had only moments to wait before she heard the slow footfalls and soft whistling.

"Punctual as ever, Miss Cavendish. Apologies for my tardiness," said the inspector, raising his bowler hat to her.

"The tower bells have not yet chimed the hour. No apology needed." She noticed that he had a small lamp attached to his belt and could not help remarking upon it. "What a useful thing! Is that given to all police officers? I have not seen you wearing it before."

"Every constable is given one, for his duties at night, though I also find mine useful in dark places. They are cleverly designed so as to maintain their light safely even should the policeman find himself in the midst of a fray. I brought it with me as I intend walking the beat myself this evening. In pursuit of my inquiries, you understand."

"I should dearly like to obtain one. Might it be possible to purchase such a thing from the constabulary somehow?"

He raised his eyes at this strange request. "I shall look into it for you," he promised. "Now I am intrigued to hear your reasons for requesting a meeting in this place."

"It was good of you to agree to come here. I hoped that what you saw, what you heard from Joe Colwall the other day, well, that it might have caused you to consider my theories. Or at least, not to be quick to dismiss them."

He looked at her levelly and she knew she had read him right. Not a man to act impulsively, he was more likely to act after consideration of new clues.

"I will come straight to it, then, Inspector, for I know your time is valuable and has many demands upon it. I hope that you will see your investment of both time and faith in me will be well rewarded and, ultimately, help you in your work greatly."

"That does indeed sound a worthy reason to be challenging my arthritic bones in this chillsome place. Please, continue."

"These are the facts as I see them. There once existed a tribe of people in an area close to Egypt called the Essedenes. They were known as warriors. They were also known for devouring their dead parents." She paused to allow him to take this brief but shocking point in, before continuing. "It appears they not only practiced this singular form of cannibalism, they also were successful in the art of necromancy."

"The raising of the dead?"

"Quite so. This they succeeded in doing even though their own people died out centuries ago. It is thought, and in some parts recorded in ancient texts, that as they were on the point of extinction they sought immortality by the casting of necromantic spells, or curses, if you prefer, which would enable them to rise again at a point in the future."

"One point? This point?"

"Actually, no, we must believe several points, as they have done so already."

"And this you learned from manuscripts in the collection?"

Hecate hesitated. She did not wish to complicate her evidence further by admitting to gaining some of her information from cooperative ghosts. Not yet, at least. "To an extent, yes. I will return to that point later. If you could bear with me . . ."

He nodded slowly.

Hecate picked up the thread. "The souls that came out of this very crypt are called Resurgent Spirits. They have, as you saw for yourself, the strength to burst forth from their coffins and mausoleums, to render any remaining bones dust, to shatter wood, marble, and stone with equal ease, and to disappear into the night."

"I saw the result of something, indeed."

"Which is why I wanted us to meet here. I wanted you to think about what we saw, you and I, and how you led me to the inescapable conclusion that the tombs had not been broken into but broken out of. You remember the scale of the destruction?"

"I do," he said, agreeing to the memory at least if not yet granting she had the cause.

"Once free to roam the city, these risen souls seek out hosts, living people—the powerful and the wealthy—they will take possession of and so become Embodied Spirits. This, I believe, is what happened to Sir Richard, or would have, had he not been interrupted by Joe Colwall."

"Lowly Joe Colwall."

"Imagine the being's ire and frustration. It had set out to take over the life of a rich, well-respected gentleman and instead it stepped into the body of a penniless farm laborer whose sole purpose was the care of his increasingly poorly wife."

"A situation that drove the creature to commit murder."

"In part, for it is my understanding that the spirits are at their most violent and volatile when they are on the point of transition, or in the short time thereafter."

"And why now? Why wait so many centuries, to raise the dead in a place a thousand miles from where the people originally lived? This tribe you speak of . . ."

"The Essedenes."

". . . their mortal remains cannot have been here," he said, gesturing slowly but expansively at the shelves of caskets and the tombstones set into the floor.

"You are forgetting, this is not the first time they have risen. To my knowledge they have done so successfully at least once before—in an abbey in France—and escaped capture. They may have repeated this over centuries with varying degrees of success."

"But again, why now?"

She stopped pacing and looked at him, taking a deep breath. "The significance of the date remains obscure, though I understand it has to do with what might be considered auspicious numbers. I believe I am close to discovering other elements essential to the plans of the necromancers. And when I do, well, then I hope . . . I pray, that I will also discover the means to stop them."

"And until then, what would you have me do? You did not ask me here only to tell me your theory, I think. What is it you want of me, Miss Cavendish?"

"I will find out why the date is significant to these foul beings, and I will find their weakness, and then we, you and I, together, using our diverse skills and knowledge, we will be able to stop them, I am certain of it. But I need time. And in that time I fear others will suffer. We need to know the whereabouts of the other Resurgent Spirits. I know you remain to be convinced of the less tangible causes for the murders. I understand your reluctance to accept such theories. . . ."

"Both my training and my life's work have taught me to rely on—"

"Proof. Evidence. Yes. I know. Would you believe the evidence of your own eyes, Inspector?"

"They have not yet deceived me," he said cautiously, sensing he was being led somewhere.

"I have told you of my theories regarding spirits called from their resting places. Within these very walls, in fact," she said, pacing the crypt, running her fingers along the cold, ancient stones that surrounded them. "I have not mentioned that these are not the only spirits I have encountered here. There are others who inhabit the cathedral. Benign ones, you will be pleased to hear."

She paused to see if he would react but he remained silent. She went on.

"It is not an exaggeration to say some of them have become my friends. I see them daily. I converse with them. I tell you this at the risk that you will now consider me quite mad. That you will dismiss, in fact, all the carefully argued points with which I have presented you thus far. Why, do you suppose, I might take such a risk?"

"I am eager to hear the reason for it."

"It is because I can offer you proof. And if I can prove what I say about my ghostly friends, you may be more likely to accept what I have told you regarding the Resurgent Spirits."

"As ever, you have my attention, Miss Cavendish."

She smiled at him. "I am grateful for it. Would you be so good as to step into the middle of the room, toward the front, so that you are in an empty space. At least, it will appear that way to you."

He did as she asked, positioning himself away from any of the stone tombs and not close enough to reach out and touch the old altar.

"Will this do?"

"Perfectly. It will no doubt surprise you to hear that you are not, in fact, inhabiting that space alone. To your left stands Corporal Gregory. A fine young soldier who fought in the Napoleonic Wars. His uniform really is quite splendid. I am sorry you cannot see it. The good corporal stands always ready to protect the cathedral, and those of us within it. He has the ability to place himself as an invisible shield, so strong, so unyielding, that you would not be able to move through it. I offer you proof of this. All that is required of you is that you now try to take two strides to your left."

He looked in the direction she was pointing. He could see nothing. Calmly, he moved to walk toward the south wall, raising his foot. He progressed no more than half a step before meeting an invisible barrier. Astonished, he raised his hands and pressed against this solid air. He could neither move it nor pass through it. He turned to stare at Hecate.

"How is that for proof, Inspector? Of course, I did promise you something you could see, the evidence of your own eyes. If you would now look at the altar. Despite it not being used for services, the tradition of keeping two candles in place upon it remains unbroken. The candlesticks are of base metal only, but with a little silver plate. Mrs. Nugent was, for many years, charged with the task of keeping those candlesticks at their bright, shiny best. She retains the ability to move small objects, when she wishes, for she has never stopped her diligent work. She is going to remove the dust from one of them now. Do you see?"

As they both watched, the nearest candlestick rose up into the air. Hecate could see the phantom duster picking it up. The inspector could see only the thing moving, inexplicable, upward, turning over slowly, and then gently settling down in its rightful place once more.

Hecate waited, allowing the detective to recover from what she imagined would be no small shock. To his credit, he did not run screaming, nor stagger back, nor, indeed, display any of the emotions of fear or wonder he might be experiencing. He pushed his hat a little further back on his head. He moved forward and picked up the candlestick, examining it closely, before turning to face Hecate once more.

"Astonishing!" he declared.

"And convincing, I trust?"

"Oh yes, Miss Cavendish." He nodded slowly. "I can only applaud your tactics, for I cannot imagine any man living who would not be persuaded by such a demonstration."

"You will help me, then?"

"I will take all steps that are within the power of my office, I promise you that." A thought seemed to strike him. He unbuckled the small lamp from his belt and passed it to her. "I should like you to have this. If it will assist you in some way . . ."

"Thank you!" she said, taking it from him.

"When you have more information, any news in fact, regarding this matter, I should be grateful if you would bring it to me at once."

"You can rely upon it, Inspector," she beamed. "For we are a team now, are we not?"

He seemed to consider this for a moment, looking at her as if coming to terms with this curious situation. "Indeed it seems that we are, Miss Cavendish. Just so."

Without any further word, he tipped his bowler hat to her and took his leave, pausing to glance once more at the candlestick upon the altar before continuing on his way, whistling softly as he climbed the stairs from the crypt.

# 17

ON THE NIGHT OF THE BALL, HECATE'S THOUGHTS WERE NOT IN THE least taken up with the idea of dancing. Dressed in her ball gown, she knelt on the floor of her bedroom, surrounded by more books she had plundered from her father's collection. His career as an archeologist had furnished him with a splendid library of his own, which had been a source of joy for Hecate all her life. As a child, good behavior and successful endeavors were rewarded with access to the shelves and the invitation to choose a book. When she had turned eighteen her father's gift to her had been to have free access to the collection. Over the past three years, particularly since starting work at the cathedral, she had often had recourse to it. Edward Cavendish had a discerning and singular taste when it came to adding to his library. Given that most of his interest lay in the long ago and often the far away, the titles he selected were written either by or about arcane, obscure, and little known people. As Hecate leafed through the pages of one volume after another, she scoured the indices for mention of the Essedenes and their Resurgent Spirits. When the clock in the hallway downstairs struck the hour of nine, she had still not found a single entry. With a sigh she sat back on her heels. She had hoped for at least something, some scrap of information that would add to what little she already knew and help her to better explain it to anyone else. She needed Inspector Winter to listen to her. She also knew she wanted to share what she was convinced was happening with John. She was utterly certain he was not behind the summoning of the spirits. She was accustomed to sharing her work with the lost souls with him. Keeping such a secret did not sit well with her.

There came a knock upon her door and her father called out her name.

"Come in," she replied.

Her father was still a handsome man. Not as strong as in his youth but retaining a trim figure and a zest for life that went a long way to counteracting the effects of middle age and his somewhat threadbare evening suit.

"The carriage has arrived and your mother is eager for us to depart. I have been sent to fetch you. Ah," he said, taking in the scattered books.

"I'm afraid I'm not quite ready, Father."

"I see your mind has been elsewhere." He stepped into the room and shut the door behind him. "Have you found whatever it was you were searching for?"

Hecate got to her feet, picking up books and stacking them neatly as she did so. "Not yet. But I haven't given up."

"Of course not. Although, now might not be the time . . ."

"Is Mother fretting?"

"Your mother does not fret, she merely seeks to . . . enliven us, so that we are not lacking in our preparedness for these social events." He joined in the picking up of the books, helping her find places to put them. He noted the title of one of the older volumes. "My, my. I doubt this has left its place on the shelf for a number of years. We have searched the collection. I do not think you will find anything further regarding the Essedenes."

"No, I believe you are right," she said, taking the book gently from him and placing it on her dressing table.

Her father took a pipe from his pocket and put it between his teeth, narrowing his eyes at her. "I see a fatigue in my girl, and I prescribe a night off. No more dark thoughts. This evening is about simple enjoyment, the company of friends, music and dancing. It will do you good," he insisted.

She smoothed down her dress, which had become a little crumpled from her sitting on the floor. She doubted the creases would show among so many frills and layers. As with every ball she had ever attended, her mother had chosen a gown for her. It was of good quality, but would have been inexpensive, due to its being so out of fashion. The frothy pink flounces with ruches and swags of paler pink lace trim, contrasted with black velvet ribbons at her waist and neck, coupled with short white gloves and more lace in her hair looked, even to Hecate's undiscerning eye, horribly dated. The color—her mother's idea of youthful prettiness—worked to make her pale skin tone appear washed out, her freckles more pronounced, and her red hair quite shocking. She felt neither sophisticated nor attractive.

"Very well," she said. "For you."

"You look . . . charming!" he said, with convincing warmth.

Hecate caught a glimpse of herself in the full-length looking glass.

"I am to present myself to the world as a sugared almond. What manner of husband does Mother hope me to attract? No man whose opinion would be worth the hearing could have his head turned by such nonsense."

Edward took her hands in his and squeezed them.

"A good man will see beyond the disguise," he said.

"Are there such men?"

"Indeed. I believe you know one or two."

"If you mean John, he will not be at the ball. Clementine's mother does not consider anything less than a bishop worthy of including on her guest list. If you mean Phileas"—she smiled as she felt his grip on her hands tighten fractionally—"well, I doubt he would care what I wore, so long as I promised to love his blessed cows."

They were laughing at this when Beatrice entered the room.

"Must I employ a herding dog every time I wish to gather this family into a carriage?" she wanted to know.

This made her husband laugh all the louder. "Make it a cattle herder of some sort, my dear. That way you might usher Hecate straight into the arms of one of her suitors."

Hecate prodded his stomach playfully.

"You are simply eager to secure a lifetime's supply of roast beef!"

Her mother gave a tut of exasperation. "Hecate, where is your stole? Your fan? Your purse? You could at least try . . ."

"I am sorry, Mother," she said, snatching up the various items she was required to take with her. "There, I'm ready now."

"Off we go!" Her father pocketed the unlit pipe and offered both women an arm. Together they went downstairs, swept up an enthusiastic Charlie, and made their way outside.

Clementine had insisted on sending her closed carriage to collect the

Cavendishes and it was causing quite a stir in the street. Residents of Hafod Road were well to do, but they were not sufficiently wealthy to ignore the glamor of such a conveyance, particularly with a fine pair of grays pulling it, and when the driver and footman in attendance were dressed in the Twyford-Harris livery. A small crowd had gathered to watch the family in their finery. Hecate felt even more uncomfortable under such scrutiny. Charlie was grinning from ear to ear. Her father gave a somewhat regal wave as they set off.

"Edward!" his wife hissed at him.

"Fear not, my dear. I am merely playing to the gallery."

Hecate recalled John's comment during his visit to the house. "John believes you could have a career on the stage, Father," she told him.

"Capital idea! What say you, Beatrice?"

"I say you should not encourage Hecate in such silliness. And I am surprised at Reverend Forsyth."

"Really, Mother? I thought he could do no wrong in your eyes."

Edward laughed. "Ah, but tonight, your mother has her sights set on more exotic prey!"

Beatrice frowned, not in the least enjoying the joke at her expense. "I am well aware you believe I think of nothing else but finding a suitable husband for Hecate. I assure you I have other matters to occupy my time, not least Charlie's health and how we are to meet Dr. Francis's ever increasing fees." When her family looked suitably chastened she went on, her tone deliberately lighter. "However, this is to be quite the occasion, by all accounts. My dearest wish for this evening is to see my daughter enjoying herself among bright company, looking delightful. Which she does." She treated Hecate to a smile that was all the more precious for its rarity.

The horses were fit and fast so that they sped through the town, across the stone bridge that spanned the river to the south, and turned east. So effective was the suspension of the carriage that even along the rutted, muddy road, the passengers were not unduly jostled or jolted. The sky was cloudless and the moon bright. Hecate watched the nocturnal scene that flowed past the window, noting how pretty the countryside looked bathed in a pearly light with deep moon-shadows fringing the hedges and trees. Despite her mother's hopes, she did not expect to enjoy the ball. Ordinarily she would have at least looked forward to the fun of Clemmie's company, and been pleased to see Charlie out and about. On this occasion her mind was so filled with more important things she would find it particularly tiresome to have to make polite conversation and dance with men in whom she had no interest.

As if reading her thoughts, her brother asked, "Will you give the first dance to Phileas? Say you will, Hecate. You know it would please him."

"I will dance with him if he asks me, Charlie, but not more than twice. He has the heaviest tread of any man I have ever waltzed with. I don't think my feet would withstand a polka."

Edward put in, "But he adds such zest to a party, do you not think so?"

"Zest?" Beatrice looked baffled. "Of what use is that?"

Edward shrugged. "None whatsoever, which is what makes it so appealing."

Twenty minutes later they turned onto the smoother going of the driveway that curved across oak-dotted parkland to bring them at last to Holme Lacy House. As Mrs. Cavendish was given to reminding everyone, the Twyford-Harris family home—mainly constructed in the seventeenth century but with earlier origins and later additions—was the largest manor house in the county. Its E-shaped design and Georgian improvements of portico and columns at the entrance gave it an imposing scale and symmetry that could not fail to impress. With a trail of slowly moving coach lamps leading to it, tall lights placed among the topiary and hedges of the gardens, and every one of its myriad windows lit up, the great house appeared as a burst of starlight in the dark landscape, a brilliant, glowing point of activity and celebration. As their carriage drew level with the flight of stone steps to the entrance, Hecate thought about the many young women like herself who had arrived there for a ball through the preceding centuries. Each of them both excited and nervous, their expectations and hopes high. She glanced at her brother. Without the weight of their mother's expectations upon him, he was free to enjoy the spectacle and fun of the event. She was glad to see him already cheered by it. For his sake, for her mother's, and for Clemmie's, she would do her best to be an appreciative guest.

A footman appeared on silent feet to open the door. Edward Cavendish exited the carriage first, turning to help his wife down the step which had already been positioned for her. Hecate smiled at Charlie, who jumped out, turning to offer her his hand, grinning at the absurd formality but enjoying the fact that his sister had allowed him to play the part of a gentleman. Together they joined a stream of new arrivals, ladies with fans in hands, skirts hitched up to climb the steps, each on the arm of a gentleman, all eager to escape the chill of the night and join the revelry. Music drifted out through the open windows of the ballroom.

The hall of the house was every bit as impressive as the exterior, with a floor of Italian marble, a grand staircase, artfully positioned ferns on pedestals, glorious flower displays upon tables which were themselves objects of great beauty, and richly colored paintings in gilded frames. Hecate remembered what Clemmie had told her about not wanting to inhabit a drafty stately home and wondered how much more grandeur and wealth there could be.

"There you are!"

Hecate turned at the unmistakably gleeful sound of her friend's voice, to see a slender vision in pale blue muslin hurrying toward her. Everything about Clemmie's gown was chic and stylish and flattering, and showed off the beautiful young woman to her very best advantage. Her elegant long white gloves, sleek chignon, and tasteful sapphire earrings completed a look that was as sophisticated as it was charming. Hecate felt even more awkward and dowdy than she had earlier, and thought that if she had not loved her friend so much she might have hated her a little at that moment. The two greeted each other warmly and slipped away from the throng and into the morning room. Ordinarily, this was a place Lady Twyford-Harris might entertain guests or work on her watercolors, taking advantage of the good light. On this occasion, however, the room had been pressed into service for all ladies attending the ball. It was at their disposal, so that they might remove their stoles and capes, apply a little more rouge or powder, or avail themselves of the assistance of one of the lady's maids on hand to repair hairstyles that had suffered on the outward journey. It was also, naturally, a place to exchange the latest news and gossip. Such was the chatter of the women and girls present that the music from the nearby ballroom was all but drowned out.

Clemmie took Hecate's arm and led her to a corner, allowing a maid to take her stole as she did so.

"I am so pleased to see you," she said. "I swear, Mama's guest list gets duller by the year. I have pointed out that a spring ball, being out of the season, should include as many new and interesting people as possible. Instead, determined to avoid anyone of the middling sort who might actually be good

company, she consults *Debrett's Peerage* and allows the men to compete for
Bore of the Ball."

"They can't all be that bad."

"Says the girl who would rather be at home with her nose in a book. Anyway, at least Phileas is here. He's been asking for you. I told him you were deliberately making him wait, so that you could make a grand entrance."

"Clemmie!"

"The poor man is quite lovesick, you know."

"Nonsense."

"It's true, I tell you! He has been badgered into dancing three waltzes and
a polka but you could tell every minute of it pained him."

"I expect it pained his poor dance partners, too."

Clemmie laughed. "One of them was Nettie Watson—her feet are even
bigger than his!"

Giggling, the two made their way to the entrance of the ballroom. Being a "ball that wasn't a ball" as Lady Twyford-Harris kept insisting, arrivals
were not announced. This rare modicum of informality allowed the friends
to slip into the crowded room almost unnoticed. Even a reluctant socialite
such as Hecate could not fail to be delighted by the loveliness of the venue.
The ballroom was rectangular, with all four walls paneled in rich, glowing
oak. The ceiling was a magnificent example of Georgian plasterwork, intricately detailed, icing-sugar white, and touched with gilt here and there. There
were two crystal chandeliers illuminated by over a hundred candles between
them. While the house itself might have gaslighting, Lady Twyford-Harris
would not permit any such vulgar, blurry, fume-laden lights in her precious
ballroom. In point of fact, the chandeliers were not the most striking feature
of the place. This was, without doubt, the great glass dome in the center of
the roof. The candlelight from beneath it, and the starlight from above, reflected off its many angled panes, making it a spectacular, lofty centerpiece
to the room. The orchestra comprised a piano, two violins, a trumpet, and a
viola. They were playing an energetic mazurka.

Clemmie squeezed Hecate's arm and spoke to her behind the cover of her
opened fan.

"Look if you dare! Phileas is thundering up and down with little Alice
Hopkins!"

They made an unlikely couple: the gentleman farmer, broad shouldered, his shock of unruly hair made madder by the dance, towering over the diminutive young woman whose own feet scarcely seemed to touch the polished wood floor.

"She looks so fragile next to him!"

"Her mother's face is a picture." Clemmie nodded toward the portly woman standing to the left of the musicians.

"I think she might be questioning the wisdom of throwing her daughter at Phileas. No amount of apple orchards can be worth having your feet trampled," said Hecate.

When the music came to a halt Phileas led his somewhat breathless dance partner back to her place beside her mother. Both appeared relieved to be able to fall upon propriety which suggested two dances in a row with the same person were poor form. As he bowed and backed away, he caught sight of Hecate. At once, he was transformed by a broad smile. One that she herself found impossible not to respond to as he approached.

"Good evening," she said, giving him her hand to kiss. "You seem to be having a fine time."

"I do my best to give that appearance out of politeness to my hosts," he assured her, taking two glasses of champagne from a passing footman and offering them to the young women. "I have merely been availing myself of the opportunity to hone my dancing skills while awaiting your arrival."

Clemmie laughed. "After all, Phileas, you are renowned for your dancing."

"Naturally I am." He smiled, enjoying the joke at his own expense. "For I am a sportsman, and is not dancing a sport?"

"Most certainly it is not!" Hecate pretended to chide him, sipping her iced wine.

"Not, you say?" He twirled the end of his mustache thoughtfully. "And yet we are to engage with the music and steps with the same gusto and enthusiasm one might employ for a day's stalking or hunting."

"Really," she tutted. "You surely cannot confess to seeing the ladies here as prey?"

"The ladies?" He gave one of his bellows of laughter, startling an elderly guest into dropping her lorgnettes. "Pah! I have never felt more like a hounded rabbit than when in the clutches of Nettie Watson!"

The musicians began to play a waltz. Phileas bowed in front of Hecate with overplayed formality.

"Miss Cavendish, will you do me the honor of giving me this dance?"

She responded with an equally fancy curtsey, earning a hard stare from her mother and a grin from her father. As she was led to the floor she noticed Charlie with two boys his age stealthily helping themselves to champagne. Phileas slipped his arm around her waist and the two fell into step to the gentle rhythm of the music. While not an elegant dancer, he was able to deftly steer her around the crowded dance floor, partly because others made a point of getting out of his way, but also because of his genuine concern for his partner. He smiled at her.

"You look ravishing."

"No, I do not."

"No? Enchanting, perhaps?"

"I very much doubt it."

"Dash it all, Hecate, I'm trying to pay you a compliment. You might at least play the game."

"It's good of you to bother, but I am unable to take myself seriously while dressed as the Sugar Plum Fairy."

He laughed loudly and spun her in an unexpected twirl. When she recovered from it she was laughing, too. He saw that she was enjoying herself and held her just a fraction tighter. Hecate surprised herself by finding she liked his strong arms about her. She felt safe, and only then realized that she had not done so for some time. For all her concern about the Essedenes, she had, until that point, convinced herself that she feared the wider, more public consequences of what they were doing. Now, when she allowed herself to feel protected, she had to admit to herself that she knew she was in danger. She was at the center of events, there was no denying it. The closer she came to discovering who had summoned the spirits, the more of a threat she presented to their plans, the greater peril she put herself in.

As they neared the far end of the ballroom, she became aware of a break in the flow of the dancers. When she turned again she saw that two couples had stopped and the gentlemen were standing toe to toe, apparently engaged in an altercation.

Phileas steered her away. "The earl's friend is in a black mood," he observed.

Hecate corrected him. "That is his cousin, Viscount Eckley."

"You know him?" he asked.

"I met him for the first time only a few days ago. He seemed a mild-mannered sort."

He gave a harrumph. "Anything but mild now, I'd say. Must be in his cups."

As they watched, the men were persuaded to leave off arguing. The viscount marched from the dance floor, leaving his partner to awkwardly make her way back to her seat unaccompanied.

The evening continued in the way that balls so often do. Amid the merriment and drinking, some hearts were broken and others were mended. Matrons and spinsters made wistful spectators of both the actual and the metaphorical dancing that was necessary for the furtherance of alliances and betrothals. Determined mothers worked fans at their throats, not for one moment taking keen eyes off their daughters and their prospects. The older menfolk engaged in gossip and ribaldry out of earshot of their wives. The men as yet unmarried vied for the attention of the prettiest or the wealthiest young women, their priority dependent on their own status and manner of means. A girl who was both beautiful and rich would begin the evening enjoying being the most sought-after person at the ball, and end it weary of clumsy dancers, fortune hunters, and pleasant men whom she felt bad about despising for their lack of fire.

After two hours, the ballroom had become noticeably hot, and the scent worn by the ladies, the cologne favored by the gentlemen, and the general warmth of so many people built to a strength of smell quite challenging. Hecate, dancing with Phileas for the third time despite her intentions, could not be certain which she was more in need of: fresh air or food. It would soon be time for supper to be served. She surprised herself then by finding herself idly wondering what sort of dancer John was. He might not attend private balls, but surely he would be invited to country dances. Just for a moment she imagined being held close by him. Her mind was a confusion of unnecessary musings.

Phileas noticed a subtle alteration in her demeanor.

"You look vexed, Hecate. Are you tired?"

She was tired, but not from the physical activity of the evening. She was tired of how complicated being an unmarried woman seemed to her at that

moment. There were so many more important things for her to concern herself with, and yet her mind was forever being bothered by thoughts about
the men of her acquaintance. Perhaps the answer was, after all, to marry
Phileas, please her father, and have done with it. Or marry John, content
her mother, and secure her continued place in the cathedral. Such pragmatic,
cold reasoning depressed her spirits. She was glad when the musicians ceased
playing and an announcement was made declaring supper to be available in
the adjoining dining room across the hall.

Lady Twyford-Harris knew well the needs of her guests. Not for them some
trifling canapés or morsels of rarefied foods. Where a lesser hostess—perhaps
one not so confident in her place in the world—might have tried to impress
with smoked fishes and seafood and complicated ices, Clementine's mother
provided proper sustenance. There were plates of roast potatoes, floury bread
rolls, pickled eggs, and stuffed portobello mushrooms. Dishes of curried rice
and honeyed vegetables competed for space on the laden tables, at the center of each was placed three great roasts—a marmalade ham, a juicy joint of
beef, and a goose. To save guests the bother of waiting to be served or having
to struggle with knife and fork, these meats had been carved in advance and
tied together with ribbons in a simulacrum of their natural shapes. Several
hours of dancing or standing, coupled with an application to drinking, rendered the ball goers in dire need of good, hearty food, and that was exactly
what was on offer. Soon the hungry guests were fair swarming around the
tables, piling their plates high.

Hecate and Phileas found Clemmie among the feasting throng.

"Honestly, Hecate, it's as if no one has been fed for a week, the way they
pile in."

Phileas rubbed his stomach. "You surely would not begrudge a man a decent plate of food after a hard evening of dancing."

"You are so gallant," Hecate told him, then said to her friend, "You can't
blame them. Your mother provides such good food."

"Even so, they are hardly the starving masses. I mean, look at the state of
Eric Francis."

"He is quite large," she agreed.

"He makes Phileas look slender, and yet I swear this is the second time he
has filled his plate."

But Hecate's attention was elsewhere. She had the sensation she was being watched and turning saw that the earl of Brockhampton's cousin was quite blatantly staring at her. She tried a smile and a nod of greeting. He continued to stare and she shifted uncomfortably beneath his unwavering gaze.

"Goodness." Clemmie had noticed his strange behavior. "Whatever is the matter with that man this evening? You'd think Lord Brocket would keep a tighter rein on his relations."

Phileas, his eyes still on the food, replied, "He's a busy man. Spends a lot of time in Parliament. Perhaps the weight of his responsibilities is taking its toll. Can't be bothered to police minor members of his family when he should be enjoying himself."

Clemmie shook her head. "Whatever his troubles, he has no business letting the viscount regard Hecate in such a way. He looks as if he might eat her!"

Phileas turned then to see what she meant and was alarmed by what he saw.

"This is too much. Excuse me, ladies, I shall have a word in his ear," he said.

"No, please don't." Hecate reached out to stop him but he was already on his way.

He had not gone more than two strides when Lady Brocket appeared at her husband's side. She spoke softly to him, placing a hand on his arm as if encouraging him to intervene. When he did not respond she stepped over to Viscount Eckley and appealed directly to him. To Hecate's horror, the man shrugged her off with such force that she stumbled backward, only saved from falling to the ground by the swift actions of a nearby footman.

"Eckley!" Phileas was not the only one to admonish him. "What the devil are you doing, man?"

The viscount barged past Phileas and the other men who had stepped in to berate him, and strode straight toward Hecate. She felt held tight to the spot where she stood, even though she knew herself to be in harm's way. It seemed to her that everything happened with supernatural swiftness. There was Phileas, calling after Lord Brocket's cousin. There were the other guests, trying to grab hold of him. There was Clemmie clutching at her friend. The man striding toward her appeared oblivious to the chaos he was causing. Hecate saw the wildness in his eyes, and the blood in her veins ran cold. Just as it seemed he would lay hands on her in his terrible rage, Phileas ran through the crowd and launched himself in the manner of a flying rugby tackle. He brought Viscount Eckley crashing down, the pair landing in the middle of one of the long tables of food. Amid shrieks and cries of shock from all quarters, above the sound of splintering wood, shattering glass, and breaking china, it was still possible to make out roars of protest. He thrashed and kicked as three other men fought to restrain him. At last they had him on his feet and, grasping his arms tight, propelled him from the room. As he left he turned to take one more look at Hecate. As did the earl.

Clemmie was at her side again. "Oh, Hecate! That dreadful man . . . to come at you in such a way . . . It is unthinkable! Such behavior. Dearest, are you hurt?"

"No," Hecate murmured, the thudding of her pulse against her eardrums still ragged.

"Are you certain? Oh, Hecate, what a thing to happen! He was about to assault you, we all saw it."

"I promise you, I am unharmed," she said, taking her friend's hands in hers. She smiled in what she hoped was a reassuring way. She had not, it was true, been injured, as the viscount had been stopped before he could reach her. It was not the actual thwarted attack that had left her so shaken. What had struck her to her very soul was the look he had given her as he was marched from the room, that dreadful, cold, deliberate seeking out of her. Beyond even this, though less overt, what she found more disturbing was Lord Brocket's small, chilling smile.

# 18

BEATRICE WAS STILL PROTESTING AS SHE took her seat in the carriage for the journey home. "It is not to be borne. Edward, have you no opinion on the matter?"

Edward sat opposite his wife. "I am content to listen to yours," he told her.

Charlie was bright-eyed from the drama. "Did you see the way Phileas brought him to the ground? The viscount was no match for him!"

"Charles, be quiet. Your sister being attacked is not entertainment."

"I am unhurt, Mother," Hecate assured her. "Charlie is right; Phileas stopped him."

"A hero!" her brother insisted, earning a stern look from his mother.

Edward leaned back in his seat as the carriage turned down the driveway and the horses picked up speed. "The man was clearly the worse for drink. I will speak with Brocket."

"Who should have been equal to the task of keeping his cousin in check," said Beatrice, pulling her wrap more tightly around her shoulders, a shiver running through her body as she did so. "There was something deeply unsettling about that man's manner."

For once, Hecate was in agreement with her mother. She had encountered drunks at parties and balls before, though none had launched quite such a personal attack on her. It was not this that had shaken her, however. It was how he had regarded her as he was led away. For she recalled now, where she had seen that sly grin before. It was the exact same expression she had seen on the face of the man who had once been Joe Colwall. It was the triumphant smile of an Embodied Spirit.

By the time they reached Hafod Road, all the occupants of the carriage were weary. The lateness of the hour, the exertions of dancing and chatting, together with the shock of what had happened, had combined to dampen their spirits and bring on fatigue. It was a quiet party, then, that returned home, handing their hats and coats to Stella. The maid had been paid to stay on to help her mistress, and ordinarily would have enjoyed listening to her recount details of a ball. On this occasion, she took in the somber state of the family and knew better than to start asking questions. There was, in addition, something she had to tell them.

"Mr. Cavendish, a letter has arrived," she said, indicating the silver platter on the hall stand.

"At this hour?" Edward picked up the folded paper and turned it over. "The earl's seal," he muttered.

The others crowded around him, waiting. He unfolded the letter and read its contents aloud.

"'*My dear Cavendish, I am at a loss to sufficiently express my regret at the unacceptable way in which my cousin deported himself this evening. Kindly pass on my sincerest apologies to your daughter. I am only glad that no harm came to her, though that is not, for one moment, to lessen the shock that she must have felt. The viscount is a poor drinker and had overindulged. I make no excuses for him, but assure you that I will remonstrate with him in the strongest terms.*'"

"Remonstrate!" Beatrice snorted. "The man should be sent home. We do not need his sort in our society."

Edward continued. "'*By way of an apology, and to assure you of the continuing high regard in which I hold your family, would you all do me the honor of visiting here at Brockhampton for tea, on an afternoon of your choosing? Ever your respectful friend . . .*' etcetera, etcetera." He looked up from the letter. "Well, it is an apology at least."

"Tea at Brockhampton!" Charlie was delighted. "May we go?"

"Certainly you may not. Nor may your sister."

"But, Mother . . ."

Edward held up his hand. "I will go next week. Speak to the man myself.

It need not be a family occasion. He is an acquaintance of long standing and we will encounter one another at chamber of commerce meetings and so forth. Better to clear the air." He folded the letter and put it in his pocket, steering Charlie toward the stairs. "Now, to bed."

Hecate followed on, exchanging glances with her father. She knew better than to challenge her mother on the matter at that moment, but she was determined, no matter what her mother's opinion, that she would be accompanying her father to Brockhampton. She followed up the staircase, reaching out for her father's hand before he turned for his room.

"Did you see, Father? Did you see what the viscount truly is?" she whispered.

"I saw he was crazed."

"In the same way Joe Colwall is. I've seen it. I know an Embodied Spirit when I see one. I must talk with you."

He was on the point of following her toward her room when Beatrice paused at the threshold of their bedroom.

"Edward? Please come to bed. I am very tired and have no wish to be disturbed later."

He squeezed Hecate's hand.

"Tomorrow," he said.

Reluctantly, Hecate nodded. "Very well. As soon as I return from my picnic with John. But, Father, promise me you will permit me to go with you to Brockhampton."

"I hardly think it necessary, nor advisable."

"You will, once we have spoken. Please, Papa."

He hesitated and then, seeing the earnest look on his daughter's face, said, "Tomorrow, you can convince me."

"Tomorrow," Hecate confirmed, reaching up and kissing him quickly before returning to her room. Though it was very late she knew she would not sleep easily. She had notes to write and plans to make.


At ten o'clock, John arrived in the cathedral gig. From her bedroom window, Hecate saw him draw up. She grabbed her hat and ran down the stairs, not wishing to involve her family in lengthy exchanges of pleasantries. Fortunately, they were all still in their rooms, none of them having got to their beds much before two, the events of the ball no doubt keeping them awake for sometime after. She trotted out through the front door. John smiled at her and reached out a hand to help her up onto the seat beside him.

"A lovely day for our picnic," he said, smiling. "Of course I arranged it so."

"I would expect nothing less from you, knowing you have such a connection with the Almighty," she teased, having earlier decided she would keep the mood of the outing light. The information she was planning to share with him was dark enough, and she did not want him frightened for her safety. It was sufficient to have her mother fussing over her. She needed John as an ally, not a protector. And besides, despite the shock of what had happened at the ball, she was excited. If her theory was correct, she knew where to find an Embodied Spirit. At last she had the chance to confront one, to challenge him, if necessary. She was not so foolish to think that she could do such a thing without help. John was a part of that. So was her father. She glanced back at the house. As soon as she returned she would speak to him about the viscount. "Let us be on our way. I have no wish to wake Mother."

He picked up the reins and the skittish horse lunged forward, tipping Hecate back in her seat and forcing her to hang on to her hat. As Bucephalus trotted along the Mordiford road and away from the city, she felt her fatigue of the night before begin to lift. It was refreshing to have the cool air of the morning in her face, the pretty countryside around her, and John's reassuring presence.

He adjusted his broad-brimmed black hat the better to shade his eyes from the morning sun, and inquired about the ball.

"Was it, after all, an enjoyable evening?" he asked, unaware of the drama that had taken place, referring rather to Hecate's own professed dislike of such events.

"For the most part it was a ball like any other. There was dancing. Clementine looked exquisite. People enjoyed Lady Twyford-Harris's excellent wine and food. But . . ."

"But? Do I sense a scandal waiting to be told?"

"Not quite, but certainly the occasion could not be called dull," she replied. "Lord Brocket's cousin caused a scene."

"Oh? I do not know the man. A scene, you say. A little too much champagne, perhaps?"

Hecate paused before giving her answer.

John glanced at her, sensing her hesitation.

"There was more to it than that," she said. "But to explain now would be to tell the story backward. There is a great deal I have to share with you, John. Things of importance . . ."

"And these have to do with the lost souls you spoke of?"

"Yes and no. Let us wait until we have reached our picnic spot. I have forgone my breakfast to be out with you. . . ."

"A true test of friendship."

"Is it not?" She smiled at him. "I will be far more eloquent when I have eaten something." She turned and lifted the lid of the picnic hamper that was secured to the back of the gig. "Goodness! Did you leave anything in the kitchen for your fellow vicars?"

"One or two of them could feel the benefit of missing a meal," he said with a shrug.

They continued in comfortable silence. After another half mile or so, John slowed the horse to a walk and steered off the path and across an opening between the trees. He found a shady spot, jumped down, and tied the horse to a young oak.

Hecate sprang down from her seat without waiting to be helped.

"What a charming place," she said. "Reverend Forsyth, if I did not know you better, I might think this is where you regularly bring young women in order to impress them." She turned about, waving an arm to indicate the loveliness of the glade. There was just enough of a space between the trees to allow sunlight to reach the ground where soft grass grew, free of brambles. On three sides the woodland deepened. In front of them, the opening expanded, giving the view of a low hedgerow and beyond it gently sloping meadows. Sheep grazed, their lambs gambolling and playing in little gangs, running up banks or leaping off a fallen tree. A robin sang from a nearby bough. "Everything is . . . perfection," she said.

"You don't think the lambs too much?"

"They are a distraction. I might prefer watching them to talking with you."

John lifted down the hamper. "Then I shall win you back with vicarage pie and ginger beer."

She helped him spread out the tartan rug and they sat down. Hecate felt at ease with him, despite their young acquaintance. For her, this was of more importance than he could know. More than his blue eyes or nimble wit. To be herself in another's company, the absence of pretense or effort, was no small thing. He set the food down and she helped herself to a plate and a slice of the pie. It was a mix of pressed cold meats beneath a topping of pasty, and was named after country vicars who had little money to spare. The pie would have been made of leftovers from a more lavish roast earlier in the week, perhaps, or donations from parishioners.

"This is very good," she said, taking another bite while he pulled the rubber stopper from the ginger beer and poured two cups.

"The vicars choral used to have their own cook, but economies had to be made. When she retired she was not replaced. Fortunately, two of our number took to the tasks of baking and preparing meals splendidly. They manage very well with the assistance of a scullery maid, and our fare has improved considerably. The ginger beer is particularly sweet," he said, passing some to her.

She drank, nodding, feeling further revived. They ate on in silence until she had cleared her plate and licked her fingers clean.

John smiled at her.

She caught the look. "You think me unladylike?"

"I think you . . . singular."

Hecate removed her hat, dropping it onto the grass, and leaned back on her elbows.

"Are you ready to tell me now?" he asked.

"Are you ready to listen?"

"To you? Always."

She sat up again, realizing the subject matter was too serious to be discussed while lolling.

And so she told him. She told him of how the Essedenes had looked at her from the map and how terrifying that moment of connection had been. She told him of how she, Brother Michael, and her father had learned all they could about the fearsome tribe and their necromantic practices. She explained how what she had learned in the British Library had given her and her father reason to suppose things would only get worse if they did not act. She told him how she believed Joe Colwall was now host to a Resurgent Spirit.

John listened attentively, interrupting only to ask for more detail or to clarify a point. When she came to telling him about the viscount at the ball he took off his hat and ran his hand through his hair.

"So you see," she went on, aware that she was speaking a little too brightly, knowing she was unsure how he would respond, "I am of the opinion that Viscount Eckley is now an Embodied Spirit, and that his cousin knows this."

"But, Hecate, the more I hear of this the more I fear for your safety."

"I am not facing this alone, John. I have my father, my friends at the cathedral . . ."

"Your ghostly friends?"

"Quite so. And, I very much hope, I have you."

"Yes, yes. Of course you do. Of course. And yet I do not see how I might help. Indeed how any of us might stop these dreadful . . . spirits."

"My father brought me up to be a woman of action. To strive for things. To be ambitious, much to my mother's displeasure. For any chance of success, he impressed upon me, one must be prepared. He told me of times during his archeological expeditions when it was this preparedness, this planning, that had saved his enterprise, and on occasion his life. I have no intention of tackling these risen spirits unless I believe I can defeat them. To that end I must equip myself with what I need."

"Which is?"

"Knowledge. Regarding their habits, their aims, their weaknesses."

"What weaknesses might they have?"

"According to Father Ignatius's letters, they have a low tolerance of alcohol. . . ."

"Which would explain the viscount's unwise behavior. Surely he cannot have wished to draw such attention to himself."

"One would think not. It seems, in addition, animals are uneasy near them, which may at least give us an indication of their presence. Most importantly, the monks had some success using the services of an exorcist."

"Ah." He smiled at her. "There I am most definitely your man!"

"Remember I said 'some' success." She let him think about this and then added, "Father Ignatius wrote that one of the priests who had tried to perform the rites was himself lost to the Essedenes' spirits. Our endeavors will not be without risk."

His expression was serious. He reached across the rug and placed his hand over hers.

"What manner of priest would I be to shy away from those risks? What manner of friend would I be to think for one moment of letting you face them without me?"

He paused and she resisted the urge to speak, for she sensed he had something important to say.

"In my years as the appointed exorcist for the cathedral I have been called upon to perform my duties infrequently, but each occasion has been memorable for its own details. Its own heartbreak. Its own dangers. Those who seek help for one they believe to be possessed do so only after a deal of reluctance to accept such a thing might be true of someone they know, perhaps someone they love. I recall one such case. I was newly arrived in the city and had been at my post a little under a year. This was not, however, the first distressed family who had requested I attend their home, so that I was not unduly concerned. I had been instructed in the rites of exorcism. I had assisted the outgoing incumbent before his departure and performed two services on my own. All had gone according to expectations and brought some comfort and good outcomes. The family who lived south of the river, however, were another matter entirely. They had requested my services and a date had been fixed upon for the following week, but their grandmother's condition worsened quickly, so that they implored me to visit them on the Sunday night after Evensong. I remember it was raining heavily, and I arrived at their cottage dripping rainwater from my hat. At the door, the man of the house, Mr. Fisher, did not so much as comment on my state but took me by the arm straightaway and hurried me through to the parlor at the back of the house. This was the room of his mother, Mrs. Doris Fisher, a woman in her later years, frail and bent. I did not find her as one might expect, folded in a chair, nor lain upon the brass bed, snug beneath the patchwork coverlets. Instead I found her crouched in a dark corner, her arms flung above her head as if warding off blows. She was agitated and muttered continually, though I understood nothing of what she said. Her son had scarcely had time to apprise me of her condition when she leaped forth. He cried out a warning to me, but I was caught off guard and the poor creature, her face contorted with demonic fury, knocked me off my feet. We fell to the ground, whereupon she set about attempting to bite me, Mr. Fisher all the while doing his utmost to pull her away."

"How shocking! You must have been at a loss, for you could not defend yourself for fear of hurting the old woman," Hecate said.

"Precisely. I mustered my thoughts, bringing my training to mind, holding my crucifix before me as I spoke aloud the words of the exorcism, for there was no doubt Mrs. Fisher was host to a foul presence."

"Did your words quell the creature?"

"They inflamed its fury, so that it raged and ranted, twisting this way and that with such energy I feared it would prove too much for the old woman's brittle bones. I had no choice but to continue. There came a moment when I was able to pull from my pocket a bottle of holy water and fling the contents forward. The demon spirit hissed and writhed but could not remain where it was. In the next second, it left the poor grandmother's body, revealing itself to be a gray whirlwind. It flew to the open window and out, leaving a rancid stench in its wake."

"You had defeated it!"

"I had driven it from its temporary home."

"And the old woman? Did she survive the ordeal?"

He could not look at her then. Instead he held her hand tightly, casting his gaze down upon it as he continued.

"She was greatly fatigued, but unhurt. I helped her son put her to bed and then took my leave, assuring him I would visit the following day. I recall how grateful he was for my assistance."

"Understandably so," Hecate said.

"The rain had stopped. I walked from the cottage shaken but satisfied that I had been successful. There was almost, I am ashamed to own it, a spring in my step. Alas, my pride was ill-deserved. I had not gone thirty paces when I heard, coming from the house I had just left, the most terrible screams and cries. I ran back. Up the path, through the unlocked front door, into the parlor . . . what I saw there, the sight that met me, will stay with me forever. It seemed the demonic spirit had not fled, but had merely hidden, awaiting its moment. As I left the house it swooped upon that hapless family, this time taking possession of Mr. Fisher. In a matter of seconds it had claimed his mind and control of his body, compelling him to strangle his own mother, squeezing the last breath from her. The cries I had heard were from him, as he came to his senses. Unable to bear what he had done, he had retrieved his shotgun from its place above the mantel. Before I could stop him he had put an end to his own life."

"Oh, John . . ."

He looked at her then. "I tell you this not to frighten you, Hecate, but as an illustration. . . . I know the dangers. I will not leave you to face them alone. I give you my word."

Hecate felt a surge of affection for him. She was aware she was going against her father's wishes in sharing so much of what she knew with John, but he did not know the man as she did. He was not there, looking into John's eyes at that moment, seeing their sincerity. She trusted him.

"I am fortunate indeed to have you as an ally," she told him. Out of deference to her father she omitted to tell him one detail: She did not speak of the fact that they believed someone was summoning the spirits. She did not tell him that the list of people who had access to the means to summon them was very short. She did not share with him the fact that his own name was on that list.

"I wish you had spoken to me of this sooner," he said, still holding her hand.

"My theories were so poorly formed. I wanted to wait until I could speak with more certainty. Until I was ready to take action."

"But, from what you tell me, there is still much we do not understand."

"Which is precisely why the opportunity to go to Brockhampton Manor is not to be missed."

"To enter the lions' den . . ."

"I am certain the viscount is an Embodied Spirit. The earl must be aware of what is taking place under his own roof. His letter to my father suggests he wishes to maintain a pretense of normality. To hold his place in society. This is the perfect chance for us to learn what their motives are. To discover what they plan to do next."

"And if the viscount tries to assault you again?"

"I doubt his cousin will let him drink to excess a second time."

"And Joe Colwall, was that Embodied Spirit inebriated when he took a hammer to his poor wife? It is a hugely dangerous course of action."

"Which is why I need the diocesan exorcist to accompany me. Will you, John? Will you come to Brockhampton with me and my father?"

"I would rather you did not go at all."

"But you see that I must."

On impulse, she lifted his hand to her lips and kissed it lightly. He regarded her with a look of the utmost tenderness.

"If you are not to be stopped, then you must be aided," he said. "You have come to matter a great deal to me, Hecate Cavendish," he told her, his voice soft and low. He reached up and pushed a stray lock of hair from her forehead.

She experienced a shiver of delight at his touch. Surprised, a little unnerved, she dropped his hand and got to her feet, assuming a lighthearted manner once again. "A fact which I shall prevail upon shamelessly. Now, help me pick some primroses to take home. My mother may not be so easily persuaded. Flowers can only strengthen our case."

# 19

THEY DID NOT, IN FACT, HEAD DIRECTLY FOR HOME, BUT WENT INSTEAD to the constabulary. Now that John had a date for Mrs. Colwall's funeral he needed to inform Inspector Winter of it. Hecate was touched to learn that the detective wished to attend the burial. It seemed a kind and respectful thing to do, and she wondered if he did the same for all the victims of crimes he investigated. On arriving at the police station they were surprised to see a closed wagon waiting outside and an air of commotion about the place. The inspector himself emerged from the building ahead of a body on a stretcher.

Hecate hurried over to him.

"My dear Inspector, what has happened?"

"Step aside, if you please, Miss Cavendish. Thank you," he added, as two policemen loaded the stretcher into the back of the carriage.

John joined them and offered his assistance.

Inspector Winter replied at his customary slow pace. "I am afraid you are too late to offer the comfort of prayer here," he said, indicating the deceased as the door was secured behind the stretcher. "Joe Colwall passed from madness to death alone and unobserved."

Hecate gasped. "But what caused his death?"

"Dr. Francis confirmed a heart attack," he explained. "No doubt precipitated by the stress of his insanity and the violent events that madness had brought about."

John shook his head sadly. "A sorry business indeed, though at least the family will be spared the difficulty of a trial and execution."

Hecate stepped forward to speak quietly, aware he would be reluctant to discuss the matter further in public. "You are still convinced of insanity, then? Might not such a sudden death, when I recall no mention of Mr. Colwall having suffered from any heart problems in his life . . . well, does that not strike you as odd? As an unsatisfactory explanation?"

He looked at her. "I am aware you have your own theories regarding Joe Colwall's state of mind, but I would remind you they are just that. Theories. The facts of the matter are that a respected and experienced doctor of medicine has declared a failure of the man's heart to have brought about his demise. That same physician added a note to the death certificate to the effect that the stress of the deceased's situation and recent history was likely what brought about this fatal event."

"'Likely,' Inspector?" Hecate would not be so easily dismissed. "Are you now prepared to accept 'likely' as fact?"

Before he could respond to this the sergeant stepped forward.

"Excuse me, sir, but I thought you should know. Constable Mitchell is missing."

"Missing, Sergeant?"

"Yes, sir. He appears to have left his post and cannot be found anywhere in the building."

"And his post was?"

"Mitchell was given the duty of taking the meals to the prisoners, sir."

Hecate could not help herself. "In which case your missing constable would have been the last person to see Joe Colwall alive. He has quit his post without being given leave to do so, and the prisoner is found dead in his cell. Surely the two events cannot be unconnected?"

The inspector inflicted a look upon the sergeant that left him in no doubt as to his opinion of sharing information of this sort with a member of the public. He raised his bowler hat to Hecate in the manner of a respectful but firm dismissal. "If you will forgive me, there is much that demands my attention. Good day to you, Miss Cavendish. Reverend Forsyth." And with that, he turned on his heel and retreated into the police station, closely followed by his sergeant.

Hecate and John watched the carriage pull away in the direction of the mortuary.

"A sad business indeed," John said again.

"Yes," Hecate murmured her agreement. "Sad indeed."


By the time Hecate reached home she felt weary to her bones. After waving John off she went through the front door and was greeted by the maid.

"Where is everybody, Stella?" she asked, taking off her hat.

"Master Charles is in bed, miss. Shall I put those in water?" she asked, taking the small bunch of pale yellow flowers from her.

"Is he unwell?"

"Oh no, miss. Cook sent him up a tray earlier and he ate three slices of her best Bakewell tart."

She smiled. "It appears he is recovering from the exertions of the ball rather well then. And my parents?"

"Out visiting. They are expected home for dinner. Would you like me to fetch you anything, miss?"

"No, thank you, Stella. I shall go to my room."

The maid returned to her duties in the kitchen and Hecate began to climb the stairs. She had not gone more than half a dozen steps when the front door opened and her mother bustled through it, every inch of her agitated. Edward followed a little more calmly but it was clear even in his demeanor that something was amiss.

"Mother, whatever has happened?" Hecate asked.

"All propriety has gone forever, and good sense along with it!" she declared, snatching her gloves off, pacing the hallway as she did so. "There can be no coming back from this!"

"Father?" Hecate appealed to him for a more helpful explanation.

"Your mother fears there is no hope for the world nor any of us doomed to dwell in it," he said, taking his pipe from his pocket and loading it somewhat hastily.

Beatrice tutted, drawing her pin from her hat and brandishing it like a sword of justice. "Make fun of me all you care to, Edward. I am right to be appalled, and you know it. Never have I heard of such . . . This cannot be left unchallenged," she insisted, taking off her hat and all but throwing it and her gloves onto the credenza.

"Father, will you please tell me what on earth has happened?"

"Lord Brocket—" he began, but his wife could not contain her rage.

"No, let me tell it. A man could not help but frame the thing as a subject for ridicule and derision, but it is not. Mark my words, this has grave significance. Yes, His Lordship, and let us begin with that! That a member of the nobility should . . . No, I cannot speak of it!" she cried, tears filling her eyes as she sat heavily on the nearest chair.

Hecate descended the stairs at speed. The sight of her mother on the point of weeping was so unusual, so shocking, she dared not press her further on whatever it was that had so upset her. Instead she put her arms around her. "There, Mother, do not distress yourself so." She turned to face her father, her expression imploring him to make sense of what her mother had been saying. She experienced a deep unease about the fact that whatever it was had to do with the earl of Brockhampton.

Edward took a moment to finishing loading and lighting his pipe. He puffed, taking in a reviving pull of smoke, the aromatic fumes, so familiar to everyone in the household, having a slight calming effect on all present. When at last he spoke he did so in measured tones, wary of setting off Beatrice again.

"It appears he has put out his wife."

"Put her out?"

"He has sent her from his Brockhampton estate with two carriages of her belongings and declared to all the world that the marriage is over."

"Good grief! Poor Lady Brocket. She has always been such a supportive wife. I cannot imagine she has done anything to warrant such terrible treatment."

Beatrice could not remain silent. "She is blameless! The man is cruel and selfish beyond words."

Edward continued. "There is more."

Hecate passed her mother a handkerchief. "He has thrown out his wife and publicly stated his intention to divorce. What more can he do to her?"

"Oh the humiliation!" her mother wailed into the lace square.

Edward took another drag on his pipe before saying, "He has installed his mistress at the hall."

"That woman!" Beatrice had found her rage once more. "What manner of person must she be? She must lack morals, lack any knowledge of God, lack any understanding of what is right and decent. Edward, under no circumstances are you to set foot in Brockhampton Hall. No, not for any amount of business nor for the sake of old friendship. He has put himself beyond the pale."

Hecate found herself lost for words. Such behavior was beyond scandalous. Marriages did fail, but respectable members of society would go to great lengths to keep such matters private, for the sake of all concerned. To evict a wife from her home, to publicly spurn her, these things were dreadful. To move another woman into that family home and openly live with her was outrageous. Whatever her mother's view on the matter, more than ever she knew that she and her father must go to Brockhampton as soon as possible.

Such was the consternation in the house, particularly on Beatrice's part, it was decided they would all take supper in their rooms. So it was that Hecate was able to catch Edward on his way upstairs.

"We must speak," she whispered to him.

"Indeed we must. I shall join you in my study in an hour."

"May we meet instead in the attic?"

He looked at her quizzically but did not challenge her choice.

"Very well, daughter. The attic it shall be."

By the time the two met, dusk had turned to proper dark. Hecate lit two oil lamps so that she could search while they spoke.

"Did you leave Mother sleeping?" she asked, kneeling next to a large tea chest.

"She scarcely touched her supper, despite Cook sending up poached eggs and a little salmon to tempt her. Sleep is what she needs now." He sat on the one available chair and took out his pipe, loading it with practiced ease as he watched Hecate sorting through boxes. "Are you searching for something in particular?" he asked.

"Yes and no. I wish to equip myself for our trip to Brockhampton."

"A wise move."

She stopped digging and turned to face him, sitting back on her heels. "You raise no objection to me coming with you?"

"It presents us with the perfect opportunity to study an Embodied Spirit. We cannot pass it up. Even though it be a perilous course of action."

"Precisely my thinking. Do you believe the earl is responsible for raising the spirits? I mean to say, if he is knowingly harboring one . . ."

"I am suspicious of him, and yet I cannot, thus far, see what he has to gain by doing such a thing. He is a powerful man already, though I know him to have ambitions of high office in government. What part violent phantoms could play in his plans I fail to comprehend."

"Well, even if he is involved, he could not have acted alone. He would still need someone with access to those forbidden books to assist him. Someone inside the cathedral. And another thought occurred to me. How do we know all the spirits are coming out of the cathedral crypt? I mean, we know those tombs have been broken out of. We know there are Resurgent Spirits at large. Was the one who now inhabits Viscount Eckley released from the crypt, or are they able to be called at a greater distance?"

"But still from the cathedral? I'm not sure. . . ."

"There is a great deal about which we are unsure, Father."

Hecate thought then about telling her father of the keys she was having cut. She was uncomfortable keeping it from him. And yet there was so much else to think about. Better, she decided, to wait until she had the keys in her hand. He was less likely to condemn a *fait accompli*.

"Have you any Hecate-related artifacts?" she asked him. "A carving, perhaps? I have my brooch, of course, but anything else might be helpful. . . ."

"I did recall another book that might be of interest." He rose and disappeared behind the stacks of boxes toward a row of shelves. "I had not thought it useful earlier as it was her history and mythology we were investigating. Ah, here it is." He returned and handed her a green leather-bound volume.

Hecate read the title.

"*To Commune with the Goddess: For Followers of Hecate.*" She looked inside. "Spells!" she said, smiling up at her father. "It is a book of spells."

"One might call them that. Others might say prayers. Others, incantations. The naming of such things was ever contentious. But it does not detract from the value of their content, particularly in this instance. Wouldn't you agree?"

"Most certainly, I would. These are fascinating!"

Edward pulled things from the boxes, his pipe clamped between his teeth, tobacco fumes drifting through the cramped space. "What else have we here . . . a sword stick?" He wielded a cane, drawing from it a fearsome blade.

"We are not soldiers, Father. And that will be of no use against a spirit," she pointed out, still absorbed by the book.

He set aside the sword and pulled out a small shovel, a bag of tent pegs, a box of candles, and an old leather belt.

Hecate glanced up. "Oh! Let me see that. Is it military? Don't they call them Tom Brownes, or something similar?" she asked, standing up to take it from him, unrolling the somewhat stiff leather.

"You are thinking of Sam Brownes, which were indeed military in their origins. But no, this is something quite other. I recall purchasing it among a chest of interesting pieces in Constantinople. On a homeward journey. Notice the small pocket set into it? And the loops. It is an apothecary's belt."

She held it closer to the light. The leather felt thirsty beneath her fingers, but she could tell it had once been supple and was worn from frequent use. It was twice the width of a normal belt, with two modest brass buckles in place of one large one. There were some metal D rings fixed to one part, a slender pocket with a toggled flap over it, and a row of narrow loops of leather. "How was it used?" she asked.

"Apothecaries often traveled some distance to their patients. While they might have carried a chest of medicines, this was for their more immediate needs. Or possibly things they preferred to keep close. The rings allowed for all manner of attachments, such as pouches of herbs, small knives, and so on. Those leather loops were for vials of potions, medicinal ingredients . . . poisons, probably. They would be held secure, and be unlikely to break."

Hecate put it around her waist and pulled it tight.

"It fits. Were the apothecaries in Constantinople small?"

"They might well have been women. Here, let me . . ." He adjusted the position of the belt. "Now you can reach your vials with your right hand, and the pocket and suchlike, quite comfortably, I think."

"It will suit my needs perfectly! May I have it?"

"It is yours. As is the task of explaining to your mother why you are wearing such an outlandish garment. What do you plan to put in it?"

"I have ideas. I will ask John for some holy water."

"Will he not think that a strange request?" Seeing her expression he removed his pipe from his mouth. "You have shared with him what we have learned regarding the Essedenes? Hecate, we agreed you would not. . . ."

"I have not told him we know someone is responsible for summoning the spirits. Or that there is a list of possible suspects."

"A list which still bears his name, however faintly."

"You do not know him as I do. He is my friend. He has agreed to come with us to Brockhampton. Let him do so, Father. Let him prove his loyalty and his worth." When he hesitated she went on. "After all, what better ally against dark spirits could we ask for than an exorcist?"

"Hmmm. It is hard to argue against that. Very well. I will let Brocket know we are to visit."

"Mother will protest."

"I hold your mother in the greatest esteem and the deepest affection, but had I permitted her objections to shape my life I should never have left England. Now, if you are going to wear that thing, you'd best restore it to its proper state. You will find a tin of dubbin in the stables."

# 20

ON MONDAY MORNING HECATE LEFT THE HOUSE BEFORE ANY OF THE family were up. She had arranged to be at Mr. Sadiki's shop "early," which was an unhelpfully vague hour. She had decided he would prefer they conduct their business before normal opening times. This suited her, as she would avoid facing her mother at breakfast. She was not looking forward to the moment when her father announced that it remained his intention to visit Brockhampton, much less the moment when he revealed Hecate was to accompany him. They had agreed to couch it as a mission of mercy, taking Reverend Forsyth with them and the civilizing presence of a woman to see if the man could not be redeemed, if only for Lady Brocket's sake. And to afford him, and the viscount, the opportunity to make a formal apology to Hecate. She doubted her mother would be won over by any of these arguments and was content to leave it to her father to manage. The other advantage of calling for the keys early was that she would not be late for work. She continued to be as diligent and reliable an assistant as she possibly could, to give Reverend Thomas no reason to complain about her work. He was firmly on the list of suspects, having the best access to the secured books. She wished to do everything she could to gain his trust, and do nothing that might alert him to her suspicions if he were in fact guilty. In addition, the more he was prepared to leave her alone in the library, the greater the opportunities she might have to use the very keys she had risked so much to obtain.

Although it was before eight, the door of the shop was unlocked. The proprietor was already in position behind the high counter, and she suspected he had been waiting for her. In front of him was a cloth bundle, which he began to unfold as she approached.

"Good morning to you, Mr. Sadiki. All ready for me, I see. Splendid! How swiftly you work." She was aware she was talking too much. There was something unnerving about the old man's stare. She had no reason to feel uncomfortable, given how helpful he had been, but, nonetheless, she found she was nervous in his presence. She told herself this was not unreasonable, given the clandestine nature of their business. She leaned forward to examine the gleaming keys. "My, they do look very nice indeed." She picked up the largest one. "I should have given them some manner of labels, I suppose. How remiss of me."

The old man adjusted his spectacles. In his habitually hoarse voice he explained, "The two door keys are easy to distinguish because of their size. The smaller iron one is the only key with such a short handle. The golden one is, I believe, readily identifiable."

"Oh, the handles . . . you have worked patterns into them. These are beautifully done. They are quite lovely." The end of each handle had been turned with a spiral of metal, no two the same in width or depth, so that it would, in fact, be possible to identify them blindfold.

"This way you will never confuse them with the . . . originals," he said, holding her gaze when she looked at him. "These are your keys. Lend them to no one else."

She nodded. "I will treasure them. I am very grateful. Now I must settle up. How much do I owe you?"

"There is no charge," he told her.

"But, Mr. Sadiki, I could not possibly let you do all this work and not pay you for it!"

He deftly rolled the keys in the cloth, positioning folds between each one so that they would not scratch against each other or rattle when carried in a bag. He passed her the bundle.

"No charge," he repeated. "If I have gained nothing by the transaction I cannot be held to blame for it."

She thought to protest again, or to restate her claim that these were copies of her father's keys, but his expression changed her mind. He had helped her, unquestioningly, knowing that she had been lying to him. It had been her Hecate brooch and her own name that had decided him.

"You have been very kind. Thank you," she said again. She put the little bundle into the deep pocket of her coat.

"Use them wisely," he said.

"I will," she promised. "I will."

The Bishop's Meadows, while still a place owned by the church and where the incumbent bishop might graze his horse, had long been a public park and a popular spot for walks and picnics with the people of Hereford. Hecate leaned her bicycle against a tree and began to pace up and down the riverbank. The tower bells chimed the hour. Of course she had been early for her rendezvous with Clementine. She did her best to quell her impatience, deciding to sit on one of the wrought-iron benches nearby. She had no sooner sat down when she spotted her friend, a vision in a dress of sky blue set off by a pretty straw hat worn at a jaunty angle, walking toward her, waving cheerily.

The two friends embraced. Hecate smiled.

"You smell of roses," she said. "Expensive ones."

Clemmie laughed. "Do you think my mother would permit me to leave the house wearing cheap scent? Now, I am agog to hear what you have to say after your mysterious note."

"Not that mysterious, surely. I have asked you to meet me in the park before."

"Hecate, you wrote that you needed my help with something important!"

"And so I do. Let's sit. The point of my asking you to meet me—other than for the pleasure of your company . . ." Hecate began, "is that I need to borrow your carriage. Or rather, your mother's carriage. For a daytime trip. Friday, to be precise. Might it be available, do you suppose?"

"I suppose it might, as long as you tell me what you want it for. I sense intrigue!"

"You won't like it."

"In which case I absolutely demand that you tell me!"

"Father and I are to visit the earl of Brockhampton."

"That man! After what happened at the ball and after what he has done to his dear, harmless little wife? Hecate, darling, have you taken leave of your senses?"

"John is coming with us."

"Can it be cathedral business? I shouldn't have thought a man who has so utterly destroyed his own reputation would be someone Dean Chalmers wants to associate with."

"He doesn't. That is, this is a matter more specifically to do with my work in the library. And the map," she added, knowing she could not properly explain but feeling the need to offer something.

Clemmie shook her head. "You are making no more sense than you did before."

"Please, can I ask you to simply trust that my reasons are good ones?"

Her friend regarded Hecate closely. "Now you sound worryingly serious."

"It is serious," she replied. "This is important."

"I see. Well, I don't know him personally at all, really, but our families are acquainted, naturally. Papa sees him at Westminster, of course, when the House is sitting. They have dined together at Rules from time to time, I believe, but only in the way men from provincial towns do when they are in London. And Mama invites him to balls. That is to say, she *used* to. He can consider himself firmly crossed off any future guest lists. Poor Lady Brocket." She looked sadly into the middle distance. "How tragic that a marriage should end in such a way. Do you suppose they loved each other once?"

"What difference would that have made?"

"Oh, Hecate, how can you ask that? Two people who have loved each other, deeply, over many years . . . such a bond, such shared history is not lightly cast aside."

"Not even for a young, beautiful mistress? I thought the upper classes were quite accustomed to such behavior."

"A discreet alliance, conducted in private, perhaps . . . but such blatant mistreatment of his wife. And to install a new woman with the marital bed still warm . . ."

Hecate laughed. "Your interest in romance is impressively unshakable. Well then, may we have use of the carriage?"

"Of course you may. I suppose you will be safe with both your father and

John Forsyth. Though you might do better to take Phileas. He defended you valiantly at the ball."

"On this occasion I think John might be of more use."

"How very . . . useful of him."

"I thought you approved of John. What has he done to change your mind?"

"He has done nothing, which I suppose is rather the point. I don't disapprove of him. He is handsome enough, but . . ."

"He has been a good friend to me. He . . . understands me."

Her friend got to her feet, and held up her hands. "Stop. I beg you, do not attempt to convert me to the idea of John Forsyth as a suitor for you."

"That's not what I'm asking!"

"Well, not *now,* not at this moment, but the matter is there, beneath every conversation we ever have about him. Him or any single man of your acquaintance." She spread her arms to indicate the loveliness all around them. "Look at this," she said, waving a hand at the sparkling river, the trees drooping with blossom, the sky of Wedgwood blue, the handsome buildings of the Bishop's Palace and the cathedral reflected in the water. "The world is full of just such beauty, Hecate. Full of things that make your spirits soar and your heart sing. Does John make your heart sing?"

"Oh, really, Clemmie, you are straying from the point. I didn't ask you here to talk about John, or any other possible husband. Why must you always take our conversations in the same direction?" Hecate was about to say more, feeling the need to explain how her own opinion of John had altered, how their friendship was starting to deepen, how she had, in fact, begun to regard him as someone more than a friend, but something in her friend's expression, some small change in the way she was looking into the distance, indeed the way that she was not entirely present, gave her pause. She stood up and peered at her more closely. "Clementine, has something happened?"

She grinned. "Not some*thing,* but some*one!*"

"You've met someone new?"

She nodded energetically. "He was at the ball, but I don't suppose you even noticed him, with all that was going on. You were dancing with Phileas when I danced with him and then later, after you had left, we danced again. And much later, when Mama was occupied with seeing off the last of the guests, he and I took a turn about the rose gardens, and oh, Hecate, he is the most wonderful man!" she insisted, spinning around, arms akimbo, laughing.

"I have never seen you so . . . lit up. For pity's sake tell me who he is."

Clemmie grabbed both her hands and held them close. "His name is Wilhelm von Kessler and he's the most handsome, most charming, most amusing man I've ever met."

"Not English, then? Does your mother mind?"

"Of course not, he's a count." She waved her hand dismissively. "Everyone knows counts are two a penny in Austria but a title is a title and Papa is already planning hunting trips. Oh, Hecate, I'm in love!"

"And does Count . . . ?"

"Von Kessler."

"Does he feel the same way?"

"Yes! We got along famously almost at once. By the end of the evening I was certain. We spent Sunday together and by teatime he had declared his feelings to be the same! His poor father died last year, so he inherited the estate and the castle and everything, even though he is not yet thirty. He is only here visiting an uncle or we might never have met. And now we have, and he is perfection!"

Hecate had known Clementine all her life but had never seen her look more radiant, more beautiful. Was this what falling in love did to a person, she wondered. Was this transformation what everyone underwent when they found the right person?

"I am so happy for you," she told her again, and meant it. "Now, will you send the carriage on Friday afternoon? Once I have been to Brockhampton and seen to the cathedral business, then I shall be free to hear more about your romance."

"Very well, I shall do as you ask. As soon as you have done with your fusty old maps you can come to Holme Lacy and meet Wilhelm. Oh, I hope you will like him!"

"When he makes you so happy, how could I fail to?"

# 21

THE MORNING OF MRS. COLWALL'S FUNERAL SAW A MARKED DROP IN temperature, the sunny spring weather choosing that very day to falter. Instead of the sharp light of the previous weeks the sky was smudged with grubby clouds. Hecate had traveled the short distance to the village of Mordiford with John, as he was to officiate at the service. They made a somber pair sitting in the gig, he in his dark vicar's robes, she in the black dress and matching bonnet kept for just such occasions. He had dropped her at the Colwalls' cottage, where she was to meet Mrs. Tribbet and accompany her to the church. She found the sister of the deceased composed but weary from grief. Her small, neat form seemed even more petite and more frail enveloped in black.

"'Tis so good of you, Miss Cavendish, to make time for me."

"I am pleased to be of use. With there being no other relative close by, well, we could not see you walk to the church unaccompanied now, could we?" she said, waiting while the elderly woman shut and locked the front door. They walked to the end of the garden path and stood at the gate to wait for the hearse. Hecate noticed one or two villagers emerging from their cottages. A funeral precession would always draw onlookers, most stepping out to pay their respects to a deceased neighbor, some eager for the social interaction such an event, however small, would offer. In this case, however, there was the added excitement of a murder in their midst. She fervently hoped there would not be obvious gawkers.

"There will be tongues wagging," Mrs. Tribbet declared, as if knowing the direction Hecate's thoughts must be taking. "And there will be those who disapprove of the way I have seen fit to do things."

"She was your beloved sister. Decisions about her funeral were yours to make."

The old woman took a lace handkerchief from her cuff and fretted with it. "But not to have had her at home . . ."

"Please, do not distress yourself."

"I could not bring her back here," she was at pains to explain. "I could not! After what had happened to her . . ." She turned to look at the charming little house, her expression showing that she saw only violence and sorrow there. "I shall be pleased never to set foot inside the place again, as soon as everything is done."

"The Chapel of Rest at Mr. Ford's funeral parlor has about it a dignity and modesty of which I am certain your sister would have approved. You have no cause to reproach yourself."

The old woman straightened her shoulders and put away her handkerchief. "Well, she will go from her house to the church. I insisted upon that much at least," she said, and as she spoke they could hear the sound of a carriage approaching.

The open wagon carrying the coffin was so plain it was more cart than hearse, but the pair of black horses pulling it sported plumes atop their bridles, and the driver and the undertaker were smartly turned out with tails and toppers. They halted at the cottage gate and the undertaker jumped down, removing his hat to bow low to the chief mourner. Mrs. Tribbet greeted him somberly and stepped forward to inspect the lilies on the casket. She reached out to make a minor adjustment to the flowers, though it was impossible to detect a difference in the arrangement afterward, and Hecate knew the poor woman had simply given in to the impulse to place her hand upon her sister one last time.

They presented a meager and pitiful cortege. The single carriage moved at a level pace so that the undertaker, cane in hand, could walk in front of it, and the two women could follow behind without unseemly haste. Neighbors came to their doors or gates, the men doffing their caps, the women signing the cross over their hearts or lobbing single flowers onto the coffin as it passed. Hecate was relieved to see they were sincere in paying their respects and knew this was a comfort to Mrs. Tribbet. Mordiford being a small village, they arrived at the church in no time at all. John was waiting for them at the lych-gate, prayer book in hand, his white cassock disturbed by the breeze that had got up. The verger, the sextant, and a local man, all in their cleanest black jackets, stepped in to join the undertaker as pallbearers and carried the coffin into the church.

Inside, Hecate was surprised to see quite a number of people. They filled at least half a dozen pews. Beside her, holding her arm, she felt the chief mourner grow and strengthen just the smallest bit, heartened by the turnout, as they followed John down the aisle and made their way to the front pew. Hecate nodded a quick greeting at Inspector Winter, and another at Dr. Francis. The service was short and simple. There were prayers and two hymns, both sung with sweetness, particularly "Abide with Me," which provoked several among the congregation to tears. John spoke of Mrs. Colwall in a speech that fell short of being a eulogy, but gave thanks for her life and acknowledged the good she had done with it.

The service moved on to the burial. Mrs. Colwall was laid to rest in a quiet corner of the churchyard just beyond the shadow of the ancient yew tree. Hecate held tight to Mrs. Tribbet at the graveside, as the elderly woman seemed on the point of crumpling. John did not rush through the burial rites, but neither did he linger, sensing perhaps that the living were more in need of his care than the dead.

At last it was over. A large woman in a profusely beribboned hat declared herself to be a forgotten school friend of both sisters, and led Mrs. Tribbet back into the church where John had said he would find a glass of sherry in the vestry to revive them both. Hecate experienced a sense of relief at no longer having to be both physical and emotional support to the grieving woman. A calm presence beside her made her turn and she found Inspector Winter raising his bowler hat to her.

"Miss Cavendish," he said slowly, his somewhat lugubrious manner for once perfectly fitting the setting and occasion. He replaced his hat on his head. "A good turnout, all things considered," he observed.

Hecate nodded. "I doubt Mr. Colwall will be afforded the same level of respect."

"I anticipate the congregation will make up in numbers what they lack in sincerity," he said, referring to the fact that there were likely to be more gawkers and sensation seekers than friends or acquaintances.

She noticed a tall, well-dressed man in his middle years. He stood out as being cut from a different cloth to the rest of the gathering.

"Who is that? Do you know?"

"That is Desmond Thurston."

"Sir Richard's son?"

"Just so."

"Oh, we should speak with him!"

"We should?" He regarded her quizzically, his face questioning both the suggested course of action and the way in which she had drawn him into it.

"Indeed we should," she insisted. "The link between the two is yet to be properly explained and yet I am convinced the Essedenes are at the heart of it." She was already striding across the grass, threading her way between headstones, knowing that he would not be able to resist following.

She introduced herself, hand outstretched.

"Mr. Thurston? My name is Hecate Cavendish, assistant librarian at the cathedral. My father was a friend of Sir Richard's. My condolences to you. You know Inspector Winter, I understand?"

Desmond Thurston was sufficiently confused by the speed of the introduction not to question its purpose.

"Yes, of course, good morning, Inspector," he said, letting go of Hecate's hand to raise his hat.

It was only then that it dawned on her how awkward such a meeting might be for the two men. Sir Richard's murderer had not yet been caught, and the responsibility for the case lay with Inspector Winter. She was relieved to see there was no tension between them, however. She supposed this was in part due to the fact that Mr. Thurston would be conscious of where he was and why, and would deport himself accordingly, whatever his own grievances. She also knew this meant he might be more easily questioned, his guard temporarily lowered.

"Were you acquainted with the deceased?" she asked.

"I was not, but my father knew the couple well. I am here on his behalf, as it were."

"An unlikely friendship, if you don't mind my saying so."

"Joe Colwall grew up in a cottage on my grandfather's estate. His own father was head gardener there. He and my father would fish together. Later he came to work in the gardens at Hampton, and then moved away when he was offered a position in Mordiford, at Park Farm."

"I see." Hecate was determined to press him for more details. "And they continued their friendship even as adults?"

"They did, yes, despite the differences in their social standing. My father had a soft spot for Joe. In fact . . ." He hesitated and then continued. "After my father's death, when we were examining his accounts and putting his affairs in order, well, we discovered entries in his ledger that were . . . surprising."

"How so?" she asked.

"There were monthly payments, not large, but generous, made by my father to Joe."

"For work done, perhaps?"

"It appears not, no. The fact was, with Mrs. Colwall's increasingly poor health, Joe was needed at home and could no longer work. They had fallen on hard times and my father helped them."

The inspector was surprised. "I would not have considered Mr. Colwall a man eager to take charity."

"Nor was he. It transpired the payments were given monthly, by my father, in person, apparently in private. According to my mother, he went to the last market of the month without fail, always returning late, in the small hours, in fact. Those were the days the payments were entered into the ledger. All except the last one, on the day of his death. It is a curious business indeed. But an action typical of my father. He was a man given to acts of kindness. As I have said, my father and Joe Colwall were lifelong friends. Now, if you will excuse me." He raised his hat, the conversation at an end, and moved on to greet another funeral goer who had been trying to attract his attention.

For a moment Hecate and the inspector stood in thoughtful silence and then he spoke.

"In light of this information, Miss Cavendish, I do not doubt you will have a theory."

"Indeed I do."

"Let me see, you think Joe turned on his benefactor, demanded more money, perhaps, but Sir Richard refused. His old friend, desperate and rejected, snapped and attacked him. Then later, in despair of their future, he killed his invalid wife."

"Do you believe that possible?"

"Do I think the sane Joe Colwall who had been a friend to this man all his life, and a devoted husband, capable of such actions? No, I do not. Do I consider the raving madman in my cell might have behaved in such a way? Certainly I do." He paused then, waiting. When she did not say anything further he prompted her. "Come along then, Miss Cavendish—your theory; let's have it."

"I think you know it by now, Inspector."

"I have a hankering to hear it from you. In the cold light of day. Humor me."

"Joe Colwall happened upon Sir Richard just at the moment he was being attacked by the Resurgent Spirit. So interrupted, it bungled its attempt to secure a wealthy host, poor Sir Richard expiring in the assault. It was then the spirit took Joe as his host, turning the mild, caring husband into a violent creature who would go on to bludgeon his wife to death. Do you still consider my theory fanciful?"

"Sadly, I do not, Miss Cavendish. I do not."

"Hecate!" John called to her from the porch of the church.

Taking her leave of the inspector she walked over to him.

"A lovely service, John. Mrs. Tribbet was pleased."

"I am glad to hear it. May I speak with you for a moment?"

He led her away from the thinning crowd, around the tower of the church to the shady north side where the cold kept people from lingering. He surprised her by taking her hand and drawing her into the privacy of a little doorway.

"I received your note," he told her. "I will be at your house for two o'clock on Friday for our trip to Brockhampton."

"I am grateful for your support."

"And your father? He understands the dangers?"

"Better than anyone else might. Do not be concerned, John. We both feel that His Lordship will be eager to show an acceptable face."

"You think not to confront him directly, then?"

"No. Father will present himself as a concerned friend and business acquaintance. We will offer him the chance to apologize for what happened at the ball. You might suggest speaking to him on the matter of his marriage?"

"Yes, I can do that, though with little expectation of a good outcome."

"None of us believes he will mend his ways, but it provides us a reason for our visit. We will wait for His Lordship to break cover."

"Hecate, I want you to have this."

John took a small, flat box from the pocket in his vestments and handed it to her. She opened it to find a little gold crucifix on a short chain.

"Oh, it is very lovely, John, but I could not possibly . . ."

"It is for your protection. We are engaged in dangerous work, and that work is of a spiritual nature. You know that, else you would not require the services of an exorcist. Please, for me, say you will wear it."

She was touched by his concern. It was a modest piece of jewelry, pretty, delicately worked, and would not be a hard thing to wear. She was not certain how much she trusted it could protect her, but John clearly believed that it could. Perhaps, she thought, that was all that mattered.

"Very well. For you, I will wear it."

On hearing her words he visibly relaxed. Taking the necklace from her, he reached forward and placed it around her neck, securing the clasp carefully.

"It belonged to my grandmother," he told her. "You remind me of her, sometimes. She, too, was . . . a rare bird."

Hecate smiled. "I've never been called that before," she said. "It is a very thoughtful gift. Thank you. As a matter of fact, there was something I wanted to ask you. . . ."

"Yes?"

"Could you possibly obtain some holy water for me? Only a very small amount. A cupful would do."

"Hecate, you would never attempt to perform an exorcism without me, would you?"

"No, no, nothing like that. Only, well, it seems you and I are of one mind: It is sensible to equip ourselves with what defenses we may find."

"Quite so." He nodded. "I shall acquire some for you."

"Capital!" she said without thinking, surprising herself in her use of her father's favorite exclamation. Was she becoming more and more like him, she wondered. Noticing the seriousness in his expression she briefly squeezed his hand. "Come along, we shall be missed. Can't have the parishioners forced to go in search of their vicar on such a day." She stepped away from him then and he followed her back to the front of the church.

As she readied herself for work the next day, Hecate felt a new excitement. Today she would use her keys. Reverend Thomas had an appointment in the afternoon that would leave her alone in the library for the first time in many days. She would seize the opportunity. It would be so much better to examine the books without first having to give some reason to the librarian as to why she wanted them, or to have him watch her as she read what she found. As she left her bedroom she felt hope rising within her. Surely the library would, ultimately, provide her with what she needed to send the dangerous spirits back where they belonged. Her new access to the treasures it held began today. As had become her habit, she pinned her cameo brooch to her dress, pausing for a moment to feel the smooth shell of the goddess's portrait and spare a thought for her namesake.

Her happiness was to be shattered, however, upon finding her mother already at the front door, greeting Dr. Francis as he entered.

"Mother?"

"Oh, Hecate, your brother is unwell. He complains of a sore throat and in the night developed a cough. Dr. Francis, would you come straight up, please. Hecate, do not dally on the stairs, child, let the doctor pass."

Her mother might have expected her to step down into the hall but instead Hecate turned on her heel and trotted up ahead of Dr. Francis. She found Charlie sitting up in bed, his color high, his skin blotchy, a worrying dampness about his brow. He attempted a smile on seeing his sister but fell into a bout of coughing. She sat on his bed and took his hand while the doctor walked to the other side, setting his bag down on the chest of drawers.

"Now then, young Master Cavendish, your mother tells me you are in the wars again." As he spoke he leaned forward and took the patient's hand in his own, expertly assessing both pulse and skin temperature. He was a man unremarkable in appearance who wore his learning lightly.

"I have a head cold, Doctor, nothing more," Charlie insisted.

Beatrice had come to stand at the foot of the bed, her face stern with disapproval, as if she could rid her son of his ailment simply by dint of her will and her standing in the household. It was not in her nature to show her fear, and the doctor had her trust. Nevertheless, all present in the room knew how quickly a simple malady could become a life-threatening illness for Charlie. Dr. Francis completed a swift examination.

"Plenty of rest, nourishing food in small quantities. Mrs. Cavendish, I will leave you with a syrup to soothe the cough. While it can be effective, it is best Charles does not exert himself in a way that might provoke a bout. Cold compresses on the throat may be helpful. Here is another bottle of tonic, three spoonfuls a day." He paused to smile as Charlie pulled a face. "As long as the patient is able to complain of its less-than-pleasant taste he should give us no cause for concern." He snapped shut his bag. "Mrs. Cavendish, call me if you have any concerns. I leave him in your exemplary care. Good day to you," he said, nodding to Charlie as he left the room.

"Do you feel hungry?" Hecate asked her brother. "Shall I have Stella fetch you some cake?"

"Really, Hecate"—her mother was unimpressed—"what is required here is nourishment, not indulgence."

"I should have thought anything to tempt Charlie to eat was a good thing. Surely we must keep him happy, keep his spirits up."

"There is too much emphasis put on enjoyment in this house, over and above what is good sense. Broth is what is called for. I have Cook making some now. Charles may have a bowl after he has taken his tonic," she declared, fetching the bottle and a spoon from the bedside cabinet.

Hecate and the boy exchanged grimaces. "Never mind," she told him, "I'll bring you back a pie from Askews when I come home. Would that be more acceptable, Mother?"

Beatrice brandished the spoon. "You mean to go to your work?"

"Naturally."

"When your brother is unwell?"

"But . . . surely, Mother, I am not needed here. . . ."

"This is your family. This is where you are needed most, but it is obvious your priorities lie elsewhere."

"Would you have me shirk my responsibilities?"

Her mother poured the tonic and advanced toward her son with the filled spoon. "I have made my opinion clear on the matter," was all she would say.

Hecate understood her mother's terseness was brought on by anxiety over Charlie's health. She knew that however much she tried to hide it Beatrice was filled with fear, knowing how quickly her son could deteriorate, the memories of previous perilous journeys from just such simple illnesses as this one still vivid and frightening for the whole family. Even so, she was hurt by her mother's words, stung by what she considered an unreasonable attack. Seeing there was nothing to be gained by arguing further, Hecate backed from the room, giving her brother a small wave and what she hoped was a reassuring smile.

## 22

IN THE LIBRARY THE MOOD WAS WORKMANLIKE. REVEREND THOMAS was deeply involved in finishing the entries in a ledger for the meeting of Chapter that afternoon. As master of the library it fell to him to report on the state of the finances regarding the care and repair of the collection, as well as putting forward request for monies needed for future projects and acquisitions. Hecate, having completed the repairs on the small map, had been given a pile of books to clean and mend. They were none of them particularly valuable or noteworthy, but as pieces of the library they had their small part to play and as such were deserving of the same care as their more illustrious shelf-fellows. She sat at her desk, her woolen crossover tightly tied, aware of the restlessness of the inhabitants of the *Mappa Mundi* beside her. The unbroken sunshine of the day fell through the rose-shaped window directly onto the small prayer book in front of her. The leather binding was in good condition, but some of the stitching had worn through. Such an item would not be sent away for expensive rebinding, so Hecate must do the best she could to reinforce what stitching remained so that the pages did not become loose. She worked beneath the watchful eye of the griffin. There was something kittenish in the way its gaze followed the movement of the thread as she stitched, as if he might pounce at any moment. She could not resist toying with him, jiggling a spare length of cotton beneath his beak. Sure enough, he found it irresistible and jumped forward to snatch at it with his ghostly claws. Frustrated by his inability to actually catch the thing, the griffin fluffed up his feathers with a growl and hopped up to sit on her shoulder instead. Hecate laughed, earning a brief but stern glance from Reverend Thomas.

At once she felt guilty. Not for the momentary lapse of concentration on her work task, but for enjoying such silliness while Charlie lay at home unwell, and while the Resurgent Spirits still progressed unchecked. By the time the moment came for the master of the library to leave, Hecate was nearly bursting with the effort of remaining patient. When at last she heard the door to the north aisle closing behind him, she immediately took the bundle of keys from her pocket. She laid it on her desk and unwrapped it. She was unable to resist picking up the glowing brass keys to the cabinet. It was so tempting just to try . . . but no. She would stick to her plan. She took the chain key with her and moved quickly along the rows of shelves until she came to the ones she wanted. Brother Michael came to stand at her side.

"You have a key! This is wonderful. How did you persuade the good reverend to trust you with it?"

"I'm afraid I did not," she told him, running her finger along the shelf of books. "Instead, I took matters into my own hands. Ah-ha! This is what I am very eager to take a look at."

She pulled a slim volume from the middle shelf, turning it to check the title: *Prayers for Protection.*

"A prayer book?" Brother Michael was a little surprised.

"Of a particular kind," she told him, slipping the chain through until it was free and then taking the book to study on her desk. "I read about this in one of my father's historical studies. It was often used by nervous archeologists when they were about to enter a tomb. Many believe curses were placed on the thresholds of such places. Whether this was a rumor to scare away grave robbers or a fact is still open to debate. In either case, those risking their lives and their souls to unearth the resting place of kings thought it couldn't hurt to protect themselves. This book is mentioned several times as containing powerful words."

"Are they Christian prayers?" the monk asked.

"Some are," she said, carefully turning the fragile pages, "and some . . .

are not." She felt Brother Michael peering over her shoulder to read. "I have no wish to offend your sensibilities," she said gently. "You may find some of the contents . . . not in keeping with your own beliefs."

"Oh, have no concern on that account. The library is a repository of the collective knowledge and beliefs of man through centuries. How limiting would it be to confine the contents to one way of thinking only?"

"It is not a particularly old work, so, fortunately for me, it is written in Modern English. Oh, this is precisely the sort of thing I had hoped to find! Look . . . 'When Confronted with Bad Spirits.' That would seem to fit the bill. A short prayer . . . 'I shall not falter, shall not yield to one not of this realm. My feet stand on firm ground, my heart is whole and strengthened with love. My mind is a fortress, built against wicked words. . . .' This is excellent. I shall write it down." She took out her notebook and quickly copied the lines onto a new page. "Now, which one next? Ah, this one specifically mentions dangerous spirits sent to cause mischief! Interesting."

The griffin would not let her work in peace but stamped about her desk.

"Little one, I need to be quick. You shall have my attention when I am done. . . ."

Brother Michael drifted over to the map.

"My dear child, I am aware you are about important work, but I fear your attention is needed elsewhere."

She turned to see that the *Mappa Mundi* was indeed alive with activity.

"Good heavens! Look at that! Every single being is moving."

She left her desk and went to stand in front of the map, the griffin circling her as she did so. She had never before witnessed so much restlessness among the figures and drawings. The image of the cathedral continued to glow and pulsate. The river upon which it stood undulated as if truly flowing. The Essedenes glared as they devoured their victims. Several of the mysterious people in the right-hand margins were disturbed, testing the confines of their given spaces. The good souls being led up to heaven crowded against each other in their haste to move forward. Even the angels looked anxious and fearful, their wings fluttering.

The griffin gave a squawk and swooped, all but attacking a small dragon on the map.

"Hush now," Hecate sought to calm him. "We are all agitated. It will not do to fight among ourselves." She reached out a hand and he perched on it, hopping up her arm to settle on her shoulder, but he could not be persuaded to purr.

Brother Michael shook his head. "I cannot believe this bodes well," he said.

"It is understandable they are alarmed. The very order of things is being turned upside down. There is so much wisdom here, Brother Michael. So much ancient knowledge and experience . . . I know the answers are here, but there is so much taking place. It is as if all that the map has recorded is distressed by the activity of the Essedenes. Some seem to be trying to get at them, see here?" She pointed to some armed men situated a little higher on the map than the terrible necromancers. "Ordinarily they are completely taken up with fighting off our little friend here," she explained, indicating the image of the griffin in front of them. "Now, however, they are looking south, their swords drawn as if prepared for an attack below."

"Which is where the Essedenes sit and feast."

"Yes. And then there are others who appear to be attempting to communicate with me. They have turned their gaze outward, and one or two of them are signaling in various ways. Look, these for example."

Brother Michael leaned forward to bring the images she was pointing at into focus.

"Ah, the knight raises his hand not to the instructor behind him, but to the fore. Toward you, in fact, my dear."

Hecate shook her head. "They are all trying so hard. . . . Why can I not see it? See here, too, even the bear has turned to stand on his hind legs and move his paws as if he were scrabbling to get out of the map and reach something. His gaze is in exactly the same direction as . . ." She drew her finger down the map to another image. "Saint Augustine, here. He's usually lying down, looking up toward Christ, his hands clasped in prayer."

"But now he lifts his hands to point outward. Again, toward you."

As the monk spoke, Hecate began to pace back and fore in front of the map, watching it all the while. As she did so, something occurred to her.

"Wait!" she said. She checked once more the direction of the gaze of both the bear and the saint. She took two paces to the left, then half a pace back. "Now it is as if they look directly at me," she said.

"To hold you in their prayers and thoughts, perhaps?" Brother Michael suggested.

"But see, if I move just half a pace to the left, or right, they do not alter the angle of their vision. See?"

The monk nodded. "That is curious, when they are making such an effort to look at you."

"But what if they are not looking at me? What if they are looking at something *behind* me?" She spun around, striding across the room, causing the griffin to take to the air, circle, and settle on the top of the map frame. She made sure to take the exact line of the saint's gaze. It reached an end at the first row of bookshelves. She searched the volumes there.

"Is there something of significance?" the monk asked.

"Quite the opposite. These are the parish records of expenditures for two churches in the city over a period of fifty years, and are quite recent. They could not be more mundane." She strode back to the map and turned again, checking the line. "Perhaps I have the geometry wrong. We need string," she decided, hurrying to a drawer beneath her desk and finding a ball of twine. She brought it back to the map, holding it up to the depiction of St. Augustine. She hesitated.

Brother Michael was horrified. "You cannot mean to deface the map with a pin?!"

"Fear not, I will not cause any damage. But I must have this end secured in the exact place." She cast about for a method of doing just that without marking the map. She dared not use a pin, and glue would cause lasting harm. "If only I had someone who could hold it in position."

"Alas, I have not the ability." He gave a rueful smile.

"It is not your fault, Brother Michael," she assured him. An idea came to her. "But there is someone who could help us." She tied the end of the string into a loop and held it up to the griffin. "Lift your foot, little one," she told him. When he hesitated she added, "Please?"

The creature fluffed out his feathers but did as she asked. With great care, Hecate placed the loop of twine around the leg of the phantom beast. She knew the griffin to be one of the more substantial ghosts in her family. He had not real strength, but he had a certain resistance at the edges of his form. Just as she had hoped, the soft, light string was not too heavy for his particular ethereal construction. The loop held in place.

"Now," she said, stepping back, "if you would be so good as to drop down just a little and hover in front of Saint Augustine . . ."

The griffin opened his wings and descended.

"That's right, that's far enough. Just there. Perfect!" she told him.

The mythical beast was not ideally designed for hovering, but, with a deal of flapping and squawking, he succeeded in keeping at least the relevant leg in place, his talons extended so that the loop could not slip off.

Quickly, Hecate unraveled the twine from the ball, following the line of sight. When she reached the shelves, she passed the string between the books and hurried around to pick it up on the other side.

"Is there anything of greater import there?" Brother Michael wanted to know.

"Nothing. I am going to continue until I reach something that suggests itself," she told him. The second row of books was equally dull and unlikely to be of assistance. The angle of the line meant that after these shelves, the next point of contact came with the far wall. Or, more precisely, a cupboard attached to the far wall.

"Have you discovered something?" the monk asked as he drifted around the end of the shelving and came to stand beside her. When he saw what she was looking at, he gave a small but unmistakable gasp of shock.

Hecate looked at him. She, too, knew what the cupboard contained. "It makes complete sense," she said.

"Yes but . . . the forbidden books!" Brother Michael took a step back as if the very proximity to the volumes he was speaking of might put him in peril.

"I cannot ignore the guidance of the map, I must act now. Do not be fearful, Brother Michael. They are, after all, simply books."

For once the monk's friendly, benevolent demeanor changed. When he spoke it was with true passion. "The texts housed in that case are locked not to protect them from people, but to protect people from *them*. This you already know."

"This is a cathedral, a Christian building. I understand that some works of writing are not acceptable. . . ."

"Acceptable!" He raised his arms and then let them fall by his sides in a gesture of exasperation and frustration. Hecate had never seen him so animated.

"You evidently have no conception of what it is we are discussing. This is not about matters of blasphemy or indecency or works that might move people to revolution. No. Within that cabinet are collected some of the oldest, most diabolical, most dangerous volumes in any collection anywhere in the world."

"Be that as it may, my father and I believe it houses the text used to raise the Resurgent Spirits. If I had any doubt, the map has rid me of it. You can see where it is directing me. I have to follow where it leads. It is our only hope of stopping the work of the Essedenes." When she saw that he remained unconvinced she went on. "I will be cautious, I give you my word, but I need to find what I can that could help us, wherever and whatever that is. Any dangers those books might contain cannot be greater than the one we face now. Remember the abbey in France. Remember your brethren," she said, instinctively placing a hand on his arm, only for it to descend through his cowled sleeve.

The sound of the griffin complaining at being left in place interrupted them and the twine fell slack. Hecate reeled it in and the griffin flew to the top of the nearest shelf where it set to nibbling at its leg as if to scratch an itch left there by the unfamiliar contact of the string.

"Thank you, my little friend. You did very well indeed," she said, watching it fluff up its feathers by way of response. She returned the string to its rightful place, Brother Michael drifting after her. She took the smallest keys from the opened bundle and walked quickly to the cabinet. The brass felt smooth after the rougher iron of the larger keys. It fitted the lock perfectly as she had known it would. The padlocks both opened with surprising ease, considering how rarely they might have been turned. But then again, she reminded herself, in recent times someone had been opening the cabinet. There was one final lock; the narrow central one, positioned in the middle of the gold plate. She carefully pushed the tiny gold key into position and turned it. There was a click, sharp and high, and then another, as the sophisticated lock yielded. She hesitated, as if expecting some powerful reaction to breaching these defenses. None came.

As she opened the cupboard door she detected the anxiety emanating from the monk behind her. If she had been asked at that precise moment how she felt she would have confessed to a small amount of trepidation, but a large amount of excitement. And hope. Hope that she could find a way to stop the Resurgent Spirits hurting anyone else. Hope that she would never again fear for the lives of the people she loved. The interior of the cabinet was lined with lustrous mother-of-pearl so that it gleamed as the light from the room fell upon it. There was a single shelf dividing the space. Hecate noticed a sweet smell, slightly heavy, reminding her of warm toffee. She counted only five books: one large, laid flat in the bottom of the cupboard; three slim, modest-sized and leather-bound stacked upon each other; and one tattered, green, its spine cracked, propped against the pile of smaller books. The griffin, its curiosity getting the better of it, flew down to perch on her shoulder and peer in. Hecate reached toward the green book. Nervousness made her movement clumsy, so that as she touched the scuffed cover she knocked the book from its upright position, causing it to fall flat on the shelf. As it did so, there came a faint but distinct sound, as if a string of a thousand tiny bells had been pulled. Hecate found herself waiting, though for what she could not have said. As the sound faded the silence that followed was unnerving. She took hold of the book and started to slide it off the shelf.

Only now did she come to understand the nature of what she was dealing with.

The book resisted her attempt to move it, pulling against her at first and then wrenching itself free of her grasp. It opened of its own accord, emitting a shrill scream as it did so, turning and twisting upon the shelf, its pages a blur of movement, flicking this way and that. Hecate flinched as the shrieking became louder. She snatched at the book, trying to grab hold, to force it to be still and quiet, but it moved with astonishing speed. At last she grasped a corner of the front cover and held on for all she was worth, trying to clutch it with her other hand.

But the book had other defenses.

In an instant it had opened itself flat and a scaly clawlike hand burst forth from its center. Before Hecate had a chance to react, the hand had grasped her wrist, closing its long talons against her flesh.

She cried out, beating at the terrifying thing with her other fist, desperately trying to pull free.

Brother Michael started to pray. She was aware of frantic activity and noise from the *Mappa Mundi*. The griffin, determined to defend her, swooped into the cabinet and launched an assault on the claw, scratching with its own spectral talons. Despite their insubstantial nature they appeared to inflict some pain on the guardian of the book, perhaps because of its own magical composition. It let go of Hecate and instead snatched at the griffin, taking a fierce hold of its leg. The mythical beast squawked and flapped as the book slammed shut against it, unable to close completely, but trapping the griffin even more firmly.

"Oh, no!" She grabbed the book again and wrenched it from the cabinet, falling to the floor and kneeling upon it as she wrestled the covers open. The griffin tried to fly free but the gnarled claws still had hold of his leg.

"Let him go!" she shouted, struggling to maintain her grip on the book as it bucked and leaped. She saw that the little griffin was tiring, shedding phantom feathers as it beat its wings in a futile effort to break away from the claw that now began to drag it down into the book. "No!" Already she felt the cover slipping from her fingers. In a moment the griffin would be lost. He was being pulled deeper and deeper into the book. She knew then that she could not save him using strength alone. Forcing herself to think, to find another way, she stopped struggling. She allowed her mind to expand, to open itself to see other possibilities, and as she did so she heard a low, steady hissing sound. Detecting a movement at her breast, she glanced down to see the tiny golden snake on her cameo brooch was moving. It wriggled free of its gold link, doubling then trebling inside, its forked tongue flicking as it detected its prey. As she watched, the tiny serpent coiled and then struck, sinking its fangs into the wrinkled skin of the clawed hand. The guardian of the book released its catch in a spasm of pain and the griffin flew free. The book set up its shrieking again, but the defender was defeated, victim to the snake's venom, inert and harmless now. The book itself put up a further fight, snapping shut its covers, but Hecate wrestled it back onto the shelf, the loyal serpent shrinking down to size and slithering back to its place on her brooch as she did so. She slammed shut the door of the cabinet, leaning heavily against it. Her heart rate had not slowed to its normal rhythm before she heard footsteps on the turret stairs. Her hands still shaking, she locked the cabinet, replaced and closed the padlocks, and hurried back to stand at her desk, just as Reverend Thomas entered the room.

Hecate scooped the keys into their bundle and slid the cloth into her pocket, greeting the librarian with a bright smile.

"Ah, Reverend Thomas. A productive meeting, I trust?"

He gave a harrumph which might have been a yes or a no, evidently too out of breath to form a proper answer as he lowered himself heavily into his chair. He took a handkerchief from his cassock pocket and polished his spectacles, narrowing his eyes at his assistant.

"Have there been any interruptions to your work?" he asked at last.

"Oh no. None at all. All quiet here," she assured him before taking her seat and continuing with her task, aware of the griffin settling, trembling, on the highest bookshelf it could find. She turned her head away from the continuing frenetic activity of the ancient map, doing her best to appear calm and focused, while all the time her mind was filled with thoughts of how close she had come to losing her little friend, and of how she might never succeed in tackling the contents of the locked cabinet.

# 23

HECATE FOUGHT THE URGE TO RUN DOWN THE STAIRS FROM THE LI-
brary. The shocking behavior of the banned book had raised many questions
in her mind, and there was one person in particular she believed might furnish her with the answers. Without stopping to speak to anyone, she fetched
her bicycle from the cloisters and pedalled at speed across the Cathedral Green
and along East Street. In moments, she was at the key cutter's shop. The sign
declared it to be open, but there were no other customers. It struck her that
she had never seen anyone else so much as enter or leave the place. The interior was shrouded in its customary gloom, so that her eyes had to adjust to
the low level of light. When they did so, she was startled to see the proprietor
already standing behind the counter, watching her, almost as if he had been
waiting for her. Almost as if he had been expecting her.

Hecate strode across the shop floor, unpinned her cameo, and placed it
on the counter.

Mr. Sadiki did not react.

"The time for hiding secrets behind caution and formalities is past," she
said, sliding the brooch across the worn wood toward him. "Tell me what
you know."

"The brooch has revealed something of its strengths to you?" he asked in
his thin remnant of a voice.

"Sufficient for me to realize it is no ordinary adornment. More, even, than a talisman. There is magic in it. I believe that you have always known this."

He nodded. "I recognized it at once."

"And yet you did not think to share with me what you knew?"

"'Twas not for me to speak. Hekate's jewel will reveal itself only to one worthy of it. Only to one meant to have it."

"But my father bought it before I was born."

He gave a stiff shrug. "The brooch will find its way to the one who should wear it. That has always been its purpose."

"Always been?" She began to feel nothing was making any sense. She had hoped for answers but every time the old man spoke she found she had another question. She put her hand to her brow for a moment, considering with care how to phrase her questions. "Mr. Sadiki, you say you recognized the brooch. When last you saw it, who did it belong to? It has been in my father's possession nearly twenty-one years, and he bought it from someone who hailed from Cairo."

"I have not always lived here," he told her. "My work has seen me travel through distant lands over many years."

"So you saw the brooch somewhere in the region where my father was working as an archeologist? Was it perhaps in some manner of shop? And if so, how was it that you understood its . . . qualities? And how did the tinker know of my imminent birth? Or that my father would choose the name Hecate for me? My mother always insisted she favored Alice. . . ." She stopped, aware that she was gabbling. She reached out and touched the brooch, feeling anew its strange vibration, remembering the moment the serpent had come to life. Come to life to help her. "I want to understand," she said quietly. "I need to understand."

He stepped to one side, lifting the wooden flap of the counter, beckoning.

Hecate picked up the brooch and followed him through the low door into the room at the back of the shop. It was a homely space, unremarkable, with a black range in the hearth, coals glowing red beneath a smoke-blackened kettle suspended on a chain. The air was tainted with soot and boot polish. There was a table, wooden chairs, a workbench beneath a window to the rear. The old man took the seat nearest the fire and indicated she should take the one opposite. Once they were both settled he began to speak, his gaze not on her, but turned toward the embers in the hearth, as if the story were written there.

"I was born in Paris, and that was where I learned my trade, in the Arab quarter. My father instructed me in boot repairs and key cutting, for we have always outwardly presented ourselves as cobblers and suchlike."

"Outwardly?"

He glanced at her sternly, making it plain interruptions would not be welcome.

"It has been the honor and the duty of my family to assist the Goddess of the Moon in her earthly work. We have done so for generations. We were given our name then, the meaning of which is *faithful*. And so we have always been loyal as Hekate's own hounds. Often centuries pass and we are not called upon. Others among my forebears have given their lives in her service. We follow Hekate's jewel, so that we are on hand. So that we are ready. I came to reside here in Hereford the year of your birth." He paused, shifting his frail frame in his chair as if his old bones bothered him.

Hecate waited, though her mind was bursting with questions, determined to stay silent until he had finished speaking.

"I had seen signs, recently, that a darkness was upon the city. The desecration of the tombs in the cathedral to begin with, and then the killings started. . . . The more I learned the more certain I became that the curse of the Essedenes had been invoked once again. That Resurgent Spirits stalk the streets, looking for their new homes. When you walked into my shop and I saw the brooch, and heard you confirm your name . . ." He looked at her again, as if he himself had questions, to which only she could provide the answers. "You are a child of Hekate, though you did not know it. Not a child in the sense you might understand, no. You have parents of your own. You are a mortal being. These things are true. What is also true is that you have in you the spark of the goddess herself. That fragment of light that searches for centuries to find its next home. To find the woman who will be the beacon in the darkness, who will stand as the goddess does, on the threshold of night and day, betwixt life and death. It found its home in you before you were born. The vagabond Phoebe, who sold your father the brooch, was a seer, a wise woman, who had heard the whisper on the autumn wind—that the goddess had found an earthy home once again. She knew before your father did what your name would be. She was sent in search of him. In truth, he was not difficult to find, his reputation telling of his whereabouts, the souls he disturbed in his digging among the dead calling to her. The moment she put that jewel, bearing Hekate's image, into his palm, the moment its magic leached into his skin, was the moment he named you. In that instant, your destiny was set in motion. And now the time is upon us when you are called to act. And act you must, for the city is in great peril, and you alone can beat back the darkness that threatens to engulf it."

Mr. Sadiki seemed to slump then, to fold in upon himself. At first Hecate thought he was ailing, and that the burden of his secret and the effort of at last sharing it had taken its toll. But then she looked again and saw a lightness in his expression and knew that it was relief she saw. That he was glad she had found her way to him. His story, *her* story, was astonishing, and yet it made perfect sense to her. Indeed, it made so many other things make sense, too. She felt no fear, only excitement. She imagined what her father would make of these revelations and knew at once that he would believe her and that he would stand ready to help her.

"Thank you," she said, leaning forward in her seat, "for your trust. You have given me a great deal to think about, and yet I still have questions, if I may . . . ?" When he nodded she continued. "You say you grew up in Paris. . . . There was another occasion of darkness, of risen spirits, in France, a little over a century ago. Does the location of that event have anything to do with where your family found themselves?"

For the first time, he smiled. "The goddess was right to choose you, for bravery without wisdom is a blunt instrument."

She smiled back. "On this occasion we have my father and the British Museum to thank. So, your ancestors, did they try to stop the Essedenes at Piedmont Abbey in France?"

"Some were slain in the struggle. That cursed place!"

"You consider the place of holy men was cursed?"

"Look to its founder! De Furches had wickedness running through his veins, as do all his descendants. No amount of money spent on building abbeys would change that. 'Twas but a veil to be drawn over their own truth. They were as far from Christian as it is possible to be. No, their souls were forfeit to an older god, for they had long ago allied themselves with the power of the Essedenes."

"You mean, they knew of the necromancy? Of the raising of spirits?"

"Knew of it and practiced it. For generations they have summoned the dead and placed them where they chose. Shoring up their power at court, or winning battles with an advantageous strategy whispered in a general's ear, or ridding themselves of a barren wife to further their own line . . . In such ways the evil has continued. De Furches cursed his own family with his greed, for the Essedenes protected their interests. The nobleman might have thought the ancient necromancers served him; the reality is his descendants are ever bound to raise spirits, every hundred years, be they willing or no."

"And your forefathers knew this? They fought at the abbey?"

"They did. One of my ancestors survived, with few allies. Their success was only partial, for some Embodied Spirits escaped and fled throughout Europe."

"And did they take with them a particular book?" she asked, her mouth dry as she waited for his answer.

He nodded again. "You have felt for yourself the strength of the magic that surrounds it."

"I have encountered its defenses. I can only guess at the power of its contents. I believe it contains the words necessary to return the spirits to their rightful places. I must gain access to it, but . . ."

"The Essedenes did not leave their legacy unprotected. Had they done so, you and I might not be here this day, conversing on this very subject."

"I have to find a way to subdue the book and use its contents, Mr. Sadiki. Can you help me? You have done so much already, making the keys for me without question, sharing what you know. How can I get past the magic that guards that book?"

"Alas no key can help you with this, so it is beyond my doing."

"The serpent knew what to do, but it only vanquished the dreadful creature that stood guard. The book itself was too wild, too resistant, to be read, let alone studied quietly. Do you think something else on the brooch might help, perhaps?" She still had it in her hand and now held it up to the blurring light of the oil lamp on the table. "The key . . . ? The moon . . . ? The goddess herself . . . ? But I cannot see how. Do you believe there is a way?"

"I believe that if there is, you will be the one to discover it."

"There's something else." Hecate was eager for more answers and felt that her host was tiring. "The first contact I had with the Essedenes was through those depicted on the *Mappa Mundi*. And the map has communicated with me more and more as the situation has grown more grave. The figures on it have helped me. It seems to me that the map and the Essedenes' activity are linked but confusingly so. The drawings of the Essedenes were alarming, their contact with me not benign at all, and yet otherwise the map has guided me, protected me even. Tell me, was there a similar ancient world map at the abbey? I know there were others which have not survived the years."

Mr. Sadiki nodded slowly. "Not all the secrets of the Essedenes' methods are yet known, despite the efforts and sacrifices of my family. But you are correct; the proximity to such a map is a common factor in the activity of the curse."

"As a force for good or ill?"

"Both, naturally. Things are rarely so simple as to be black or white, night or day, bad or good. You of all people know that it is within the liminal realms that most of us dwell."

"Of all people?"

"The goddess stands upon the threshold and lights the way. As do her followers."

The old man got to his feet. Evidently, the meeting was at an end. She followed him out into the shop. When they reached the door she turned to him.

"Thank you, Mr. Sadiki."

"I regret I cannot help you with the book, but if you have need of more keys, or should you have more questions . . . you are welcome here. Any time of day or night."

"Oh, there will undoubtedly be more questions, you can rely upon it."

As she went to leave he put his hand on her arm.

"Remember, wherever a poisonous plant is found, its remedy grows nearby, often cloaking its importance in drabness."

Without allowing time for her to press him on such a cryptic statement, he closed the door behind her and she heard the heavy bolts put into place.

Phileas was late. Hecate was not surprised, and yet still she had to suppress irritation. Why was it that some people were unable to be punctual? She knew that his intentions were good, but his life tended toward the chaotic. Her mother said it was his want of a wife. She herself doubted any one woman could bring sufficient order to his existence to effect much alteration in the man. When at last she saw his phaeton turning into Broad Street she felt any irritation fade away. His likability would ensure he was always forgiven, and therefore change was not necessary.

"Whoa! Whoa, girls, steady now!" He could be heard persuading his two fine dapple grays to a halt alongside the west gate to the Cathedral Green. He cut a dashing if somewhat outlandish figure. The phaeton carriage had been popular years earlier as a racy and quite dangerous style of transport, favored by young men with a thirst for speed. In recent years it had been superseded by more stable and comfortable conveyances, but Phileas would not part with what had been a favorite carriage of his father's. The two mares who pulled it were highly strung and underemployed, so that their one desire any time they were taken out was to go as far and as fast as possible.

He tied the reins to a brass hook by the driver's seat and leaped down, greeting Hecate with an elaborate bow, doffing his bowler hat as he did so.

"Apologies for my tardiness, Hecate. We encountered not one but two flocks of sheep being relocated along the Mordiford road."

"Were any sheep or shepherds mown down in your haste?"

"Not a single one. On the contrary, I took an aging ewe aboard to save her legs."

"How thrilling for her."

"When set down again, she seemed relieved to have been spared the walk."

"Or happy to reach her destination alive," Hecate teased, accepting his hand as he helped her up into the seat beside his own.

He jammed his hat back on and picked up the reins. As they set off at some speed west along King Street, she found it impossible not to compare her outings with John in the cathedral gig with this breathless journey with Phileas. The modest, two-person carriage and poorly trained, lowbred horse that pulled it seemed to suit John's lack of interest in anything frivolous or ostentatious. The way Phileas's yellow silk waistcoat matched the painted livery of his flamboyant conveyance was typical of his personal flair and sense of fun. She had, of course, considered asking John to take her to Grayfriars but several things had persuaded her that Phileas was a more fitting choice on this occasion. To begin with, there was her father's continuing concern about John's name being on their list of suspects regarding the raising of the spirits. While she herself did not believe him to be guilty of such a thing, she did not wish to clash with her father on the point more than she could avoid. And then there was the fact that she had been so busy of late she had seen very little of her old friend, and she missed his company. In the midst of so much darkness, he offered light relief, and she was thankful for it. Besides, she had told herself, the housing development on the west side of the city was his project and he would be so proud to show it off to her. It mattered not that her main need to see the site was to fully understand what was taking place regarding the exhumation of the ancient graves there. Could it be that some of the Resurgent Spirits were emerging from such a place? She had been so fixed on the cathedral crypt, was it possible she had missed other places where the necromancers had used their skills? She hoped she would be able to find out what she needed in the course of letting Phileas take her on a tour of the old abbey location.

The site in question was only a few streets from the cathedral and she could easily have walked it but had not wished to deprive him of the obvious delight he took in fetching her in his precious phaeton. They flew through the town at a reckless rate, avoiding collisions due to the fleet-footedness of the horses and their master's deft handling of the reins. He was so at ease and aglow with the joy of the ride he was able to shout greetings and even raise his hat to familiar faces he spotted along the way. When they arrived at their destination, Hecate found she had been gripping the handrail so tightly her knuckles were white. He helped her down, his face beaming.

"Safely delivered!" he announced. "Here"—he offered her his arm—"the going is uneven, so much groundwork and whatnot being underway."

She accepted the support, aware he was enjoying the curious glances they were garnering from the workmen as he strode forward with a young woman on his arm. The sight of a figure near one of the remaining small buildings made her stop short.

"Is that Lord Brocket?"

"What? I believe it is, yes."

"Has your enterprise here anything to do with him?" she asked, immediately concerned.

"I should say anybody's enterprise hereabouts has to do with him. Or rather, he was to do with it. The man has his finger in many pies, d'you see? A voracious appetite for business."

"Is that so?"

"Indeed, there is little that goes on by way of development in the city, I daresay the entire county, that His Lordship does not have an interest in."

"But he has stepped outside of society. His behavior . . ."

"Ah, but society is not business, now, is it. I say, mind where you put your feet. Mud and dirt and all that."

They were indeed picking their way through a place that was more earthworks than construction. There was a smell of wet ground, freshly turned. On the far side, Hecate could see stacks of timber and quantities of bricks awaiting their moment. For the most part, however, the landscape was mud, holes, discarded stone, slick boards, and masculine activity. Men wielded spades and shovels or pushed barrows. To the right a team of shire horses were being hitched to a felled tree. This scene of industry played out to an accompaniment of whistled tunes, shouts of warning or encouragement, stomping boots, scraping shovels, and squeaking barrow wheels. The men sported the ubiquitous uniform of the laborer; clothes that were mud colored before and after a day's work, heavy hobnailed boots, and greasy cloth caps. The foreman of the works was easily identified by his short black coat and his bowler hat, which he raised in recognition of his superior. Phileas returned the gesture and then fell to explaining the plans to Hecate.

"It should only take a further week or so to finish the clearing of the ground. Most of the stone has already been moved, as you can see. It's an ample site. Thirty dwellings are planned, each with its own yard, coal bunker, and privy. And there are trees to be planted along the central avenue, here and there," he said, waving his arms expansively, doing his best to paint a picture for her.

She was happy for him. Happy for the obvious pride and excitement he felt at being in charge of such a worthy social project. She feared "avenue" might be somewhat a grand description for how the place would actually look, but she could not hold his enthusiasm against him. She thought then that this was a rare chance for a man of privilege who enjoyed a life of ease, able to dabble in whichever enterprises took his fancy, to put himself to good use. To be seen as someone more than a dilettante. She admired him for valuing this.

"Tell me, where exactly was the old abbey?" she asked.

"Well, there were really only ruins of one or two walls. They have already been removed," he explained, pointing toward the piles of stones near the entrance to the site. "We will have them crushed for ballast and used in the footings of the new houses. The abbey itself stood over there," he said, indicating the central area.

"I should like to see," she said.

"Truly? There is nothing left save marked ground."

"Indulge me," she insisted, pulling him gently with her as she stepped forward.

He hurried to guide her onto the nearest run of wooden boards, keeping her out of the worst of the mire.

"There really was little to see of it even before we set to work. The building was deconsecrated many years ago," he told her as they came to a halt.

He was right; there was nothing of note to be seen, save the scarred earth where the last of the stone had been removed. Hecate looked about her.

"Where was the burial ground?" she asked.

"Oh, what we know of was to the right, there, beyond where the abbey would have stood. Though of course there were very few actual marked graves."

"Nonetheless, you had to seek permission to exhume any remains, did you not?"

He raised his eyebrows at her and twirled the waxed ends of his mustache. "Certainly, all our actions have been most proper in that regard."

"And complete? Have you opened all the known graves?"

"'Pon my word, Hecate, you do have an uncommon interest in such things," he said.

"You can hardly be surprised, given where I work."

"I suppose not. Well, we have indeed taken up all the remains that had marked positions. As I said, every propriety was observed, all highly dignified, and so on and so forth."

"And the unmarked graves? Can you be sure you have located all of them?"

"No, point of fact, we cannot. Not until we have dug all the footings, which will possibly, fair to say, reveal more . . . um . . . unfortunates. Very old remains, you understand? No living relatives or anything of that nature."

"So, that area there, that looks like the last piece of ground to be dug. There could be more deceased to be discovered there, could there not?"

"It is possible, yes. Dash it all, Hecate, don't go treading through the morass. Hold up!"

She strode off the boards, her leather boots slapping on the wet mud, grateful for her shortened skirts. She had to move swiftly to avoid her feet getting sucked in. She could hear Phileas's heavier tread squelching in her wake. As she reached the point where the workmen were slicing through the ground with their spades, she experienced a sudden shiver and thought, for a fleeting instant, that she detected a spectral presence standing on the perimeter. She was not accustomed to encountering souls so far from the cathedral, so that she was momentarily thrown. She listened, and considered how the place affected her demeanor. Was there, she wondered, any trace of the sense of menace and evil she had detected that time in the crypt? Nothing seemed to present itself.

"Hecate, for pity's sake, how am I to explain to your parents that I watched you disappear into the mud? Have a care."

She leaned forward as far as she dared, peering into the gaping hole that the men had created. She could see no bones, nor any remnants of what might once have been coffins or tombs. While she did not detect that overpowering dread, she could sense an unease in the atmosphere, a disturbance above Phileas's mild panic for her safety.

"Where do you take them?" she asked, wheeling about.

"What?" He teetered as he came to stand next to her.

"The remains that you find. Where do you take them?"

"For the moment, all have been placed in caskets and taken to the Chapel of Ease in Eign Street. Once we have finished our excavations they will be removed to the new municipal burial site out at Breinton."

"Some several miles from the city center."

"One or two. I don't suppose it will matter to the . . . to those we find."

"It may or may not," she muttered, half closing her eyes, squinting in the direction she had detected a possible ghostly presence.

"Good Lord, look who has come among us!" Phileas exclaimed.

She turned to see who he was looking at and was astonished to witness John picking his way across the boards toward them. She had only mentioned her planned visit in passing, without date, time, or details. Had he watched her leave and followed her on foot? It seemed a strange thing for him to do.

"John," she said as he drew close. "What brings you here?"

As he had been brought up to do, Phileas fell back on good manners to ease a slightly awkward situation. The two had met before, so were not complete strangers. Hecate was aware, however, that her father would have mentioned Reverend Forsyth as part of her new life in her place of work. And her mother had not been above referring to him in front of Phileas in a way that deliberately placed him as a possible husband for her daughter.

"Ah, the good Reverend. How kind of you to pay us a visit. It is always heartening for we men of business to have the support of the church. Puts our endeavors in a good light, don't you know?"

"Mr. Sterling," he said, raising his black hat briefly. "Hecate," he said, smiling.

"Why are you here, John?" she repeated her question baldly, annoyed that he should perhaps have thought her incapable of going anywhere without him anymore.

"The dean asked me to see for myself that the exhumations have been done according to his instructions. Of course, I have every confidence in Mr. Sterling's overseeing of the work, but, well, you know how Dean Chalmers likes to proceed with caution. He thought it only fitting someone from the cathedral should be sent to confirm—"

"So he sent you," Hecate interrupted.

John smiled calmly. "He sent me."

Phileas was determined to keep the encounter pleasant all around. "Good of him, and of you, Reverend, to spare the time. As you can see, we are nearly finished in these . . . ah, peculiar aspects of the construction. Scarcely a dozen more yards to dig. Oh, my foreman is hailing me. Forgive me, I shall return in an instant. Hecate, if you care for me at all, you will refrain from hurling yourself into the swamp."

So saying he hurried off to address his foreman's concerns, leaving the other two alone together.

Hecate spoke to John in a low voice so that their conversation would not be overheard by the workmen.

"I was quite capable of doing this myself, John."

"Doing what, precisely?"

"Coming here to inspect the exhumations. I wished to confirm or disprove a theory, concerning the Resurgent Spirits."

"Which is?"

"That they have all been summoned via and from the cathedral. I wanted to come here to see if I might sense that . . . threat. That dark presence that I detected the day the crypt was desecrated."

"And did you? Sense anything, I mean?" he asked, his face showing concern.

She wondered, then, what he would make of the conversation she had had with Mr. Sadiki. How would he feel if he knew he were in the presence of one chosen by an ancient non-Christian goddess to do her work? It was then she realized, with a calm, happy certainty, that it would not change his opinion of her. It would not change the way he felt about her. He might not understand everything, any more than she herself did, but he understood what she was trying to do. He knew of her gift, and of her mission, and he did not question its value.

In that moment she felt all her crossness toward him evaporate. He trusted her judgment. She tried to imagine explaining to Phileas what she planned to do. For all their mutual fondness and familiarity, she simply could not see how she would ever convince him of her secret, of her gift. How could she expect such a thing of him, in all fairness? John, on the other hand, had already accepted all that she had told him about her family of lost souls. He had already proven himself a valuable ally in her work to stop the Resurgent Spirits. With him she could do what she had been called to do, without secrecy, without explanation. In that moment she saw that it was he, and probably *only* he, who could marry her without taking from her that aspect of herself that had come to mean more than anything. She decided that she must be honest with him, though. When she shared her experiences of the banned book and what Mr. Sadiki had told her with her father, she would make sure that John was included. There must be no more secrets between them.

By the time Phileas returned, she and John were already making their way back along the boards toward the site entrance.

"Hecate!" he called, puffing slightly in his hurry to catch up. "Leaving so soon?"

"Thank you so much for the tour," she said, taking his hand. "It has been fascinating. You are doing something very worthwhile here."

He twirled his whiskers again, shifting from one foot to the other. "One must do one's bit, what? But why the haste? I had thought we might call in at the Black Lion for a bite to eat. What say you, Reverend Forsyth? Or is such a place beneath the dignity of a man of the cloth? Don't want to get you into trouble."

"It's an attractive offer. Alas, I am required at Evensong," he replied.

"Another time, perhaps. Just the two of us then, eh Hecate? Cheer you up after all this talk of dead bodies and ghoulish things like that?"

Hecate let go his hand. As Brother Michael had once said, there were some divides that could never be crossed.

"Not today. I am expected home."

"Then allow me to take you in the phaeton."

"No need to trouble yourself. I must fetch my bicycle from the cathedral. I can walk back with John. Thank you again," she said, turning before he had a chance to put up further argument.

When she and John were properly out of earshot she had a question for him.

"Did the dean really send you? Only, it seems something of a coincidence that he should do so today, on the one day I am there. And as you know, I am no lover of coincidence."

He hesitated for a moment and then replied.

"He did send me, but only after I suggested it."

"Oh. I see. You did not think me capable of inspecting the burial site without you?"

"On the contrary, I knew you to be perfectly able. No, I'm not proud of it, but the fact is . . . I was jealous. It . . . it did not sit well with me that Phileas would get to spend time with you. I confess I worry that he is someone your family sees as a suitor. Someone you have known a long time. I fear our own new friendship . . . Well, I did not wish him to have further advantage."

Hecate stopped walking and stared at him. She had never seen him so vulnerable, so lost for words. His honesty, and his obvious deep affection, moved her.

"I should not encourage such jealous behavior," she said.

"I would not expect it of you."

"You were wrong to deprive poor Phileas of his moment."

"I was. And yet . . ."

"And yet?"

He looked at her directly then, as if trying to read in her expression her true feelings.

"And yet I would do the same thing again in order not to lose you."

A lively party of factory workers, freed from their shift, swarmed along the street, breaking the quiet tension of the moment with their ribaldry and noise, allowing Hecate a chance to collect her thoughts. When they had moved on she stepped close to John and took his arm. She would share with him everything, she had already decided that. And she knew the perfect moment in which to do so. A moment which had the added advantage of involving her father, for she believed the only way to avoid feeling divided by the two most important men in her life was to bind them together in a common cause. A cause which had herself at its heart.

"Oh, I am much harder to be rid of than you might think. Now, come along, or Mother will blame you for my being late home, and that wouldn't do at all, would it?"

# 24

SITTING WITH JOHN AND HER FATHER IN THE TWYFORD-HARRIS CAR-
riage, Hecate waited until they had left the city boundaries before she spoke up.

"Now that I have your undivided attention, there are things I should like
to tell you," she explained. "Things I need to tell you, regarding the Essedenes,
and regarding myself."

"Why, daughter, you sound quite mysterious," said Edward. His tone was
light, but she could see concern in his eyes. He knew her too well. As he waited
for her to speak he took out his pipe and loaded it thoughtfully.

Beside her, John shifted in his seat. "I am happy to be taken into your
confidence, of course. Might what you have to say better equip us for today's
mission?"

"It might," she agreed. "Though I shall leave you both to judge for yourselves if you think our work here more or less dangerous because of it." Her
statement silenced both men. She had been uncomfortable keeping her actions with the keys from her father, but now she came to confess to what she
had been doing she felt guilty, too, and not a little ashamed. He deserved her
trust and her honesty. They both did.

"After our trip to London, Father, we agreed that the most likely place for
the writing used to summon the Resurgent Spirits was the locked cabinet. We
were correct, and the map confirmed it to me." When his expression suggested

he would like clarification on this point she pressed on. Some details would have to wait for another time. "I needed to gain access to that cabinet's contents, as I believed—indeed I am now certain—that the same book holds the incantations required to return the Resurgent Spirits to their rightful place. As we do not yet know the identity of the person performing the rituals to invoke the Essedenes' curse"—here she avoided glancing at John, ashamed to have ever allowed her father to include him on a list of possible suspects— "there was no one I could trust to grant me sight of the cabinet's contents. Which is why I had a set of keys cut. Keys that would open the way to the library and the cabinet itself."

"But"—Edward was shaking his head—"how were you able to have keys copied when you did not have the originals?"

"I made impressions and took them to a key cutter."

John spoke up. "When I saw you leaving the cathedral that evening . . . you had taken the keys from the vestry?" There was real hurt in John's tone. "You made me complicit in deceiving the dean."

"I was grateful for your discretion, John."

"Given when I was unaware of your actions."

"Would you not have helped me had you known?"

"Well, I . . . that is not the point."

"Forgive me, but I believe it is entirely the point," she said, putting her hand on his. "I do not believe either of you would have condemned my actions. Not if you fully understood their necessity."

Edward puffed pointedly on his pipe before demanding that she give them the name of the unscrupulous key cutter who would undertake such illegal work.

"Before you pass judgment on him, Father, hear what I have to say. Mr. Sadiki is no ordinary locksmith. His family have served Hekate for centuries. He recognized my brooch, heard my name, and only then agreed to help me."

"Or so he would have you believe!" John suggested. "How convenient for him, to be offered an excuse to make money from . . ." He hesitated, quietened by the look Hecate gave him.

"Two things render your thinking on this redundant, John. The first is that he would accept no payment, even though he furnished me with a number of keys, and at short notice. The second is that he had knowledge beyond anything he might have ordinarily come by."

"Such as?" Edward asked.

"Such as how you came to buy my brooch. Where you were when you bought it. Who sold it to you. And how the second you took possession of it, you could do no other than name me for the goddess who I also now serve."

"Good Lord! He knew of the tinker woman?"

"Her name was Phoebe. She, too, was one of Hekate's followers."

John reached over and took her hand in his. "You say you serve her, my dearest Hecate. . . ."

"Do not fear for me. I am not lost to all Christian hope. I am as I have ever been. The girl you both know. The only difference is, now I know myself better."

The astonished silence that followed her revelations was broken only by the rumbling of the carriage wheels and the hoofbeats of the horses. When the men did speak again, they did so together, their questions overlapping, their exclamations and reactions competing for her attention, their looks of amazement colored with concern, sometimes with hurt, occasionally with anger.

Edward waved his pipe to underline his sentiments, his care for her safety fighting with his wish that she had consulted him before acting. "To open that cabinet alone . . ."

"I was not alone, Father."

". . . am I no longer to be trusted with your confidence, daughter? Why did you not come to me, share with me your intention?"

"I am sorry. . . ."

John spoke up. "Why spurn help from those who you must know would give their support if asked?"

"It is precisely because I knew neither of you would refuse me. Had I asked, John, I think you would have helped me make copies of those keys and gain access to the library, and in doing so you might have ended your career, were our actions discovered. Might have lost your position at the cathedral. I would not put you in such a situation, not for my sake. And you, Father, you would have assisted me in actions that could have ruined your professional reputation, a renown you have spent your life building, only to be tainted by an illegal act. I would not have you remembered for one misdeed on my account, all else you have strived for forever forgotten."

Both men considered her answer in silence. Hecate seized this pause to move the conversation onward.

"I am truly sorry if my actions have disappointed you. Either of you. These were not . . . ordinary decisions to make."

"We do indeed find ourselves in extraordinary times," Edward acknowledged. "And times of great peril."

Hecate moved to take the seat beside him. "Which is why I need your help now. Today I believe we beard the lion in his den. What we learn here could answer some of our many questions. It might put us on the right path to stopping Lord Brocket's plans with the Essedenes and the Resurgent Spirits. Mr. Sadiki said there is a cursed family—the de Furches—who summon the dead using the Essedenes' words every hundred years. We know someone with access to that cabinet is using the banned book and we suspect they are acting on the earl's instructions. Two unconnected families, or is there a connection between the two? Could it be that the earl's family are related to the one responsible for the desecrations at Piedmont Abbey? This is our chance to find the truth. We must present a united front."

Her father placed his hand on her shoulder.

"My dear daughter, you know you always and ever have my full support. It could never be otherwise."

John looked at her. "It is because of you I am here, Hecate. You must know you can depend on me."

Her father's mind had already turned to practical matters.

"Of the utmost importance is that we have access to that book. I share your belief that it contains the words that summon the dead, and is therefore most likely to contain the counter curse or spell."

"Spell," John muttered the word. "How strongly that speaks of witches."

Hecate tried to read his expression. "I am being guided by the Goddess of Witches."

"If your Mr. Sadiki is to be believed."

"We have no reason to disbelieve him," Edward said.

"And what of the brooch?" Hecate pointed out. "It was the serpent that saved the griffin. Hekate's serpent. Whichever way you look at it, Father is right when he says I must overcome that book's defenses." She sat back in the seat. "The question we must put our minds to is, how is that to be done?"

Her father was quick to offer the contents of his own library again, or another trip to London and the British Museum. "We have scoured both for references to the Essedenes themselves, and to necromancers in general. What if we were to search for assistance in countering enchantments that guard dark magic?"

"I cannot imagine there would be many books in such a category," said John.

Hecate's face lit up. "That's it!" she said. "Of course!"

"What have I said?" John asked.

"It is what both of you said. Such a book would be a rare thing, and we might not find it in a library or museum."

"Might we not?" Her father was unconvinced.

"It would only be of any use in close proximity to the book which was ensorcelled, do you see?"

"As a key must be readily available to a lock," John suggested.

"Or a piece of a puzzle at hand to fill a blank space," her father agreed.

Hecate grinned. "Or the remedy to a poisonous plant growing close at hand," she said, thinking of Mr. Sadiki's words and the drab, unremarkable book that lay on the lower shelf of the locked cabinet.

Brockhampton Manor was markedly smaller than Holme Lacy House, but no less impressive. What it lacked in size and grandeur it made up for in age and significance. If Clementine's family home was the largest house in the county, Lord Brocket's was certainly one of the oldest. Its black-and-white timber frame and limewash, beneath a stone tiled roof, with its own miniature moat and gatehouse, had their origins in the mid-fifteenth century. Its stone chapel, now fallen into ruins, was thought to date from the early eleven hundreds. Even the lonely gable wall with the tall, pointed arch of its window space held a romantic charm and a strength of presence that had stood the test of time. Such was the ancient provenance of the place, and the renown of the family it was home to, those later, grander, redbrick Georgian constructions with their classical allusions, could not compete for importance. The family were as old as the manor house, their connections unrivaled, their reputation impeccable. Until now.

Hecate could not fail to be moved by the beauty of the place as they approached it. She did not wonder that the earl had rejected the more modern

house that his grandfather had built elsewhere on the estate and chosen this
as his home. Surely a man who was born to such a house could never entirely
besmirch his name.

"All will be well," Hecate promised them. "We three together, in daylight,
are surely safe enough."

Her father put away his pipe. "Brocket will, I'll wager, be keen to keep what
friends are prepared to be seen in his company still," he pointed out. "It would
not strengthen his case were anything untoward to happen to us."

The driver brought the horses to a halt. A footman emerged through the
gatehouse but Hecate was out of the carriage before he could perform his duty
of opening its door for her. If he was surprised by her appearance he managed
not to show it. She was wearing her best day dress, made of a fine cotton print,
dark green with tiny brown leaves. Being of the day, it had a bustle, which
she had left in place, as there was no time to make the adjustments to length,
the gown having been designed for this extra padding. Stella had helped her
shorten some of these swags so that her long brown boots were exposed. The
purpose of this minor alteration was not for appearance, however. It meant
that she could more safely ride her bicycle in the dress, should she wish to. It
also meant she could more easily run, should she need to. She had pinned her
precious Hekate cameo to the lapel of her dress, the day being too warm for a
coat or jacket. The gold cross that John had given her hung around her neck,
visible in the open collar of her dress.

The three followed the young man under the arch of the gatehouse. They
passed through it only briefly, but as they did so Hecate was assailed by a feeling of dread. From the stairs to the right she heard her name being called by a
chorus of unknown souls. She glanced at her father and John but it was clear
they had heard nothing.

They were led down the garden path, and into the house itself. The footman left them in the great hall, assuring them that their host would be with
them very soon. The room had a vaulted ceiling, with a gallery across one side,
but it was not grand in the way some fine houses were. The overriding sense
of the place was one of timelessness. The walls of the interior were timbered
in the same way as the exterior, with dark beams and here and there runs of
burnished oak paneling. One wall was taken up by an enormous fireplace,
and three latticed windows looked out over the moat. The furnishings were

antique and valuable rather than fashionable. The effect was quite medieval, and Hecate doubted it had altered greatly for centuries. There were several portraits, one or two particularly large and bearing a patina of age and grime. Hecate stepped closer to inspect the severe faces of the nobles looking down upon them. One was identified as John Buckler and dated 1872. There was an elderly woman with no inscription and another painting of a child, but the one that caught her attention was of a handsome man, his clothes suggesting the sixteenth century. There was nothing remarkable about his appearance; it was his name that made her grab her father's arm.

"Look!" she whispered urgently, directing him to the nameplate set into the frame. "James Habington. The name that was mentioned in Father Ignatius's letters. Do you remember? He said a young preacher had come to the abbey to help and his name was—"

"Habington! I knew I had heard the name before. I recall now that His Lordship mentioned his ancestor during a talk he gave to the chamber of commerce. He has always made much of his lineage and of how ancient his family is. Never passes an opportunity to tell us how long his forefathers have inhabited Brockhampton."

"Father, it cannot be a coincidence. I will not have it! We know Lord Brocket is harboring Embodied Spirits, and now we know his family connection to spirits being summoned goes back centuries!"

"But how does this sit with your key cutter's assertion that some Frenchman's family is at the heart of it all? Habington is an English name."

"It is, but only think, there has been a dwelling on this site for centuries. . . . Consider the chapel. The style suggests it was built in the eleven hundreds."

"After the Norman Conquest of 1066."

"When most of the important land was given to invading nobles. Nobles with French names, Father."

"If both your Frenchman and Habington have their origins here . . ."

"We must look for anything bearing the name of de Furches. Perhaps there are some old graves in the chapel. . . ."

Their conversation was interrupted by the earl himself striding through the door.

"Ah, Cavendish, Miss Cavendish, Reverend Forsyth, how pleasant to have visitors," he said, his whole manner that of an acquaintance practiced in the art of social sincerity, hand outstretched in greeting. He took Hecate's hand and gave a stiff formal bow over it, leaning to touch it to his lips. She was glad she was wearing her kid gloves. His touch, even through the leather, caused her to shiver. Now that she knew what he was about, she felt she was in the presence of someone capable of extreme deeds.

"Lord Brocket," she said, returning his greeting as neutrally as she knew how, a little wrong-footed to see how at ease he was. How good humored, almost jovial. But then, she told herself, her father was in all probability correct. The earl would wish to maintain the pretense that nothing serious had taken place, that his behavior and that of his cousin were things that could be smoothed over and accepted, given time.

"I have not received many guests of late. As you might imagine, recent circumstances have somewhat shortened the list of people who might consider me friend."

"Circumstances!" John was unable to help himself. "You phrase the events as if you yourself were not their instigator."

"Ah, I see the reverend gentleman has come to chastise me. To rescue my soul, perhaps, or at the very least my reputation," he replied, continuing to smile, casting a glance in Hecate's direction when he uttered the word "soul."

Her father stepped forward. "Come, come, man. You must have known your actions could not go unchallenged."

"Is that why you are here?" He made a point of addressing this question to Hecate. "To challenge me?"

She felt a deepening revulsion for the man with each passing moment she was required to spend in his company. He was not, she was certain, himself an Embodied Spirit, but there was something malevolent in his gaze, hidden behind the charming, aristocratic smile. Before he could form an answer her father spoke again.

"We've come to see if you might not reconsider. Your behavior . . . you realize it has set you quite apart from society."

"Ah, society." There was pity in the earl's tone. "How limiting to have to shape one's life according to the dictates of *society*."

John moved to stand closer to Hecate. "We hoped you might take this opportunity to grant Miss Cavendish the apology she is due. Your cousin's behavior at the ball . . ."

"Was deplorable, yes." He gave a nod of agreement. "A man who cannot hold his liquor should not be given unfettered access to it. I confess, I hold myself as much to blame as he, and therefore"—he put his hand over his heart and bowed again—"please, my dear Miss Cavendish, accept my most sincere apology."

"Yours I accept. I should sooner hear one directly from your cousin, however. Is he at hand?"

The earl frowned at this but did not let his annoyance infect his voice. "He can be called upon. Indeed, you are right, he should be held to account." He pulled a bell rope by the fireplace and when a footman appeared instructed him to ask the viscount to join them.

"You suffered no lasting ill effects, I trust?" he asked her.

"None."

"I am glad to hear it. Though not surprised. Cavendish, your daughter strikes me as a singular young woman. One in possession, perhaps, of unusual qualities, beyond those of her appealing appearance. Would you not agree?"

Hecate felt John tense beside her.

Edward took out his pipe and helped himself to a match from the box on the mantelpiece as he spoke.

"Look here, Brocket, we've come as a show of the concern that exists in the light of recent events. I have to tell you"—he paused to light the tobacco and draw smoke through the stem of his meerschaum—"that concern is chiefly for Her Ladyship. Such sympathy as there is for the situation does not, I feel obliged to let you know, extend to yourself. You might want to think about how poor public opinion could impede your political progress. I know this is where your ambitions lie. There is always a price to be paid for trampling over the accepted boundaries, the limits of what is expected of a privileged public figure."

The short speech was direct and challenging but the earl did not get the opportunity to respond to it. At that moment the door opened and Viscount Eckley entered the room with, to their surprise, a handsome woman of middle years on his arm.

"Ah, cousin. And my dear, there you are." The earl's smile broadened. "Permit me to present Mrs. Veronique Fletcher. Her late husband had a fine estate a little west of Shrewsbury, you might recall?" he asked, leading the woman forward so that she could greet their guests. When she spoke, her voice was soft and bore traces of her French ancestry. She dipped a shallow curtsey.

"I have heard so much about you, Miss Cavendish," she said, her dark eyes taking in Hecate's unconventional dress with a somewhat amused sweep.

Two things struck Hecate at once. The first was that her mother would declare the woman to be all mistress and not in the least bit wife. The second was that Veronique Fletcher was, beyond the slightest doubt, also an Embodied Spirit. She could sense it so strongly she had to prevent herself from taking a step back. There was a vibration about her that she recognized at once. Not the unstable madness she had encountered in the man who had been Joe Colwall, nor the drunken aggression the viscount had displayed. This was something more fundamental, more settled, and all the more unnerving for that. Hecate watched John closely as he took her hand in greeting but he did not react in any way that might suggest he felt it, too. His expression remained polite but somewhat stern, his own disapproval of the people in whose company he now found himself affecting him on an entirely different level. Her father seemed equally unperturbed though he could not fail to be struck by the woman's flamboyant and handsome appearance.

"Now, cousin," Lord Brocket beckoned to the viscount, "don't you have something to say to Miss Cavendish?"

Viscount Eckley stepped forward, once again not faring well in comparison to his nobler, more self-assured relation. He was sober, but strangely unsteady.

To Hecate's relief he did not take her hand. Her pulse quickened. There was a coldness in his presence, which he shared with Mrs. Fletcher. A chill that surrounded them both and seeped into anyone who came close. She was aware of a nausea taking hold of her, a visceral reaction to the two beings in front of her. Again, she had to force herself not to recoil or retreat. Her father came to stand next to her, and she was grateful to have him close.

"So, Eckley, what have you to say for yourself? My daughter is waiting," he said, his tone the most severe she had ever heard him use.

The air in the room seemed to crackle.

The viscount could not muster a smile, but he spoke politely enough.

"Hugely regretful, sorry business, embarrassment to myself and my dear cousin. Stupid of me, caught up in the fun of the evening, don't you know?

Sincere apologies . . ." and so on. He added a bow for good measure, though nothing could make his words sound genuine.

Hecate dearly wished she could remove the focus from herself and so quickly accepted his apology.

"Excellent!" Lord Brocket declared that particular matter closed with a clap of his hands. "Now, my dear," he said, addressing his mistress directly, making no attempt to hide his obvious affection for the woman who had usurped his wife, "I was about to offer our visitors some refreshment. Shall we take tea here, or the morning room, perhaps?"

"Oh, but it is such a beautiful day. Let us have some lemonade, or ginger, perhaps, or some cider, outside. A table by the moat would be more refreshing, after such a journey. Would that please you, Miss Cavendish?" she asked.

Hecate, having no clear plan as to how to proceed, decided being out of doors might put her hosts at ease and so allow her to question them more directly. It would also give her a little more time to assess the nature of their relationship. Was Brockhampton Manor to play a part in the Essedenes' plans? Could its ancient heritage and connections be something they sought out in particular, or had the geographical location an importance to them she could not yet see?

"Thank you, I should like that," she said.

The bell was rung, servants instructed, and Hecate, her father, and John were led outside. All was suddenly bustle and activity. As the party walked toward a lawned area beside the moat, footmen and maids scurried by, carrying table, chairs, and trays of drinks and cakes. The new lady of the manor might be lately arrived and spurned by society but she was evidently at ease when commanding servants. They were on the point of taking their seats when Hecate's attention was drawn back to the gatehouse. It was a curious building, almost a replica on a small scale of the manor itself. It had been constructed with a quirky lopsidedness, but otherwise it accurately mimicked the black beams and whitewashed walls of the main house. It served no practical purpose but had been added to the property as a show of wealth and the fashionable taste of the day.

It was not, however, its appearance nor its function as a statement of status that interested Hecate. Her interest lay in the atmosphere she had experienced as she walked through it, and the unmistakable ghostly voices she had heard.

"Your gatehouse is a charming building," she said. "I should very much like to take a closer look."

Her father's attention was piqued. He knew her well enough to understand her interest in the gatehouse must be important.

"Yes," he agreed, "an intriguing construction. The archeologist in me cannot resist digging around in ancient places. How about it, Brocket?" he asked, already walking away from the table.

The earl sat down. "I'm sure Veronique would be happy to show you. Vicar, why not stay here, see if you can't redeem my soul? Fifteen minutes long enough for you?" The invitation was meant to provoke and insult. To his credit, John maintained his unruffled exterior.

"Challenge accepted," he replied, earning a bark of laughter from his host.

"It would be my pleasure to show you," Veronique said quickly. "Edgar, don't let the reverend die of thirst. We three will enjoy the little house together and leave you three to your talk." With that she took Hecate by the arm and steered her away.

It took a great effort of will for Hecate not to snatch back her arm to free herself from the spirit's cold grasp. She was relieved it was but a short distance to the gatehouse, but that relief was short-lived. As they stepped across the threshold this time she was immediately aware of an unnatural drop in the temperature. She glanced at her father and could tell at once that he felt it, too. Sunshine fell through the windows yet the interior contained none of the warmth of those rays, even when she stood within their light. While Mrs. Fletcher chatted away politely regarding details of the building's history, she herself heard little of what she said, for she was overwhelmed with a sensation of dread. The voices began to call to her, louder and more insistent with each passing moment. She followed the other woman up the short run of stairs to the first floor as a moth to a flame, appalled by the atmosphere of the place but unable to resist looking closer.

"This upper floor has been employed for many purposes down the centuries," Veronique told them. "Some mundane, such as a storehouse for gamekeeper's traps, others more . . . interesting." Her smile had lost its easy charm and instead emitted something Hecate could only describe to herself as menace. "It's said that séances have been held here. Successful ones, I should imagine, as the place is thought to be haunted." She gave a light laugh which had no more warmth to it than her smile.

It was then that Hecate noticed something unusual about the beams on the far wall of the room. She walked forward to examine them more closely. Her father saw what she was looking at and moved to stand beside her, reaching out to touch the strange marks upon the wood.

"We have seen these before!" he whispered to her.

She nodded, recalling their visit to the British Library and the curious drawings on the monk's last letter. The shapes marked on the beams were identical.

"Tell me," she said, pausing to clear her throat as her voice was choked with alarm and she did not wish to show it, "what do these symbols signify?"

Veronique glanced casually at what she was indicating. "Oh, they are nothing so important, merely scorch marks of clumsy builders centuries ago. Look, do you not think the carving of the window frames attractive?"

Hecate fought confusion. She was in no doubt that the person opposite her had been summoned from her grave, had hunted for her intended host, and was now an Embodied Spirit, here at the behest of whoever had called her, prepared to do their bidding. The game the two of them were engaged in was wearying. How long, she wondered, would the pretense be maintained? She had hoped to buy time to think, to decide whether or not to confront them with the truth, but now, standing in the gatehouse, she was unable to think clearly. Her surroundings were so oppressive and so sinister they must surely have some vital significance to the ancient beings that were now striving to tread the earth once more. And those marks, too quickly dismissed by Mrs. Fletcher, were surely the key to the puzzle.

"My dear, are you quite well?" the other woman was asking.

At that moment Hecate made her decision. To show her hand, to directly confront two Embodied Spirits in what appeared to be a significant place for them would be foolish. The danger was too great. She recalled the violence and wickedness that had roiled forth from the possessed Joe Colwall. She did not have iron bars and burly policemen to protect her now. She would continue to go along with the subterfuge. She would not give away the fact that she knew what her hosts were. She had been naive to think that having her father and John with her would provide sufficient protection. All she had done by taking them there was put them in danger. The few things she had that might protect her from the spirits might not work against the two of them, with Lord Brocket acting against her, and in this place of terrible, dark power. She decided they would complete their visit, and leave as soon as possible. And the first thing she would do upon returning to the library would be to search for the meaning of the symbols burned into the beams, for these were surely proof positive of a connection between Brockhampton Manor itself and the Essedenes' plans.

"I am a little thirsty, perhaps," she said, turning to descend the stairs. "Even a covered carriage can be quite warm in this sunshine. If you don't mind, I think something to drink . . ."

"But of course!"

They rejoined the others, Hecate experiencing a lightening as if she had shed a heavy weight with each step she took away from the outwardly charming gatehouse. She did her best to appear untroubled but knew that John would notice the change in her. She hoped the others would not see it. As they took their seats and a maid poured lemonade, she put on her brightest smile. Her father, following her lead, found subjects upon which to make light conversation. They had, after all, received the apology they had come for, and Edward had said what needed to be said regarding the earl's actions. Etiquette demanded that they now observe the niceties of an insignificant social engagement. Much as it frustrated Hecate, she was for once happy to fall back onto what passed for civilized behavior. At least when safely back in the carriage she would be able to discuss everything she had discovered with John and her father.

Viscount Eckley, however, had other ideas. As she sipped her drink Hecate became aware he was watching her. The polite conversation around the table continued but he was silent, his attention entirely upon her. She lifted her eyes to meet his, intending to present a calm, unruffled expression. What she saw challenged her ability not to react in horror. The viscount's skin tone altered as she watched, quickly becoming deathly pale, his eyes darkened as he glared at her. And then he smiled. It was the most unnatural, mirthless grin she had ever seen, his mouth widening to an impossible stretch, so that his face appeared almost split in two as he revealed far more teeth—sharp and white—than were normal. Teeth which he slowly, deliberately licked with a deep red, unnaturally long tongue. She looked away, wishing to see if her father or John were aware of their host's repulsive transformation. Her glance told her it was invisible to them, but as Mrs. Fletcher came into her line of vision she saw that the woman was similarly grotesquely altered. The Embodied Spirit dipped her head almost coyly, raising her glass of lemonade in a toast as if acknowledging Hecate's horror, her own mouth as wide and revolting as that of Viscount Eckley's. Hecate turned to the earl. His own face was unaltered, save for the knowing look he gave her as he witnessed her reaction to the revelation. It was, Hecate knew, a direct challenge. There was to be no more pretense between them. They might present their acceptable selves to the rest of the world, but to her they revealed their true, terrifying selves. This display, directed only at her but in the presence of those dear to her, sent a clear message.

*We have no fear of you, but you should fear for your very life.*

She refused to let them see her frightened. Keeping her hand steady she picked up her drink.

"A toast to our hosts," she said, ignoring her father's somewhat surprised expression. She got to her feet, raising her glass. "May you both find the futures you deserve," she said, earning a muttered "*hear hear*" from the viscount, baffled silence from John and her father, and sweet smiles from the earl and his mistress. She made a point of directing her words to Lord Brocket. "I shall take a personal interest in seeing that you do," she promised him, *challenge accepted!*

She gave her father a look which he correctly interpreted as a signal to take their leave. With farewells exchanged, the three of them walked toward the carriage, which had been waiting in the stables.

"Well," John said beneath his breath, taking her arm, "that was the most uncomfortable visit I have endured in quite some time. That woman! In fact, all three exude a dreadful coldheartedness, a cruelty, even . . . Hecate?"

She was not listening. Her attention was, suddenly, elsewhere. She had noticed a man crossing the yard. He was dressed in the clothes of a laborer, with a flat cap pulled low over his eyes, and yet there was something about him that did not fit. He was familiar, and yet out of place. As she watched him, he looked up, and though he was still at some distance, for an instant their eyes met. And in that instant she recognized him. A shiver traveled the length of her spine. The man turned away and as he did so the driver steered the carriage out from the stables. All four horses snorted and shook their heads, refusing to move closer to the stranger. Despite the driver's best efforts, they bounded forward, ignoring his shouts, pulling the carriage away from the stranger as quickly as they were able, united in a desire to flee from him. John ran forward to help, taking hold of the bridle of the lead horse. The stranger dived into the entrance to the stables. As the Twyford-Harris horses calmed down, Hecate heard the commotion of those in their stalls, reacting to the presence of the unknown man.

Except that she *did* know him. She recalled where she had seen him before. It was in the crypt, when she had taken tea to the inspector and his men. This was one of those very constables. It was also the same one who had gone missing. Not only was Hecate certain of his identity, she was equally certain that the hapless policeman, who had had the misfortune to be in the wrong place at the wrong time, was now host to the spirit who had fled the dying Joe Colwall and found itself a new home.

The discussion on the carriage ride home from Brockhampton was filled with urgency. When Hecate confirmed that there were three Embodied Spirits there, Edward revealed he had noticed something unnatural about the viscount and Mrs. Fletcher, but without his prior knowledge would not have known what to make of it. John had confessed he felt a bad presence that put him in mind of exorcisms he had been called upon to perform. When pressed he had described this as a coldness in their company and a deadness in their eyes. The news of the constable's transformation was deeply troubling and brought on a heated debate regarding the danger of pursuing the Embodied Spirits and how best a person might avoid becoming a host.

When at last they fell to silence Hecate retreated into her thoughts. She was disappointed not to have found any evidence of the de Furches connection, but the portrait of Habington was proof of a century-old link between Brockhampton and Piedmont Abbey. And now the Embodied Spirits had revealed themselves to her. She sat back in her seat, determined to be alert to their characteristics should they present themselves in anyone else, forcing herself to remember every vile detail of what they had revealed themselves to be.

# 25

A MOONLESS NIGHT SAW THE STREET LIT ONLY BY THE FEW LAMPS SET between the pollarded trees along it. The large, handsome houses were not so close as to shed any illumination from their lit windows, which in any case were few, so late was the hour. There were no pedestrians to disturb those who waited in the shadows. Waited and watched. Sounds of the city were fading as most of the good people of Hereford went to their beds. No hawkers' cries broke the quiet, no carriage wheels or ironshod hooves rattled over cobbles, no revellers sang their way home. The night was deepening into sleeping silence.

The watchers crept forward, emboldened by this hush, confident there was no one to detect them. The boldest of them knew they could not be seen, not even if they should carelessly move into one of the meager pools of light thrown down by the lamps. All that would be visible to the innocent passerby would be a subtle alteration in that light; a lessening in its purity; a blurring at its edges. One of the watchers, however, had reason to be more cautious, for his mundane form was, in this instance, unhelpfully solid. Unimpressively shabby. Unmistakably human.

They looked up at the redbrick house in front of them, scouring for signs of the one they hunted, agitated and eager. They began to whisper to each other with increasing urgency.

*She knows! She knows us!*

*Where is she?*

*Where is she?*

*Where is she?!*

The man among them risked another pace forward, taking care to use the laurel hedge to mask his presence should anyone look out from the house. He noted that all the downstairs windows were in darkness, shutters closed or curtains drawn. The servants' quarters in the attic were similarly dark save for a single candle on the small stairwell window ledge. On the first floor, however, two rooms were illuminated, their curtains open.

*She is a danger to us!*

*A danger!*

*Where is she?*

For a short while no movement could be detected at those carelessly unguarded windows. The watchers bobbed and fidgeted, restless and driven. At last their fractured patience was rewarded. A figure appeared, a woman, slim and small. For a moment she stood as if looking out, her fiery red hair glowing even brighter beneath the gaslight, and then she turned back into the room as if called, pausing to pull closed the curtains.

In the street the formless beings whined and keened, and from the man there came a low, rumbling growl.

As Hecate closed the curtains she could not rid herself of the sensation that she was being watched. She had thought, fleetingly, that she had seen something in the street below, but the night was too dark and she could make nothing out. Charlie had called for her, and she quickly crossed the few strides from the window to his bed.

"I am here," she said, sitting beside him, taking hold of his hand.

"Is it summer?" he asked. "Have I slept so long the holidays have come? Let's ask Father if he will take us to the sea again? I should love to swim in the sea right now," he said, beads of sweat forming at his hairline, his eyes without clear focus.

Hecate picked up a damp cloth and mopped his brow.

"Hush now. A trip to the sea is a splendid idea, but first you must get well," she told him, resolutely keeping her anxiety out of her voice. Her brother's condition had worsened over the past two days. Her mother had maintained a near constant vigil, refusing to leave his bedside unless another family member took her place, and even then only for short breaks. Now that Hecate was home to witness the tension in the household she worried that she herself should not leave again until her brother recovered.

Charlie fidgeted and she rearranged his pillows, doing her best to make him more comfortable.

"Mother says you went to Brockhampton Manor," he said, dipping back into a moment of lucidity as the fever waxed and waned. "You know of course that it is haunted."

"Of course," she agreed, smiling.

"Everyone says there is a soldier buried in the ruined chapel and on nights when there is a full moon he marches up and down. When you were there, did you see any ghosts?"

She thought about what she had seen, about what she had felt, about how dangerous she now knew the place to be. She shook her head. "It was a bright sunny day," she explained, not wishing to tell an outright lie.

Charlie looked as if he might say something else but then frowned and began muttering. Hecate lifted his head a little and encouraged him to sip some more of the beef tea Cook had prepared for him. He did so, grimacing as it went down, before lying back on the pillows and closing his eyes. Soon he was sleeping. She touched his forehead again and found it to be dry.

At that moment the door opened and her mother, dark circles beneath her eyes from lack of sleep, came into the room. Her expression asked the question she did not quite dare voice.

"He is sleeping, look," Hecate told her. "He seems a tiny bit better now, don't you think?"

Beatrice felt his hand and touched his cheek. "Has he spoken with you? Spoken . . . clearly?"

"A little, yes. And his fever seems reduced."

"It comes and goes. That he is cooler now does not mean it is certain he will not worsen later. He is always more fretful at night."

Hecate so admired her mother's stoicism and strength. She knew her heart was filled with fear and yet she would not be pitied, would not turn attention to herself. Her son's well-being was all that mattered.

"I can stay longer, Mother, if you'd like to sleep. While he is resting . . ."

"No. No, thank you, Hecate. You can go now," she said, attempting a soft-ness though her words were blunt.

Hecate nodded, got up, and left, closing the door quietly so as not to wake Charlie. Once in her own room, though tired from her long day and from her concern for her brother, she did not feel in the least bit sleepy. She found herself pacing the floor, thoughts swirling in her head, chasing one another like will-o'-the-wisps.

"This will not do at all," she told herself firmly. If she was not to sleep, then she must put her time to good use. She fetched paper, a pencil, and a stack of books from her desk and put them on the Persian rug in the center of the room. Pausing to unlace her boots and kick them off, she then knelt down and took up the pencil. On the first sheet of paper she wrote the word "Essedenes" in large letters and sketched a basic but adequate copy of the im-age from the map. She set the page aside, propped up against a small stack of books, and picked up another. On this one she wrote a list of all the people she now believed to be hosts to Embodied Spirits. So far this was Viscount Eckley, Veronique Fletcher, and the constable whose name she recalled was Mitchell. She put a date on this, and placed it on the floor beside the first sheet. Next she wrote a list of questions. How many spirits emerged from the crypt? Where were the missing Resurgent Spirits? What was the signifi-cance of the strange symbols in the gatehouse at Brockhampton Manor? How did the bodies entombed beneath the cathedral connect with those escaped from the abbey in France, or with the original Essedenes in Mesopotamia? Another list contained the names of those dead as a result of the Resurgent Spirits: Sir Richard, Mrs. Colwall, and Joe Colwall. She wondered how soon that list would grow. She wondered, also, how many there were she did not yet know about.

One of the most worrying things she had been forced to face was that the spirits could, if threatened or trapped, move from one host to another. The death of Joe Colwall and the sudden disappearance of the young constable whom she then saw at Brockhampton seemed to confirm this beyond any doubt she might have clung to. This meant that the spirit would be doubly difficult to contain or, if it came to it, kill.

It also meant that anyone who confronted an Embodied Spirit put them-selves at risk of becoming its next host. The idea made her shudder.

Sitting back on her heels she sighed, pushing stray strands of hair from her face. There was so much still to make sense of. So much still to be done.


Her journey to work the next day—an uncommon working Saturday, as she was keen to make up for her absence—was beneath a canopy of dark cloud. Gone was the spring sunshine, replaced by a stiff breeze and the threat of rain. She was compelled to wear her buff-colored Mackintosh over her blue dress and abandon her boater in favor of a mulberry wool hat which would better withstand getting wet. She had secured it as best she could with her mother's hatpin, but still she felt it unequal to the task of staying in place upon her abundant hair, tested by the bicycle ride and the wind. When she reached the cathedral she took it off, leaving it in the basket, annoyed that her bun had already begun to collapse. She began to unbutton her coat, and had not gone two strides further before John found her. He appeared so suddenly she was certain he had been waiting for her just inside the door.

"Are you well?" he asked, searching her face. "I confess I slept little myself last night, after what we saw at Brockhampton. . . ."

"We had a great deal to think about," she agreed. "I find the best cure for worry is action. And to that end I have been drawing up a plan."

He smiled at her. "Of course you have." When she made to continue on her way he put a hand on her arm. "Hecate, may I speak with you in private? It will only take a moment."

She hesitated only briefly before smiling at him. "Well then, to the tower?"

He nodded, holding up the key he had obtained in anticipation. "To the tower."

The wind that had been moderate at ground level was markedly stronger at the top of the cathedral. Her unbuttoned raincoat flapped behind her as her hair fell from the grip of its pins, both caught by the turbulent air. The metal-gray sky seemed to press down upon them. The city below was not a pretty scene of miniature houses but a series of dark channels and lines, with roofs slickened by the increasing moisture in the wind. Hecate stumbled as she walked toward the balustrades. John caught her about the waist, steadying her. She saw that he would have been happy to remain holding her, but she twisted free, gently loosening his grip to stand a pace away, smiling at him.

"What is it that you wished to discuss, John?" she asked, having to raise her voice a little above the sounds of the weather.

He hesitated before speaking as if ordering his thoughts. It was unlike him, ordinarily so articulate, to falter. When he did speak, his voice was low, his words sometimes snatched by the wind so that Hecate had to step closer to hear what he was saying.

"Ours is a new friendship, and yet I believe we have come to know each other better than many who might have enjoyed years of acquaintance. I had thought myself content here, engaged in work of value, granted liberty to celebrate and enjoy the music I love. I believed myself fortunate and happy. Until the moment you strode into my life, a person of such energy, such verve, such life! Your presence has transformed me. I have discovered a new level of existence, a new way of experiencing the world, seen not through my own eyes, but through your restless, beautiful, reckless vision. The moments I spend in your company are the ones that fill me with joy. Time spent away from you is merely ground to be trodden on my journey back to your side."

He took her hand then.

Hecate looked at him, finding herself fascinated by the intensity of his gaze. The stormy light behind him put him almost in silhouette save for the paleness of his eyes and his blond hair bright against the backdrop of gray.

"When we were at Brockhampton," he continued, "even though I do not have your gift, I experienced such a great . . . weight. My work as an exorcist has informed my opinion of this feeling, and I recognize what it means. What prompts it. And that is a dark presence and a danger. To see you so close to danger . . . I have never endured such apprehension. I was not afraid for myself. I was terrified that I might fail to protect you."

"I know there was danger, and yet, here we both are," she said.

"I knew then that my life without you would be meaningless. No, not that." He glanced upward, as if appealing to the God to whom he had dedicated his life to forgive him, to understand him. "It would be torment. I wish, more than anything, to be always at your side." He held her hand tight, moving a little closer to her. He nodded at the streets below them. "Hecate, I cannot give you the city, I cannot give you a life of ease, but I can promise you my heart. Always. I am yours, mind, body, and soul. Marry me, Hecate. Be my wife."

His words moved her. She had never been the subject of such intense long-ing, such heartfelt sentiments, and she could not fail to be deeply touched.

"John, you have caught me by surprise. . . ."

"I know, and I am sorry for it, but I could not wait. I felt compelled to speak out. Who can say what perilous times lie ahead for us? For any of us? These are strange days, my darling, and I would not have you face them with-out me, not for one second."

He lifted her hand to his lips and bestowed a lingering kiss upon her fingers.

A scintilla of excitement ran through her body.

"I cannot give you my answer now," she told him. "Will you allow me a little time?"

"Of course! Of course." He smiled then. "I am only relieved you have not turned me down flat. You have given me hope." He pulled her into his arms, looking deep into her eyes. She could feel his heart beating against hers. Her hair, free of its bonds, whipped around them as he stroked her cheek. The threatening rain began to fall, driven by the wind, so that water ran down their faces as they stood holding one another, both caught in the moment. And then he lowered his mouth to hers and kissed her. It was not a tentative, questioning kiss, but one filled with desire, with yearning, with passion, and she found herself responding to it. Even as the rain beat against them, they stayed as they were, drawing back only a fraction from that kiss, kept warm by that heartfelt embrace.

It was Hecate who at last broke the moment.

"I must go," she said simply.

He nodded, releasing her but keeping hold of her hand, leading her off that windswept aerie and down the twisting turret stairs.

# 26

STILL REELING FROM JOHN'S PROPOSAL, SHE WAS GLAD OF HER DESK and her work to settle her. So much was happening, and so many things demanded her attention. As she worked she planned the order in which she would address things, so that by the time Reverend Thomas went for his luncheon, she was clearer in her mind. She took up pen and paper to write a letter. She had spent some time going over its composition in her mind the previous night while sleep eluded her. Now that she came to write it, however, she was less certain that her words held weight. She reread it to herself.

> *My dear Inspector Winter,*
> *I am writing to inform you that I have discovered the whereabouts of your errant constable.*
>
> *If you will agree to come to our home this evening, around eight, I will furnish you with the full details. Forgive me for not simply revealing his current location here in this note, but there is much I need to make clear, and I must be certain that I have passed onto you all that I have learned in regards to this matter in a way which is both complete and sensible. Furthermore, there are details in connection with the constable's present home that I would not wish to commit to paper, lest it fell into the wrong hands.*
>
> *Please believe me when I say I remain your friend in this and all matters where I might be of service to you, the cathedral, or the city,*
>
> *Hecate Cavendish*

Satisfied she could not improve upon the wording, she folded and sealed the letter, tucking it into her pocket.

"Forgive me, Reverend Thomas," she said to the librarian, "I need to visit the—"

"What? Oh, yes, yes." He waved her away before she could name anything which could make him uncomfortable. "You might stop in at the vestry and see if the verger has the kettle on," he said, surprising her with such a suggestion. By way of explanation he went on, "Today I cannot keep the chill from my bones. Some tea, perhaps . . ."

"An excellent idea," she said, hurrying away.

Downstairs the choir was in the stalls practicing. Hecate took the route down the north aisle, the music following her. She was aware her feelings were still in turmoil after John's proposal. She found herself listening for his voice among the others. The memory of that kiss was bright and shining. She paused by St. Thomas Cantilupe's shrine, taking a moment to marshal her thoughts. The stormy light outside flattened the colors of the great stained-glass window in the transept, rendering its colors dark and somber. Solomon came to wind himself around her ankles. She picked him up, hugging him gently.

"Well, Miss Cavendish!" Mr. Gould's voice was jarringly loud and bright as it cut into the quiet moment. "I am surprised to see you having the time to stand at your leisure and bother with the cat. Or are you troubled with vermin in the library, is that it? Has Reverend Thomas sent you to fetch the animal to roust them? What a disturbance! Still, one cannot have mice in a library, no. Of course not. That would not do, would it? And what is the cat for if not to be put to such use? Indeed. Would you not agree?"

The verger's ability to use fifty words where one would do, to say so much and yet at the same time say little at all, never ceased to amaze Hecate. Also, his obvious need for someone to be in agreement with him at all times was a test to her patience. She put the cat on the floor, smiling to herself as Mrs. Nugent checked to see that he was not leaving prints as he trotted off across the ancient tiles. She brightened that smile.

"Do not concern yourself, Mr. Gould, there is no infestation in the library. As a matter of fact, I was on my way to see you."

"To see me, Miss Cavendish?" The man could not have been more astonished if she'd suggested they polka around the font together.

"I have a favor to ask."

He beamed, and a pinkness spread across his face and to the very tips of his ears. "How might I be of service?"

Hecate took the note from her pocket. "I have this letter, and alas I did not have the opportunity to send it by post. In fact, it is too important to be entrusted to the postal system."

"Important, you say?"

"Quite so. It is for Inspector Winter, see?" She handed it to him so that he could read the name it bore and take in the official library seal.

"Well! Has it to do with the events in the crypt? Has Reverend Thomas new information, perhaps?"

Hecate tried hard not to show her irritation. It was typical of him to assume any important business to be that of her superior, and, of course, a man. She herself was evidently worthy of being no more than the messenger. Her smile began to falter. She pressed on.

"The contents of the letter are confidential," she said.

"Oh, yes, of course!"

"What I can tell you is that this . . . information must get to its recipient at the earliest possible moment. I would deliver it myself, having my bicycle to enable me to cross the city swiftly, however." Here she paused to summon the humility required to swallow her own, bitter lie. "However, Reverend Thomas does not consider the task should be entrusted to a woman. It would not be fitting, you understand?"

"Oh, absolutely."

"I thought you might perhaps send for a constable? Or summon a reliable boy?"

"A boy? Oh dear me, no, that would not do!" He took a step back, his grip on the letter tightening as he did so. "There is no necessity to find another. I will deliver the letter myself."

"But, you are so busy, your responsibilities so many, we could not possibly ask . . ."

"Please, tell the master of the library not to give it another thought. It will be my honor to be of such service," he insisted.

"That is exceptionally kind of you," Hecate told him. She was satisfied on two counts. First that her note would be delivered. Second that, given it was sealed, Mr. Gould would not be able to open it and read its contents. He was still on her list, still not above suspicion.

"Is there likely to be a reply? Should I wait for one?"

"No doubt the inspector will inform you of that once he has digested the contents of the letter. While you are gone, why don't I make tea? I can take some up for the reverend and set yours on the stove for when you return. Will that suit?"

"It will suit very well indeed. Now, I will not delay a moment further," he said, turning on his heel and all but trotting away in the direction of the north door.

"Well then," Hecate said to herself beneath her breath, watching him go. "Tea."

The vestry presented its habitual combination of muddle and method. There were stacks of unrelated papers upon the desk awaiting the verger's attention; books placed seemingly at random about the room; two biscuit tins on the shelves beneath the window; and two rings of keys left unguarded on hooks by the door. Hecate filled the kettle with fresh water from the churn kept on a cool flagstone in a dark corner, and set it on the little stove to boil. While she waited she fetched china cups and a teapot and pictured in her mind the verger's breathless progress through the city streets on his way to the constabulary. She could not be certain Inspector Winter would send a reply. Her note did not necessarily require one. He merely needed to arrive at the appointed place at the chosen hour of the given day. In fact, she rather hoped he did not send a reply, for Mr. Gould would be sure to try to press it into the hand of the librarian, and it would be up to her to explain the situation without giving away her duplicity. She set biscuits on a plate beside his chair, just in case sweetening was required.

Hecate was late arriving home that day. She had not attempted to redo her hair, so that it hung about her shoulders, still wet from the persistent rain. She had received a brief reply from Inspector Winter to the effect that he would be out of town that night but would call the following evening. If he did not hear from her he would assume this time and date to be convenient. She did her best to enter the house as quietly as possible, wishing to have time to herself in her room. The back door creaked unhelpfully as she went in from the garden. As she passed the open door to the sitting room she was surprised to find her mother sitting by the unlit fire.

"Mother? Why are you in here all alone? And no fire. Let me send for Stella to lay one—"

"No need. I shall not sit long. I sought a few moments out of Charlie's room, but I shall return soon." She looked up then and took in her daughter's disheveled appearance. "What a state you are in, daughter! Must you go about looking as if you are without either home or parents?"

"It was raining. . . . I am sorry. Where is Father?"

"Sitting with your brother."

"How is Charlie?"

Her mother gave a sigh that demonstrated the depth of her weariness. "He is stable now, out of danger, so Dr. Francis assures me."

"That is good news!"

"It is. And yet . . . Dr. Francis sees him only in his extreme moments of poor health. He does not live with his condition, with this . . . sword of Damocles suspended above us, above our family, every minute of every day."

"Oh, Mother, he is feeling better! Do not distress yourself unnecessarily." Hecate took the chair on the opposite side of the hearth and sat down.

Beatrice lifted her head to stare at her daughter. "Unnecessarily!"

"Well, if he is out of danger . . ."

"That you can say such a thing tells me you have no understanding of my position! Of what it means to be a mother. Of what it means to be the one who must ensure that her children not only live but thrive. Each time your brother's health fails him we use up more of our meager funds. Do you imagine your father's wild journeys, grubbing around in the dirt of foreign countries, provided us with comfortable means? I am here to tell you it did not. It is true that the doctor's fees nibble only slowly at what there is, but just as an infestation of moths may make but a small impact initially, the end result is ruination. What will happen when the day comes Charles is dangerously ill and there is no more money? And before you speak of the earnings you provide from your work, do you imagine such sums color the costs of running this home in any meaningful way? Again, they do not. Your refusal to seriously consider marriage means we must keep you, that is the plain fact of it. It is not a simple matter of a gown here or a new pair of boots there. . . . The one way in which you could, in truth, improve all our circumstances would be to marry well."

"Mother, I—"

"No, do not speak, Hecate. I have not the strength to endure your selfish protestations this evening."

Hecate had heard such charges before but she had never seen her mother deliver them with tears in her eyes. She had not the heart to argue with her. Seeing her so beaten down by the demands, emotional and practical, being made upon her, saddened her deeply. Was her mother right to call her selfish? What, in fact, had she herself done to help the family? To help Charlie? She took a handkerchief from her pocket and passed it to her mother, who took it somewhat warily.

"Mother, when Father proposed to you, were you certain? I mean to say, how did you know you were making the right decision, in marrying him?"

Beatrice looked taken aback by the question. She dabbed at her eyes briefly while she considered her reply.

"Your father was employed by the foreign office at the time and expected to have a diplomatic career. His family are respectable, well thought of. . . . My own father approved the match, though I think my mother had higher hopes for me. And of course, there was my younger sister to be considered. She could not marry ahead of me. I . . . disliked being a bar to her happiness and advancement, particularly as there was someone who wished to marry her."

"Uncle Bertram?"

"Yes. It has been a highly successful marriage," she pointed out, evidently still pleased that she had in some way enabled it.

"So, it was the practicable choice, to marry Father? The responsible choice?"

"It was that, yes."

"But did you . . . When you agreed to become his wife, did you *love* him?"

The air in the room seemed to fizz. Hecate could not read her mother's expression and waited anxiously for the answer. When at last she spoke, Beatrice had regained her more customary composure. Her voice was level, almost matter of fact. Which made her words all the more surprising. Hecate had been half expecting something about love growing from friendship, or affection deepening with the shared joys of family life. Her mother, however, had something quite different to tell her.

"I adored your father from the outset. The first time I met him, I thought perhaps I was sickening for something, I experienced such a giddiness. To be in his company was to know complete happiness and became my greatest wish. The strength of my feelings toward him terrified me at first and then, once I was certain they were returned in kind and in sincerity, I was the happiest girl in the county. We have shared that love for over twenty-five years and it has not diminished one iota. Oh, I know you see us as a couple in their middle years, perhaps too accustomed to one another's company. You will come to understand that not everyone makes public their feelings. We do not all of us see it necessary to do so. Your father knows precisely how I feel, because it is how he himself feels." She smiled then, and Hecate was aware it was in part due to the look of amazement she could see on her daughter's face. "So you see, I was fortunate, for the right choice was also, for me, the happiest."

Hecate sat back in her chair heavily. She did not know if her mother's declaration of such a grand love was helpful or not. In some ways, it would have steered her toward a sensible choice more readily if Beatrice had spoken of a personal sacrifice of some sort. And yet, there were more people than herself to consider. Had she the right to refuse to help her family when she had the means to do so? John was not wealthy, but he had a respectable, well-to-do family behind him and a good position at the cathedral. He would keep her, she would no longer be a drain on the family resources, and she would be able to help with Charlie's medical bills. More than that, she could ease her mother's burden and put her mind at rest. One thing was certain, she could not make a decision at that moment. She got to her feet.

"Come, Mother, let me help you to bed. We both are in need of sleep, I believe." She offered her arm and her mother rose and took it and together they went upstairs.

The rain worsened through the night. After breakfast, Hecate had Stella show her how to twist her hair into a French plait. It required several attempts, but she mastered it. It was somewhat off-center, but this was not apparent if she chose to wear it pulled forward over one shoulder. Her mulberry wool hat sat atop it much more securely, the pin working through the braid. She donned her Mackintosh and was on the point of going to fetch her bicycle when her father emerged from his study.

"I have a meeting at the museum," he told her, putting on his top hat and plucking his umbrella from the hall stand. "Won't you walk into town with me? Forgo your bicycle ride, just this once?"

"Very well," she said, taking his arm. "For you."

They left the house, striding down Hafod Road together, keeping close to benefit from the shelter of his umbrella.

"I have arranged to speak with Inspector Winter later today," she told him.

"You plan to tell him of what we learned during our visit to Brockhampton?"

"It is vital that he understands what is happening, at least as far as we ourselves understand it. He must be made to see that while the spirits are being raised, no one in the city is safe. And the connection with the activity of the Essedenes' curse at Piedmont Abbey and Lord Brocket's ancestor is too strong a link to be ignored."

"You think you have found a way to convince him? He is not like you and I, daughter, nor even John. His faith lies in the tangible. His actions proceed from evidence, not theories."

"As a matter of fact I have already done so. At least as far as my communication with the lost souls goes. His acceptance of such a thing has helped further persuade him of our theories regarding the Essedenes and the murders in the cities. We cannot stop the earl on our own. We need his assistance, and he ours."

"We should surely convince him more easily if we knew the earl's goals. I still fail to see his purpose," said her father, steering her around a large rainwater puddle without causing them to slow their marching pace.

"Did you not say that he unsuccessfully ran for the post of prime minister?"

"Yes, he did. Narrowly lost, as I recall."

"I imagine having Embodied Spirits carefully placed in positions of power might assist him in that particular ambition, might it not?"

"Indeed it might. And consider how difficult it would be to remove such a person from office once legitimately installed, if he were to be supported by a cabal of such spirits," her father pointed out.

"Nigh on impossible, I shouldn't wonder."

Edward stopped, turning to her. "An unassailable position from which he could wreak havoc without possibility of being voted out!"

They stood wordlessly for some time, the sound of the rain beating upon the umbrella accompanying their splashing footsteps, both united in their thoughts.

"Hecate! Mr. Cavendish!" John's voice broke into their meditation. He was driving the cathedral gig, Bucephalus's mane wet from the journey, his head shaking rain from his ears. John pulled the reins and brought the little carriage to a stop alongside them.

Hecate stepped out from the shelter of the umbrella to speak to him. "You are out and about early."

"I have been sitting up with an elderly parishioner in Mordiford."

"They were unwell?"

"Mr. Mitford died shortly after dawn."

"I am so sorry. It would have been a comfort for him to have you there."

"Would that we could all pass from this world in such peace."

Edward raised his hat. "You are a good man, Reverend."

"The rain is worsening, I think. Can I offer you a lift to work, Hecate? I'm afraid there is not room for three."

"Oh. I had thought to walk in with Father."

John looked at Edward. Hecate watched the silent exchange. Here was the most important man in her life encouraging her in one manner of behavior, and here was the new man in her life suggesting another. Was this what it would be like were she to marry? To be forever torn between her old life and her new? Her father and her husband?

Edward put his hand on her elbow and guided her toward the gig. "Go with John, Hecate," he said.

"But—"

"We will talk more when you get home this evening. In my nice dry study. Off you go."

He helped her up as John reached down and took her hand. Once seated she turned to her father, who smiled up at her.

"Off with you, little worker bee!" he said cheerily.

"Until this evening," she said, raising her hand as John urged the horse forward and the gig pulled away. She held on to the armrest to brace herself against Bucephalus's erratic progress and the infamous Hereford potholes.

John glanced at her.

"I am so happy to see you," he said. "An unexpected delight. And a very welcome one, I must say."

"It cannot be easy, what you are called upon to do."

"As you say, I am called to do it." He smiled at her then, and her heart danced a little at the warmth in that smile. "All the same, I am grateful for the joy of your company," he said, his blue eyes holding her in their gaze.

She reached across and put her hand on his arm, feeling the warmth of him beneath her fingers, and together they traveled on to the cathedral.

# 27

IN HIS OFFICE AT THE POLICE STATION, INSPECTOR WINTER SAT DEEP IN thought. He picked up the note he had received from Hecate the previous day and read it through for the umpteenth time. News of the whereabouts of his missing constable was important to him, and he had regretted not being able to meet her sooner. However, after what he had witnessed in the crypt, after the irrefutable proof she had provided regarding her connection with spirits there, he had felt compelled to conduct his own investigations. He was not concerned with the lost souls she had described to him. By her account, these were benign, even helpful ghosts. Her demonstration of their existence had, more importantly to him, lent weight to her theories concerning the desecration of the tombs in the crypt and the reasons for the murders in the city. That these acts of violence should remain unaccounted for troubled him greatly. With no clear leads to follow, Hecate's insistence that the two events were linked, and that to solve one he must solve the other could not be ignored. On the contrary, he would be foolish not to use what facts she had given him.

And it was these facts that led him to focus on the actions of Lord Brocket. Hecate's insistence that the earl's cousin was one of the Embodied Spirits she had told him about indicated that there was a connection there that went beyond coincidence. To the inspector's logical mind such an alliance raised a question. Why would a wealthy, powerful individual knowingly harbor a demonic, murderous being? Either he was aware only that his cousin was strangely altered and given to uncharacteristic behavior, nothing more. Or, the earl knew precisely who, or rather what, he had taken into his home. In search of answers, Inspector Winter had taken the Birmingham train to the town house of Viscount Eckley and presented himself there, knowing the man to be absent. He had been able to question the somewhat alarmed housekeeper regarding her master's relationship with his cousin. It took mere moments to establish that there was little affection between them. When pressed further, the housekeeper revealed that in point of fact the earl frequently snubbed or belittled his relative. Recently, however, he appeared to have had a change of heart, inviting the viscount to stay at Brockhampton. On the train journey home the inspector had come to the conclusion that it was not fond regard that prompted Lord Brocket's sudden interest in his cousin. The earl would certainly not tolerate the younger man's loutish and difficult behavior without good reason. Given the earl's own recent scandalous actions, it was fair to assume those reasons would further his own causes. If Hecate's theories that these beings sought out the wealthy and powerful were correct, and that they did not act as individuals, but under the control of another, the earl would seem to fit that description. Could he be pulling the strings of a puppet at the cathedral who was summoning these fiends for his own advancement? Or was he himself a lesser player in a larger scheme? This line of thought brought the inspector to the unpalatable truth that someone at the cathedral could be responsible for calling the dead from their resting places, either as minion or puppet master.

He rose from his seat, his legs stiff from inactivity. Opening the door he called along the corridor.

"Sergeant Highcliffe!"

"Sir?" The sergeant appeared quickly.

"Have a constable take your place at the desk. I require your assistance."

"Right away, sir. Will we be making an arrest?"

"Not on this occasion," he said, taking his bowler hat from the stand. "I wish to pay a visit to Dean Chalmers. I often find the presence of a uniformed officer helps concentrate the mind of the person being interviewed. However lofty his state."

The sergeant hid his surprise well and went to find a constable to stand in for him.

His superior selected a fresh pencil from the box on his desk and left his office, whistling softly as he went.

It was at the end of that same day that Hecate heard organ music. John was at his practice. The rich sounds of the great instrument soared into the vaulted ceiling, filling the cathedral with joyful notes and dramatic chords. She descended the library stairs, bidding good afternoon to Reverend Thomas, and made her way through the choir stalls. John was about to come to the end of the piece of music he was playing. She waited, standing just out of his sight, watching him. He played with such concentration, such skill. It was a gift, his flair for music. Whether singing with the other vicars choral or giving a recital on the organ, his talent was obvious. She felt proud of him then and was grateful for that. He finished the piece and became aware of her presence.

"Oh, Hecate! What a lovely surprise."

"I did not wish to interrupt your playing."

"Had I known I had such a particular audience I might have done better."

"Or I might have put you off." She moved forward and sat down on the stool beside him. He shifted up to make more room but still they were sitting close. Hecate placed her fingers over the cool ivory keys, imagining what it must be like to be able to bring forth such wonderful music.

"You have escaped the library," he noted.

She nodded but did not reply, fixing her attention on a tiny chip in one of the keys. She traced its shape with a finger, bothered by such sharpness hidden among the smooth keys, wondering if John knew that this small flaw existed. Did he wince each time he found it as he played? Or was he oblivious, being so entirely taken up with what he loved? After all, it was unreasonable to expect perfection in anything.

The nape of her neck was exposed as she leaned forward and she felt John lift his hand to touch it gently. His flesh felt cool against her own warmer skin.

She turned toward him then and the intensity in his gaze moved her.

"Hecate," he murmured, "what an extraordinary creature you are. Your coloring, your spirit, your presence . . . you are composed of the very elements."

"Take care I do not burn you, then." She smiled.

"You might consume me in a blaze and I should not care. To be so close to you, to know you . . . it would be a price worth paying."

She lifted her hand to touch his lips, compelled by feelings she did not yet understand.

"I would far rather you lived," she told him. As she watched him looking at her, watched the desire written on his face and felt his breath upon her fingers, it was as if the rest of the world had shrunk away. The sounds of the cathedral, its echoes and sighs and creaks, were muffled. Instead of feeling anxious that they could be observed or overheard by someone, other people ceased to be of importance. All that mattered at that moment was him. All that she wanted at that moment was to be with him. To hold him and be held by him.

She leaned forward and he let his arm drop behind her to pull her close, encircling her into a warm embrace.

"Hecate," he said again, softly yet fiercely, and the sound of her name spoken in such a way made her shiver. "You have it about you to reduce a man to blasphemy, for I am certain I hold a goddess in my arms."

He took hold of her hand and kissed her fingers, before he slowly, tenderly, kissed her mouth.

When she opened her eyes and looked at him again, Hecate became aware of a joy welling up inside her. She slipped from his grasp, standing up, brushing down her skirts.

"It is pleasantly fresh outside after the rain, had you noticed?" she asked.

Surprised at this change of subject, John laughed lightly. "Yes. When I passed along the cloisters earlier the gardens were looking particularly fine."

Without looking at him she said, "I believe it is precisely the best sort of day for hearing good news."

She heard him gasp.

"Hecate . . . my dearest . . ."

"I wanted to catch you on your own to speak to you," she explained quickly, "but you are so busy. I saw you in the vestry earlier, but Mr. Gould is such a tittle-tattle, and such news should be ours for the sharing, don't you think?"

He stood up. "Hecate, please look at me."

She did so, raising her face to him with a cheerful smile.

"I would not want you to make a decision in haste," he told her. "That is to say, of course I would not wish to give you pause, only . . . Such a big decision . . . such . . . not an easy thing, and . . ."

"Why Reverend Forsyth, I have never before, I think, seen you at a loss for words."

"Can you blame me? When my future lies in your hands? In the few words that you may be about to utter? I want you to be certain, Hecate. Certain that this is what you want. Not what you think you should do. Not a choice made to please anyone else. Be certain that it is what *you* want?"

She took his hands and held them both, lifting them to her lips for the very lightest of kisses.

"Do you think I can be a good wife to you, John?" she asked, equally sincerely.

"Truly, I can imagine none other," he said.

"Well then, only one question remains."

"Which is?"

"Will you tell Mother our happy news, or shall I?"


The heavy marble and rough ancient stone presented no barrier to communication between the restive spirits. In sounds that were not quite words they called to one another, each urging the other on, repeating the urgency for action, the need to rise. Both had been woken from their sleep of centuries, summoned by a force they could not resist. The moment had come for them to wake and to answer the call of their forefathers. But theirs was not a joyous awakening. This moment was not simply for their own freedom, or even for the greater task destiny had chosen for them. These two spirits had a singular task, immediate and dangerous. Dangerous because there would be no time for them to seek out hosts. No time for them to become Embodied, corporeal, secure in a new living person who wielded physical strength and social power. These two would have to act as they were, newly risen, nothing more than fierce energy, dark magic, and wicked intent driving them forward.

*We are called!*

*We must act!*

*We cannot fail or all will be lost!*

The spirits writhed and twisted in their tombs, and as they did so the bones and fragments of cloth and precious metals which were all that lingered of their earthly lives disintegrated further. Soon the coffins contained nothing but that impure, singular energy which grew and grew, the pressure on the antique caskets increasing until, at last, as if dynamited, they burst apart. The spirits sprang free of their miserable confinements, erupting into the cold, dark air of the crypt. They swirled about the low vaulted ceiling, slowly becoming denser and more visible. Not as human forms, but as a shadowy mass, pulsating and pullulating, so that they became bigger and stronger, until they had reached their full potential. Had anyone looked into the solemn space at that moment they would have seen dense shadows with no person to cast them. But the day was over, the evening beginning, and there were no people near the crypt. Not then.

The spirits moved together, forming a single mass at the foot of the stone stairs, their single thought brought to bear on the one they hunted.

*She must be stopped.*

*She must be stopped!*

*We will finish her!*

They crouched on the cold flagstones and there they stayed, listening. Waiting.

# 28

"NOT PHILEAS AND HIS LOVELY COWS, THEN?" CHARLIE ASKED AS HE climbed into bed.

"Sorry, no." Hecate smiled at him. "But at least when I am living in the cloisters you may visit me and I will show you all sorts of hidden places in the cathedral. Places most people aren't ever allowed to see. John has promised to take you up into the bell tower if you should like to go," she told him, tucking the covers in around him.

His face brightened then. "Might I be permitted to ring one of the bells?"

"Who knows, you just might!" she said.

It was good to see him happy, but the evening's excitement had worn him out, and it showed in the dark circles beneath his eyes. When she and John had arrived home and asked to speak to her parents, Charlie had, initially, been kept out of the room. Only when John had announced his intention and gained Edward's permission to marry Hecate had the door been thrown open and an impromptu party begun. Beatrice, aglow with excitement, had asked the maid to bring wine and glasses and Cook to join them in the dining room. Charlie had been a little shy with John at first, but had been won over by discovering a shared interest in historic ships. Hecate's father had taken her to one side quietly and asked a single question.

"Is this what you want?"

"It is," she had replied, and meant it, at peace with her decision, buoyed up by the happiness she saw it bring to those she loved, for there is nothing makes a person so attractive as seeing others enjoy his company.

Once everyone was assembled, Edward gave a short speech, saying how delighted he and Beatrice would be to welcome John into the family. He then proposed a toast to the happy couple and the engagement was official. Cook was seen to have to dab her eyes with her apron, and Hecate's mother was more animated and jolly than anyone had seen her for quite some time. There was a great deal of discussion regarding how the engagement should be announced in the papers and whether or not the charm of a Christmas wedding outweighed the practicality of an autumn one. John was invited to stay for dinner and Edward treated him to his best port before the evening drew to a close. In the hallway he had held Hecate's hands in his and kissed her briefly. She had been a little surprised at how much she had liked it and at the sadness she felt as she waved him off.

Now, as she hugged her brother good night, she thought properly for the first time about what it would be like to leave the family home and set up her own household.

"You're squeezing jolly hard, Hecate," Charlie complained.

"Sorry," she said, ruffling his hair. "Get a good night's sleep." She reached up to switch off the gaslight.

"Not all the way off," he told her, sounding much younger than his years, betraying a little of the fear he lived with due to his illness.

She left the light at a glow, the soft beam of illumination falling upon him as he lay down, lighting him like an old master painting.

"Good night," she said as she left, closing the door quietly as she went. She crossed the landing and was about to go into her own bedroom when something made her stop. At first she thought it was a sound, like the dull thudding of heavy treads upon the stairs. But then she realized it was not a noise as such, rather the shuddering of footfalls through the floorboards beneath her feet. This sensation was accompanied by a smell, sour and dank, putting her in mind of rotting potatoes or an unwashed chamber pot. While her mind was taking in these strange occurrences, instinct flooded her body with fear. The desire to run conflicted with the absolute certainty that she must remain completely still, if she were not to somehow give away her own presence to whatever it was that now crept up behind her. Her hand was on the door handle and she felt unable to release it, as if to do so would be to let go the one thing that kept her anchored, that prevented her being snatched away. It was then that she felt a slithering touch upon her waist. Glancing down she could see nothing, save perhaps a deepening of the shadow in the pulsing gaslight of the landing, but she could distinctly feel pressure at her sides, right and left, as if two unseen arms were pulling her into a foul embrace, gathering her close to the thing that crouched at her back. She opened her mouth to scream. No sound escaped, as a further blackness crept across her face. She could feel it moving over her eyes, into her nostrils, between her teeth.

*A Resurgent Spirit! No!*

She knew what fate awaited her if she did not act. She recalled in a vivid flash the raving face of the man who had once been Joe Colwall. She thought of the cold menace that emanated from Veronique Fletcher and Viscount Eckley. She imagined what it would be like to be inhabited by such evil, to have it crush her own soul, to lose herself forever to such darkness. Even as she fought to take her next breath, her mouth now stopped by the thickening blackness, she felt increased pressure around her throat. She knew what would happen next. It would only be a matter of moments before she was robbed of air so that she would fall into a faint and be defenseless against the spirit.

She could not let that happen. She *would* not let that happen.

She forced herself not to give way to panic but instead to think of what her father had taught her regarding protecting herself from attack. An assailant will expect a fight, he had said. Best not to give it to them. Against all her instinct, Hecate allowed herself to go limp. She slumped forward against the door, no longer trying to take a breath, simply breathing out slowly, letting her head sag against her shoulder. She could not know if the spirit was confused or surprised by this, or even, indeed, if it had the capacity for such responses. What she did know was that it appeared to hesitate, to pause in its action, as if having to reassess what was needed, when the fight it was expecting did not come. In that fraction of a moment, Hecate acted. She dropped down and then flung herself into a ball, rolling down the stairs as she wrapped her arms over her head. She was aware of the bruising impact of her cheek and head and back against the wooden treads as she fell. More importantly, she felt the foul phantom recede as she moved out of its grasp. At the turn in the staircase, she grabbed the bannisters, stopping her fall. Turning, she looked up and saw the dark mass undulating and twisting as if searching for her. Hecate hauled herself to her feet, fists balled, teeth clenched.

The shadow became more dense and even appeared to gather into a shape that resembled a figure. As it did so it moved toward her again.

From deep within herself Hecate felt a rage and a strength building that she had not known she possessed. She thought of Hekate and how the goddess had told her to be brave.

"Leave this place!" she screamed at the spirit. "Return to where you belong!"

The spirit reared up, recoiling, its progress stalled.

From the drawing room came the sound of raised voices and running feet and then her father calling her name. Before he had reached the bottom of the staircase, however, Hecate's momentary relief had already turned to horror.

As she watched, the seething, formless being moved to the left, not down the stairs toward her, but in the direction of the next room, where it slid with terrifying speed under, around, and through the door.

"Charlie!" Hecate screamed, tearing up the staircase and flinging open the door into her brother's bedroom.

She was too late. Charlie's body lay motionless, his arms flung wide, his eyes closed, as the last remnant of the spirit seeped into him.

"No! Charlie!" She ran to the bed, taking up his hand, patting his cheek. "Charlie! Charlie, wake up. Wake up!"

Her father came running into the room.

"Hecate, in the name of God, what is happening?"

"A Resurgent Spirit!"

"What? No!"

"Oh, Father." She turned to face him, her eyes filled with tears of despair. "It has taken Charlie as its host!"

"You saw it?" He strode to the bed, sliding his arms under his boy and lifting him up. "Charlie?" he called to him, heartbreak in his voice. "Can he hear me?" he asked her.

"I don't know. I don't know! It tried to take me but I got away and then I saw it come in here, and oh, Papa!"

"Edward?" Beatrice called up the stairs. "Whatever is going on up there?"

Hecate felt her brother's brow. "He is cold as marble!"

"Dear God, what is to be done?"

Her mind raced, searching what little she knew of the spirits for some guidance, for some hope.

"An exorcism!" she said. "Father Ignatius said in his letters that while most did not work, some were successful."

"Such poor odds," her father murmured, but he was already carrying Charlie toward the door at a run, shouting for Stella to go to the street and hail a cab.

In the hallway, Beatrice cried out, her hands flying to her face. "Charles! Oh my boy . . . !"

Edward watched her clutch at her son as he lifted him carefully through the hall and out of the front door. "My dear, he has taken a turn for the worse. We must find help."

"Let me call Dr. Francis!" she pleaded.

Hecate gently removed her mother's hand from Charlie's sleeve.

"We will get him the help he needs, Mama."

"Hecate! What happened to your face? You are bleeding."

"It is of no consequence, do not concern yourself. You must trust us to do this," she said, looking deep into Beatrice's panic-filled eyes. She had not time to say more, as her father, already in the road, called back to her.

"Hecate, make haste, we have a cab!"

The timely arrival of the hansom was due to the fact that it was conveying Inspector Winter, summoned by Hecate's note, to their house. He took in the scene of drama with a practiced eye.

"What's to be done?" he asked, moving aside to allow Edward to step aboard with his son.

"We must get him to the cathedral, to Reverend Forsyth!" Hecate explained, climbing in behind her father.

He put a hand on her arm.

"Is this the work of your fiendish spirits? You think the reverend can save him?"

"It is his only hope," she said, lowering her voice for fear her mother might hear.

He jumped up beside the driver.

"The cathedral, quick as you can," he told him, and the carriage sped away.

Inside, Hecate took her brother's face in her hands.

"Charlie," she whispered, putting her mouth close to his ear. "My dearest one, hold fast. Hold fast!"

Though it was but a short journey, each minute that passed was torture for herself and for her father.

"We must find John," she said simply.

Edward nodded but when he spoke his voice contained a note of warning. "Hecate, remember what else Father Ignatius wrote . . ."

"That the first exorcist himself succumbed to the spirits. I have not forgotten," she replied, and they spoke no more of it.

On arriving at the cathedral Hecate ran ahead to the cloisters. She knew which door remained unlocked at night to permit the residents freedom to come and go from their little houses. She raced along the ancient covered walkway until she came to John's dwelling and hammered upon the door. He opened it in seconds, having only just reached home himself, his eyes bright with surprise at seeing her.

"Hecate . . . good Lord, have you been attacked? Whatever has happened . . . ?" he asked, reaching out to touch her bruised cheek.

"It is Charlie," she gasped, refusing to let fall the tears she felt blurring her vision. "A Resurgent Spirit has taken him!"

"God save us! Where is he?" he asked, already turning to pick up a lamp and take his key ring from a hook on the wall. He ran with her back along the cloister, their footsteps dogged by jarring echoes as they went.

They found Edward and Inspector Winter waiting for them at St. John's door. Charlie stirred a little, moaning pitifully. For a second he opened his eyes.

"Hecate?" he called out, his voice hoarse.

"I am here!" she said, taking his hand. "And John is here to help you. Do not be afraid."

"It is so dark," he said, even though his eyes were open and the light of the lamp was falling on his face.

"We must take him to St. Thomas Cantilupe's shrine," John instructed.

"Not the main altar?" Edward asked.

"St. Thomas was renowned for the number of miracles that happened in the presence of his relics. I believe it is a miracle we are in need of this day," he said.

Hecate ran with them as they went, a worrying thought making her speak up. "But, John, there are no longer any relics in his tomb."

He snatched candles from the stand as he passed, lighting them from the solitary burning one and handing them out. "Pilgrims have prayed at his shrine for centuries. We have his presence."

"Will it be enough?"

"Let us pray so," he said.

Edward laid Charlie down upon the cold flagstones next to the distinctively carved tomb, removing his own jacket to place beneath the boy's head.

"Hecate," John said, "stand at your brother's head. Mr. Cavendish, at his feet, quickly now. Inspector, take the boy's hand, if you please." As he spoke he fell to his knees beside Charlie, the lamp set down on the floor next to him.

Hecate experienced a chill so deep it caused her bones to ache. She looked up at John then, torn between her devotion to her brother and her care for the man she was to marry.

"John," she said quickly, "you must know . . . there is danger in what you do. For yourself. Great danger."

He looked at her, his face full of compassion and resolve, and in that moment she thought that she had never loved him more.

"This is what I do, Hecate. This is who I am." He spoke to all of them when he said, "Whatever takes place, do not move from your posts. No matter how alarming the events, we hold Charlie here between ourselves and St. Thomas, under God's benevolent love. We must keep him within that blessed space. Keep your hands upon him now."

They nodded their agreement and did as he bid them.

"Hecate," Edward called to her quickly. "Be on your guard. If John succeeds in expelling the demon spirit, it will look for another home."

"Yes, Father. We must all be ready."

It was at that moment that Hecate saw Brother Michael had come to stand beside her father. And then, taking form swiftly and silently, Corporal Gregory, who stood straight and strong beside her. One by one her other ghostly friends appeared, Mrs. Nugent and Lady Rathbone, coming to stand facing her. Without a sound, and seen only by her, they came to strengthen that circle, to lend their support, to show their love for the girl who was a friend to phantoms.

John had begun the words used in an Anglican exorcism, speaking out in a clear, strong voice. In front of them, Charlie started to move. At first he merely turned his head, or lifted a hand, but gradually his whole body writhed, his eyes remaining shut tight, his mouth working silently.

"The power of Christ compels thee!" John repeated the line three times, and each time Charlie thrashed more violently.

Hecate could not help crying out for fear that her brother's frail body would not withstand the process.

"Hold firm, daughter," Edward told her. "Inspector, do not for one second loosen your grasp."

"I have him, Mr. Cavendish!" he promised.

It was then she heard the whispered prayers of Brother Michael, the soft words of comfort from Lady Rathbone, the call to courage from Corporal Gregory. Each in their way did what they could.

John's voice became ever louder, the words of the rite spoken with increasing urgency. At one point he stumbled over them and glanced at Hecate.

"John . . . is it working?"

"The possession is entrenched, even now. . . ." He shook his head. "I have never before encountered anything so strong."

"You have to help him! Please, do not falter."

"I will do my utmost. . . . I will do all that is within my power, but, Hecate, I have to tell you, there is something of immense evil at work here."

"*Please!*" she said again.

He nodded and raised his hands, speaking with yet more determination and fervor.

"Begone from this innocent child! The Father, Son, and Holy Ghost drive you from this place! In St. Thomas's name, I command you! In the Lord's name, I command you! The power of Christ compels thee!"

Charlie's eyes sprang open. At first Hecate thought this a sign he was waking, but when she looked again she saw that it was not her brother's eyes that gazed up at her. Instead she found a dark, fearsome presence showing itself, flicking this way and that as if searching for the cause of its distress. She saw the gaze lock onto John. Charlie's body lifted from the ground where it lay, wrenching itself free of the hold of those who were doing all they could to keep him in their grasp. He levitated, arms dangling, legs jerking, as it rose above their heads. Instinctively she and her father moved beneath it, as did her spectral family, arms upstretched as if they might catch the boy were he to fall. The creature inside him turned his head to glare at John, spitting in fury, but still it would not be dislodged.

John ceased reciting the words of the exorcism that he knew by heart and instead raised his voice in a prayer to the cathedral's own saint.

"Hail Thomas, good shepherd, patron of the flock of Christ and teacher of the Church, lend your help to the sick, I beg you, and confer on devout minds by your intercession, the light of grace . . ."

This was too much for the spirit to endure. Not yet fully Embodied, the call to the holy bishop who had once prayed on that very spot was something it could not resist. With a shriek it left Charlie's body, manifesting as a black swarm of fat-bodied flies that flew in a whirlwind, filling the upper reaches of the transept.

Edward cried out in alarm as Charlie fell. The lost souls held fast their place beneath him, Corporal Gregory using his shield of protection, slowing his descent and cushioning his fall, so that his father was able to catch the boy in his arms.

"Charlie!" Hecate clutched at him, gasping with relief as she felt a more natural warmth return to his skin.

She turned to John. "It worked! You have saved him."

John's face lit up with joy. He smiled. He opened his mouth to speak.

And the swarm descended.

Hecate screamed.

"John! Protect yourself!"

He stepped back, throwing his arms up in a futile attempt to defend himself. In an instant, the vile entity had found its new home. He clutched at the wooden cross that hung around his neck. Even above her own screams, Hecate could hear him reciting prayers, calling on St. Thomas and God to help him. But the demon fought back. As she and her father watched helplessly, John was raised up, as Charlie had been. But he went higher. Up and up, past the shutters of the muniments room, above the walkway to the bell tower, up and up until he was under the bosses and arches of the vaulted ceiling of the transept.

"Father, we must help him. Say the words of the prayer he used. Say them with me!"

"Hecate, have a care! If the demon leaves him now he will fall to his death."

"And if it does not?" She ran forward so that she could see him more clearly, calling up to him, not daring to pray, yet terrified of doing nothing. She saw him continue to hold up his crucifix. She saw him struggle to take a breath. She saw that he would not give in to the thing that would take his soul, no matter the cost. He made his choice. For a split second he looked down and their eyes met. Hecate's heart lurched. He kept both hands tightly on the cross, though the rest of his body danced and spun, twisting and twitching until it was suspended upside down. She could hear him shouting out the words of the prayer, over and over. Louder and louder, though he had no air left in his lungs.

There came a terrible shriek. A fierce, furious sound that filled the great cathedral. Hecate saw the dark spirit leave John's body and fly between the shuttered boards of the belfry, out into the night.

And she saw John fall.

The sight of him plummeting, his black robes fluttering, his hands still holding fast to his cross and his faith, his beautiful blue eyes closed, his mouth moving in prayer, before his body hit the unforgiving stones of the cathedral floor, would be seared upon her memory forever.

# 29

THE MOMENTS AFTER JOHN'S DEATH WERE TO REMAIN A BLUR TO HEC-
ate for some time. Days later, she would recall running toward him, and her
father grabbing hold of her, stopping her, making her look at him instead, and
telling her that Charlie needed her. That she must go to him. She had allowed
herself to be steered back to her brother, who murmured her name, so that
she once again knelt beside him and took his hand. Inspector Winter and her
father had tended to John, though there was nothing to be done. By the time
the dean and two of the vicars choral, alarmed by the sounds coming from
within the cathedral, came running, the detective was taking off his coat and
draping it over John's body.

She remembered later, quite vividly, curious, isolated things. The smell of
extinguished candles, their bitter smoke lingering. The gentle voice of Brother
Michael as he said ancient prayers for the fallen priest. The sound of boots upon
flagstones as John was carried away. The feel of Charlie's hand in hers as together they made their unsteady progress along the north aisle, out of St. John's
door, and into the cab that had been summoned to take them home. So profound was her shock at John's tragic death that she did not feel sorrow or grief
or even anger at that time. All those things were to come later.

Once home, Edward put Charlie to bed, while Beatrice led her shaken
daughter to the drawing room where a fire had been lit. Hecate did her mother's

bidding and settled in a chair by the hearth, sipping the tea that had been brought. She knew her mother was struggling with the drama of the night in so many ways. She had seen her son dangerously ill, whisked away, later to be told they had taken him to the cathedral because there was a specialist doctor staying there who was able to help him. While she was making sense of this information, she had been told of John's death, Edward explaining he had gone up to fix a loose part of the shuttering that had been interrupting earlier choir practice. Hecate, in her stunned state, was doing her best to be gentle with her mother, understanding that her manner of navigating her own shock and grief was to fuss over her daughter.

In truth, she had not the strength, at that moment, to resist. She sat in the chair, her body still and quiet but her mind a tumble of thoughts. A tangle of if only's and what if's. What should she have done differently? What could she have done to save John? How could she come to terms with losing him in such a way? How could she forgive herself for asking such a dangerous thing of him? The idea that he was dead because he acted for her was torment. And yet, her mind reasoned that John would have helped anyone if asked. He risked everything because Charlie was in peril. He was a man who had dedicated his life to loving and helping others. He could not have done other than he did. It gave her a crumb of comfort to know that he would be pleased that her brother was saved. That he would do the same thing again even had he known the consequences.

As she allowed her thoughts to strike and parry in this way, she came to see that blame was of no use, and that the choice to step into the path of danger had been John's own. Gradually, in place of confusion and angst, a heavy calm descended upon her mind. Her heart, however, was another matter entirely. For now the numbness began to lift. The pain she felt at losing someone who had become so dear to her would not be so quickly soothed. The sorrow she felt for the way his life, his future, had been snatched from him would, she believed, be her constant companion forever. She would have liked to weep, to release her grief in a flood of hot tears, but none would come. She felt suspended between the drama that had befallen her and the coming weeks of sadness. She saw then that this limbo, this pause, was something she could, something she *must*, use. There would be time for grieving. Time to mourn

John's passing, both publicly and privately. But this was not it. Now she must act. If she was not to see another and another and another of her loved ones put in peril or cruelly taken from her, she must act. And she must do it alone.

She was relieved to finally be permitted to take refuge in her room but had no plans to sleep. She had made up her mind and nothing would turn her from her course of action. She would not let one more person come to harm attempting to help her. She would not risk those she loved. She would act on her own. It was time for her to do what had to be done, to answer the call that Hekate herself had spoken of. It was for *her* to do, *her* risk to take, *her* courage that was needed. She waited until she was certain the rest of the household was abed. Getting up from the chaise where she had been resting in her nightclothes as a ruse should her mother or father come to speak with her, she went to stand before the looking glass.

"Well then," she said to her sorrowful reflection. "To go into battle requires that one wear battle dress."

She put on a chemise, cotton bloomers, and a corset, before adding a petticoat, and then stepping into her black mourning dress. It was the only piece in her wardrobe Stella had not yet shortened, so Hecate selected two sturdy skirt hitches. When pulled short, the hikes gathered the front of the skirts, lifting them to her knees, out of the way. She quickly put on her long brown boots and laced them up. Her cameo she pinned to the bodice of her dress, the creamy carving of Hekate in sharp contrast to the dark bombazine beneath it. Her broad apothecary's belt fitted snugly around her waist, three vials of holy water waiting in the loops. She fetched a large iron ring she had been keeping for the purpose and threaded the cathedral keys onto it, before fastening it through one of the belt's D rings. The police lamp she attached via its loops onto the right side of the belt, facing it forward so that it would provide the best light while she was moving. From her top drawer she selected a pair of brown woolen fingerless gloves, tight fitting and warm while allowing her to perform fiddly tasks.

She paused to check herself in the mirror. Her hair was still in its French plait which would keep it out of her eyes. Years of habit made her feel the need for a hat. She went to her cupboard and searched through hatboxes until she found what she was looking for.

"Yes," she said to the lady's riding hat, "you will do nicely." She cut off the veil so that what remained was a sturdy, low top hat. It would provide a modicum of protection from blows to the head. The lapis pin was long enough to secure it in place. As she looked in the mirror again the gold cross at her throat caught the light. She touched it, thinking of John, feeling that he would be with her. She wondered then about what her father had once said regarding talismans and amulets. He believed that they worked because of the faith that the wearers placed in them, suggesting that it was the strength of that faith that caused them to have effect. This worried her. Was her faith strong enough? Stronger than John's had been? She held a different view. Perhaps that faith lent the wearer courage, and that courage saved them. Or perhaps, she thought then, it was the love with which those things were imbued that gave them power. The gold crucifix from John's beloved grandmother passed on to her. The brooch her father had kept for her all those years. The hatpin given to her by her mother. The keys made by a stranger who would take no payment. The lamp provided by an ally in her mission.

She shrugged on her Mackintosh and took a black band from her dressing table. The paleness of her coat bothered her, given that she was now in mourning for her fiancé, so the armband pinned in position felt fitting. She needed one more thing. A short search unearthed the Spanish embroidered shawl which had been a present from Clementine. She snipped off the tassels and looped it around her neck, knotting it to a carefully judged length. The ghastly memory of the black mass of the Resurgent Spirit entering John's body flashed before her. She closed her eyes against it, but still it remained. Steeling herself, she raised the scarf to test that it would sit properly over her nose and mouth. It might afford only some small protection, buy her some moment of time if a spirit came close, but some was preferable to none at all.

"Better to be prepared than to suffer for the lack of preparation," she muttered, repeating one of her father's maxims.

Leaving the house as quietly as she could, knowing which creaking stair or wobbling floorboard to avoid, she strode to the stable to fetch her bicycle.

The rain had stopped, though high cloud remained. The night was moonless and a thin mist swirled throughout the streets as Hecate rode swiftly through the city. In no time she was parking her bicycle at the entrance to the cloisters. Pausing for a moment, she listened for voices or footsteps. Hearing none, she lit the policeman's lamp at her hip and walked briskly along the covered walkway. She kept the light low, hoping it would not catch the attention of any of the vicars choral as she made her way to what had been John's front door. She turned the handle and the door opened. Inside, everything was as it had been only two short days ago. Two days in which so much had changed. She stood, taking a breath, experiencing the sharp memory of John standing just there, when he had opened the door to her. When she had taken him to meet his end. She closed her eyes, as if she might shut out the painful thought, the piercing blue of his eyes, the love for her that was always there.

"Not now," she muttered to herself. The single key to the cathedral was on its hook. The first hurdle had been jumped. She took the key and forced herself to leave John's home without a backward glance. When she returned to the south door, she found Solomon sitting there. He greeted her with a soft meow. She smiled, leaning down to stroke his bright fur, grateful for the comfort of his warm, unquestioning presence. "Come along then, little one," she whispered to him, "you can help me this evening."

Instead of enjoying her attention, however, the cat let out a low, fierce growl, flattening its ears against its head.

Hecate knew at once it was not responding to her. She stood up, whipping around, dropping the cathedral key as she did so, its clatter on the flagstones echoing down the cloisters.

Viscount Eckley stepped from the shadows, jauntily swinging his cane.

"In such a hurry, my dear?" he asked, taking another step toward her.

"I . . . left something in the library," she told him. "I am returning to collect it." She fought the urge to move back a pace, knowing she must not be out of reach of the key. "What brings you here at this late hour, Viscount?" she asked.

"Why you, of course. Did you think we were unaware of your actions? Did you truly believe we were not observing your every move?"

"Did you truly believe you would be permitted to proceed with your murderous plans unchallenged?" she asked.

"And who is it who will stand in our way? You? Your father? A policeman who might be better put out to grass? I admire your courage, my dear, but you must realize you are unequal to the task, all of . . ."

She did not wait for him to finish his little speech. She dropped to the ground, snatching at the key. The Embodied Spirit, however, moved with terrifying speed. He struck with his cane faster than a striking snake, pinning the key ring to the ground before she could reach it.

"As I say," he went on, "your ambition outreaches your ability." He smiled then, another hideous, wet, toothsome grin.

Two things happened simultaneously. Solomon, aggravated by the increasingly close proximity of the spirit, attacked the cane, hissing and clawing, throwing himself at it. Small though he was, he succeeded in unbalancing the viscount, causing him to draw back his stick, cursing at the animal as he did so. At that same moment, Lady Rathbone swooped through the door, throwing herself at the viscount, dress and hair billowing, screaming as she did so, distracting him for a crucial instant. And in that instant, Hecate grabbed the key, unlocked the door, and ran inside. Solomon stopped fighting and darted in beside her just as she flung herself against the door in an attempt to shut it. She had the latch in place, but the viscount was too quick and too strong. She had no chance of getting the key in the lock as he hurled his body weight against the door, leaving her with no option but to run.

She was glad of her lamp, the interior of the cathedral being in darkness save for the few sentinel candles here and there which burned at all times. Fortunately, she was so familiar with the layout and so aware of any raised flagstones that might trip her that she made swift progress. She tore past the Lady Chapel and was drawing level with the top of the crypt stairs when, to her horror, she saw both Lord Brocket and Constable Mitchell emerging from the subterranean level. She came to a skidding halt.

The aristocrat raised his top hat. "Good evening to you, Miss Cavendish. Kind of you to unlock St. John's door for my cousin. I relied upon the constable's talents with lock picking to tackle the smaller mechanism of the outer and inner crypt doors. Now, why don't you save a deal of unpleasantness, hand over your set of keys, and come with us?" he asked, his hand outstretched.

Hecate could hear the viscount's footsteps behind her. If he reached her, if they took hold of her, all would be lost.

"Are you not ashamed to have fallen so low?" she asked him. "To rely upon these summoned ghouls to do your bidding, to work to your plan, to set yourself above all others even though it be at the expense of innocent lives?" As she spoke she paced, turning, never allowing herself to be placed between her adversaries, playing for time when she could seize the opportunity and run for the turret door. "Have you lost all sense of what is right and what is wrong? Of what is good and what is wicked? Are you content to simply follow the path of your ruthless ancestors?" she asked him, all the while watching, waiting for her chance.

"Your naivete is quite charming. Alas, when you have lived as long as I have, you will better understand that goodness will only get you so far."

She thought of John's sacrifice to save Charlie. She thought of where they stood at that moment. "A curious philosophy to proffer considering where we find ourselves," she pointed out, gesturing to the glorious building. "There is always a right path, Your Lordship. It is up to us to choose to take it."

She glanced toward the north transept and saw Corporal Gregory appear, striding forward, coming to stand in front of her. He drew his sword. Both Embodied Spirits reacted to his arrival. Lord Brocket, unable to see him, was distracted by their attention being drawn by something not revealed to him. Hecate saw the smallest hint of doubt in his expression.

"There is righteous help to be found to counter the evil you wield," she said, backing away with a nod to the young soldier who raised his sword with a battle cry.

As her ghostly ally produced his protective barrier, she turned and ran, racing down the north aisle, Solomon bounding from the quire to catch her up. Hands trembling, she lifted the key ring on her belt and selected the key for the turret door. Even as she opened it she could hear shouts and cries behind her. Corporal Gregory would not be able to hold off her pursuers for long. She charged up the stairs, counting them as she went, driving herself to go faster. She had not reached the halfway point before she heard the heavy tread of the viscount on the bottom stair, lumbering up the stairwell behind her. Fear lent wings to her heels, but the climb was so steep, she was no match for the speed of the Embodied Spirit. Guttural cries and growling echoed up the turret until at the final window the viscount was only strides behind her. He hurled himself up the stairs. Hecate gave a shout as she felt him grab her ankle. She fell forward, her knees and shins connecting painfully with the stone of the stairs. Frantically she kicked and squirmed but the spirit merely tightened his grip. He began dragging her back down the stairs. She twisted

around so that she was facing him, gasping at the vile appearance of his transformed face, his mouth open, teeth bared, not, she realized, with a smile this
time, but with the intention to bite.

Anger rose within her. She would not let this hideous creature defeat her.
She had not come so far, lost John, seen her brother nearly taken, risked so
much, only for it to end in such a way.

"I think not!" she said, plucking her mother's pin from her riding hat. She
took a firm hold of the lapis lazuli handle and brought the sharp end down
with as much force as she could muster, right through the viscount's hand. The
spirit roared in rage and pain, releasing its grasp on her ankle as she swiftly
pulled out the pin again, holding it tight. Hecate sprang to her feet and ran
on, reaching the library door with the spirit's screams reverberating off the
turret walls behind her. She fumbled for the key on the ring, found the right
one, opened the door, leaped through it, Solomon with her, slamming the
door and turning the lock. Seconds later came the sounds of both Embodied
Spirits flinging themselves against the door. It would not yield. Hecate stood
shaking, still holding her mother's pin.

Brother Michael appeared at her side.

"My child! What has befallen you? Who hunts you? Those creatures . . . !"

Hecate turned her back on the shouts and curses coming from the stairwell and deftly returned the pin to her hat.

"Those creatures are precisely the reason I must do what I came here to
do," she said, dusting down her skirts and striding toward the locked cabinet,
the griffin flapping down to accompany her. She detached the lamp from her
belt and set it down upon the small reading desk that was fixed to the wall.
Lifting the key ring, she selected first the padlock key.

"Well then," she said, as much to herself as Brother Michael, who was peering over her shoulder. "Let us begin."

As before, the cabinet opened without resistance, Mr. Sadiki's keys working
each lock smoothly. The door opened with only a faint sigh from the old, worn
hinges. This time, Hecate went straight for the insignificant-looking book on
the bottom shelf. Its pages were dust dry, their edges starting to crumble, but
what was written inside was at least legible. It appeared to have been scratched
with a sharp nib in some haste with no importance given to decoration or even

neatness. She flicked through the pages, deciphering the Old English without too much difficulty as simple words had been used. She quickly came to the instructions she had so fervently hoped for. She read them aloud.

"*'To overcome dark defenses when accessing a spell to undo that which should never have been done.'* How aptly put," she said, running her finger down the page to the necessary incantation. She stepped as close as she dared to the enchanted book, holding the other one up so that she could read it while keeping its more dangerous fellow in her line of vision. She would not for one moment take her eyes from it once she began the words, for she could not imagine it giving into its fate quietly. She was aware of the griffin retreating to a safer distance.

"*'For all that is good, for all that must be protected, let not this barrier to truth and justice remain.*

*No more shall this stand, else nefarious deeds will prosper.*

*Yield to the one who seeks the remedy, and let peace prevail once more Yield!'*"

Hecate waited.

Brother Michael ventured an opinion. "So few words for such a violent adversary. Will it suffice?"

"That is all it says. There is nothing else." For good measure, she read the words again, shutting from her mind the growling and scratching that continued at the library door. When she had finished the incantation a second time, she closed the book and replaced it on its shelf. Slowly, cautiously, she reached out toward the necromancers' book. As her fingers touched the leather binding she noticed that all noises at the door ceased. The Embodied Spirits were evidently sensitive to the workings of the book. Hecate braced herself and withdrew it from the shelf. It put up not the slightest resistance. She smiled at Brother Michael, picked up her lamp, and walked back to her desk. She glanced over at the map. It was fairly wriggling with life now. Solomon sat on the edge of her desk, while the griffin flew up to perch atop the nearest shelf. Brother Michael drifted to stand beside Hecate. She glanced at him, took a breath, and then opened the book.

This time there was no reaction, no guardian fiend, no magic that would stop her.

The next discovery was that it was written in Latin. Hecate grinned. While not fluent, her father had seen to it that her education was a classical one. She would be able to pick her way through it and could rely on Brother Michael if she was uncertain. She flicked through the rough leaves and selected one at random, attempting to translate the title at the top of the page.

"*'For the purpose . . . of . . .'* What is that? *'Seeing . . . For the purpose of seeing that which . . . stays'* no, remains, *'that which remains . . .'*" She let her finger slide down the page to the first paragraph which appeared to be made up of a list. This time, instead of translating, she attempted to read the Latin aloud.

"*'Veniant, cum vocati fuerint . . . faciant quod iussi sunt. . . . habeant decem vires. : . .'*"

"For the love of God, child, stop! Read no further!" cried Brother Michael.

"What? Oh, yes, I see what you mean. . . ."

"That is a necromancer's spell. You are summoning the dead!"

"I will have to be more careful. Clearly reading things out before I have translated them is unwise. At least there can be no doubt we have found the right book. This must be what was used to summon the Resurgent Spirits."

"Let us hope that the reverse instruction will be contained within the same manuscript."

"Perhaps you could cast your eye over the contents page? There may be something there of use?"

"Of course," he said, leaning forward, clearly prepared to tackle the frightening text if it would stop her inadvertently raising more spirits from their graves.

While he looked, his lips moving as he silently read the list of entries, Hecate watched his face closely for signs of alarm. She was momentarily distracted by thinking she heard something, an unfamiliar sound coming from the stairwell, something above the curses and hammerings upon the door of the thwarted viscount, and no doubt his cousin and the constable. She held up her finger to her lips and Brother Michael stopped reading. Solomon and the griffin both turned to look in the direction of the door. Hecate listened hard, but hearing nothing more, dismissed it as the workings of her imagination and signaled to the monk to continue.

They had just settled into concentrating on the book once more when a single bell began to toll. Hecate and Brother Michael stared at each other.

"Lady Rathbone," she said.

"She has raised the alarm!"

Brother Michael might have said more, but at that moment Corporal Gregory appeared before them. The soldier was not given to visiting the library, and he was clearly agitated.

"Miss Cavendish," he spoke in an urgent whisper, "danger is close! I urge you to leave this place while there is still time!"

"Corporal Gregory, I thank you for your concern for my safety, but we are about important work. I cannot leave."

"I tell you, something that means you harm has broken free of its bonds in the crypt!"

"More Resurgent Spirits!" Brother Michael whimpered as he spoke the words.

Hecate would not be rattled. "All the more reason for me to find a way to stop them while I have the chance."

The young soldier looked horrified at her decision but then accepted it. "In that case, I will stand guard while you do what you must," he declared, turning to put himself between the desk and the door, his sword drawn.

Hecate turned to the monk. "Let's look for anything mentioning how to stop a spirit that has been summoned. Or anything that might pertain to the Essedenes themselves. Quickly now," she urged him.

He did as he was bid, shaking his head as he scanned the contents. "Oh, wait."

"You have found something?"

"Here it mentions placing a spell upon a grave called the 'Centurion's Call to Arms. . . .' That might be relevant."

"If it refers to summoning somewhere in the text, then yes, you may be correct," she agreed, trying to keep up with his reading.

"And this . . . oh! This talks of '*Mortuus est reversus*'!"

She looked at him then. "'Returning the dead'! Brother Michael, you are a genius! I would hug you if it were possible."

His bashful smile was short-lived.

At that moment, Solomon began to emit a low growl. Slowly, he rose to stand, arching his back, staring in the direction of the door. He flattened his ears, hissing as if trying to scare away something that was clearly terrifying him. Hecate could not see anything, but she could sense something.

As she watched, the door appeared to bulge and buckle. For a moment she thought it would give way, allowing Lord Brocket and his dreadful allies into the library, but it held. What it was not proof against, however, was the swirling, fetid mass that was another Resurgent Spirit.

Solomon sprang from the desk and ran to take cover beneath it. The griffin took to the air. All the creatures and beings of the map stirred and fretted. Brother Michael shrank backward. Hecate found herself rooted to the spot, kept there more by shock than bravery. Corporal Gregory showed great courage, brandishing his sword, the brass buttons of his red uniform glinting in the patchy light from the single lamp as he held his position, determined to do the thing he was born to do, the thing he had vowed never again to fail to do: to protect. While his steadfastness could not be questioned, his ability to withstand the foe he now faced was in doubt. Through the wooden door came a twisting morass. In the gloom it appeared as a deeper lever of shadow; a pulsating cloud of darkness. Hecate thought at once of a murmuration of starlings, or a swarm of bats as they swooped through the night sky, before her mind inevitably recalled the flies that had attacked poor John. These were not harmless, mortal creatures. Before them was something unmistakably malevolent, and even in its shapeless state it was evident to Hecate that its focus was herself. What was more, given the scale of the thing, she feared what she faced was more than one single Resurgent Spirit.

Instinctively, she took a step back. The menacing mass moved forward. Corporal Gregory stood ready to defend his friend, but Hecate knew there was nothing he could do that would prevent the progress of what they faced.

"Stay back!" the young soldier shouted. "I will not permit you to pass!"

"No, Corporal, you cannot fight this thing. Do not endanger yourself, I beg you!"

"I will not desert my post!" he insisted.

Even as he spoke, the dark spirits advanced. Within seconds they had enveloped him. He fell to the ground, stricken, his sword falling from his hand, his eyes wide in horror though no more words came from him.

Hecate knew she must act to save him. She was certain the spirits were only truly interested in her. Seeking to draw their attention away from the soldier, she darted to the right of the desk. Her action worked. The mass lifted from the young man's ghostly figure. Too late, though, she understood that they wanted not only her, but the book, too. The mass divided, half moving toward the desk. Hecate leaped back toward it, reaching out for the vital book. She was aware of Brother Michael moving his arms in a frantic attempt to beat back the spirits but his efforts were ineffectual. As she made one more lunge across the desk she felt the oppressive weight of the spirits pressing down upon her. She held her breath, so as not to inhale the toxic air of the things, lifting her scarf into position over her mouth, and snatched up the book. With it in her hand she turned to flee but was thrown to the floor by the spirits' force.

Winded by the fall, she curled into a ball, still clutching the book, determined that she would not give it up. The room was a chaotic blur of movement and noise. The spirits swirled and twisted; the creatures of the *Mappa Mundi* fought against their confines, squawking, yapping, and crying out; Brother Michael could be heard praying fervently; Solomon spat and hissed as he clawed at the terrible being that was doing its all to attack Hecate. The griffin launched swooping attacks, fierce but futile, and she watched appalled as he was thrown back against the wall with such force that he fell to the ground and lay stunned and motionless.

"No!" she cried out, trying to get up. She was on her knees when the spirits began to rain objects down upon her. First the things from her desk came hurtling through the air. She tucked the book inside the bodice of her dress and put her arms over her head to protect herself, yelping as an inkwell struck her elbow. Then her attackers tried to wrench the books from the shelves but the chains prevented them from doing so. Thwarted, they sought to push the bookcases over. Hecate scrambled across the floorboards, scurrying out of the way just as the first of the shelves crashed to the ground. More followed. She got to her feet, but found she was trapped against the far wall, the fallen bookcases blocking her path. In their determination to attack both her and the book, the spirits had knocked over the lamp which had shattered. Brother Michael shouted in alarm but was powerless to stop some of the parchments, papers, and scrolls that had been scattered catching fire. Hecate knew a fire could spread through the library in moments. While she looked for something with which to smother the flames, she saw the marble statue of St. Esmond lifting slowly into the air. It was the largest piece of statuary in the muniments room and almost certainly the heaviest. The spirits raised it higher and higher and now their purpose became clear. In seconds they would send it crashing down upon her. She knew she should call for help, try to climb over the shelves, do something to save herself, but she felt unable to act, paralyzed by the inevitability of what was about to happen.

She summoned her courage.

"I think not!" she told the vile being that would see her crushed. She forced herself to move toward it, leaping over the fallen shelves, screaming as she did so, her own voice terrifying to herself, even through the scarf. It was like the battle cry of the member of an ancient tribe, or the shriek of a furious witch. She flung herself into the very midst of the dark mass. As she did so she pulled a vial from her belt, removing the stopper and emptying the contents into the spirit. The being let loose its own screech of rage and pain, whirling around her, dropping the marble bust, seeking to rid itself of the holy water. She emptied another at it as she found her feet. It writhed and shrieked, dividing into two. She had been correct that the size indicated more than one Resurgent Spirit.

"You do not belong here!" she shouted. "You will not hurt anyone else. Not while I live!"

She had to jump to one side to avoid the fire that was now taking hold of the stack of papers under her desk and growing at an alarming rate. One of the spirits swirled about her. She raised her voice, reciting the words of the protective prayer she had memorized from her father's book. As she did so she removed the stopper from the last vial, waiting until the spirit was tight around her. Just when it seemed it would squeeze the breath from her, she flung the contents at it. The being recoiled, screeching, breaking into small pieces, falling to the floor. For a moment, Hecate thought she had killed it, but the pieces took the shape of beetles and swarmed under the door, fleeing from the room and down the stairwell.

The creatures and people of the *Mappa Mundi* gave in to cheers and whoops and yaps of delight.

She peered through the thickening smoke, but the other spirit was nowhere to be seen.

Hecate felt relief weaken her legs. She concentrated on steadying herself, taking hold of one of the fallen bookcases as she clambered over it. She ran to the corner of the room to collect the fire bucket. Upending it, she poured the heavy sand over the main part of the small but dangerous blaze that had taken hold. There was a puff of smoke but the flames continued to sprout. She ran to the other bucket and repeated the process but by the time she had done so she knew she was losing the battle.

Hecate turned and bent over the fallen griffin, calling to him. To her relief he stirred and flapped up to sit on her shoulder where he clung on tightly. From beneath the table came a mewing.

"Oh, Solomon!" She crouched down, peering into the gloom at the terrified cat. "Come along, little one, come. We must get out. We must get help!" The smoke was already beginning to make her splutter. She knew there were more fire buckets downstairs, and she could run to the vestry and raise the alarm. She could not be certain anyone would respond to Lady Rathbone's ringing of the bell. If she did not act swiftly the whole collection could be lost. "Please, Solomon, you have to come with me." When still he did not move she reached forward. At the same moment, Brother Michael blew his cool, ghostly breath from the other side, causing the cat to spring forward. Hecate scooped him up and ran to the door, pulling at the handle. It would not move. She tugged frantically, gasping and coughing as she did so, Solomon setting up a wailing.

"I cannot open it!"

"It will not yield!" Corporal Gregory shouted. "That dark spirit has sealed it with cursed magic!"

Hecate fought down the terror that was rising inside her. The fire was now consuming the edge of the desk and a stack of maps that had been stored beside it. There was a fierce heat coming from it in addition to the suffocating smoke that now took the place of the dark spirits high in the room. There was no need for a lamp, for the fire cast its own lethal light. She knew however much they wished to, her ghostly friends were powerless to help her. It was up to her to save herself and raise the alarm. She ran to the small door set in the wooden interior wall. It had not been opened in years, and as it led onto a void dropping thirty feet to the floor of the north transept, Reverend Thomas always kept it locked. If she could open the door, she could climb down to escape the blaze and get help to extinguish the fire. She looked at the ring, but she knew she did not have the specific key. The smoke began to fill the room more and more. Perhaps one would fit? Many of the internal doors had the same mechanisms.

"Oh, which one, which one?" She tried the stairwell door key. It would not go into the hole. Each time she guessed incorrectly she wasted vital seconds.

Solomon ceased wailing, the smoke subduing him. On her shoulder the griffin fidgeted. "I can't find one to fit!" she told them, desperation coloring her voice, the smoke making her cough and causing her eyes to stream.

It was then she felt a supernatural coolness touch her hand as Mrs. Nugent took shape beside her. "There now, young mistress, fret not. You have the key you require," said the mop-capped cleaner with a reassuring smile.

"But which one? Where?"

"This one, here," she said, laying a ghostly finger on Hecate's brooch.

She looked down in time to see the tiny golden key attached to it begin to glow and pulsate. She held out her hand to catch it as it grew in size and then fell from its position on the cameo into her palm.

Hecate gasped, quickly grasping the key and inserting it into the lock. It fitted perfectly. With a soft clunk the mechanism released and the door swung open.

Hecate gave a small cry of triumph.

The other side presented a terrifying drop two floors down to the flagstones, the height causing her to feel dizzy. The griffin tightened his grip on her shoulder. She clutched the doorframe. There was a narrow ledge along part of the great window. It was no use to her, but wide enough for a nimble cat. She picked up Solomon and leaned out, averting her eyes from the drop, setting him down carefully on the ledge.

"Off you go, little one. Make haste!" she said, giving him a little push.

The fresh air revived the cat and he did not hesitate to dash across the window, his deft paws not faltering once as he used another part of the tracery as a landing point, and then another, quickly jumping down to safety.

"Yes!" Hecate cried.

And then she saw them. Viscount Eckley and Constable Mitchell had realized what she was trying to do and had descended the stairs and were now at the bottom of the great window, looking up at her, Lord Brocket coming to stand behind them seconds later.

As she watched, the Embodied Spirits began to climb.

She turned to see the room was filling with smoke which was also now billowing out past her. What was worse, the air from the open door was feeding the flames of the fire. The room presented a tragic scene. The ceiling was obscured by a pall of smoke, several of the bookcases lay broken upon the ground, everywhere were charred pieces of paper floating through the hot air. And the map! The beings that inhabited it were now stricken with terror. They cried out, the animals squawking or braying, trying to escape their given spaces, the top of the vellum starting to blacken as the ever-thickening smoke and soot descended.

"The map!" she whispered.

And as she did so, the griffin let go his grip on her shoulder and flapped into the room.

"No! Come back!" she called.

It turned and looked at her with a baleful expression but it did not come. Instead it flew to the ledge of the frame surrounding what was, after all, its rightful home, and there it perched, waiting for the end, prepared to be destroyed along with all those with whom it shared its rare existence.

"No! No!" Hecate could not stand it. Her mind was made up.

She stepped back into the library and closed the door behind her, locking it against the possible arrival of the Embodied Spirits. As she removed the key from the lock it shrank back to its normal size so that when she touched it to the brooch it was able to instantly fasten itself back onto its rightful place. As quickly as she could, Hecate removed her coat, her hands trembling. With all the doors closed, she believed there was a chance she could smother the fire. Thanking her mother for the good quality raincoat, she used it to beat at the flames. At first she seemed to be having no effect at all and the flames licked at her boots as she stamped on them, but then, gradually, inch by inch, she began to see progress. She had succeeded in suffocating some of the fire. She knew she must press on, moving forward a bit at a time. She must save the map.

It was not, however, the flames that presented the greatest danger, but the smoke. For all that she was defeating some of the flames, the smoke increased in thickness, robbing the room of breathable air. She knew that the fire had caught some extremely flammable substances, such as varnish and glue, and these were giving off harsh, acrid fumes, making her cough and splutter. She dropped to her knees, trying to avoid the worst of the smoke, but it was harder to beat at the flames when she was nearer the ground. Dizziness began to assail her.

There came a hammering on the library door. Not the Embodied Spirits this time, but help, real and wonderful. She recognized her father's voice.

"Hecate! Hecate, open the door!" he shouted as he tried the handle.

She knew it was not locked but held shut by the actions of the Resurgent Spirit.

"Papa . . ." She tried to call to him, but was robbed of her words by the smoke. She heard the dean's voice and more hammering on the door and her father's increasingly frantic shouts but she could not reply. She could not get to her feet.

Brother Michael was beside her. "My dear child, you must get up. You must!" The poor monk was close to tears of frustration and despair.

Hecate tried to push herself up on part of a fallen bookcase but it was too hot. She withdrew her hand with a gasp. The *Mappa Mundi* continued to undulate as its inhabitants gave way to rage or panic depending on their character. Through the deepening smoke she saw St. Augustine's hands raised in prayer. She saw the bear roaring in fear and fury. Then, as she watched through smarting eyes, she saw the great bull at the center of the map turn face out and paw the ground as if about to charge. She had never seen the bull move before. As she felt herself drifting into a faint she recalled that the beast was depicted breathing fire and this amused her, for the last thing she required at that moment was more flames. To her astonishment, she saw that the bull was rapidly growing in size. In seconds it had doubled, then trebled in width, so that soon all other images were hidden behind it. Its huge face filled the entirety of the map. And still it grew bigger and bigger, until all she could see of it were its red flaring nostrils.

Hecate thought then how curious it was that time could stand still in extreme moments. She felt a preternatural calmness descend upon her as she crumpled to the floor. She had no more reserves of strength as the smoke overwhelmed her but she felt neither panic nor fear, only a sad acceptance of her fate.

It was then that the great bull snorted. There was a pause and then the fire-breathing beast inhaled. It was an in-breath of mighty, magical force that drew from the room all the smoke, and all the air, sucking them deep into its vast lungs, more and more until at last there was none left. The flames faltered and died. The fire was suffocated. The deadly smoke removed. All sounds in the room ceased.

Hecate clambered to her feet. Gulping for breath as air returned to the space and the bull diminished, resuming its place on the map. She stumbled through the muddle of shelves and burned paper and singed books.

"Hecate?" Edward rattled the door handle again. "Hecate!"

"It is not locked, Father," she said, her voice hoarse, her mind still cloudy from lack of air and surfeit of smoke. Her thoughts were jumbled. The fire was out, the room clearing, the spirit had fled. Why, then, was the door still prevented from opening? She rubbed dust from her eyes, blinking as she looked around the room.

She felt rather than heard the movement beside her. She did not dare turn. Out of the corner of her eye she could see the dark mass rising up from the floor, thickening and swelling as it grew to become a looming, pulsing shape between her and the map.

She could hear the dean and her father calling to her and fighting to free the door, but she knew they could not help her. She was trapped in the room with the second Resurgent Spirit, and it was not finished with her yet. To her horror, it twisted so that its attention seemed to shift toward the map. The shadow began to creep over the ancient vellum, seeping into the cracks and crevices, spreading itself to cover the entire surface.

"Leave it alone!" she shouted. "Do not touch that! Your quarrel is with me. Here I stand!"

But the spirit only delved deeper into the map's corners and grooves, intent on overtaking it completely.

Hecate pulled the book from her dress and held it up.

"You want this, don't you? Look, here is your precious book. See?"

The being paused in its progress and twisted again. Whether it could see or not Hecate had no way of knowing, but it detected the book, and changed its focus.

"That's it. Come along now. If you want it, you will have to take it from me," she said. Her scarf had dropped from her face. She quickly pulled it up again to cover her mouth and nose. She had no holy water left. Nothing with which to attack the vile entity which was slowly moving toward her. She stood motionless. There was nowhere to run to, after all. Nowhere to hide. Her ghostly friends could do no more for her. She must face the spirit alone. She felt it reach toward her, its darkness forming elongated fingers that stretched toward the book, which she drew back close to herself, enticing the spirit forward. At last it was before her, but a hand's span from her face, looming above and around her, coiling as a snake ready to strike.

But Hekate was the Goddess of Snakes.

Hekate was the Goddess of the Night who lights the way, guarding the threshold, standing sentinel at the crossroads, holding the keys to unlock the door from one world to the next, from the living to the dead.

Hekate was the Queen of the Liminal Realms.

And Hekate had her hounds to protect her.

From behind the spirit, deep within the world of the map, came the sound of barking, growing louder and louder.

"Help me, Queen of Ghosts. I need you now!" she whispered, and heard again the goddess's voice in her mind. She forced herself to recall again one of the prayers of protection she had written in her notebook.

*Let not the darkness prevail! I am a child of the light and hold the hand of the blessed!*

She shouted at the spirit then, and when she did so, the voice that came forth was not hers alone. She heard it resonate with a chorus of souls, some known to her, some not, as if her spectral family, sensing her peril, had come to her aid. Above all of these, though, it was her namesake, Goddess of Witches, whose voice she heard most clearly as it reverberated through her.

Hecate raised her voice above the noise in the room. "In the name of the Goddess of the Night, I send you back to Hades. Back to the darkness. Descend to the depths and cross the River Styx. Return to the realm of the dead! Hekate commands you! I command you!" she cried raising her hand, glaring into the swirling body of the spirit. "You do not belong here! Take your foul, heartless soul and slither back to your rightful place!"

She sensed its hesitation and took courage from it, moving forward even as the spirit swayed and undulated. It drifted back and she took another step. It began to resist and thrash about. In its rage it wrenched the book from her hand, flinging it into the pile of fallen shelves and debris. She did not falter but stepped on.

The baying of the hounds increased to a terrible, cacophonous level.

"They are coming for you!" she told the spirit, "Hekate has sent her fearsome dogs and they will drag you to hell!"

Finally the spirit gave in to its fear. It rotated with such speed it caused a whirlwind, snatching up papers and books and loose objects from the room, almost knocking Hecate off her feet. She battled forward, reciting the chant she remembered from Hekate's book of spells, her words almost drowned out by the snarling and barking of the hounds, whose faces now filled the map, teeth bared, red eyes glaring.

The spirit formed itself into a cloud of locusts, rattling and clicking as they circled the room once more before crashing through one of the rose windows and disappearing out into the night.

The door, no longer ensorcelled, was flung open and her father and Dean Chalmers charged into the room. The dean was paler than some of Hecate's beloved ghosts. Her father looked as if his heart might break.

"My dearest girl! Are you injured?" he asked, slipping an arm around her shoulders to support her.

The burn on her hand made her wince. She tried to take steadying breaths. The air in the room smelled of smoke and tasted gritty. "The map . . . !" As soon as she attempted to speak she was stricken by a fit of coughing and had to wait for it to subside.

Edward sought to reassure her. "The map is safe, the fire is out. Hecate, whatever has taken place here?"

The dean spoke up. "The door was not locked, and yet it would not open. We were alerted by the bell being rung. I came from the cloisters and noticed the destruction in the crypt. More tombs have been broken."

Her father told her, "I had come in search of you. We saw the smoke coming from this direction and could hear you shouting, but, oh my dear child, we could not open that door. I feared we might lose you!"

Hecate struggled to regain her voice. "Thank heavens the map is safe. Oh, the library, look at the mess . . ."

"Your safety is paramount," the dean insisted, adding shakily, "Whatever would we have done had you perished?"

"I am quite well," she assured him. When Edward took her hand to examine the burn she said, "It is of no consequence. It will heal. But the books . . ."

He held her arm, unconvinced that she might not yet faint or fall. "There is no real damage done," he told her. "It appears worse than it is. The shelves can be righted, the desk replaced. Perhaps one or two minor items have perished, but the map is remarkably unscathed. Look."

She turned to study it and let out a small cry of joy and relief. For all that had taken place in the room, the *Mappa Mundi* did indeed appear to be undamaged. Everything was in its rightful place, the bull reduced to its more ordinary tiny scale, all the figures quiet as if subdued and tired by recent events, but not hurt or ruined. Only the city of Hereford still pulsated with a low golden light, at least to Hecate's eyes. She knew the others would be unaware of its strange activity.

"What I do not understand," the dean's voice cut into her thoughts, "is why you were here at such an hour? And on your own? Did Reverend Thomas ask that you work at night? It seems a curious thing for him to do."

"No," she said, realizing that she would have a great deal of explaining to do, "the reverend had no knowledge of my plans. There was something I had to do. Something that could not wait."

"Hecate," Edward spoke quietly to her. "Why did you not come to me for help?"

"After what happened to Charlie, and to John . . . I would not put you at such risk again, Father. I could not."

The dean picked up a scorched book and brushed some of the sooty marks from it. "This book is not part of the chained collection," he said.

"It is not, and I know I was not supposed to have it, but, oh . . ." Now that the immediate danger was past and she recalled what she and Brother Michael had discovered before the spirits entered the library, she became animated. "Dean Chalmers, I know this will be difficult for you . . . for anyone . . . to believe, to understand, but I promise you, I had good reasons for what I did."

She wanted to tell him she had not been alone. Wanted to tell them both how her wonderful ghostly family had helped her, had saved her. Wanted to explain that she would never have succeeded without them. But she could not. A weariness crept over her. She suddenly became aware of how she must appear. She was standing in the middle of a room that was blackened and dirty and in parts damaged because of her actions. She had risked things that were not hers to risk. She had acted in a way she knew would be against the wishes of both Reverend Thomas and the dean. She had been secretive and impetuous. Her hair and dress were singed, her face filthy, her hand burned, her outlandish clothes torn and soot covered. Unsteadily, she pulled herself from her father's hold. With as much dignity as she could muster she retrieved her ruined coat from the embers and shook it out. It was unwearable. She straightened up.

"I understand that there will be much more to say on the matter, but I would be grateful if it could wait until morning. I should very much like to go home," she told them.

"Of course," Edward said, removing his own coat and slipping it around her shoulders. The dean helped clear a path so that she could more easily step through the debris.

"I must contact Inspector Winter," he said. "He will need to examine the crypt again. How many more times must this happen? As for the library . . . what I remain puzzled by," he said as he righted a chair, "is why the door, though unlocked, would not open."

Hecate opened her mouth to explain but her father spoke up.

"All questions can wait for tomorrow," he insisted.

She was relieved not to have to talk further, on two counts. For one thing, she was exhausted and her burns were starting to trouble her greatly. For another, she had still not uncovered the identity of the person responsible for summoning the spirits, and one of the possible suspects was currently standing in front of her. What gave her strength was the fact that the crucial book was still hidden beneath one of the fallen shelves. She could retrieve it when she returned. She allowed herself to be led out by her father, agreeing that they would meet the next day for further discussion.

HECATE SLEPT LATE THE NEXT MORNING. WHEN STELLA BROUGHT A tray of breakfast to her room it was almost noon. Her burns were bothering her, so she allowed the maid to help dress her into a dark skirt and blouse, her mourning dress being beyond repair. She was accepting another cup of tea when Clementine arrived, sweeping through the door, full of love and compassion.

"Dearest Hecate, I came as soon as I heard!" The two exchanged kisses, the pale peach silk of one dress contrasting starkly with the dark garb of the other. "Such terrible, terrible things to happen. First John's fall, and then the fire with you nearly lost to us forever . . . You poor lamb," she said, taking the seat opposite. "And your mother gives you tea. Would you not prefer brandy, to steady your nerves?"

"I'm not sure they are in need of steadying. Truth be told, I am once again numb. As if my feelings are frozen in the moment before John . . . before he fell."

"Mama woke me the minute she received your mother's note. She was quite incoherent, I have to say. I was able to learn little of sense save that poor John was dead and that you had been with him in the cathedral. . . . Hecate my dearest, do you wish to talk about it? And Mama spoke of an engagement!"

Hecate smiled wanly. "It's true. We were engaged only the evening prior."

At this Clementine burst into tears. "Such cruel luck!"

"Please, do not distress yourself on that account. I'm sure I will survive being known as the girl who had the shortest engagement ever. Save your prayers and your sorrow for John."

"Of course." She nodded, dabbing her eyes with monogrammed lace. "Of course. It is not my place to give in to tears when you are being so very brave. Is there anything I can do? Anything at all?"

Hecate set her teacup down on the table beside her. "As a matter of fact, there is something."

"Only name it."

"I want to see John. To say goodbye. Could you face coming with me? Only I fear I will not persuade Mother otherwise."

Clemmie nodded, blinking away more tears. She got to her feet, reaching out her hand. "We shall go together. No one will stop us," she promised.

John had been taken to the chapel in the cloisters. As Hecate and Clementine were escorted along the stone covered walkway toward the ancient door set within the quadrangle, she flinched as she passed John's little house. She had stood in that doorway the last time he had touched her, when he had reached out to stroke her bruised cheek. Her hand went to her face, instinctively tracing that same place where he had so lightly rested his fingers. It was incomprehensible to think she would never feel his touch again, never hear his voice. They came to the chapel entrance and went inside. It was a single room, no bigger than a family drawing room, but with a high ceiling and long slender windows letting in sunshine. At the center a modest wooden catafalque had been placed, with John's body, in his vicar's robes, laid out upon it. Edward had been adamant that he should not be left unattended. The vicars choral interpreted this as a sign of love for their fallen brother, and an act of respect from the man who was to have become his father-in-law, so they readily agreed. The vigil had been kept through the night by his fellow vicars. When Hecate and Clementine were led into the little chapel they found candles burning and the dean himself keeping watch over John. Hecate experienced a moment's panic. Dean Chalmers, for all that he was her father's friend, was still on her list of suspects. Had they unwittingly delivered John's body into the care of the very person responsible for his death? She was relieved to hear that at least two sentinels had been in place at all times. The dean offered his condolences and then left the women to say their goodbyes. Clemmie was content to hang back, not wishing to intrude upon

Hecate's time with her deceased fiancé, and reluctant, in any case, to stand any closer to a dead body.

Hecate stepped forward. John looked heartbreakingly young. He had landed on his back, the impact of the fall killing him instantaneously. What damage his poor body had sustained was not on show. Skilled morticians had already visited, for he was carefully positioned upon cushions and cloths which had been artfully folded, so that none of his injuries was evident. He looked for all the world as if he were asleep. His hands were folded over his chest, resting upon his crucifix, causing a jolt of memory for Hecate as she recalled how he had clung to the symbol of his faith even as he fought for his life. She removed a glove and put her hand over his. She thought she had prepared herself for this moment, but she had not. The cold lifelessness of his flesh undid her. She wept then, tears of sadness for the love she had glimpsed gone forever, for the friend she had lost, for the life together they would never have, for the unfairness of a future snatched away from such a good man. Her tears fell unchecked as she sobbed, dripping onto him, leaving tiny wet marks upon his clerical robes which caught the uneven light of the candles as they soaked into his garment. She found she had not the strength to stop weeping, nor to move, until Clemmie came and put an arm around her, gently making her release her grasp of John's hand, turning her friend slowly away, and helping her from that sad, lonely place.

Another day passed before Beatrice would agree that her daughter was sufficiently recovered to face a meeting with the dean, and then only after some nimble footwork on the part of her father. Hecate once again parked her bicycle at the entrance to the cloisters. Her dress and coat were receiving Stella's attention in the hope they might be repaired and cleaned, so she wore instead her navy wool skirt and a dark jacket of her mother's, another armband stitched in place. Beatrice had refused to let her leave the house wearing her riding hat, so she had returned to her rather battered boater. The burns on her hand remained painful but some ointment and a carefully applied bandage meant she would be able to ride her bicycle home later. Her father had pushed it for her on the journey to the cathedral.

"I shall leave you here," he told her, putting away his pipe.

It had been decided that, prior to Hecate being brought before the dean, Edward would speak with him. Her position at the cathedral hung in the balance. Her father's support was vital.

"Thank you again, for agreeing to speak with him."

"I can only do so much. I have known the man thirty years: If his mind is made up he will not be swayed."

She nodded, lowering her head. "On top of which, we do not know, even now, whether Dean Chalmers has his own agenda."

Her father sighed. "Just as you were reluctant to have poor John remain on our list of suspects, so it does not sit well with me to think of the dean in such a way. But, I must accept that, until we have proof to the contrary, he remains in doubt."

"All the more reason why I must fight to keep my position in the library," she said.

She watched her father stride along the cloister in the direction of the dean's office. She would not have much time before being called, so she hurried through the south door. She moved quickly, not wanting to encounter Mr. Gould at that point. The morning service was over and most of the vicars choral were either back in their houses, taking a late breakfast, or out attending to their parish church duties. She thought about the space at their table where John once sat and pitied them the pain of their grief. Heading down the stairs toward the crypt, she paused to whisper to Corporal Gregory.

"Are you quite recovered?" she asked him.

"I am, miss. And yourself? Your hand . . ."

"Will mend. Thank you, Corporal. I could not have prevailed without your help."

"I regret I was not able to do more," he told her.

"You played your part," she said. "In the end, that is what counts."

She descended into the crypt. It was in a pitiful state, two more tombs having been rent asunder as the Resurgent Spirits escaped their bonds. She wondered who had summoned them, and from where. Had they been down among the catacombs at the very moment she had been in the library? And had they made a copy of the sacred book? She was eager to retrieve it from where it lay among the bookshelves but could not do so until she was permitted access again to the collection. She picked her way through the splinters of wood and crumpled iron bars. What strength such dark magic contained! It frightened her now to think of what she had faced, and she was grateful she had not felt that fear at the time.

She heard footsteps. Slow, deliberate strides. She recognized the soft, tuneful whistling that accompanied the footsteps.

"Inspector, so good of you to come," she said to him as he entered the crypt.

"Miss Cavendish." He raised his bowler hat to her. "Naturally I would answer the call of a fellow detective," he said.

"Oh? Is that how you see me?"

"Not an official one, of course, but if ever the word could be accurately applied to someone . . . your endeavors have been . . . remarkable," he said.

"Thank you. It . . . means a great deal to me that you think so. Particularly today. Particularly after . . ."

"Yes. Allow me once again to express my condolences. Reverend Forsyth was a good man."

Hecate found she could only nod. If she allowed herself to dwell upon John's death for more than a moment, she might succumb to tears. Now was not the time.

He stepped a little closer, lowering his voice. "In matters regarding our investigations, we must continue to play our cards close to our chest."

"Indeed, I think that the wisest way to proceed."

"In any case," he said, "I should imagine being brought before Chapter to explain yourself is a daunting prospect."

"Mercifully it is not the whole Chapter. Dean Chalmers was persuaded by my father in a note last night that the events in the library would be best kept between as few people as possible."

"Are they aware I am to attend?" he asked then, his bushy brows betraying a certain concern. "Well . . . I thought it best to present you as my *bona fides*, my professional expert, if you like . . . at the moment of the meeting."

"Ah."

"It is unorthodox, I grant you, but then . . . but then, what about any of this matter could accurately be called 'orthodox'?"

"Not a great deal."

"It may interest you to know that I interviewed the dean recently."

"You suspect him?"

"Lord Brocket is not acting alone, we know that. However, the dean gave nothing away. He remains under suspicion, though. My presence might . . . unsettle him."

"I don't want to believe he is a part of this."

"Time will tell," the inspector said, offering her his arm. "Shall we?"

She took it, thankful for his support and his new confidence in her, and together they walked to the dean's office.

The modest room Dean Chalmers had chosen for this purpose was set in the cloisters, to the south of the cathedral. Hecate hesitated. She knew that her father would, by now, have told the dean everything they had agreed upon. That Hecate had been so affected by the tragic death of her fiancé she had not been in her right mind. Her distress had led her to a course of action that she now saw was reckless. At first Hecate had resisted this plan, not at all at ease about being portrayed as an unstable woman. Edward had pointed out that their options were limited if they were not to give away too much of what they knew to both the dean and the master of the library, who would also inevitably be in attendance. Reluctantly, she had accepted that this was the best hope they had of her being permitted to keep her position. Now, as she stood outside the office, she realized she would be at a further disadvantage to defend herself in the imminent meeting, as she would not know how successful her father's conversation with the dean had been, nor what, if anything, had been shared with Reverend Thomas.

Inspector Winter turned to her. "It might be best not to keep the dean waiting, don't you think?"

She nodded. "Of course, forgive me . . ."

She knocked on the smartly painted red door. Upon hearing the dean's reply, they went in.

On the far side of the desk sat Dean Chalmers, Reverend Thomas, and her father. There was no chair provided for herself, and as they were not expecting the inspector, none for him, so that the two were required to stand. She felt as if summoned to the headmaster's office at school.

It was Reverend Thomas who broke the small, surprised silence.

"I had not expected to see you here, Inspector." He turned to the dean. "Is this another instance of my being kept in the dark?"

"Not at all, not at all. I am as surprised as you are," the dean assured him.

"Forgive me," Inspector Winter put in. "I am here at the request of Miss Cavendish. It seems there was not time to alert you to my planned attendance."

Hecate opened her mouth to speak but a stern look from her father changed her mind.

"Very well," said Dean Chalmers, "I think we should begin. The facts as I understand them are that Miss Cavendish, acting entirely on her own, gained entry into the late Reverend Forsyth's home, took his set of keys, went to the vestry, and obtained the keys to the locked cabinet in the muniments room. Her intention was to gain access to the banned books in the search for some manner of evidence regarding the terrible and as yet unexplained death of her fiancé, Reverend Forsyth."

"God rest his soul," put in the master of the library.

"Indeed, indeed," agreed the dean. "I am further given to understand by Mr. Cavendish, that, in her shock, his daughter came to believe that certain creatures on the map were signaling to her, and that she must act, as it were, on their behalf. Miss Cavendish, have I said anything thus far with which you would disagree?"

"No, Dean."

"Good."

"Such disregard for both propriety and the safety of the collection!" Reverend Thomas could not help voicing his opinion of her behavior.

The dean sought to keep him calm. "If you wouldn't mind, Reverend, I will come to you for your thoughts shortly. Now, it is while you were reading one of these books that things took a turn for the dramatic, is that right?"

"Yes, Dean."

The master of the library refused to stay silent. "Which is precisely why such books are kept under lock and key and not put within reach of those who have no notion what they are doing!"

"I am so sorry, Reverend Thomas." Hecate felt it was right to apologize but had to dig her nails into her palm to prevent herself saying anything in her own defense.

"Sorry does not mend charred manuscripts or salvage ruined copies of important books. Sorry would not have saved the map or the library from fire," he pointed out.

"It was not my intention to put any part of the library at risk, I do hope you will believe me," she said, looking at both the dean and the librarian. "As Father says, I was not in my right mind. My thinking was . . . disturbed."

"Well," the dean asked, "can we be sure you are clearer in your thinking now, my dear? I mean to say, the tragic events which appear to have been the catalyst for your behavior are so very recent."

"I assure you, I am much better now. Of course, I will grieve for Reverend Forsyth for a very long time, but that initial shock has passed. It is as if I have awoken from a dream state," she assured them.

Reverend Thomas folded his arms across his ample stomach, his face stony. Hecate wondered if his anger was for show, was genuinely connected to his love for the library, or might be an indication of his own guilt. It was impossible to say. It was he who spoke next.

"In my opinion, Miss Cavendish has forfeited her right of access to the collection."

"Oh, no!" Hecate was horrified.

The dean nodded. "It is very soon. Perhaps a period of absence . . ."

Her father came to her rescue.

"Permit me to say, I know my daughter. She will recover more quickly if she is kept occupied. What is more, she feels, as do I, it is only fitting that the task of restoring the library to good order should fall to her."

"I wish very much to put things to rights," she agreed.

There came the sound of Inspector Winter clearing his throat, causing all to turn in his direction.

"You have something to share with us?" the dean asked.

"If I may," he said, stepping forward from the corner of the room where he had been standing. "You suggest that Miss Cavendish acted recklessly. . . . Neither she nor her father would dispute that. What is also agreed upon, however, is that this behavior was out of character. She has never before given reason for concern nor abused the trust placed in her by yourselves. In fact, she has, from what I am told, been an asset to the cathedral, and more specifically to the library, working diligently and respectfully throughout her time here." He paused while the assembled company took in his points. "Furthermore, I myself have come to see that Miss Cavendish has about her a talent for detail and logic rarely, if I may say so, found in so young a woman. It would seem to me these are attributes that would be of great benefit to a librarian. As Mr. Cavendish says, best to keep such intelligence and eagerness occupied." He gave a slow nod to indicate he had said all he had to say, before moving back a step, his angular frame cutting a quiet figure in the corner of the room once again.

"Thank you, Inspector, for the benefit of your wisdom. Miss Cavendish, while I do not condone your actions, I understand that you were greatly affected by the tragedy of Reverend Forsyth's death. I am also mindful of the fact that you suffered an injury, and have taken into account your genuine regret at the damage done to the library. Therefore, I am content to direct you to the work of cleaning up the muniments room and restoring the contents as best you are able. You will also"—here he glanced in the direction of her father—"make good on any costs for repairs and suchlike arising."

Hecate squirmed at the thought that she had caused her family extra expense, but was grateful her father had, clearly, offered the dean this recompense.

"I do not think it either necessary or prudent to dismiss you from your post," he added.

"Thank you, Dean," she said, already trying to decide how she could repay the money her father would have to pay out.

When the master of the library grumbled under his breath about this decision, his superior turned an uncharacteristically stern gaze upon him until he fell silent.

"Very well." Dean Chalmers got to his feet. "Miss Cavendish, you have a deal of hard work ahead of you; I suggest you begin at once. Reverend Thomas, thank you for your assistance, I am sure your gout must be causing you much discomfort, so you will be pleased to hear you are now free to return to your home. Inspector Winter, if you would be so good as to stay and talk with me, I have many questions regarding the most recent desecration of tombs in the crypt. We must, I think, work as one if we are to be successful, would you not agree?"

"Indeed I would," he said.

So dismissed, Hecate began to walk toward the door.

"One more thing," Reverend Thomas called after her. When she had stopped and he had the attention of all present he asked, "You succeeded in opening the locked cabinet. The books it contains are both dangerous and valuable. I have attempted a swift inventory of its contents and I found one volume to be missing. After searching the damaged shelves, papers, and suchlike, I discovered it. As the cabinet has yet to have all its contents replaced and locks checked, I took it upon myself to guard this particular volume. I have it in my keeping," he told her, lifting it from the folds of his robes.

She checked the impulse to step forward and demand he give her the book. For a moment she contemplated denying all knowledge of it. She glanced at her father and knew that he saw her struggling to find the right thing to say. The truth was, she had no right to it, and Reverend Thomas had evidently recognized that it was of particular importance. In which case, there was little she could say to change anything. In that moment so many thoughts crowded her mind. Would she ever gain access to the book again? How could she and Brother Michael translate the relevant texts if they could not take it from the cabinet at the next opportunity? Did the master of the library's interest in the book strengthen the case against him, or was he merely doing his job? The main thing, she told herself, was that it had survived the fire. Now that she knew of its existence, knew that it must contain the words to return the spirits to their own realm, she was confident she would, when the time was right, gain access to it again.

"I am relieved that none of the important works have been damaged," she said at last.

"I will be responsible for the care of this item of the collection," Reverend Thomas announced. "As master of the library it is my duty to protect such rare works. Until the room is returned to good order I will secure it in the safe inside the sacristy, with your permission, Dean. That way we can be certain it will not fall into the wrong hands."

The dean agreed this was a sensible course of action and the meeting came to an end.

Outside, Hecate hugged her father and thanked him for all he had done on her behalf.

"Couldn't see my worker bee out of a job," he told her. "Now, hurry back to that blessed library of yours and tidy it up. I want to express my thanks to Dean Chalmers. We must keep him on our side."


Hecate stood on the threshold of the library and did her best not to give way to despair. Everything sat beneath a layer of soot and the place was thick with the lingering smell of burned paper and singed wood. She took a step, leaving the door open in the hope of freshening the air within. The sight of the damage and chaos shook her anew. It was now that she experienced some of the fear that she perhaps ought to have felt when she was so nearly killed. She noticed her hands were shaking and her mouth was dry. What would have happened had not the bull from the *Mappa Mundi* acted to save her? Would she have been overcome by smoke? Would her body have been burned along with the entire library collection and the map itself? She wondered then if the bull had acted for her salvation or its own. She shook off thoughts of terrible alternative outcomes, reminding herself whose child she was. Mr. Sadiki had been quite clear. She drew her strength from the goddess she now served. It was Hekate's strength, given to her to use, that had ultimately seen her fend off the Resurgent Spirit. She could feel that strength with her still.

She picked her way through the debris to stand in front of the map, experiencing a wave of relief at the realization that it had suffered no damage save for a little dirt from the smoke. She reached out and touched the gritty surface, already planning what she would use to clean it and restore it.

"Don't worry," she murmured, "I will soon have you looking as good as new once again."

She heard a small movement and looked up to see the griffin perched on one of the rafters that had been exposed in the fire-damaged part of the ceiling.

"Hello, little one. Do you like it up there? A new place for you. Do not grow accustomed to such a lofty perch. I intend returning this room to its original state, and that includes replacing the ceiling." When the creature made no response she became worried that it might be fearful of her after what had happened under her care. She held up her arm. "Come along. We have work to do. Won't you help me?"

The griffin tilted his head, lifting one foot and then another to move sideways along the beam. And then, its decision made, it swooped down, ignoring her arm, and landed directly on her shoulder. It immediately set about nibbling her ear, its phantom beak applying only the very lightest, tickling touch.

"Well then," she murmured, stroking its puffed up chest.

And so she set to work. Mr. Gould and two of the vicars choral had earlier lifted the heavy cases and shelves and set them into their rightful positions. The chained books they had slid back into place. Most were unharmed save for some smoke marks, one or two were torn or had broken spines, but there was nothing beyond repair. Hecate considered calling Brother Michael but decided against. She did not want to put him under pressure to help her again so soon after such a terrifying night. He had warned her against opening the cabinet of banned books and she had ignored his warnings and his beloved library had nearly been lost because of her actions. Better that she let him come to her in his own time.

She knelt on the floor and began sifting through the fragments of paper, scrolls and small maps and drawings that lay scattered about. They were none of them of any great significance, but she was sad to see that some had been too badly burned to be saved. She fetched a wooden crate and began to fill it with the ruined scraps. As she did so, one snagged her attention. It was among a stack of loose leaves that had once been secured by a ribbon at one corner. There was some writing, very faded, possibly in Old English, and then line drawings. Something about them caused a jolt of recognition to awaken her interest. She looked more closely at the curious, simple shapes. And then it came to her; these were the same symbols she had seen burned into the mysterious gatehouse at the Brockhampton estate. The same ones she had seen in Father Ignatius's letter.

"Well, look at these!" she said to the griffin. "Perhaps now I can find out exactly what they mean and why the Brockhampton estate is so important to the Essedenes."

Hearing footsteps on the stairs, she folded the paper and tucked it into her pocket.

A shadow filled the doorway. Her father entered the room.

"Goodness, Hecate, the dean was not letting you off lightly, was he?"

"Have you finished your conversation with him so soon?"

"He was eager to inspect the new damage in the crypt. I shall speak with him later."

"I am fortunate he has allowed me to keep my post as assistant here, but oh, Papa, look at it all. . . ."

He took in the sorry scene. "Indeed, it will not be the work of a moment to make sense of this muddle. As luck would have it, I am not required at home and do not have an appointment until this afternoon so I am at your disposal."

She smiled at him as he reached over and gave her arm a reassuring squeeze.

"You are not on your own, my little Hecate," he told her.

"No, you are right about that, Father," she agreed, the griffin tightening his whispery grip on her shoulder. "Here, I am never alone."

It was gone six by the time Hecate stepped out of the south door and retrieved her bicycle. Edward, true to his word, had stayed to help until four o'clock when an appointment at the museum called him away. Together they had made good progress on restoring order to the library. There would be days of work ahead, a glazier to mend the hole in the window and workmen to repair the ceiling. Her father had promised to purchase a new desk. Most other things could be restored, and at least now it all seemed manageable.

A gentle purring alerted her to Solomon's presence.

"Hello, little cat," she said, bending down to stroke him. "No ill effects after the other night? Not much more than a few singed whiskers, I see. I think you may have used up one of your nine lives though." On impulse, she picked him up and gave him a tight embrace. His purr increased in volume. The comfort of him brought her close to weeping for John, making her wonder how much she would have to harden herself against such simple sources of solace if she was not to be often overwhelmed by grief. She kissed Solomon and let him go again, watching him trot off toward the vicars' vegetable patch in search of mice. There was a bloodred sunset in the west, the sky blazing above the walls of the Lady Arbor. Rooks circled the beech trees prior to roosting for the night. A pair of turtle doves, high in the eaves of the cathedral tower, cooed as they nestled up together. Hecate breathed in the sweet evening air which carried on it the scent of early roses from the cloister gardens. She looked up at the mighty building beside her, watching for a moment as its ancient stones took on the glow of the sunset. At one of the windows in the tower she glimpsed the figure of Lady Rathbone and imagined her wandering wistfully among the bell ropes. Corporal Gregory would no doubt be back at his post, his endless vigil continuing. Mrs. Nugent was most likely at that very moment fussing and fretting over some of Solomon's sooty paw prints. She hoped that Brother Michael would emerge to inspect her work in the library and approve of her efforts so far.

She gave a deep sigh. At that moment, the collection was secure. As was the *Mappa Mundi*. The cathedral, and the lost souls it was home to, was safe. For now. She had witnessed destruction come so very close but had withstood the assault. There would be danger ahead, she knew that. John had paid the highest price as his part in protecting her. Her punishment for having put him in peril was to carry the pain of his loss in her heart.

The Essedenes' plan to stop her and destroy the book had been thwarted, if only temporarily. Where their greater goals were concerned they would not be easily defeated. She was heartened to think that she now had the help of both Inspector Winter and the mysterious Mr. Sadiki. She would not face the battles to come without assistance. She had her phantom friends to watch over her, too. And she had the map itself, with its strange, magical beasts. She knew its creatures would protect her if they could and it struck her afresh how singular a blessing it was to be able to communicate with them. Her connection with the ancient treasure would have its further part to play in the battle that lay ahead, of that she had no doubt.

She accepted that she had put herself at the center of the fight. She remained the greatest threat to the Essedenes' success, and the ambitions of Lord Brocket and his family. They would not suffer her to live. It was as simple as that. A scintilla of fear shot through her. She allowed herself to experience it without giving way to panic. She was right to be afraid. Her adversaries were powerful and wicked. She must grasp that fear and turn it first into courage and then action. John had been tested and had not faltered. She would always be in his debt. She owed it to him to prevail. All those she loved would be in danger until she had defeated the Resurgent Spirits and their ruthless masters. She would not fail them.

"Well then," she said aloud, to herself, to any of her ghostly friends who might hear her, and to those foes who even now lurked in the shadows waiting for the moment her guard was down. She turned her head quickly, thinking to catch whatever it was that moved in the periphery of her vision, beneath the arch of the cloister doorway. There was nothing to be seen, but that did not mean that there was nothing there.

Hecate felt a fierce determination take hold. She would not give in to sadness or self-doubt. She would serve her namesake and do what was required of her. She was no fragile woman to be frightened or turned from her mission by wicked creatures. They did not, she concluded, truly know with whom they were dealing. She had the Goddess of Witches leading her, her phantom friends watching over her, and her earthly team at her side. There was work to be done.

On impulse, she removed her hat, took out her pins, and shook her hair free of its plait before mounting her bicycle and pedalling away across the Cathedral Green. As her hair flowed behind her in the wind it was as vibrant and as wild as the sun-streaked, darkening sky above.

# ACKNOWLEDGMENTS

IN WRITING THIS BOOK I HAVE BEEN SO FORTUNATE IN RECEIVING TRE-mendous support from people connected to Hereford Cathedral. My thanks go to Rosemary Firman, who was the cathedral librarian at the time of my research and assisted me in finding all sorts of wonderful books. I am indebted to Chancellor Canon Chris Pullin, now retired, for the time he took to answer my many questions. Special thanks go to the archivist at the cathedral, Elizabeth Semper O'Keefe, who has taken up my quest for facts with such enthusiasm. She provided a wealth of information, gained access for me to fascinating areas in the cathedral, delved deep into the archives for details regarding clergy and interesting characters long gone, and generally made the whole process of research for this book so much fun. Thank you!

My gratitude also to John Marshall, Mayor's Officer at the Town Hall, for his time, knowledgeable talk, and for access to Lord Owain's sword. That story line has been saved for a later book in the series.

I would like to point out that, even after all this wonderful assistance toward historical accuracy, I am a writer of stories, and this is a work of fiction. As such, it contains liberties taken with the facts, and mistakes borne of creative endeavor, all of which I claim as my own.

As always, my heartfelt thanks to my editor, Peter Wolverton, for his tireless efforts to help me find the best way to tell my story. As the first book in a new series we faced very specific challenges, and I would not have risen to them half so well without him, or without his editorial assistant, Claire Cheek. Thanks to you both. We got there in the end!

There is one character in this book who carries a special significance. A dear reader lost three family members tragically and approached me to see if her nephew (who was only a small boy at the time of his death) could be memorialized as a character in one of my stories. I was pleased to be able to do this, and he now has a small but important part in the series, the cathedral cat bearing his name; Solomon.

# ABOUT THE AUTHOR

Skyla Holman

PAULA BRACKSTON is the *New York Times* bestselling author of *The Witch's Daughter* and *The Little Shop of Found Things*, among others. Paula lives with her family in the historical border city of Hereford in the beautiful Wye Valley. When not at her desk in her writing room, she enjoys long walks with the dog in a sublime landscape filled with the imprints of past lives and ancient times.